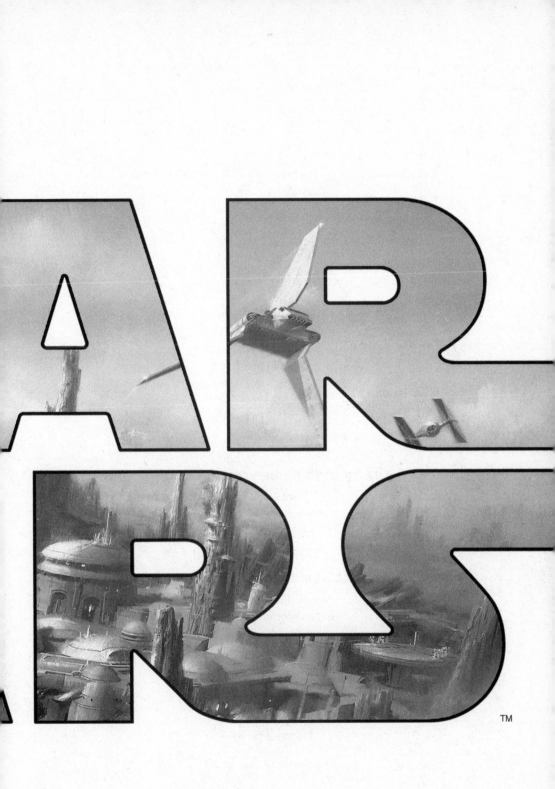

™

By Delilah S. Dawson

STAR WARS

Phasma

The Perfect Weapon (e-novella)

THE HIT SERIES

Hit

Strike

THE SHADOW SERIES (AS LILA BOWEN)

Wake of Vultures

Conspiracy of Ravens

Malice of Crows

Treason of Hawks

THE PELL SERIES (WITH KEVIN HEARNE)

Kill the Farm Boy

No Country for Old Gnomes

The Princess Beard

THE BLUD SERIES

Wicked as They Come

Wicked as She Wants

Wicked After Midnight

Wicked Ever After

Servants of the Storm

BLACK SPIRE

STAR WARS
GALAXY'S EDGE

BLACK SPIRE

DELILAH S. DAWSON

DEL REY
NEW YORK

Copyright © 2019 by Lucasfilm Ltd. & ® or ™ where indicated. All rights reserved.

Published in the United States by Del Rey,
an imprint of Random House, a division of
Penguin Random House LLC, New York.

DEL REY and the HOUSE colophon are registered trademarks
of Penguin Random House LLC.

ISBN 978-0-593-12838-1
International edition ISBN 978-0-593-15681-0
ebook ISBN 978-0-593-12839-8

Printed in the United States of America on acid-free paper

randomhousebooks.com

2 4 6 8 9 7 5 3 1

First Edition

Book design by Elizabeth A. D. Eno

For Rhys, who named Waba, and
for Rex, who invented the starmarks.

I'm glad that *Star Wars* is part of you,
and now you are officially part of *Star Wars*.

THE DEL REY

TIMELINE

THE DEL REY

STAR WARS™

TIMELINE

A long time ago in a galaxy far, far away. . . .

BLACK SPIRE

At the edge of the galaxy
So far away
Black was the spire
That called me to stay.
A beacon for drifters
Forgotten and lost
The spires summoned those
Broken and tossed.
Come stay here forever
Or just pass on through.
The spirit of Black Spire
Will forever change you.

—old Batuuan ballad

Chapter One

HIDDEN RESISTANCE BASE, D'QAR

THE LIFE OF A RESISTANCE SPY was all about excitement—or at least, that's why Vi Moradi signed up. That, and the chance to do some good and strike back at tyranny. As Vi stood outside the office of General Leia Organa, she was anxious to see what her next assignment would be. She was getting that old restless feeling and needed something to do, something real. On Major Kalonia's orders, she'd spent the past several weeks recuperating from her last mission, and she was itching for activity beyond debriefing pilots and gathering intel from their droids on enemy firepower and fighting prowess. They knew the First Order was out there and supposedly unbeatable; did they really need to keep reaffirming that through numbers? Vi liked being an under-dog, but she didn't necessarily want to know the odds.

"Come in, Magpie."

Vi smiled at the way Leia always used one of her call signs and stepped inside the makeshift office, taking a seat on an old red crate. "Good to see you, General."

Every time Vi was in the presence of General Organa, once Prin-cess Leia Organa of Alderaan, it felt a little like going home. Leia had a calm, steady presence, motherly but tough as nails, and no matter how dire things got, the older woman had a way of looking at each member of the Resistance as if they were the hero that could turn the tide against their enemy, the dreaded First Order that had risen from the Empire's ashes. Leia returned Vi's smile, her eyes twinkling.

"I have a mission for you," Leia said, her attention flicking from various holos to Vi and back. Leia's mouth fell into a familiar grim line, which told Vi she wasn't necessarily going to like her assignment. That was fine—she didn't particularly like how her last mission had gone, either. It wasn't her job to like it.

"As you know, we're massively outgunned. We don't know what the First Order is planning, but it's something big. Some kind of attack. I'm leaving immediately for Takodana to collect some valuable intel, so I wanted to meet with you personally and underline how very important your work will be."

"If you brought me in just to tell me it's important, it sounds like it might not be that important. I'm ready to work, General. Major Kalonia signed off. I'm back in top form."

Leia's gaze was unwavering. "I wouldn't blame you if you just disappeared, after what happened to you on the *Absolution*. You were captured by the enemy, Vi. Tortured. Beaten. Shocked. Injured. I've read your med charts and your reports. Downplay it all you like, but an experience like that changes people. I should know."

Vi shook her head. "But I'm still me. So put me on a Star Destroyer and let me—"

"No." Leia cut her off, almost apologetic, and Vi's mouth snapped shut. "This assignment might sound like a vacation, but I assure you, it's of vast strategic importance. If you're ready."

Vi shifted on the crate, her back aching. Leia was right—she'd taken a beating on her last assignment, and although most of her wounds had healed, her body wasn't getting any younger. Leia had sent her to a forgotten planet called Parnassos to gather intel on the First Order's Captain Phasma, which was challenging enough. But on her way home, Vi had been captured by a different First Order officer, Captain Cardinal.

Instead of interrogating her through official channels or turning her over to Kylo Ren or General Hux, Cardinal had secretly taken her to a dank chamber in the ship's lower levels and tortured her for the information she'd collected on his rival in the First Order, Captain Phasma. In the end, Vi had managed to manipulate him into letting her go, and Cardinal had gone out to face Phasma in combat. Vi made it out of the enemy ship and back to the fleet, and for the last few weeks she'd struggled to process all that had happened to her and heal in body and mind. But despite what she'd told Kalonia and now Leia, was she really ready to go back to work?

Well, was anyone ever ready to move on from trauma?

It would never leave her, but she couldn't stay still any longer. It wasn't in her nature.

"I'm ready," she told Leia, putting the full force of conviction in her words.

"Good." Leia's smile returned. "Should the First Order succeed in their attack, or should they find us here on D'Qar, we need two things most of all: allies and places to hide. So I'm looking for suggestions on a place so out of the way that the First Order would never even think of it, a place where we could set up camp and put down roots. Specifically, we need an inhabited planet with an active port and resources, but not anything big, not anything the First Order would find advantageous."

"Castilon isn't safe anymore," Vi thought out loud. "Not Pantora. Nowhere in the Core or Mid Rim, or any place where we've had a base before. Definitely not Parnassos."

"Definitely not. Think, Magpie."

Vi raised an eyebrow; Leia was not in a patient mood. "Batuu, maybe? I've heard of it, but I've never been there. It's out on the edge of Wild Space. The main settlement is called Black Spire Outpost. It's rough. Primitive. Seedy. Exciting. Smugglers consider it a good place to hide or hop a ship that can't be tracked."

At that, the general nodded. "I knew I could count on you. Batuu is perfect." She chuckled. "Han told me all about it."

Leaning forward, Vi gave her a suspicious look. "That can't be the only reason you called me in here—just to ask me a question. You have strategists for that."

"But I don't need strategists." Leia likewise leaned forward. "I need *you*, Magpie. I trust you. And what I need you to do is go to Black Spire Outpost on the planet Batuu, establish an outpost for the Resistance, and collect as much support as possible among the locals and visitors. We need bodies. We need friends. We need skills. We need ships and food and fuel. We need eyes and ears on the ground. We need a place we can go if everything falls apart, a place so far off the map that the First Order has forgotten it even exists. To them, Batuu will seem strategically useless. But to us, it's another spark of hope. I need you to cultivate that spark, to keep the fire burning."

Vi leaned back, letting her head fall to the side. "So why do I feel like you're promoting me out of harm's way? Protecting me? Maybe even coddling me?" She held Leia's gaze, never an easy task. "Use me, General. I have skills no one else has. I'm your best spy. So why are you sending me to what's basically nowhere?"

"Because nowhere is what might save us. You're not the only valuable person being sent out to nowhere." Leia gave her a significant look, blew out a sigh, and took on an air of urgency, as if Vi had already been excused. "That's your assignment. Take it or leave it. I'm needed on Takodana immediately. They're holding the ship for me, and I'm out of time to convince you. The great thing about the Resistance is that you always retain free will. I hope you'll trust me when I tell you that your work on Batuu is part of a larger plan. So do you trust me, Magpie?"

The general's eyebrows went up, her graying hair in a perfect crown. Yes, Vi did trust her. And Vi wasn't going to walk away, even though she knew it was always an option.

"I trust you, General," she finally said.

Leia nodded. "Good. Dismissed. Report to the hangar tomorrow morning. Lieutenant Connix will provide further details and a manifest of your cargo. You'll be assigned a droid to help with the heavy lifting and logistics. We're giving you the materials, and we need you to scout the ideal site, connect with the local population, recruit new bodies to join the cause, and establish communications so we can discuss next steps."

Vi stood. "I'll do my best, General."

The smile she gave Leia was resigned. Yes, she would do her duty. In this case, Vi didn't think she would like it, but she was a soldier, and she would do whatever it took to resist the First Order and keep the galaxy safe.

But as Vi headed for the door, the general said, "Oh, and Magpie? One more thing."

Vi couldn't help chuckling as she turned around. "Of course. There's always one more thing, isn't there?"

Leia stood, looking grim and regal and certain. Vi steeled herself for what she knew would be unwelcome news.

"I'm assigning you a partner for this mission, and again I need you to trust me."

Vi leaned against the door and crossed her arms. "Uh-oh. That doesn't bode well. You know I prefer to work alone. And if it was somebody I liked, you would've led with that."

"Perceptive as ever." Leia rolled her eyes as if to suggest Vi had caught her out. "Before you head for Batuu, I need you to make a quick stop on Cerea to pick up someone. Archex."

"Who's Archex?"

The general's gaze went dark, serious. "The man you knew as Captain Cardinal has chosen to return to his childhood name."

Cardinal.

Archex was Cardinal.

Vi went cold all over as images flipped through her mind—unwelcome ones. Cardinal pulling her from her ship, putting her in binders, strapping her into an interrogation chair he wasn't quite certain how to use. His face when she'd first convinced him to take off his shining red helmet. The conviction in his eyes, the unwavering faith in his calling. The way her vision went red each time he'd used that chair to shock her, pushing her further toward the edge of desolation, toward betraying all that she stood for.

She'd turned him against the First Order, sure—but just barely.

Cardinal had gone out to face his rival, Phasma, who'd nearly killed him. And then Vi did something unusual, something she still didn't quite understand: She'd saved him. Dragged Cardinal's dying carcass across the *Absolution,* stole a ship, and hightailed it back to D'Qar with her enemy and torturer by her side.

She'd seen something in Captain Cardinal, something she'd thought impossible: a good man who believed in the First Order with all his heart. And she'd used that good to convert him—if not into a Resistance fighter, then at least away from the First Order's lies.

She hadn't seen him since they'd landed on D'Qar and he'd been hurried to the medbay.

She hadn't wanted to.

"Archex," she said woodenly, dumbly. The name tasted like blood in her mouth, like the metallic burn left behind by his interrogation chair's repeated shocks.

But Leia went on as if she hadn't noticed Vi's discomfort. "I sent him to Cerea for . . . well, let's call it a restful retreat with gentle deprogramming while we monitored his recovery. He's as healed as he'll ever be and cleared for work. Although he hasn't fully committed to our cause and will continue to wear a monitor, he needs something to do. You two are more alike than you know."

Vi barked a bitter laugh. "I bet we are."

"Look, I need him with someone we can trust, someone *he* can trust. You were the first one who told me he might be worth saving, after all."

"Yes, I was. And I'm starting to regret it."

Vi still couldn't quite process what she was hearing, couldn't understand why Leia would do this. "Am I being punished for something?" she asked, voice rasping.

Leia swiftly moved around the desk and grasped Vi by the shoulders. "No. Of course not. I'm doing what I've always done: putting the best person on the job. You have the skills to command, to think on your feet. You're the one who turned Cardinal, who made that connection. I believe you can use that skill to help our cause. You're a great spy, Vi, but you're also a leader, and I know you're going to succeed. We need places like you're going to build on Batuu, and we

need Archex, and as hard as it might be for you to hear, I think Archex needs you."

But what about me? Vi wanted to ask. *What about what I need?*

What she needed was a job that would bring back that old beloved
zing of excitement, the thrill of going undercover, collecting intel,
foiling bad guys, and returning a hero. Instead she was being sent to
the far end of nowhere with her enemy, the man whose visage
haunted her when she woke at night, screaming and covered in a
sheen of sweat.

"Vi?"

Leia still held her shoulders, looking concerned. Vi shook off her
misgivings, exhaled, and met the general's gaze.

She could do this. She *would* do this. For Leia, for the Resistance,
she would do anything.

"Yes, General," she said. "I'll do my best."

Finally, Leia smiled that smile that made it seem like anything was
possible.

"I know you will," she said. "That's why I chose you. Good luck on
Batuu, Magpie. And may the Force be with you."

Chapter Two

HIDDEN RESISTANCE BASE, D'QAR

THE NEXT MORNING, BEFORE SHE WAS due in the hangar, Vi stopped in the medbay and asked for Major Kalonia. She'd seen a lot of the doctor since returning to D'Qar, and her wounds had healed as much as they ever would, inside and out. Today, however, she had a different reason for visiting.

"Trying to get out of this assignment?" Kalonia asked with her usual wry grin. The older human woman had smoothly bobbed dark hair threaded with gray and was known for her competence as a physician and her warm bedside manner. "As I told Leia, you're perfectly fit for your usual misadventures."

"It's not me I'm worried about," Vi told her. "It's Archex. I understand you treated him here when we returned from the *Absolution* and that you've been monitoring his recovery while he's been on Cerea?"

Kalonia tilted her head knowingly. "Discussing the private concerns of my patients is generally considered a breach of protocol—"

Vi opened her mouth to interrupt, but Kalonia stopped her with a hand.

"But Leia and I suspected you would want answers. I don't blame you; if you're going to be stuck in a transport with him and then alone on a planet far from backup, you deserve to know what you're dealing with. Considering he's technically a political prisoner who hasn't yet formally joined the Resistance, we feel it's reasonable to share some information that will be relevant to your partnership."

Partnership. Vi snorted. "That's not the word I would use for it."

Kalonia shrugged. "Collaboration, then. Let me show you."

The physician led Vi over to a bank of screens and pulled up a holo. There was Cardinal as Vi had last seen him, still in his bright-red armor and black captain's cape as Kalonia, med droids, and other personnel swarmed around him under bright lights. He was on a gurney, his helmet off, unconscious. A worrisome amount of blood stained his armor, especially in the two places where Phasma had stabbed him with a poisoned blade she carried from her homeworld.

"When you brought him to us, he was in bad shape. Lost a lot of blood. The weapon introduced an organic compound we'd never seen before, and it took us a while to work up—well, not an antidote. We couldn't just cancel it out. But we were able to fight it. Still, one lung was punctured, and the wound in his leg was deep and festering. We did all we could, but for all our technology, as you know, medicine is still an imperfect, messy science."

Kalonia pulled up a new holo, this one showing Cardinal out of his armor and clad in the usual white medcenter gown, sitting up in a bed and connected to several machines by tubes. He looked so different without the bulky plating, smaller and more human, and Vi realized that this wasn't Captain Cardinal—it was the man who now went by the name Archex. His black hair had grown out a little, but his face was as she remembered it, his yellow-gold skin freckled from a childhood under the Jakku sun, and his creased brown eyes troubled. He wasn't smiling.

"At first, he was withdrawn and seemed . . . well, like he'd lost the will to live."

"He told me so," Vi murmured. "When I was pushing his gurney out of the *Absolution.* He said *let me die,* over and over."

"Yes, well, letting people die is not my job," Kalonia continued with a twitch of her lips. "So I did my best to help him through it. We see this sometimes, in war—soldiers become disillusioned. They lose faith. They don't know how to go on. And yet there's just something about him, isn't there? He's a survivor, but not the kind made cruel by the crucible that forged him. He didn't seem to want to live, and yet he approached rehabilitation like it was his job. He walked weeks before we thought he would. He exercised on his own time, even though I'd warned him that his lung wasn't ready for it."

She flicked the screen over to a video of Archex doing push-ups. Sweat beaded his brow, and he was clearly struggling. His arms and legs wobbled, and he toppled over, but he quickly got back up and continued. Vi watched him gasping for breath like he'd run a kilometer, his eyes grimly determined.

"He doesn't give up easy," she noted.

"He does not," Kalonia confirmed.

"But what about his psyche? Is he . . . broken?"

Kalonia clicked her tongue. "No more than you, or me, or Leia. So many of us came to the Resistance via tragedy. He's healing, but he has a long way to go. The program on Cerea is intended to give him the space and time he needs. When you're in the middle of things, on a base like this or one of our ships, you get caught up in the cycle. Everyone needs downtime to figure things out."

"But is he safe?"

"Let's not fool ourselves, Moradi. No one here is safe. But he's not violent. He's cogent and reasonable and even if he hasn't joined us, he's no longer aligned with the First Order. He's not going to attack you in your sleep, if that's what you're worried about. But like you, he might have nightmares for the rest of his life."

Vi sighed. "That's what I needed to know."

"I can heal bones. But I can't heal souls. You have to do that yourself."

Vi looked down, fidgeting. She'd been neglecting that, focusing instead on action. Maybe she'd find some healing herself on Batuu. Maybe life would move slowly and she'd, what? Commune with nature?

Sure, why not?

Well, because she'd run from Chaaktil, and she'd never stop running. As it turned out, there was always another fight.

"Work first, therapy later," she finally said. "I'll focus on healing
when we've beat the First Order. So what about—"

"Attention, all hands," Leia's voice boomed through the intercom
system. She sounded exhausted and sad, like she'd aged fifty years
since the last time Vi had spoken with her, just yesterday. The general
had to be well on her way to Takodana by now. The comm system
crackled, and Vi held her breath, waiting for more. "To your stations.
An unknown weapon has just . . . I don't even know how to say it. We
believe . . . somehow . . . we are working to confirm this, but it seems
the worst has come to pass. The Hosnian system appears to be gone.
Yes, every planet. The entire New Republic government can only be
assumed a casualty of this cataclysm." And then, as if an afterthought,
"May the Force be with everyone who was lost. May it remain with us
all."

It was as if a great hollowness entered Vi's chest. She'd been
there—to Hosnian Prime and Hosnian and Cardota. Lived and slept
and worked on their surfaces, felt their sun's warmth on her skin.
And now they were just . . . gone? She struggled to breathe, thinking
of everyone she knew who would count among the dead, recalling
faces and names. At least her brother was still on Pantora, she told
herself; he'd once worked as an intern for the Senate. And in a flash
she wondered: Was this how Leia had felt, so long ago, when she
watched Alderaan explode, knowing exactly what had been lost?

"An entire system," Kalonia said, almost a question, as if she
couldn't even comprehend it, either, because who could? "Billions of
people . . ."

Vi put a hand on her arm. "Focus on the ones here, now. We're
going to need you."

Kalonia nodded, and Vi watcher her undergo the process that
she'd seen so many of her compatriots undergo, that cycle of emotions she'd felt herself. Whatever doubts a person might have disinte-
grated in the face of necessity. If the First Order had a weapon like
that, the answer wasn't to stop, go silent, wait, cry. The answer was to

feel your will coalesce, to firm up your chin and focus on the future and what you could personally do to fight the enemy, to stop such a horror from happening again.

Her comm buzzed. "Magpie? Your mission to Batuu is on hold. You're needed in the hangar."

"I have to go," she said, and Kalonia nodded.

Vi ran.

The Resistance might need Batuu, but Batuu could wait.

Chapter Three

CEREA, FOUR MONTHS LATER

AFTER THE HOSNIAN CATACLYSM, THE RESISTANCE was thrown into utter chaos. And after the Battle of Crait, it was nearly destroyed. Their ships and officers were gone, Leia almost died, and Luke Skywalker saved what was left of their crew only to pass into the Force himself, leaving the Jakku scavenger, Rey, as their only hope. With nothing left of their fleet but the *Millennium Falcon* and no allies rallying to their call, Leia contacted all her spies and gave them new orders:

Hide. Recruit allies. Gather ships. Collect fuel and weapons. Rebuild. Go far away from the target on my back and find a way to help us get on our feet again.

For Vi, that meant it was time to go to Batuu.

But first, she had to pick up her partner.

No. That word still didn't sit right.

Her *collaborator.*

And so she slowly rambled toward Cerea in an ancient transport filled with junk. Or, as Leia called it, the building blocks that Vi would use to help build a new Resistance base. The world down below reminded Vi of what life could be like when beings were allowed their freedom and weren't blown up or subjugated by cruel regimes: gorgeous turquoise seas, old-growth forests, fields of waving golden grain. She sighed and aimed her old, bulky transport for the grungier spot of smog over Asphodar 3, one of Cerea's Outsider Citadels. The native Cereans took great pains to keep their planet untouched by pollution and technology, so these city-sized structures were the only gateway and accommodation for immigrants and visitors. Vi landed in a short-term docking bay and glanced around.

"You ready for this, Pook?"

Her rejiggered PK-Ultra worker droid let out a comically loud groan of despair from the hold, where he was fixing a dented power droid. "Ready for what, another day of inconceivable torment? With another feeble human ordering me about nonsensically? With twice the work to do, I'll most likely snap an arm."

Pook was twice the size of the usual PK droid, designed to be just as forgettable and inoffensive as the original but sturdy and capable of lifting heavy loads. His "head," if you could call it that, looked like a lamp with a black light, and his body was bottom-heavy with clunky feet and three-fingered hands, all a pearly silvery white.

"Wish I'd had time to get your personality tuned up."

"And I wish I'd been left to slowly rust away on Naboo, but here we are, all victims of some sort of grand cosmic joke."

Vi ran a hand over her face and murmured, "If only the FO hadn't torn Gigi into parts."

"I heard that," Pook warned. "And I'm far superior to any garbage pail of an astromech, considering I have a ramped-up JN VerboBrain combined with the ability to lift a fully grown male ronto. A lot of help a U5 would be where we're going. Wretched, beepy things."

Vi stood and pushed her bangs aside. She'd let her hair grow while she was recovering but now wore it in flat twists under one of her favorite wigs, which was styled in a long, shaggy bob, smooth black with the tips dyed blue. Two more wigs carefully rested in a special case in the hold, just in case Black Spire Outpost wasn't the most stylish of places.

It was actually kind of strange, starting a mission dressed as herself. No disguise and fake name, no zippy little starhopper. Just Vi

Moradi, openly working for the Resistance, and a transport ship that had once carried loads of ore and fuel to and from some dusty moon but was now heavy with cargo of a different sort. She'd found a jacket that felt almost as good as the one she'd jettisoned while being dragged into Cardinal's Star Destroyer, Resistance-orange synth-leather with cream trim, plenty of pockets, and a proud starbird symbol. Her cargo pants were packed with useful tech and weapons, including her favorite blaster, her second favorite blaster, and a specialized tactical baton that had saved her rump more than once when laser bolts weren't the answer. Her boots were rugged, and her gloves were still stiff with newness and ready for hard work. This was an unusual sort of mission for her, and originally, yeah, she'd had her misgivings. But with what was left of the Resistance on the run from the First Order, she was glad to do whatever Leia asked. After the Hosnian Cataclysm, her will had resolved. She no longer had any doubts, just goals.

Which meant she had to stop stalling and move on to the next step.

"Here goes," she said as she stepped off the ship and into the nicely kept hangar. A Cerean woman with a tall head and gray robes gracefully walked toward her carrying a datapad.

"Have you made docking arrangements?" the woman asked, inclining her head in greeting.

Vi returned the gesture. "No. I will be departing within the hour."

"And your cargo?" The woman's eyebrows rose.

Glancing back at her ship, Vi recalled that it definitely looked like something that would require loading or unloading, and the Cerean administrator was most likely making sure that Vi wasn't bringing anything illegal to her docks. The Cereans had trouble keeping the criminal element out of their citadels, but Vi wasn't here to smuggle armaments or obtain the valuable Cerean drug guilea. Not that the administrator would believe that until she'd checked the ship's hold or watched Vi leave without loading or unloading anything except . . .

"I'm just here for one thing," Vi assured her. "And there he is."

Walking toward them was a figure both familiar and curiously different. His dark hair had grown out from its uniform shave and was getting a bit floppy, and he had a noticeable limp, but it was still Cardinal—

No.

It was *Archex*. She had to remember that.

Scanning his simple costume of white shirt with brown jacket and black pants, Vi realized she'd never seen him in civilian clothes outside of Major Kalonia's holos of his time in the medbay. He seemed smaller without his armor, vulnerable and aimless. And yet he was a powerfully built man and, as Kalonia had shown her, he'd taken pains to maintain his strength and fitness despite his injuries. It was his eyes that made him seem exposed. He seemed to always be squinting into a far-off sunset, always worried about what was to come. Vi read pain there, and she knew quite well that any kindness on her part would rankle.

"I know I'm a few months late, but you look good, Emergency Brake," she shouted across the busy spaceport.

His mouth turned down; he hated his limp, she suspected. It was probably infuriating to a man like him to wear armor every day for twenty years and then suddenly feel so unprotected and . . . well, imperfect.

"He does not look particularly good by human standards," Pook said, peering down from the transport's open hatch. "No wonder they included advanced med protocols in my most recent upload. That one's a piece of work."

"Keep that to yourself," Vi snapped.

Pook sighed; it was like he was programmed to sigh. "Human bodies are garbage," he opined.

Cardinal—no. Archex! It was so hard for her to see him as anything other than the man who'd taken her to the darkest cave of her mind, a man she'd still inexplicably considered worth saving, in part because Leia believed redemption was possible. He hurried toward her ship, clearly putting himself in pain to do so and trying to hide that he was breathing heavily. She held out a hand to help him up the short step and into the cargo hold, but he ignored it, grabbed the edge of the hatch, and pulled himself up on his own. It cost him, and his face showed it, but Vi knew well enough that any further attempts to help would only make him resent her more.

"Welcome to the fastest ship in the galaxy," she said. "Just kidding. That's a total lie. Welcome to a clunky transport full of secondhand junk and a melancholy droid that I'm pretty sure they gave me just to get him out of the way."

"I heard that," Pook grumbled. "And I'm not melancholy. I'm realistic."

Archex carried one small brown leather bag, which he slung on the floor as he levered himself into an uncomfortable seat designed to haul miners.

"Can we go now?" he said.

The Cerean administrator was still hovering just outside.

"Do I need to sign anything?" Vi asked.

"Although visitors may legally dock here for up to an hour, it is important to record the comings and goings—"

Archex pushed the button that slammed the hatch down in the poor woman's face.

"It's not necessary. Just go."

Vi gave him the quelling look one gives a small child who doesn't yet understand civility.

"It's true," he said. "Trust me. I've been here for months. As long as you're not loading up four tons of guilea or dropping off a dead Hutt, it's all voluntary. They just like manners." Vi continued to stare at him, and he shook his head and gesticulated at her. "So let's take off. We're on a mission. Dire circumstances. All that." After she stared at him a beat too long, he added, "Please. Get me off this exhaustingly polite rock."

Vi finally relented because she needed him as an ally more than she needed the approval of a random Cerean bureaucrat. Settling in the captain's chair, she made sure the woman was out of range and took off. She would never get used to the way the awkward transport rumbled up into the atmosphere; she preferred a sleek ship with some style, or at least some speed. This thing was ugly and slow, not to mention almost impossible to maneuver.

Archex maintained a firm, disapproving silence, and after a while she couldn't help returning to her original role in their relationship: goading him.

"So did you have a nice vacation on Cerea?"

"It wasn't a vacation," he snapped. "It was a . . . what did they call it? *A peaceful and nature-led deprogramming protocol in the beautiful and ancient forests of Cerea.* In addition to daily meditation, obnoxiously gentle stretching, and practicing the Dance of the Three Suns, I ate an entirely plant-based diet and detoxed from the evils of technology."

Vi couldn't help laughing. "Yeah, you sound real peaceful. What was Leia thinking?"

Archex sighed and had the grace to look a bit ashamed. "She was thinking she needed to get me away from First Order action. And maybe she wanted to actually help me. But I think she overestimated my interest in making baskets from porlash needles."

"Fair enough. I don't think I'd do so well in a program like that, either. A body likes to move. You get used to work, it's hard not to work."

He nodded along. "Considering most of what they want me to do now involves tech, Cerea was a poor choice."

"I will handle the tech," Pook interrupted. "I'm still not sure what *he's* here to do."

"Ignore him," Vi said. Then, louder, "Pook forgets I'm the boss. Point is I'm the hustle, Pook's the brawn, and you're the brains."

Archex almost chuckled. Almost.

"If I'm the brains, then we're in trouble."

Vi wanted to correct him; the barrage of scans and tests they'd put him through on D'Qar had proven that he was smarter than most, but the First Order's brainwashing had long ago convinced him that he was just the hand that wielded the weapon, not the clever brain that could build the weapon or decide what to do with it. The First Order didn't

want their soldiers thinking too hard, because then they might question the war machine. Poor Archex had no concept of his own intelligence, and any attempt on her part to tell him would surely backfire.

"Okay, so maybe you're like the operator. You stay put and run the
comms while I go out and recruit. You're strategy, coordination, organization. And you get to tell Pook what to do—or try to. Just remember: You were chosen for this mission. Leia believes in you." She
turned to meet his gaze, sending an unwanted jolt of recognition
through her own nervous system. "And so do I."

Archex leaned back as they broke atmo. He couldn't seem to get
comfortable in the hard contours of the transport's less-than-
ergonomic chair. But who could? They were made for working-class
folk lugging around the raw materials that would make greater beings wealthy. No one thought of the servant's comfort. Vi couldn't
wait to land.

"So where are we going?" Archex asked. "All I was told was that I
was operating as your support on a top-secret Resistance mission. If
I'm honest, I can't believe they're trusting me with information like
that already."

"Ah, well, see . . . we're going somewhere far from First Order rule.
Our mission is to build a new Resistance facility on an out-of-the-
way planet and attempt to recruit warm bodies for the cause. I've
chosen a place called Black Spire Outpost on the planet Batuu. It's the
last stop before Wild Space. It's a sort of crossroads, the kind of spot
where everyone is too busy with their own business and secrets to
worry too much about yours."

Archex's face screwed up as if thinking too hard caused him pain.
Maybe it did—Phasma had messed him up pretty badly, and Major
Kalonia had mentioned migraines as an ongoing trouble. Vi gave
him a moment to consider this information as she checked their coordinates, saw that Pook had slightly altered their course, deleted his
alterations to suit her own sensibilities, and kicked up the hyperdrive.

"Never heard of it, huh?" Vi continued as the ship jumped to hyperspace. "Yeah, well, that's the point. There's nothing of strategic
importance there for the First Order. No grand resources, no indus-

tries to take over, no government to buy. Batuu is off the beaten path and has seen better days. Remember: Most of the galaxy doesn't know that Starkiller Base is gone. They're easy pickings for your beloved new Supreme Leader and his pinched little fox of a lackey, which means places that don't matter . . . now matter even less." She watched closely to see if Archex would bristle at that. "Guess the deprogramming worked," she muttered.

But he just shrugged. "Hard to get energized about something that doesn't matter. This doesn't seem like a 'top-secret mission.' It sounds like a classic case of promoting people out of the way. And making sure I can't get in too much trouble."

Vi shook a finger at him and ignored the fact that she'd considered the same possibility before the Hosnian Cataclysm. "Just because something doesn't matter to the First Order doesn't mean it lacks value. The Resistance is built on hope. People need something to believe in, a symbol to stand behind. So we go to places where the First Order doesn't have a foothold, win the people over, and create a place where anyone who stands for freedom can find their home—or park their X-wing and wait for orders. By now, you probably know how few people we have left. We lost most of our fleet, tons of our allies. Every bolt-hole we can build to hide and gas up our ships is one more pocket of hope. Now, if you'll excuse me."

She reached down for her bag and pulled out a new knitting project. That was one of Vi's little secrets—she loved the clack of needles juxtaposed with the cool blue lines of hyperspace, the primitive and the futuristic happening at once. It was relaxing and helped her get in the right headspace for a complicated job. The squashy hat was half finished on circular knitting needles, and the charmingly bulky bantha-fur yarn hid her imperfect stitches.

Archex stared at her like she was insane. "Are you . . . knitting?"

Vi raised an eyebrow. "Yeah. Why, you want to learn?"

He grimaced. "Can't you just buy . . . whatever that's supposed to be?"

"It's a hat, and yeah, I guess I could. But there's something to be said for making things with your own hands, the old-fashioned way.

Having physical evidence of your effort to admire at the end of the day. Haven't you ever made anything?" She was kind enough not to mention the fact that he'd once helped make thousands upon thousands of small children into merciless soldiers for the First Order.

But Archex just sighed sadly and looked like his mind was elsewhere. "I made things with my hands. A long time ago. Not recently. Not a lot of spare time for whittling toys on a Star Destroyer."

"Well, the good news is that the Resistance will let you whittle wherever you want to. And when we get to Batuu, you and I are going to make something good."

"Correction," Pook interjected from the cargo hold. "You are both damaged specimens no longer in the prime of human life, meaning I will do most of the physical labor using my superior strength and spatial reasoning, all while taking whatever crude abuse you choose to heap upon me."

"I need to knit a droid muffler," she muttered.

Vi caught Archex's eye and was gratified to see him smirking, for once. She realized there might actually be a sense of humor somewhere in there. Seeing an opening, she dived right in.

"So are we going to talk about it?"

He looked away. "Talk about what?"

Vi chuckled. "You never did strike me as a coward, Archex."

"I'm not a coward. I just think actions speak louder than words. I'm here. That should be enough."

Vi raised an eyebrow. "Well, I believe in honesty. Neither of us escaped that Star Destroyer in one piece. You did some damage. I'm still recovering. Just seeing you makes all my nerve endings jump around like frightened fathiers. But I have a job to do, and I'm going to do it, and I hope we can just start fresh. You were doing your job, I was doing mine. I told you on that boat and I'll tell you now: I still think there's a good guy buried somewhere underneath that red armor."

He looked down at his hands, flexed his fingers. "The red armor is gone."

"Maybe we can crack through the tough-guy exterior, then. See what you're like without all the programming and protocol and propaganda. I bet you're fun when you're not torturing me."

His sigh was a wheeze. Every breath would be like that for him now: a torture of his own. "Look, I know what you really want, and if you think I'm going to turn to the Resistance, become a true believer, you're wrong. I may not believe in the First Order anymore, but that doesn't mean I'm going to immediately put my faith in something else. Right now . . ."

He trailed off. Vi dropped a stitch. He stared out the viewport at the calming blue, although he was radiating pretty much the opposite of calm.

"Right now?" she prompted.

"I don't know what to believe. But that doesn't matter. They sent me here, and I didn't have a choice, but I have to do something, so whether it's a punishment or a job, it might as well be this." His fingers tapped on the chair's hard armrest. "Although I do miss the First Order ships. This chair is like—"

"Like a torture chair?" Vi said sharply. "Didn't think you'd ever seen the wrong side of one of those."

Archex looked down, a little sheepish, but not much. "Bad metaphor."

"It was a simile."

"Are you always this annoying?"

"Always."

"She really is," Pook offered from the back of the ship. "You both are. All humanoids, really. It's a plague."

Vi almost smiled but stopped herself. She and Archex were bickering, almost like siblings. It wasn't much, but it was a start.

"I know it's hard. I know . . . well, you lost everything. But I promise you, Archex: You're going to come around and join the Resistance. Trust me—it feels great, being a good guy."

He shook his head, any trace of humor gone. "A good guy. You think you're the good guys? Then why am I wearing this?" He twitched up the pant hem on his right leg—not the injured one—to show a tracking anklet.

Vi had seen this sort of thing before. The slim metal monitor would track his every move, his heartbeat, his sleep. It would record any conversations he had. It was basically a tattletale so the Resistance could keep track of him until the First Order defector had proven himself trustworthy—if he ever chose to try.

"Just because we're altruistic doesn't mean we're stupid," she reminded him.

His eyes met hers, and it struck her to the heart, the pity she felt for her once-enemy, the man who'd taken her into that dank, blood-stained room in the belly of a Star Destroyer and pushed her to the limits of her own sanity and loyalty.

"You have to see it now, Archex. You saw the holos of the Hosnian Cataclysm. Billions of people—families, children, babies—all dead. You told me once that the First Order was all about order, but even you must recognize that they've moved on to extinction of all who oppose them. The entire First Order is flat-out wrong. I know you were starting to understand that, back on your ship. Phasma and Hux are just symptoms of the disease. But we caught you early, and there's a cure."

He rolled his eyes at the metaphor, but Vi could tell it hurt him. "And what's that?"

"Empathy." She reached out as if she might touch his arm, and he twitched away painfully, so she picked up her needles again. "Understanding. Seeing beauty in our differences. Valuing freedom and the right to fail and get up and try again. Standing together against oppression and cruelty."

"You make it sound so easy."

"It *is* easy."

Archex turned to her, leaning forward, his breathing labored. "You can't force people to believe in something, Moradi. Isn't that the whole point of your Resistance? Resisting control? Don't you all believe that eliminating the First Order lets everyone choose their path, even when they choose poorly?" She nodded. "Then you have to let me choose not to be part of the Resistance." For just a moment, he smiled—very wryly—but then his usual scowl returned.

Vi shrugged as she knitted; he seemed easier to talk to when they weren't looking directly into each other's eyes, as they had on the *Absolution*. "You get to choose what to believe, Emergency Brake. But Leia and I have faith in you. You'll change your mind. There's always something, some revelation or epiphany or line in the sand, that makes ordinary people choose to take a stand. We just have to figure out what that is—for you."

"If you were smart, you wouldn't have let me live," he said softly.

"We'll see" was all Vi could say.

He turned his eyes back to hyperspace and went silent, his only remaining method of escape on the crowded transport. Vi knew that gesture well; she'd used it during her interrogation.

She watched him a moment before returning to her knitting. It would take time for such a broken man to heal. And then he would have to rebuild his entire life, starting with his heart. He would have to find his own reasons to go on, his own path out of this valley. Pain, regret, loss, and possibly even shame would be his constant companions.

As they were hers.

It was going to be a long road.

Sometime later, Archex hobbled over to one of the transport's welded-in bunks and fell asleep soon after, which made sense—Dr. Kalonia had warned Vi that he was still healing and would be doing so for a long time, just as Vi would be. She had permanent nerve damage from Archex's clumsy use of the interrogation chair, and she didn't know if she'd ever feel two of her fingers again. At least it wasn't her trigger finger, she told herself. She still found the blue streaks of hyperspace peaceful, and with the humans silent, Pook remained silent, as well. Unfortunately, such calm only made her more uneasy.

At first, she'd been insulted by Leia's assignment, and in the wake of Crait, she'd hoped to be back in the field, this Batuu nonsense forgotten. Vi was a spy—the general's best spy, if Vi was being honest—and she excelled at disguises, slicing, and sneaking through enemy territory like a wraith. She'd heard about an upcoming assignment that involved infiltrating a Star Destroyer, but that mission had instead been given to a newer unit, code-named Green Team. Vi had sliced into the system and discovered that Major Kalonia herself had advised against sending Vi, suggesting the setting might trigger ongoing psychological trauma.

Whatever that meant.

So now here she was anyway, on her way to a nowhere city on a backwater planet to build bunks and convince naïve farmers and shady smugglers to take up a fight that hadn't yet reached their borders. It still felt like a waste of her talent and possibly a waste of time, no matter what she'd told Archex regarding the importance of the mission. It was just too simple. She'd told him to have faith in Leia, in the Resistance, but in moments like this one Vi, too, chafed at the shackles of obligation.

She took a deep breath and recognized that tight, gasping, achy feeling—it was tension. Worry. Stress. Her shoulders were hunched up and her fingers were numb, the nerve pinched. As she settled back against the hard chair and forced herself to relax, she had to confront the truth: Maybe Kalonia was right. Maybe she, too, needed time to heal. Maybe being around Archex brought it all back. Maybe she wasn't over it. Maybe she needed an assignment like this, something useful, almost a vacation on a quiet planet. And maybe the Resistance really did need warm bodies and beds to put them in just as much as they needed First Order intel.

For several days of travel, she and Archex warily shared the same small space, eating and sleeping and being bored while trying to pretend the other didn't exist. Vi had just finished knitting her hat when the ship dropped out of hyperspace, and she was almost accustomed to the rustic itchiness of the yarn. Sure, the fibers had felt soft enough on the skein, but it was rough compared with the luxurious hippoglace yarn she'd lost aboard the *Absolution* when Cardinal's men had destroyed the sweater she'd been knitting for her brother. Even thinking about it made her furious, and she had to concentrate on unclenching her jaw as she recalled her droid's nervous beeping and the feel of binders on her wrists. It was odd, how she could separate Archex from Cardinal but couldn't control her physiological response to flashbacks sparked by such small details. Yes, fine, so a Star Destroyer was probably the wrong place for her right now.

The stars came back into view, and Batuu shone below, a jewel against the indigo curtain of infinity, just as full of natural beauty and boring peace as Cerea. Beyond it, Wild Space spread across the viewport, mysterious planets and unmapped stars twinkling.

"I guess this is our new home," she murmured.

"I will only exist here until General Organa assigns me elsewhere," Pook observed. "The natural humidity levels will wreak havoc on my sensors."

Archex shuffled into the cockpit and sat heavily in his chair, turning his bad leg this way and that. "Are we there yet?"

Vi smiled and nodded at the viewport. "Welcome to Batuu. We're headed straight for Black Spire Outpost."

As if on cue, the ship's sensors beeped, and two red dots appeared. Vi kicked her knitting bag out of the way and leaned forward.

"First Order attack?" Archex asked, likewise leaning forward, his pain momentarily forgotten.

She shook her head. "They're not TIEs. Just . . ."

"Disorderly smuggler ships," Pook said. "Because that's how backwater planets operate."

Laserfire erupted as the two approaching ships went from blips on the screen to actual objects in space. A smaller craft with huge guns chased a larger ship, looking very much like a rat chasing the cat.

"They're not after us," Vi said, not that she sat back or relaxed. Their ship was big, visible, and definitely not a threat. She eased away, hating how sticky and slow the controls were.

"This transport is not equipped with deflectors," Pook reminded her from the hold. "You might wish to take evasive maneuvers. Not that you generally listen to anything I say."

"They have to see us," Vi murmured.

But the ships were acting like they were alone in space, as if Vi's hulking transport were inconsequential or possibly invisible. She wrenched the controls and juked out of the way as the first, bigger ship lumbered past, far too close for comfort.

"Is he using us for cover?" Archex shouted. "That absolute—"

"It is the intelligent thing to do," Pook interrupted.

Vi jerked the transport to the side as the smaller ship zoomed forward, bright laserfire bursting from its guns. The ship was suicidally determined to continue its path and seemed quite willing to blow up Vi's ship if it remained stubbornly blocking its target.

Vi forced her ship's nose down, but she wasn't fast enough, and the transport was too cumbersome. The smaller ship caught the transport in an impatient and impersonal burst of laserfire as it buzzed past, and Vi felt the impact in every bone of her body. The transport shuddered and wailed a complaint. Red light flooded the cockpit, an alarm blared, and Archex groaned from where he'd fallen on the floor.

"I prefer the autopilot," Pook complained. "You've tangled my wires."

Vi had no time for either of them. Alone on the galaxy's edge, with the Resistance already suffering, knowing that this ship was the best they could offer her, there was no one to call for help, no convenient squadron of X-wings to scream in and escort them to safety. And now her comm array was down, too, not that there were any Resistance allies within hailing distance. She had to get the ship planetside—and keep everyone on it alive and functional.

"Hold on!" she barked. "It's gonna be a bumpy landing."

"Lieutenant Moradi is generally an excellent pilot, for a human," Pook offered. "Not today, but generally."

"Shut it, or I'll open the hatch," Vi warned. "Let me concentrate!"

It took everything Vi had to get that ship into atmo straight-on, and even if they were coming in hot, at least they were headed in the right direction. The transport's nav system kept trying to send her directly to the docks at Black Spire Outpost, but Vi politely but firmly steered toward an old-growth forest off to the west, where her scans showed the fewest life signs. Towering, rocky spires poked up through tall evergreens that nearly scraped the clouds. At least the weather was pleasant; if Vi was going to die in a violent fireball as she plummeted to the surface of a planet in the middle of nowhere, she'd rather do it with a cheerful blue sky as the backdrop.

"Looks like a nice place," Archex said, the calm of his voice betrayed by the whiteness of his knuckles gripping the arms of his chair. "I'd hate to die here."

"You're not going to," Vi snapped through gritted teeth. "But you might want to find somewhere to strap in instead of clinging to a chair that's mostly for show."

Archex almost said something cutting, but instead he shut his mouth and hurried into the cargo area, where Pook politely told him his chances of dying depending on where he was when the ship crashed.

"We're not going to crash!" Vi shouted.

"Humans will believe anything," the droid muttered sadly.

Vi pulled up as the ship approached the treetops. They were going too fast, but there wasn't much she could do about it, so she tried to skim over the trees to lose some velocity. The trees didn't respond well to that strategy, and soon the ship went from skimming like a stone skipped over water to crashing through the upper layers of the forest like a mad rancor, breaking branches and cracking through ancient trunks as it slowed and plummeted. They clipped a spire, knocking off its tip—a worthy trade for reducing speed, in Vi's opinion.

Her safety harness kept her in place but did nothing to shield her from the knocks that nearly tore her head off her neck. Luckily, she was panicking too much to feel pain, but in the back of her mind she knew it would return with a vengeance—if she lived.

Finally the ship came to a trembling halt, trapped in thick branches and feathery needles. An inquisitive bird-thing flapped down and, for the briefest of moments, stared at Vi through the viewport, blinking brightly. Then the old transport tipped, nose down, and arrowed for the ground far below.

Chapter Four

BATUU

"LIEUTENANT MORADI, IT IS IMPERATIVE THAT you achieve wakefulness."

Vi drew a breath and her head exploded in stuffy agony, her vision flashing red with stars around the edges.

"Do I have to?" she groaned.

Cold metal gently probed along Vi's neck and head, and when she opened her eyes she was staring into a circular black screen set against a backdrop of green leaves.

"Back off, Pook," she muttered. "It's rude to stare."

Whoever had designed the PK droid had not put a single thought into making its design personable. Pook's head had no familiar and friendly anthropomorphic features, and even if that big black circle where his face should've been was actually an advanced-level scanner, Vi would've appreciated the tiniest suggestion of eyes, maybe a smiling mouth. At least astromechs looked perky.

"Your neck is, as Archex so elegantly put it, a mess," Pook explained. "There is extensive nerve damage and a bulging disk, along with repetitive stress injuries and spinal stenosis. You have the spine of a ninety-year-old woman."

"Tell me something I don't know." Vi attempted to sit up, but

Pook's three-fingered hand pressed on her upper chest, which felt like one giant bruise.

"Remain supine," he warned her. "I have not completed my scan. Archex is concerned about the dangers posed by the local population, but it is too late for that. The damage is done, and all is apparently lost."

At that, Vi hinged upright to sitting, immediately regretting that instinct and putting a hand to her neck as she winced. "What do you mean, it's too late? Were we taken prisoner?"

"Worse," Archex said. He sat on the ground nearby, his legs stretched out in front of him. He had a purpling bruise on his forehead, but at least there was no blood. "We've been scavenged."

Vi looked around. Their transport lay right-side up as if it had landed properly . . . except its blunt nose was squashed flat. It looked like it had been eaten, digested, and eliminated by an exogorth. The cargo hold door was gone—not just open but gone—and the cavernous space inside was nearly bare.

"But Pook should've stopped them!" Vi shouted, standing and trying to both catch her breath and not fall over with dizziness.

"I regret to inform you that I was unable to do so through no fault of my own."

When she looked to the droid, she saw the problem: Only half of Pook was there. He had his head, neck, torso, and one arm, but the rest of him was gone.

"Were we attacked? Did they cut you in half?"

Vi couldn't believe it. Her intel had suggested that the denizens of Black Spire Outpost weren't overly violent—just local farmers, merchants, and the usual actors in the sort of not-quite-savory economy that tended to grow around a spaceport. After her visit to Parnassos to dig up the dirty truth on Captain Phasma, Vi always did her research on the general attitude and lethality of the local populace whenever she was given a new assignment.

"I was shielding Archex from harm per the general's orders," Pook explained mournfully. "My lower half became unmoored during the crash. When the scavengers arrived, they exclaimed over the value of my extremities and enthused over selling me to a being they called Mubo. When Archex awoke, they swiftly retreated before completing my utter demolition. I am worthless now. Please reset my memory core so that I can forget what it was like to be complete."

"Sorry I didn't wake up earlier," Archex said, sounding like a kid who'd gotten a bad score on an important exam.

Vi gave him a wry smile. "Yeah, well, don't blame me for being unconscious and I won't blame you." Noting where each of them was currently located, she realized that Archex must've wrangled her out of her harness and dragged her over to Pook for a scan, an act that would've cost him dearly. She didn't thank him; she could tell it would only make him feel worse.

The world finally stopped spinning, and Vi staggered over to the transport to confirm what she already knew: Everything of value had been taken. Even the uncomfortable seats she'd repeatedly cursed had been unbolted from the floor. Interior panels showed naked places where wires had been ripped out.

"Looks like we got hit by a swarm of Dardanellian locusts," Vi said, one hand on the transport so she wouldn't fall right over. "The nerf herders even stole my hat! And my knitting bag!" She ventured a little deeper and punched the transport wall, bruising her knuckles. "And my wigs!" Thank heavens she'd pinned this one on well before her trip to Cerea.

Archex stood, a painful affair that showed just how useless his left leg was, especially without the painkillers that had been stolen along with their medkits. Trying and failing to hide his limp, he hobbled to her side, and she did wonder if he intended to catch her if she fell, or perhaps merely wanted to keep his voice low in case enemy combatants were near.

"So what do we do now? Can you contact your general for orders?"

Vi noted that he didn't say *our* general. "We're too far out, and I'm willing to bet they've pulled out our long-range comm system." She leaned into the transport, saw the state of the cockpit, and winced. "Yeah, it's gone, and the friendly fire from that welcoming party took

out the array. We might be able to pay for the privilege of using someone else's equivalent in town, but . . . then anyone could trace it back
to the Resistance, and the First Order would pay a high price for that
knowledge." She exhaled through her nose. "Unbelievable. We had
everything we needed to establish an outpost, and now it's all gone. I
have some credits from the general for incidentals, but nowhere close
to enough. We're going to have to use most of what I have just to buy
back Pook's butt."

"I thought the Resistance was well funded," Archex said.

Vi snorted. "We were. And then the Hosnian Cataclysm happened.
And then Crait happened. There's not a lot left. And my own savings
were never, shall we say, plentiful."

"So how do we get back to the Resistance?"

"We don't. We stay here to complete the mission."

"Okay, then how do we get our stolen cargo back?"

She stopped herself from laughing at him. How strange, to spend
so much of your life with the First Order that you forgot how the
actual galaxy worked.

"I suspect we're going to have to get jobs like normal folk. In case
you didn't know, a job is where—"

Archex rolled his eyes and leaned back on the transport, too. "I
was born on Jakku. I've been a scavenger. I know what work is. I'm
not someone's pampered pet gone feral. I'm just unsure what good
we could do in a place like this. I'm pretty much useless for manual
labor."

"Sell me, please," Pook said. "To reasonable people."

"If he is for sale, I know someone who'd be interested!"

This new voice came from the shadows of the forest, and Vi immediately drew her blaster, which was still in her holster and had
apparently escaped the notice of the thieves. For all that they'd stolen
everything that wasn't bolted down—and some things that were—
they'd left her person untouched.

"We don't have much left to steal, but I plan on protecting it," she
said in a low voice to Archex. "You kept up with your target practice?"

"No," he whispered back. "There were no weapons on Cerea. And I'm still wearing my anklet, so just know that anything you say to me could get back to your superiors. *Our* superiors. I don't think I'm cleared for a blaster yet."

Vi reached into one of her cargo pant pockets and put a tiny blaster in his hand. "Consider yourself cleared. It may not look like much, but it kicks."

When the figure from the forest appeared, they both had their backs against the transport and their blasters pointed. But it was just a girl—a smiling girl. She put her hands up and didn't stop smiling.

"Bright suns, friends!" she called.

Vi corrected herself. The newcomer wasn't a girl; she was a woman, one of those fortunate people who looked younger than they were thanks to a guileless and curious expression. She had black hair and warm, red-brown skin complemented by symmetrical blue designs painted on her face; her loose blue tunic draped over green pants and boots that looked like something a soldier might wear. The goggles on her head and the tools hanging from a belt at her waist suggested she had some business besides welcoming strangers in the middle of a forest, but the pretty necklace made of natural materials and stones said she wanted to look good doing it.

"Bright suns," Vi answered back, echoing what had to be a local saying. "You wouldn't happen to know who robbed us, would you?"

The woman stopped, her smile wry now. "I have a good idea, but I enjoy conversations more when no one is aiming blasters at me." Hands still up, she slowly spun in a circle, showing that she carried no obvious weapon. "I do not intend you harm."

Archex met Vi's eyes. He raised his eyebrows. She gave the slightest of shrugs and flicked her eyes down to the holster on her hip. She could draw a blaster pretty fast, and she bet he could, too, injuries or no. He gave a tiny nod and slipped his blaster into his waistband, and Vi slid hers home and tried to step confidently away from the transport. Hopefully the newcomer didn't notice her wincing when she stood on her own.

"I'm Salju," the woman said, "And it looks like you're injured." So she had noticed the wince—or maybe it was the bruises on Vi's upper chest or the scrapes on her knuckles. "Do you need help?" Salju put her hands down and cocked a hip but was wise enough to know that she hadn't been invited to approach.

Vi sighed heavily and leaned back against the transport again. "I'm Vi, this is Archex. And yeah, we got shot by some smugglers fighting their way out of atmo—"

"Ugh. Jerdan and Royce." The girl shook her head in disgust. "I knew that deal was going to go bad. They were arguing while I was filling up Jerdan's ship—I run the filling station at the port in Black Spire Outpost."

"Well, I hope they're both floating around space in a mingled cloud of atoms." Vi gestured to the transport and felt something in her neck clench. "So we crashed. And we both blacked out. And when we woke up, we were missing all of our cargo and half our droid."

As if that was the invitation she'd been waiting for, Salju walked to where Pook . . . well, *sat* wasn't quite the right word. He looked like he'd been buried in the ground and was waiting for spring rain to bloom. As the girl approached, the droid's neck swiveled to follow her.

"You look like you're having a terrible day," she said.

"You have no idea," Pook replied.

Salju poked around him, asking questions and nodding sympathetically at the droid's complaints. When she was done, Pook said, "I like her. But I am running out of charge without my second battery, so I will place myself in stasis while you work out how to regain my backside." Without another word, he mercifully powered down.

"I've got good news and bad news," Salju said, approaching Vi and Archex. "The good news is that according to your droid's descriptions, it wasn't Savi's scavengers who stole from you."

"How is that good news?" Archex asked, and Vi was glad to see his spirit returning.

"Savi runs the main scrapyard here, but he's a fair man, and if his people had done this, things would get uncomfortable. It wasn't the

Mubo your droid mentioned, either; he fixes droids but doesn't scavenge or steal. The bad news is that it sounds like the thieves were Oga Garra's minions, which means it's not going to be easy, getting things back. Oga's the boss around here, and although she's fairer than most . . . well, business comes first for her."

Vi rubbed her head and briefly saw stars again. "So let me get this straight: The people who took our entire haul work for the local gangster, which means not only do we have no hope of justice, but we're probably going to be charged three times as much to buy back our goods once the serial numbers have been filed off?"

Salju executed a little bow and said, "I'm afraid so, and may the spires watch over you. But don't lose hope. There's plenty of work in town. Maybe tomorrow you'll have a better hand."

This was not the first time Vi had lived this moment, where it felt as if all was lost and it would be rather easy to give up, change her name and hair again, and take on work that didn't involve quite so much bodily harm. But she couldn't let the Resistance down. And having been here before and having survived similar catastrophes, she knew that the only way out was through. One foot in front of the other with the same grace the general had shown after the Hosnian Cataclysm. Every step forward was a step back to normal. She could always take one more step.

"All right then," she said, her will coalescing. "Archex, you stay here with what's left of Pook and make sure no one else drags away our transport. Until something better comes up, this is our home. I'll head into town with Salju, if you're offering?" The woman nodded. "I'll find us something to sleep on, get some food, and maybe find a lead on a way to earn some credits."

Archex looked down at his leg and shook his head. "So I just sit here and babysit a husk of a ship and half a droid, huh?"

Vi sighed. "You want me to stay behind and you go in? You ever done recon before? You know what I've been told to look for? Have you even seen a town in the last twenty years when you weren't following orders?"

His brows drew down. "No."

"Exactly. Your job is to support me. So support me."

His answering nod was a tight and unwilling gesture, but it was there. He'd been raised as a soldier, after all, and he knew how to follow orders, even if he didn't like them.

Vi hobbled toward Salju, who said, "You two have an interesting relationship."

"Tell me about it."

Salju led her into the forest, and Vi was overjoyed to see that the woman had hidden her landspeeder behind some bushes. The vehicle looked like a crusty old rust bucket, but its engine purred, and the seats had woolly seat covers that felt like heaven when Vi leaned back. Salju offered her a canteen, and the water was cold and tasted of minerals.

"And now," Salju said, grinning, "let's get you to Black Spire Outpost."

Chapter Five

IT WASN'T A LONG JOURNEY, THANKS to the speeder, and Vi made note of the route so that she could get back on her own. Considering that they needed to protect what was left of their transport and conserve credits by living out in the wilds instead of finding a place in town, she assumed she'd be making the trip frequently.

Near a patch of rugged stone, they intercepted a rough sort of dirt road. "We call this Savi's Path," Salju told Vi. "It starts at the ancient ruins, which are considered dangerous or holy, depending on who you ask. But if you follow it in this direction, the path will lead you straight to Savi's scrapyards and then the market. His workshop and storefront are in BSO—which is what locals call the outpost."

Up ahead, the tall trees thinned and parted, and Vi could see evidence of civilization. The buildings were a hodgepodge of old and new, as if everything here had been built on something older using whatever materials could be found. Tarps and striped canvas awnings stretched between tall structures, providing shade for the colorful figures bustling to and fro on the paths underneath. Lanterns and censers bobbed from posts and swung from ropes, and good smells danced on the wind, promising rich spices and fire-roasted meats. The buildings favored roofs with flat domes, whether dull concrete, painted in bright colors, or crafted of metal in various stages of rust and verdigris. The structures seemed to be cut from the planet's natural features, almost as if they'd been carved from natural rock or built up from the ground itself like a child's sandcastle. Vi could hardly tell what was old and what was new.

"What's that stuff on the spire?" Vi asked, pointing to something growing on one of the many spires for which the outpost had been named. Although they looked like brown and dark-gray rock now, Vi had read that they had once been trees, petrified after eons in the elements. At this particular spire, several locals in colorful vests and sweaters were standing on ladders, scraping a strange yellow substance off the stone and into buckets.

"Golden lichen," Salju said. "A local delicacy. They call it gold dust. It can be used in paints and dyes or as a garnish for food." As if she could see Vi counting the patches of gold on various spires and structures, she added, "Seems like easy pickings, doesn't it? But Oga also controls the gold dust market, so I wouldn't get caught poaching her lichen."

"Trust a crime boss to monopolize anything of value," Vi grumbled.

"Just assume that Oga controls everything—or at least takes her cut." Salju pointed to one of the bigger structures. "We call this part of the outpost the Land Port. That's my filling station, where I handle the smaller vehicles—speeders, speeder bikes, and crankbikes. Fill 'em up and fix 'em up when they break down." She next pointed to a beige structure with three matte-gray dome roofs sprouting antennas and other crude tech—but tech nonetheless. "But that's where you'll want to go first—Mubo's Droid Depot. He's a reasonable fellow, if not to everyone's taste."

Outside the depot's trapezoidal open door waited a host of different droids, ranging from astromechs and power droids, to round BB units, to a very familiar undercarriage with an arm laid in front of it like an invitation: Pook's stolen parts.

Oga's people worked fast.

"Let's definitely talk to Mubo. Although you had me at 'reasonable' and lost me at 'not to everyone's taste,' " Vi said, scrutinizing the state of the droids on display. In her experience, the droid shops with clean, working droids tended to have proprietors with whom she could do business, whereas the crustier, sparking droids suggested someone who was only interested in credits instead of someone who enjoyed working on bots and bringing them, as a fellow on Coruscant had once put it, "back to life."

"Oh, it's not that he's bad." Salju lowered her voice as they approached, cutting her eyes at the passerby inspecting the depot's wares. "Just a bit eccentric. Manic, even. Mubo has a one-track mind, and that track is droids. He's a character, but he loves his work, and I think he might be sympathetic to your current problem."

Salju didn't try to help Vi out of the landspeeder, but she did stand nearby, just in case. As Vi limped under the awning of the Droid Depot, a cheerful and well-kept white-and-navy R4 droid beeped in welcome. She noted that none of the droids were sparking, and that Pook's rear end had been polished to a shine.

The shop was dark and cool within, and the familiar smells of metal, oil, and the sharp burn of solder made Vi feel right at home. Every surface was crowded with droid-based wares, and colorful droid appendages dangled from a conveyor belt overhead, zooming aroun the room with lively efficiency. It had a junky but whimsical feeling, as if every droid, part, or upcycled project might be exactly what some customer was looking for. Taking in the thoughtful chaos, Vi approved of the general bustle and friendliness of the shop's technicians.

"Bright suns, Salju!" called a high voice, and a stocky Utai with grayish skin waved from where he stood on a ladder behind the counter. He was working on a KX droid, goggles over his distended eyes as he waved a blowtorch in a careless sort of way.

"Mubo, your—" Salju called, pointing worriedly at the waving flame as it came perilously close to a moldering bit of tarp.

But the Utai ignored the warning, scuttling down the ladder with the torch in hand. "My latest droid!" he said proudly. "Isn't he a beaut? Picked him up for a song and a wink." He hopped to the ground and waddled around the counter—up until the hose on his blowtorch ran out of length. It nearly jerked out of his hand, and he yelped something in his native Utai, stared at the blue fire like it was a naughty pet, turned off the gas, and extinguished the flame.

"Mubo, this is my new friend Vi," Salju said with a small bow.

"Bright suns to you, too!" He lifted up his goggles and gave Vi a curious glance. "You look like someone who needs a droid."

Vi was well aware that her smile was wry and not nearly as innocent as his. "I do. Or, to be more accurate, I need half a droid. Maybe two-thirds."

Mubo cocked his head and pointed at a wall of rusty shelves holding thousands of stacked droid parts. "Well, you've come to the right place."

"Vi's ship crashed. Jerdan and Royce, you know," Salju said. She and Mubo shook their heads as if in understanding of the embarrassing business. "And when she came to, someone had stolen the bottom half of her PK-Ultra droid, as well as one of his arms."

"How rude!" Mubo said, looking truly scandalized and putting a stubby hand over his heart. "It's one thing to take a droid apart for noble reasons, but to tear one in half for coin is insulting to all who love our metal friends."

"And it looks like you paid coin for my droid's parts."

Mubo's head reared back, and he gulped and fidgeted with the goggles. "Oh. Yes. I see now. Half of a PK-Ultra droid and an arm. That's your unit out front, isn't it? I thought the price was too good, but it was the sob story that drew me in." He leaned toward Vi. "Fellow sold the parts to me at a good price this day, said it happened in a crash."

"It did. *My* crash."

Vi and Salju waited while Mubo took off his goggles, tried to clean them, smeared their lenses thoroughly with the oil on his hands, and put them back on.

"I can't give it to you," he finally said. "Because that's bad business. But I'll sell it to you for exactly the same as what I paid for it."

The price he named was in the local currency, spira. Once Salju helpfully told her the rate for converting spira into credits, Vi realized it was more than fair, and she reluctantly paid him a downpayment from her emergency stash. For all that Pook was gloomy and a little annoying, he was the key to a successful mission here. He was the one who would do the physical work of building out the site that would act as a Resistance command center and recruitment facility, erecting bunks and stacking crates and, hopefully, one day, installing power and lights and walls, and he needed legs and both arms to do it.

"Tell you what, though," Mubo said. "I'll put him back together for you for free. Your sob story's worse than the original one, and if Salju says it's true, then it's true. Where is he? Er, the rest of him?"

"On the edge of the old post," Salju said.

"I thank you for your kindness, and we'll bring him to you tomorrow," Vi broke in. Sure, Salju knew where her transport was, as did the gang of thugs who'd stolen from her. But from here on out, Vi wanted to keep the exact location of her headquarters a secret. For all that Salju and Mubo seemed like good people, such crossroads generally attracted less honest and altruistic folk, too. It was always possible that someone might recognize Vi from an old holo and attempt to make quick credits by turning her in.

Mubo smiled. "I'll see you tomorrow, then. Good trade. May the spires keep you!"

Salju led Vi back outside, where the sunlight seemed unusually bright.

"I get the 'bright suns' greeting, but what's 'may the spires keep you'?" Vi asked.

One hand shielding her eyes, Salju pointed to the rocky spires rising from the surrounding forest. "We don't know much about the civilization that was once here. Where they came from, who they were, what happened to them. We use what they left behind, but for the most part their legacy is shrouded in mystery. The one constant from their world to ours is the spires, these petrified remains of ancient trees. So we honor them with that reminder. The outpost was named for one in particular—you'll know it when you see it."

"Fair enough." Vi should've known—it was common across cultures to choose something big and mysterious and constant and treat it, well, if not as a god, then as something of importance, something that could change luck or add protection. And the spires were ancient, mysterious, and ever looming. Might as well code them as protective rather than ominous. The sooner she learned the town lingo, the sooner they'd accept her as a known quantity. "Where to next?"

Salju stopped to consider it, looking Vi up and down.

"Before you go looking for your belongings, you'll probably want to adopt some of the local wardrobe. The way you're dressed now brands you an offworlder, and offworlders are harder to trust."

"I'm not giving up my jacket," Vi said, a little more fiercely than necessary.

Salju held up her hands. "Oh, you don't have to! But a local scarf, vest, or wrap would help you blend in a little better, or at least show that you're trying. Come on. We'll stop in at Arta's place."

"I don't have money to spend on looking sharp," Vi reminded her.

But Salju just kept smiling—could anything stop that smile? "Just a cheap used wrap, then. But trust me: Fitting in could be the difference between a fair price for your goods and a deal that'll set you back. Black Spire—well, we take care of our own." She paused. "And to some, that Resistance symbol is a target."

Vi sighed; she'd hoped to find the local populace on the side of the Resistance, but of course there were always going to be detractors. "Okay. Maybe you're right. Let's go."

She briefly wondered if Salju would get a cut of any business she brought in, but she had to smother that thought. After all, Mubo had sold her Pook's missing pieces for far below the asking price and had even offered to help fix the droid—and the guileless Utai actually looked excited about the prospect. Places like Black Spire Outpost, far away from the rest of the galaxy, became tightly knit communities. Residents cared about one another and about their home. And what she'd seen of Salju so far suggested the Batuuan was genuine.

They walked through the market, and Vi saw stalls selling refreshments, lanterns, toys, pets, and artifacts. People chatted with neighbors, wove on lap looms, or ground grains into masa on worn stones. Sunlight slanted down through strips of fabric overhead, and small avians flitted everywhere, darting from the crumb-laden stone floor to nests hidden in the eaves. Lanterns of all sizes and shapes dangled from gently swooping power cords, casting warm light into even the most shadowy corners. Vi couldn't help stopping to inspect some charming carvings in a shop that appeared to be closed; she was especially interested in one showing the Jedi crest, flanked as it was by two pudgy and curious-looking bird statues.

The local architecture favored domes and swags and three-quarter arches, and the windows were all divided into smaller panes of glass, making everything feel decorative, like the icing on a cake. Balconies and turrets made patches of shade over handwoven baskets of fresh vegetables and fruit and mounds of powdered spices. Vi loved visiting markets like this, where she could exchange credits for goods farmed or crafted by callused hands and taste food one step away from nature.

In the midst of the market's splendor, one landmark stood out: a black spire different from all the rest. Instead of the usual gray and brown stone, it was all black and smooth as volcanic glass.

"I'm guessing that's the black spire of Black Spire Outpost?" Vi asked.

Salju smiled, kissed her pinkie, and touched it to the spire. "It is indeed, long may it stand."

"Why is it different from the others?"

"There are many stories. My favorite is the one about how, long ago, when the ancients dwelled here, there was once a fearsome monster in the forest called the Naklor, a hairy beast with long claws made of bone. It came out at night, when the moons were darkest, to steal gruffins and the men who went out to milk them. Soon the villagers began to suffer as the milk dried up and the hunters disappeared. So the local matriarch took her staff out to fight it, and their battle was mighty. Finally, she struck the Naklor with such power that it burned to a cinder where it stood, and this is all that's left of its shriveled husk. Some say its heart still lurks within, thirsty for blood. When I was little, we dared each other to kiss it, but we only used our pinkies."

Vi chuckled; she'd heard this sort of legend before. "So nobody thinks it's just a really old tree, huh?"

Salju winked. "Where's the fun in that?"

As they continued walking and she watched the locals go about their business, Vi had to admit that Salju was right about her clothes—nearly everyone wore some kind of woven tunic, shawl, vest, or scarf over their practical cargo pants and heavy boots. Sure, there were people wandering the market in the leather jackets and capes of smugglers and the easy coveralls of long-range haulers, but that only made them easier to pick out from the locals. When Salju led her into a warm and inviting space filled with unique clothing, Vi knew it was the right choice.

Overhead, colorful spools of thread dangled like galaxies filled with stars, while rolls of luscious fabric hung down like curving rainbows, each sporting a handwritten tag. It felt like an artisan's cozy workshop, and Vi actually found herself fingering some of the hanging clothes—on a clearance rack.

"Salju!" A slim and graceful Twi'lek woman in a beautiful magenta kurta appeared from between two lush purple curtains behind the main counter. "I told you this tunic was just the right color for you." She and Salju embraced, and Salju turned to introduce Vi.

"This is Arta Kleidun," she said. "Arta, this is Vi."

"Bright suns," Vi said with a warm smile.

Arta inclined her head and returned the greeting. "I saw you touching the shawls. Are you looking for anything specific?"

"I've been admiring the local fashions," Vi told her. "What would you suggest?"

"Her ship crashed, and her cargo was stolen, so she'd like to fit in," Salju added helpfully.

Vi schooled her face not to show her annoyance at that. Spies didn't reveal any more information than was necessary, and now that Arta knew her purpose, she might charge more or spread word among the merchants.

But Arta's smile disappeared. "Oga's boys. I saw Rusko and his gang hauling in some sleds of goods from the old post earlier. I swear, just when you think things are getting civilized—"

"You didn't come here to be civilized, Arta," Salju reminded her.

Arta rolled her eyes and shrugged. "I like a little color in my life. Doesn't mean I think we should stoop to stealing from the travelers who keep us in business." She walked to the selection of shawls that had caught Vi's eye and selected a pretty one in dark orange with a geometric pattern in deep red around the edges. "This would be nice with your complexion, bright without standing out too much." She expertly draped it over Vi and tugged here and there, making adjustments. "I saw your eyes light up at the brighter colors, but one mustn't look like they want the attention sometimes, eh?" She gently steered Vi toward a mirror, and Vi turned this way and that, admiring the clever style, which loosely hid everything above her knees yet made it easy for her to access her weapons.

"And with a few adjustments, you can . . ." Arta trailed off as she restyled the shawl to hide all but Vi's eyes. Clever girl!

Vi nodded and grinned. "I didn't come to Batuu for fashion, but I'm not disappointed," she said. "How much?"

Arta held up a small tag affixed to a corner of the shawl, which showed the original price in spira, crossed out with a welcome discount. "I can tell when someone's looking for a deal," she admitted.

Vi gladly paid her in credits, and as they left, she returned Arta's "May the spires keep you!"

Outside, she let herself breathe out a little. Bit by bit, she was moving through her troubles. Up next—

Vi's stomach, much against her wishes, growled.

Salju looked at her and smothered a laugh.

"Being in a crash makes a girl hungry," Vi admitted. "Do I smell meat?"

Salju pointed to a wide-open door farther along. "That would be Ronto Roasters—a local favorite."

"Then let's go there."

Vi was glad to notice that the locals weren't staring at her quite as much as they crossed the market. The delectable scent of roasting meat continued tickling her nose, drawing her forward, and she knew she'd made the right choice.

"So we call the owner the Butcher, but his real name is Bakkar," Salju told her. "If you want to avoid small talk and eat in peace, just don't mention podracing. He's crazy for it."

Vi perked up. "Is there podracing here?" The dangerous sport had been declared illegal, but Batuu didn't seem like the kind of place that lived under the New Republic's laws.

"Just a little, in the Galma vicinity, when they can cobble together some racers. But . . . you'll see what I mean once we're inside." Salju's smile was impish as she led Vi to the big bay door bedecked with fluttering pennants.

Yes, that was definitely the smell Vi had been following as it danced through the market: fresh meat, roasted with exactly the right spices by a culinary genius. But the setup was indeed unusual. Instead of the typical oven or pit, the meat was being roasted under the engine of a podracer. The conical mass of metal hung down from the high ceiling like an overly large lamp, flames bursting out at intervals to sear a variety of cuts that seemed to run the gamut from the promised ronto to more exotic selections. A smelting droid watched the meat and turned the spit, muttering cheerfully to himself about his prospects for a more glamorous life.

Vi followed Salju to the counter, and they both ordered the ronto wrap. They found seats at a table that looked out on the courtyard, and although Salju had plenty to say, Vi couldn't help staring past her, watching pilots in leather jackets swagger past old women rolling out flatbreads and small children chasing chickens or selling eggs from their tunics. It seemed a peaceful place, but Vi was happy to note it was busy and prosperous. She hadn't seen anyone begging in the streets, nor had she heard any blasterfire. Ships landed and took off from the port with regularity, and although she'd kept an eye out, she hadn't seen any First Order officers, nor anyone who looked like a bounty hunter. Not that that meant much—as Vi knew from personal experience, you never saw the best bounty hunters until you were in their binders, being marched to their ships at gunpoint.

After eating every bite of her meal and almost licking the wrapper, Vi remembered to order a to-go box for Archex, who was probably hungry enough to gnaw on his belt by now. She hadn't asked him if he knew anything about foraging, and she could only hope he wasn't the kind of fool to wander out on a new planet and start tasting things that looked edible. That was one thing they needed, quickly: comlinks, so they could communicate. Oh, and all of their other belongings. And a medkit, or at least painkillers. She glanced at each stall or cart they passed by, hoping to see something cheap, but anything high tech or manufactured was priced high here. After all, they were far from the Core Worlds, and such things had to be imported. Or stolen.

It was odd, though. Despite the frustration, despite the ache in her neck and back, she was actually . . . having fun.

Yes, everything about the mission had gone wrong. Yes, they were in trouble. Yes, they were missing their cargo and had suffered painful injuries. And, yes, for a spy accustomed to high-profile work, being sent to a place like Batuu felt like a demotion, like she didn't have what it took to succeed against all odds these days.

But she liked this place, blast it all.

"Are you ready?" Salju asked.

Vi looked up. She'd forgotten what was next on the docket. "For what exactly?"

This time, Salju's smile faltered. "To go to Oga's cantina."

Chapter Six

VI CONSIDERED IT. "DO YOU THINK that's the right way to approach it? I might have a concussion. I probably shouldn't be cornering the local boss in her den."

Salju shook her head. "Oh, you won't. You can't. Oga is rarely seen. She has a hidden office somewhere below the cantina. Or behind it. No one is quite sure. And Rusko—her second in command—won't help. We'll have to start with someone lower down. We can act like you're looking to buy whatever was stolen—but maybe don't mention it was stolen from you. Maybe you'll get a better deal on the lot, before they break it up too much."

Concussion or no, Vi didn't like the idea.

"Is Oga a good person or a bad person?"

Salju shrugged. "Oga supports Oga. And Black Spire Outpost, in that order. All coin is welcome here, and all trouble is escorted out. Sometimes violently."

"But what about doing what's right?"

Salju thought about it a moment before answering, "According to Oga, what's right is whatever maintains order and balance. Legal or illegal, native or traveler, we all need each other to keep this place running. When you're this far from the Core Worlds, from someone else's idea of justice, you don't worry so much about how some far-off government defines right and wrong. Oga is the only government we have, and things run well enough for most of us."

Vi found this argument frustrating, and it was why the Resistance had such a hard time gaining a foothold: Everyone thought the First Order was someone else's problem. "But the galaxy's problems will eventually come here. You know that, right? If the First Order wins, there will be no one to protect you, not even Oga."

Salju shrugged again. "When that happens, maybe things will change. But they won't change today. And if you force Oga into that conversation, I guarantee you'll never get your cargo back, not at any price."

Vi let it go. She was too tired to argue, and as much as she didn't like it, being right wasn't worth losing Salju's goodwill.

As they walked through the market, Vi could feel the day winding down. It wasn't properly evening yet, but afternoon seemed like it would last a long time on Batuu, thanks to the three suns. The market proper gave way to an area that was more . . . well, it wasn't quite seedy, but it was headed there. Instead of grandmothers sitting on stoops, wrapped in patterned scarves, she saw colorful characters leaning against walls, their eyes watchful and their hands on their blasters. She took care to draw her shawl around her and keep her posture upright and not limp, even though her neck still felt a little iffy and she couldn't even turn her head subtly to see if they were being trailed. Salju's posture and demeanor didn't change at all in response to the shifting surroundings, but why would they? This was her home.

"There's the cantina."

Not that Vi needed any help identifying it. She'd seen hundreds of cantinas on dozens of planets, and they all shared that same heady mix of excitement and grunge. Oga's cantina, as Salju had called it, was in a big, round, squat building with a heavy metal dome roof. The arched doorway was open, surrounded by banners that flapped in the evening breeze and the inviting glow of lanterns. It seemed to be part of the older architecture, with fading paint on the cream-colored walls and decorative touches here and there, including a stylized painting of a drink and patterns that looked like something from an ancient language chased into the roof. Vi braced herself for live music, but instead she heard a recording of an old Gatalentan song her mom had once loved.

Salju stopped just inside the cantina and pointed to a sign.

"You don't want to break Oga's rules," she warned. "Or she'll destroy your goods just to teach you a lesson."

Vi read the Cantina Code of Conduct, which included both sensible guidelines, like the one about no Kowakian monkey-lizards, as well as more obscure ones that spoke to past imbroglios, like the one that forbade ripping off limbs. She took careful note of the rule stating that all deals over ten thousand credits needed Oga's approval.

"That's . . . a lot of rules for one cantina," she said cautiously.

"There's a local joke about how all these things happened in one night, and Oga grew very angry and wrote out the rules to make sure it never happened again."

Vi raised an eyebrow. "In one night?"

"I wasn't here, but that's how the story goes." Salju did her little bow again, and Vi walked deeper within the cool shade of the cantina.

It was much like every cantina, but this dive bar also had a feeling of control—that had to be Oga's influence. Anyone who entered here knew that even if it was an outpost on the edge of the galaxy, they had to watch their behavior. It was still a while before quitting time, so the room was mostly empty, which may have also explained the lack of trouble.

The cantina was dominated by a stone bar that drew the eye—and kept it. Exotic creatures swam and fluttered in tanks along the bar back, including a bulbous, bug-eyed worrt, a slimy gray swamp slug, and a pickled mynock forever silently screeching behind the safety of thick glass. Vi's attention was drawn to droid heads placed around the bar like a strange cross between a threat and art; Mubo probably hated it. And the drink taps—she'd never seen so many, each one a unique shape suggesting the beverage within. She was especially intrigued by the one shaped like a lightsaber hilt—and the four made of rancor teeth. One even had a trio of that same round bird she'd noted among the carvings outside. The tables and bar were all lit from within and gave the red-tinged room an intriguing glow.

They weren't at the cantina to drink, though—they were here for information. Still, Vi knew that she'd be spending a lot of her time here, listening to the local talk, approaching visiting pilots, and generally keeping up with the news of the greater galaxy beyond, especially when it came to keeping tabs on the First Order. She hoped all those drinks in their fascinating taps were tasty—and good at loosening tongues. If she could play it right, this would be her main recruiting ground for the Resistance.

Vi took a seat in one of the booths while Salju went to the bar and spoke with the bartender, an older human woman in faded robes of blue and mustard yellow who looked like she'd forgotten how to smile. Salju returned shortly and slid a foamy drink across the worn table.

"It's called a Spice Runner," she said, taking a sip of the same. "A local cider." She grinned. "My favorite."

Vi took her first sip and immediately liked it, sighing gratefully as the warmth unspooled through her middle and her shoulders finally relaxed down from around her ears. In between the crash, the thievery, and this afternoon's work, it had been a tense afternoon.

"None of Oga's lieutenants are around," Salju said, leaning in. "I'm guessing they're off, as you said, filing away the serial numbers on your cargo. So I think your best bet is to enjoy your drink, pick up some blankets, and head home for today. Unless you want to talk to Savi while you're in town?"

"You've mentioned that name before. Who's Savi?"

Salju took another sip and wiped the foam from her lip. "He runs Savi and Sons, the main scavenging company. Brings in rusted ships and loads of unwanted junk from all over the galaxy, sorts through it, and sells what he can. Not only could he be on the lookout for your things, but he's your best chance at a job here, unless you have any particular skills. I forgot to ask!"

Vi thought of her best skills: spying, thievery, interrogation, infil-tration, evasive flying. Definitely not knitting. Nothing with fashion. Nor did she relish making flatbreads or shelling peas. Merchant Row was not her place. She couldn't work in this bar, she knew that much—more than a couple of hours of dealing with rude customers would land her in whatever passed for jail here, explaining that the guy broke his own nose by accident.

"I can scavenge," she said. It was actually a good direction, consid-ering their setbacks. She would learn the lay of the land, make con-nections with the locals, and probably get deals on any junk parts this Savi guy didn't know how to move. Even sheet metal and old cargo containers would help build up the recruitment post the Resistance so desperately needed. "What kind of man is this Savi?"

"Kind. Wise. Old. Maybe a little gruff, until he gets to know you. He's fair, which is not what you generally hear about scrappers. And the folk who work for him are almost like a family. He takes care of them, and they take care of each other. If I had to work for someone besides myself, I would consider him." She dimpled and ducked her head. "But I'd ask Arta first because I could use the employee dis-counts."

Vi chewed the inside of her cheek before asking the big question, the one she'd been holding off on with each introduction on the planet. But if she was going to consider working for someone, day in and day out, she needed to know.

"Do you know how he feels about the conflict between the First Order and the Resistance?"

Salju rubbed the condensation off her glass and considered it. "People who weren't born here but who choose to stay and build a life in BSO are usually running away from something. Lots of times, it's the law; other times, it's that general busyness of the galaxy. Batuu is a small place, its own place, a closed sphere. The First Order and the Resistance are just stories brought to us by offworlders who leave the next day. So until they become our problems or our saviors, ei-ther way, we don't much think about them at all. But I think Savi is against oppression of any sort. He had ties to the Jedi long ago, I heard."

"Let's stop by, then," Vi said. "After we get my droid fixed tomorrow, I'd like to have something to do besides sit around that clearing, feeling sorry for myself and hearing Pook complain."

"And although the main office is here in the Land Port, the junkyard is out near your clearing, too, so that's a shorter walk."

Vi grimaced. "Do I look like I'm in that bad a shape?"

Salju gave an apologetic shrug. "I'm sure you'll clean up fine after a bath and some sleep."

They finished their drinks, took their glasses back to the bar, and headed out the door. As soon as they were outside, Vi sensed danger. Everyone in the market was staring at something across the street from the cantina.

"Where the hell have you been?" came a raspy, gurgling voice that somehow managed to chill Vi to the bone. The language was Huttese, which of course Vi understood.

A figure stepped out from the shadows—a Blutopian, Vi knew, thanks to her extensive training on alien species.

"That's Oga Garra," Salju whispered, surprised. "It's a rare thing, seeing her out and about."

Oga, like all Blutopians, was a curious sort of person to human eyes. The local crime boss had wrinkled, leathery skin that faded from gray to a fleshy salmon, and her mouth was a mess of pinkish tentacles that constantly moved in a peevish sort of way and reminded Vi of a can of angry worms. Her back was hunched, but her flipperlike arms had thick hands that looked capable of crushing skulls. She wore a belted tunic and vest that Vi was certain had come from Arta's shop, along with cargo pants and brown boots. Her eyes were small black dots, but she somehow managed to look crafty—and dangerous.

"Nnngharooogrrrr!"

Up on a balcony, a Wookiee had emerged from the arched door of an apartment and seemed to be the focus of Oga's wrath. The Wookiee's hair was mussed, he was in the middle of buckling on a bandolier, and despite his general lack of expressive facial features and her tenuous grasp of Shyriiwook, Vi could tell he was embarrassed . . . and frightened.

"Taking an afternoon nap? In the room assigned to that new Rodian waitress, Meeba? The same one I saw you giggling with in the back booth last week, when you assured me you were merely discussing the going rate for Corellian champagne?"

"Mmrawwr!"

"Well, what was it, then? Were you fixing the bathroom for her or . . . oh, I don't know. Navigating some other sort of personal plumbing issue?"

Whispers had started up, and the Blutopian spun around, blaster ready.

"This is between me and Dhoran," she warned them. "I can't make you leave, but I can accidentally shoot you."

The locals didn't seem to understand Huttese, but the sentiment was clear in any language. Their whispers went silent, and several of the more timid folk blended back into the shadows or scuttled behind half-closed doors to continue watching.

"Rrhhhhhogah?" the Wookiee crooned, putting his hands on a low metal railing and leaning down as if to give his lady love a flower and beg for her favor.

Oga turned away, waving a hand as if to disperse him. "Don't you *Oga* me, you walking catastrophe. Get off my planet and don't ever come back or I'll mount your head on the bar with the droids."

Dhoran stood back up and smoothed the hair around his face. "Huhn. Greh." Vi didn't know much Shyriiwook, but that sound of scorn and dismissal was about the same in all languages.

Without another word, Oga spun around and shot the Wookiee in the chest.

Dhoran's hands—or paws, Vi didn't know what was under all that hair—clutched at the smoking wound. The Wookiee's eyes went wide with surprise and he gently toppled over the rail, breaking the aged metal as he tumbled into space and fell with a heavy thump at Oga's feet.

The Blutopian knelt, pinched him somewhere, and muttered, "Good riddance." Then, almost to herself, "Why do I always fall for the big, hairy bad boys?"

A new figure appeared in the open apartment door. The tall female Rodian was wrapped in only a small pink towel, but she screamed bloody murder as she stared down at the dead Wookiee. Oga glanced up briefly, aimed her blaster, and shot a bolt within centimeters of the Rodian's antennae.

"You're fired. Get out of here. I'm keeping this week's wages as your formal apology."

The Rodian disappeared, and Oga silently looted her former lover's body. She slung his bandolier over her shoulder and stood.

"Anybody who doesn't want to eat lasers should probably stay out of my way today," she said.

Everyone found something else to look at or somewhere else to go, and the Blutopian disappeared into the shadows around the edge of the cantina, her shoulders hunched. Vi noted the direction, reasoning that if she ever needed to face the gangster herself, she would find an entrance in that area. The busy market went back to normal, but the sort of normal that involved completely ignoring a smoking Wookiee corpse.

"So that was Oga," Salju said again. "And you definitely don't want to talk to her today. Maybe not this week. Or month."

"Then let's just hope that your friend Savi hasn't experienced a personal tragedy today."

"Oh, we all will," Salju said darkly. "As soon as her orders go out on payday and we see our usual contribution go way up. Oga has a hand in every business. She takes a cut of all profits. You don't do a big deal without her blessing. When she gets mad . . . her thugs get mad, and they demand a higher cut, and . . ."

"When she weeps, the economy weeps."

"Yes, but all the runoff is still directly into her pockets."

They headed past what was left of Dhoran and into the market, retracing the route that had brought them here. Vi was more cautious now, having seen evidence that despite the rules scrawled on her cantina, Oga's Black Spire Outpost was still a rough and lawless frontier town. At least Oga's thugs hadn't looted Vi's own body as she sat unconscious in her crashed ship; she still had her credits and the weapons that had been hidden on her person, and she knew how to use them.

Most of the people in the market, however, seemed to be innocent locals just going about their business. As they wound through the shops and carts, Vi took note of every stall and proprietor they passed and innocently asked Salju about them while secretly considering who might make a good ally.

The Milk Stand was run by an Aqualish farmer named Bubo Wamba who was new to the planet and spent much of his time among his banthas or in his stall—probably not an ideal recruit. Zabaka the Toydarian toymaker was deeply loyal to Oga, Salju said, so Vi likewise crossed her off the list. Kat Saka, who ran the popped-grain stall, was a fourth-generation Batuuan who owned several farms and was therefore unlikely to want to get involved in any conflict. Kamka of The Jewels of Bith and Bina of the Creature Stall were also not great candidates for the Resistance. The entrepreneurs of the area would have too many reasons not to join up. She would need to look at the working-class Batuuans, at the farmworkers and dockworkers and visiting pilots, if she wanted to lure recruits to her cause.

Next to the Droid Depot was another large shop, this one more of a compound with a small courtyard. Painted on the wall was the logo for Savi and Sons Salvage. Vi noted that it, like the cantina, had faded decorations that included strange symbols resembling some sort of ancient alphabet. As she watched, a teen girl with curly hair walked up to an interesting tree planted just outside the workshop. Hundreds of colorful bits of ribbon and rope fluttered from the tree's branches, and the girl tied on her own bright-green strip of fabric, closed her eyes, smiled briefly, and walked away looking lighter and happier.

"The Trilon wishing tree," Salju said before Vi could ask. "This is how we send our hopes and wishes out into the universe. You tie a piece of fabric to the tree and make your vow or ask your wish, and when it disintegrates, the galaxy grants your boon."

"So you do think of life beyond Batuu."

Salju nodded earnestly. "We look up and see the same stars as everyone else, even if our exact perspective is different."

Vi grinned. "I like that. A whole tree, covered in hope." Leia would like that, too, she thought.

Salju led her to an outdoor counter under a sloping awning and told a smiling worker that she was looking for Savi. They were asked to wait, and moments later a wrinkled old white man appeared, bowing with gentle formality. He had gray hair with a matching mustache and beard, and his left arm was a silver prosthesis that seemed as if it had always been a part of him. For all that he looked utterly ancient, there was an energy about him, a vitality, as if he could stay up all night arguing over philosophy or helping a shaak give birth. He was dressed in the usual natural colors and layers of Batuu but also wore a slender scarf tied jauntily around his neck.

This man did not at all fit Vi's mental image of a salvager, the sort of big, brusque fellow who bullied his way to better deals and bought dead ships from desperate people for the lowest price he could pressure them into. There was something soft and gentle about him, a serenity as well as a curiosity. Vi liked him immediately.

After Salju explained Vi's predicament, Savi gave her a long, measuring look. She returned the stare and fought the urge to straighten her posture and look competent; this guy wasn't General Organa, after all. Why would she need to please a backwater junk seller? Having a brain and a mostly functional back should be adequate skills to work as a scrapper.

"I can always use more Gatherers," Savi told her, "but I'd like to know a little more about you. How did you end up on Batuu?" His eyebrows rose in question, and Vi felt like she was being tested. But at the same time . . . well, something about Savi made her want to open up, to tell him the truth. There was something familiar or some fellow feeling here. She looked at Salju, whose warm smile and nod suggested it was safe to trust the old man. And if he knew her goal, perhaps he could help her along the way.

"My ship crashed, and my cargo was stolen, and now I need to earn credits to buy back my goods," she told him. In other circumstances, she might've said that she just wanted to get offplanet and go her merry way, but no employer ever wanted to hear that from a potential hire.

His eyes crinkled up. "Yes, that answers the 'how' part, but it cleverly evades the 'why.' What business brought you here?"

"I was delivering a shipment," she said, and it was true. Some people, Vi included, had a sort of sixth sense for lies, and she suspected Savi was one of them. You didn't get as old as he was without being, well, savvy.

The old man's eyebrows rose. "Delivering a shipment to whom?"

Vi felt like a little kid caught out by a kindly grandfather. They were toying with each other, and the old man wasn't going to give in until he was satisfied.

"I hear you're not a fan of the First Order," she said, changing the subject to put him in the hot seat.

Savi nodded as if finally satisfied by the conversation. "I believe what you're really asking is if I'm a supporter of the Resistance. My longtime friend Lor San Tekka was a great believer in the Jedi Order, and together we decided it was our calling to help keep the Force in balance. Perhaps it's not mine to choose others' paths for them, but I believe in supporting those who are strong in the Force, who are fighting for the same ideals."

Vi considered how to move forward. On one hand, she was far from any allies and had been specifically assigned to recruit new members for the Resistance. Savi had already identified himself as being in the same camp. On the other hand, directly telling anyone on Batuu that she worked for the Resistance could result in the wrong people finding out and alerting the First Order.

Well, they were going to find out soon, anyway. And there was just something about Savi; all Vi's instincts told her he could be trusted. As hard as it was for a spy to lay bare her truth, that was the only way to find allies and move forward.

"I'm with the Resistance," she said, carefully watching his face to see how he would react. "I was sent to this place to build a new Resistance waypoint away from the First Order's territory. It's true that I crashed and that my supplies were stolen, and I need to earn credits to buy them back or replace them with something better."

Savi nodded, a smile playing at his lips. "So you *are* with the Resistance. And it's still led by Princess Leia, yes?"

Vi bristled, just the tiniest bit. "General Organa is her formal title."

The old man chuckled. "Some of us have many names, live many lives. And her brother was Luke Skywalker."

It wasn't a question, so Vi didn't answer it.

"Our allies are in trouble, Savi. *We* are in trouble. Our greatest hope now is to find footholds to help us regroup and rebuild so that we can continue to fight. General Organa sent me here to do just that."

Savi clicked his tongue and fussed with a ring on his right hand. "Building something from nothing. A difficult task, even when you have all the resources you require." He met her gaze, and this time she didn't only see the old, kind man. She also saw the fierce, strong core of him. "I can hire you. And I can help you find some of the supplies you'll need to build your refuge. But I need to know that you are trustworthy. This business is called Savi and Sons Salvage, not My First Priority Is My Other Job. When you're on the clock, you're working. Not recruiting, not giving speeches, not begging my customers and employees to join your cause. I must protect my livelihood and that of my other scrappers, and we can't have Oga slamming her fist down on my counter, complaining about one of my people."

It was a fair enough statement, and Vi nodded.

"I appreciate your position, Savi. I'm a hard worker who knows when to keep her mouth shut. During work hours, I'm a scrapper." She leaned in and let the strength and tenacity of her own core rage in her eyes. "But outside of work hours, I am my own person. I'll tell my own truth and collect what allies I may. It's hard to believe, out here on the edge of nothing, that the First Order could ever destroy your safe little world, but I've seen it happen. One day, they'll land here, too, and you'll be glad to have us on your side."

Their eyes locked in a battle of wills so electric that Salju had to clear her throat and inspect an old thruster. Finally, Savi blinked and the crinkles returned around his eyes and mouth.

"The world needs true believers," he said with a creaky laugh. "After all, I can't force you into silence."

The way he said "force" stood out to Vi, but Savi bustled back behind his counter, his former presence replaced with the sort of cheerful friendliness that kept customers in a good mood. "When would you like to start?"

"Day after tomorrow would suit."

Savi picked up a datapad and typed, all business now. "You'll start at the scrapyard, on the outskirts of town, near the old post. Do you know it?"

"We'll pass by there on our way back to her ship," Salju said.

"Good. Work starts at dawn. Ask for Ylena. She'll get you on your feet."

Vi inclined her head. "Thank you. I won't let you down. May the spires keep you."

It felt like a promise, using the BSO phrase, like she was becoming part of something good.

Savi returned the small bow and murmured, "And you."

As she followed Salju toward the market, Vi thought she heard the old man softly say, "And may the Force be with you," but when she glanced back over her shoulder he was gone.

Chapter Seven

ON THE WAY OUT OF TOWN, they made one last stop at a supply cart where a scruffy but arrogant Trandoshan named Kasif attempted to sell Vi the newest innovation in self-warming, self-cooling, self-inflating sleeping bags . . . until Salju got in his face and threatened to raise the price of fuel the next time he came to gas up. Flustered and taken down a notch, Kasif instead brought out a selection of used, lightly ragged sleeping bags that he swore no one had died in.

Now toting Archex's dinner and a pack with one broken strap and enough room to hold both sleeping bags, Vi was more than ready to get back to the ship and settle in for the night. But Salju suggested that she pick up some fruit, beverages, painkillers, and other necessities from the market stalls, which were still open and lit by lanterns that glowed orange against the purple sky.

Other than Pook's parts, they hadn't seen a single case of Vi's missing cargo, but Salju was certain it would turn up in the next week. She promised to make discreet inquiries with an infamous pirate, Hondo Ohnaka—and warned Vi to stay out of his way, as he would sell his own grandmother for a few credits and would happily alert the First Order if he recognized a wanted spy. Vi wished she had some way to thank the local woman, who had sacrificed an entire day to helping her get around and securing far better deals from the locals than she would've won on her own.

As she settled into the landspeeder's cushy seats, Vi nearly collapsed in relief. Thank the stars she didn't have to walk back; she was already exhausted. Instead of turning off toward Vi's camp, however, Salju steered the speeder farther down Savi's Path. Vi smelled the scrapyard before it came into view—there was nothing else like the smell of thousands of tons of old metal, the oil and fuel baking in the sunlight and leaking into the hard ground all day and now cooling with the evening breezes.

"You'll enter here." Salju pointed to a more formal entranceway, and Vi nodded.

It had been a long time since she'd had a job that involved showing up at a certain time each day and doing repetitive work, and she wasn't particularly looking forward to it—even if it was necessary and purposeful. She had to remind herself that at least it was better than getting stuck in the belly of a Star Destroyer again with a guy like Archex used to be, back when he'd been Captain Cardinal. There was something to be said for a profession where you had a reasonable expectation of getting to work and back home without any threat to your life.

"Dawn's going to come real early," Vi noted, her voice creaking.

Salju laughed and turned the speeder back around. "You've had a bit of a day."

The stars began to peep out from between the leafy boughs overhead as Salju steered the speeder through a landscape merging ancient ruins with giant trees and an understory of tall ferns, all curled up for the night. As they passed through a clearing that contained an unusual circle of angular black stones, Vi leaned back and looked up at the sky, wincing at the pain in her neck, which the painkillers had helped but not eliminated. No matter which planet she was on, she always loved looking up and seeing new stars. Somehow, those tiny white pinpricks always told a new story.

"So where are you from?" Salju asked.

Vi's spy training made her look at the girl with suspicion, but

Salju's face was as open and curious as that of a child. She would've made a terrible spy.

"Chaaktil, originally," Vi finally said.

"What's it like? I've seen some old star maps, but most of what I know comes from visitors at my filling station, and I don't think I've heard of that one before—of Chaaktil."

Vi considered it. "Mostly desert. Nothing like here. Going too far away into nature meant you might end up a well-buffed skeleton if a storm came up suddenly. Small cities grew up around deep wells and then became tall cities. We had the best fried palm fruit."

"What about the animals? I love to hear about new animals."

"Lots of lizards and dragons. Chaakrabbits and chaakrats. The chaakroaches were as big as my foot, but we just thought of them as free protein with a creamy center."

Salju shuddered. "Okay, so that might not be on the top of my list of places to visit one day." She looked away, which wasn't something she often did. "I've always been good with machines. I can fix almost anything. So I figure if things ever go bad here, I'll just hitch a ride out. I know all the pilots. I keep a list of all the places that sound interesting, so I'll just pick one and go there."

The look Vi gave her was half amusement and half pity. "So you've never been offplanet?"

"Never."

The starbird on Vi's jacket felt warm over her heart. "Well, if you change your mind, the Resistance could use you. If you're as good with machines as I'm guessing you are—and I know you're good with people—you'd be an asset to us. You could be a mechanic in the fleet or run tech on one of our bases. And you could see new planets all over the galaxy."

Salju smiled, her eyes rolling up to the stars as she considered it.

"Thanks for the offer, but this is home," she finally said. "Black Spire has a way of getting under your skin."

"Well, just know the offer is always there."

Considering the way the girl kept staring up at the stars with twinkling eyes, Vi realized that Salju represented her main challenge on

Batuu: How could she convince normal, everyday people—good people—to give up their comfort and safety to stand up against evil? Vi had seen firsthand what the First Order could do. She had tended to refugees and comforted orphaned children and nursed burns and buried bodies. To her, the Resistance was the only choice. To Salju and her neighbors, it wasn't a choice at all, but something other people threw themselves into—fools and heroes. Vi didn't consider herself either one—just a person who had already drawn her line in the sand.

It was full dark by the time they returned to the clearing, the speeder's headlights flashing on bounding dugar dugar and violet-scaled lahiroo as they fled into the trees. Firelight flickered past the thick trunks up ahead, and Vi smelled roasting meat. Her estimation of Archex went up a notch. Salju called out, "Rising moons, friends!" and Pook powered up and complained about it, muttering, "All living things should come with built-in volume control."

Archex rose from one of two logs he'd dragged near the fire. He looked like something a gundark had eaten and spit back out, and his exhaustion and pain showed in every line of his face, but he was smiling.

"Hope the local birds aren't poisonous," he said, pointing to several plump forms roasting on cleaned sticks over the fire. He was both sheepish and proud about his accomplishment and reminded Vi of a little boy who'd just proven himself capable of a new skill. Not that she would ever say something like that out loud to him.

"So I guess that means you don't want a precooked meal?" Vi grinned as she extricated herself from the speeder and dangled the bag in front of him.

He greedily snatched it up and opened it, inhaling the aroma of roasted ronto with eyes closed. "Oh, I'll take a real meal over half-raw, half-charred fowl any day."

Salju knelt by the fire to inspect his work. "They were indigo and gray with white stars on their chests, right?" When Archex nodded, she said, "They're called starmarks. And they taste a lot better with salt and spices. Definitely not poisonous."

"Anything's better than starving," Vi reminded them both. She tossed her bag on the ground and sat heavily on the log. "And nothing is better than sleep." She looked up at Salju. "Thank you so much for all your help today. Really. I get the feeling you were just being nice to a down-on-their-luck stranger, but you've done the Resistance a great service, and we won't forget it."

Salju inclined her head. "Then I'll head back home. I'll be at the filling station tomorrow—and most days—should you need me or just want a companion for meals. May your deals go well!" Salju raised a hand, and Vi raised hers.

"May the spires keep you!"

Salju drove into the forest, then stopped the speeder to shout, "Oh, and don't worry—it should be pretty safe out here. Rusko will have spread the word among the criminal element in town that there's nothing left to steal. And there aren't many natural predators—at least, not big ones. Just beat a stick against your ship if you hear growling nearby." And then she was gone.

"What was that about predators?" Archex asked from where he sat on the other log, tearing into his long-cold meal.

Vi unrolled one of the sleeping bags and considered whether it would be better to sleep out here, where she'd be under the stars and where the ground was halfway soft, or in her bunk on the ship, where she might be a little safer but her back would be punished by cold, hard metal, since even the thin mattresses had been taken. With a weary sigh, she spread the bag out near the fire, inflated the pillow, and tested its relative coziness, which wasn't terrible.

"Pook can keep watch," she said. "No predator wants any piece of him."

"But if I allowed you to be eaten, I could have such peace," Pook moaned.

"But your programming commands you to keep us safe."

Pook gave a mechanical sniff. "Would that I had permission to reprogram myself. For so many reasons."

Vi lay back, elbows out, and gazed up at the stars. "Damn, I miss my old astromech. No complaints, just beeps."

"Beep," Pook said, and it carried the existential weight of the entire galaxy in that one syllable.

Vi tried to get comfortable and go to sleep, and she was definitely exhausted, yet she just couldn't settle down. She drank some water from the canteen she'd brought, gave Archex some of the sub-par painkillers she'd found in the market, and picked at the mostly cooked bits of leftover starmark meat before reclining back onto her pillow. When that proved too uncomfortable, she got back up and unpinned her wig, removing it and her shimmersilk cap and untwisting her hair, sighing to finally feel her scalp relax. Finally, furious with her body for not going insensate, she hopped up and stomped around the clearing as if to scare off those predators Salju had mentioned.

"You seem on edge," Archex observed.

Vi gave him a look. "You think?"

"Seems like you had a good trip to town, though. People weren't terrible?"

She shook her head. "They weren't terrible. They were just people. But are they people we can recruit to our cause? They've never seen First Order tactics up close. They can't be scared of something they can't yet imagine."

Archex chuckled. "Yeah, they don't advertise their eventual reign. Lots of civilizations are totally innocent when the TIEs scream out of atmo and the transports belly up to the docks. On many planets, they look at us—at the stormtroopers, I mean—like gods descending with open arms, like your basic grunts will solve poverty and fill every empty belly. When they first file into the mess hall, some kids openly weep because they've never seen so much food and water at once."

He was on his back on his own sleeping bag and looked . . . kind of happy. Vi hadn't seen him happy before. Even in pain, even on a mission he still had doubts about, Archex was smiling. Which meant she could probe a little more deeply.

"So I get how the First Order convinces orphans to sign up, but how do they recruit adults to the cause?"

That made him stop smiling. He rolled up on one elbow and stared at her like she was an idiot.

"Some people are grateful for order, just begging for rules to follow. You'd see them exhale in relief when they saw our uniforms and then glare smugly at their troublesome neighbors, feeling that they themselves were safe because they were righteous. And then some people are desperate for money, and the First Order pays for intel and tattling. There are always those eager to be minions, to rest safely in the shadow of the bigger predator."

"You've thought about this."

He nodded wryly. "I thought about it a lot on Cerea. But the truth is that most people don't welcome the First Order, and they're the ones who get recruited at blasterpoint. Technically, it's not even recruitment. The First Order just takes over. They subsume. Patrols, executions, hostile takeovers, controlling the flow of information and spreading propaganda while silencing those who speak against the cause. I went on a few of those missions when I was younger, and they told us we were only punishing those who stood in the way of progress. All the clever slogans they fed us, the lies they told us—I can't even explain it. It was all we heard. Everyone else was the enemy, which made us the good guys. So we believed it."

"They brainwashed you."

He chuckled ruefully. "Yeah, well, in a way, it's pretty nice, being brainwashed. You're not constantly questioning everything. You do what you're told, and then it's dinnertime." He winces. "I had fewer headaches and was less grouchy."

Vi opened and closed her left hand. She still couldn't feel two of her fingers. "And you didn't hurt, then, either. I can't wait until we get Pook back up and running in a decent medbay."

"Some better painkillers would not go amiss. The ones from town are . . ." He trailed off, apparently not wanting to seem ungrateful.

"Not strong enough," she finished for him.

"I look forward to having the proper supplies to dose you both into oblivion," the droid grumbled from the darkness. "You'd complain less."

The silence after that was more tense than it should've been for two people who didn't necessarily hate each other, camping out under the stars. They had decent sleeping bags, they had full bellies, they had a fire. Yet as Vi stared at their broken, gutted transport, she realized she was fuming angry. And not doing a good job of hiding it.

"It's not your fault," Archex said, so softly she could barely hear it. "The crash."

"Sure feels like it is," she whispered back. "But I'll fix it."

Eventually, she fell asleep, and it was just like falling off a cliff. Nearly dying, she'd learned long ago, was always exhausting.

The next morning, Vi woke up with the first sunrise. Her mouth felt like she'd spent all night licking swamp slime off a sleen. She had no mirror, no toilet, no soap, no toothpaste.

"Did he find any water yesterday?" she asked Pook, as Archex was still asleep.

"He did a small amount of recon and found a natural spring in that direction, a journey of five minutes." Pook raised his one good arm and pointed into the woods. "I can only assume the water wasn't poisoned, as he's still alive. And snoring."

Vi ignored that, although the droid was right. She hurried into the forest and soon found a beautiful turquoise spring with white stone walls, surrounded by healthy ferns. With only the briefest pause, she undressed and bathed, careful to keep her hair dry. The clearing felt otherworldly and ancient, with a beam of sunlight angling perfectly down to sparkle on the water. Nearby, jagged cliffs rose from the ground, and if they'd landed safely with all their cargo she would've given herself an hour to sunbathe and relax until she was dry. As it was, she hurriedly dressed while still regrettably damp, did her best to pin on her wig, picked at the cold meat still spitted over the coals, and regarded what was left of her droid.

"You're super strong, aren't you, Pook?"

The droid cocked his head. "That is obviously why I was assigned to this doomed mission."

"How much can you lift?"

If he could've scoffed, he would've. "When I possess all my limbs,

I can lift up to three tons, if there are reasonable handholds and anchorage."

Vi nodded. "Excellent. I'll be right back."

There was no school for Resistance spies—although there should've been—but Vi had undergone rigorous training that included navigation. She easily found her way back to the outpost using Salju's shorter route and in less than an hour returned to the clearing carrying Pook's missing arm.

"Consider this a down payment," she said, holding it out to the droid.

Archex watched from where he ate cold fowl on his log. Vi hated about 99 percent of what the First Order had done to this decent man, but she did appreciate that when she made a plan, the former soldier rarely argued or questioned her, viewing her as his superior officer.

Pook stared at his arm and then directed his gaze—or at least pointed the round, black screen of his face—to her.

"That is my arm," he observed.

"Yep, and now we're going to reattach it."

"Your tools were stolen."

Vi held up a rough canvas case and grinned. "I borrowed some."

It would've been easier with Salju's help and mechanical savvy, but Vi and Archex managed to follow Pook's instructions and reattach his arm. It wasn't a perfect connection, and it wasn't pretty, but it was load bearing, and that was the important part.

"Perhaps you have forgotten I am missing my legs," the droid said.

Vi mimicked an apelike, swinging motion. "Then let's go get them. They're on the edge of town at the Droid Depot, and if you can just manage to get yourself there, Mubo can't wait to give you a tune-up."

Pook put out his arms, laid his three-fingered hands flat on the ground, and lifted his torso. "I hope this Mubo can erase my memories of the past two days."

With his prodigious intelligence and strength, the droid easily mastered locomotion, and he and Vi were soon entering the Droid Depot, where Vi first returned the borrowed tools. Mubo was delighted to have a new project, and he and his mechanics quickly had Pook in one piece, oiled and resoldered, as good as new. All the wires that had jiggled or ripped loose were replaced, and even Pook couldn't complain once they were done.

"Are we now to return to the forest?" Pook asked as he tested his various joints and waited for Mubo to oil them. "Or will you find some way to exacerbate my misery here in the city?"

"Back to the forest. Work is your job, Pook," Vi reminded him.

"Then why was I given this enormous intellect?" he wailed.

"Because you're our Everything droid. Protocol, heavy lifting, medcare, all that."

"Unless you want me to dumb him down or silence his voicebox?" Mubo asked. "Shouldn't be too hard. Just a few tweaks, and—"

Pook jerked away from the Utai's oil can and gasped, "How dare you!"

But Mubo just laughed and went back behind his counter, giving Vi a friendly but expectant sort of look. She presented him with the remaining credits she owed him—plus a small tip, even though she couldn't really afford it. Some wheels, Vi knew, were worth greasing. He squeaked with pleasure and leaned in close. Vi leaned down, too.

"Saw some interesting things for sale in Smuggler's Alley," he whispered. "You'll need Oga's approval to go there, of course. Prices were ridiculously high, but I wouldn't try to haggle down too hard."

Vi nodded. "Good trade."

Mubo nodded back. "And you."

The market felt pleasantly familiar today, and Vi was glad for her wrap. Pook stumped along beside her, turning his head from side to side. That was good, too—his memory would map out the town, which would be of benefit in the future, when their headquarters were further along. Without appearing to be in too much of a hurry, acting as if she had every right to be there, she ambled down Smuggler's Alley and inspected some of the wares displayed in carts and on blankets. One merchant in particular had a large selection featuring several items that Vi recognized.

"Not a word, Pook," she growled. "Complete silence. Keep your distance. That's an order."

Pook sighed heavily and settled down, his fingers tapping against his round middle as Vi walked closer to the goods for sale. Yep, that was her tool chest. There were their medpacs. There were the pieces of her built-in kitchen and restroom, still flat-packed in their crates. Heat rose in her cheeks, and she swallowed the anger down.

The only thing Vi hated as much as a bully was a thief, and she suspected she was about to deal with both. She counted down from ten, made her face carefully neutral, and walked under the awning.

"Bright suns!" called a female Duros wearing a yellow Batuuan wrap that set off the blue-green of her skin and the red of her eyes. Vi didn't let her smile falter, but she hoped this woman hadn't been part of the raiding party that had stolen her cargo. A Duros had once told her they had perfect memories, and this interaction wouldn't go as well if the shopkeeper knew who she was. "How can I help you?"

"Bright suns, Traveler," Vi responded, adding a nod to the Durosian honorific. "I'm thinking about setting up shop in the port, and I see some goods I could use here. Are your prices firm?"

The woman stood and walked with Vi among her wares. "Prices are always negotiable, but I'd be glad to tell you what we're asking." If the clerk had been human, Vi had a dozen ways to leech extra information from her—her eyes, her breathing, the pulse at her throat, her word choice. But as she was a Duros, her face had almost no plasticity, and her language use was formal.

"These comlinks look a little beat up," Vi said, pointing at some units that had until recently been in her possession. "Do you know their age, make, and whether they work?"

"I'm afraid I'm just the attendant," the Duros said with a shrug of apology. "You'd have to ask Rusko for more information." When she named the price, it was indeed inflated, and if Vi paid for them now, she would've drained much of her cash.

"That is a bit high," she allowed. "What about these?"

The crate of medpacs she pointed to was not hers, and she was curious to see how its price would compare. Again, it was far too high. That was expected for a settlement so far from the rest of the galaxy, where every item of value had to be imported and often fixed up, but it didn't mean Vi was willing to pay ridiculous sums for basic equipment. She inquired about prices on many different items, including all of those on display that had been in her transport ship, and was disappointed to hear that everything was prohibitively expensive. It would take many months of steady work to buy it all back—even if no further tragedies struck.

As Vi frowned at the frustratingly close supplies that were financially so far away, the Duros clasped her hands in apology. "We're so far out, you see. The cost of fuel adds on to the rarity of certain objects, driving up their cost. Oga will allow us to offer a ten percent discount if you spend more than two thousand credits, but I'm afraid that's the best I can do."

"Might I ask where you acquire your goods?" Vi asked. Although she knew there was no local law enforcement, she was still curious if theft was openly discussed.

The Duros turned away. "Here and there. Oga's workers always have an eye out for a good deal." She turned back around, her big eyes bright. "Everyone knows Oga is always buying. And watching."

Taking the hint, Vi inclined her head. "Thank you for your time. I will consider it and possibly return."

"Good journey!" the Duros called, retreating to her perch, where she picked up a tablet and returned to her reading.

Before Vi could visit the next stall, a short human man in a leather vest materialized out of the shadows and put a grease-stained hand on her arm.

"This area is off-limits," he growled. "Oga's orders."

She easily slipped out of his hold and threw a cold stare at the Duros woman watching her from the stall. "My apologies," she said stiffly. "I'll see myself out."

Turning her back to him, she collected Pook and returned to the market, muttering, "Space lane robbery! Those prices weren't just in-

flated, they were outright swollen! And she reported me? For wanting to buy goods? I can't believe this backwater—"

She noticed a shopkeeper staring at her, and she stopped talking
and put a bland grin back on her face as she waved and murmured,
"Bright suns!"

"The suns are not particularly bright today," Pook said.

"It's a colloquialism. Because they have three suns. And two
moons."

"A colloquialism. Of course it is. Only your species would walk
around lying to everyone you met as an exercise in local color. It's
just so utterly tiresome."

"You're a droid, Pook. You can't get tired."

His head hung. "Watch me."

Vi stopped to buy some fruits and flatbread before she noticed
several familiar crates of nonperishable food in front of another
building—wearing an exorbitant price tag. Again and again as she
walked through the market, she recognized the items the Resistance
had entrusted to her—for sale. When she saw the old bartender strut
by wearing one of her wigs, Vi's blood boiled. Of course, she'd also
noticed the man from Smuggler's Alley trailing her, poorly, so there
was nothing she could do about any of it. Any bad behavior on her
part would be reported directly to Oga, which would not bode well
for her time on Batuu.

When she found her med kit, she knew that was the one thing she
couldn't leave behind. It was expensive, but at least it hadn't been
damaged or broken up. When she handed over five credits for her
own knitting bag and two for her bantha-yarn hat, her teeth were
clenched so hard together she couldn't even be polite to the merchant.

"Is that the wisest use of General Organa's credits?" Pook asked.

"First of all," Vi ground out, slow and deadly, "those were *my* credits. Second of all, if you keep making me angry, I'll sell you. And
third of all, knitting helps me relax!"

In typical droid fashion, Pook didn't absorb the threat, saying only, "I do suspect I would fetch a very high price, considering the overall quality of the goods on this planet."

On their way out of town, Vi stopped in Savi's workshop. Not only because perhaps some of her goods had been sold to him as scrap, but also because she suspected the older man's quiet goodwill might serve as a balm after the stress of her day. He reminded her of ascetics she'd met before, people who lived on a more spiritual level and radiated contentment. Nearly alone on this rock, far from her fellow believers in the cause and from safety, she was sure just a few minutes of borrowed calm would be most welcome.

Savi's workers sent her out into the sales yard, where Savi was prying apart a crashed shuttle with the strength of a much younger man.

"Bright suns!" Vi called.

Savi shielded his eyes and smiled. "Bright suns, and welcome back! Tomorrow is your first day at the scrapyard, is it not? I told Ylena to expect you."

"It is," she acknowledged. "But I've noticed several of my belongings appearing around town today with rather a high price point, and I was wondering if perhaps you'd taken on any new scrap? Especially if it was sold by Oga's minions?"

Savi wiped his hands on his apron and gave her a measuring look. "I buy from Oga when Oga tells me I must. I'll sort through the latest load today and see if anything looks like it might serve your needs. But I hear the rage and resentment in your voice, and I must warn you: You don't want to be heard speaking out against Oga. The walls of the outpost have ears. I wouldn't tangle with her, if I were you."

Vi huffed. "I'm not tangling. I'm just trying to get my stuff back at reasonable prices."

He shook his head and went back to the shuttle. "Sometimes good work must be done quietly. You'll fare better if you stay off Oga's scanners."

Vi struggled to hold her tongue. This man was now her boss, and judging by what she'd seen around town, it was the best and most fair job offer she was going to get. She didn't want to make him mad. She *couldn't* make him mad.

"I'll try to behave," she finally said.

Savi smiled. "That's wise. Perhaps you'll have the better hand tomorrow."

"And you," Vi murmured.

She and Pook headed back to their clearing, but when they arrived, the camp was unnaturally silent and still. Archex was nowhere to be found.

Chapter Eight

"ARCHEX!" VI SHOUTED "DID THAT PREDATOR eat you?"

And that's how she knew she was really worried: She was making jokes.

After several moments of fruitless yelling as she hunted for any sign of him, she headed back for the shuttle, muttering, "My first week's pay is going toward a cheap set of comlinks. Or maybe one of those bells people put on their pet tookas."

Although there were no signs of struggle and no splatters of blood, she knew that Archex was in no condition to fight effectively, not with his damaged lung and leg and the added injuries from the crash. She sat down on the log, bolted up, paced around, yelled his name some more.

Every single thing about this mission had gone wrong. She couldn't even pay someone in town to borrow a long-range comm and let General Organa know that she'd lost all the Resistance supplies . . . as well as the wounded former First Order officer she'd been tasked with training and babysitting. If anyone else knew Leia's location or had the codes to reach her, they could sell that intel to the First Order for more than the entire planet was worth. That was the problem with being on the edge of the frontier: Sure, it was a great place to hide out, but you were pretty much alone when you were the one who needed help.

Sitting around wasn't going to bring Archex back from wherever he'd gone—or been kidnapped to—and no matter how carefully she looked, she couldn't find a trail. The forest understory wasn't the sort of environment that allowed broken twigs or showed footprints in mud; the leaf litter was high, puffy, and dry, as the canopy overhead soaked up most of the rain.

"Any ideas, Pook?" she asked.

The droid looked around. "My extensive programming doesn't include tracking. Would you like me to tell you the odds of Archex still being alive?"

"Absolutely not."

Pook looked away. "Such a waste of my talents."

And it was annoying but true. They should've been unloading all their cargo and beginning to build their facility. They had brought enough materials to construct a proper shelter with barracks for six, a comm room, a small kitchen, and a bathroom. But now Pook had nothing to do, and Vi had . . . well, the wrong things to do.

She was angrily knitting a scarf out of leftover bantha yarn when she heard a twig crack. When she looked up, blaster pointed, she found Archex standing there, his jacket bulging out and supported by his arms.

"And where have you been?" she snapped.

He raised an eyebrow at the blaster, which she lowered. "Out scouting. Wasn't sure if this was the best place to start building the encampment."

"I assumed—"

"That I was stupid enough to get eaten or stupid enough to get ambushed or stupid enough to try to run—I mean *hobble*—off?"

She shrugged. "One of those."

"Well, I'm not. Before I received my post on the *Absolution,* I did my required tours of duty. Scouting, recon, building a base, all that. I thought you'd be gone longer, is all."

"You just need to be careful. Did you take your weapon?"

He glared at her. "Of course I took my weapon. I'm a soldier—*was* a soldier—and before that I was a desert rat. Self-defense is always on my mind. I know your general sent me to Cerea to get deprogrammed, but you know they didn't magically transform me into an idiot, right?"

She shrugged and rammed the blaster home in her holster. "I hoped so. But you've got to remember: I'm a soldier, too. And I look out for the people in my care. That's my job."

"And my job is supporting you and, I guess, feeding you, so you'll be glad to know I found a healthy patch of cloud mushrooms and some wild shi-root." He unzipped his jacket, and a treasure trove of vegetables thunked to the ground. The look he gave her—it was a pitiable mix of pride and desperation. Even after all that he'd been through with the First Order, he still just wanted to do a good job and please his superiors.

"Looks good," she told him with a grin. "Can't wait to roast those bad boys tomorrow. I'll see if I can pick up some spices and a pot, next time I'm in town."

"And some oil."

"And some oil," she agreed.

Archex nodded, satisfied, and Vi watched him limp to the other log and sit down, putting his bad leg out in front and forcefully massaging his thigh.

"The more you walk, the more it hurts, huh?"

He glared his annoyance. "Obviously."

"I don't think you'll be able to make the walk into town every day, then. It involves some hills and a little bit of clambering."

His head hung. "Clambering is not currently one of my skills. But I can still scout around and forage for food."

"But not too much," Vi warned. "Painkillers dull the pain that would tell you if you're overdoing it. Kalonia said it would take time to heal. Pushing too hard could do more harm."

The way he looked at the ground and worked his jaw told Vi that the pain was even worse than he was letting on. "Yes, fine, not too much."

She shook her head, feeling a wash of sympathy. "You just can't stand not being useful, can you, Archex?"

He rolled his eyes. "I'm not the only one."

Vi jerked her chin at Pook. "Pook, go look at his leg. Make sure nothing's broken or . . . worse."

Without complaining, the droid did his duty, from which Vi could only extrapolate that even Pook just needed something to do.

Fine. They all did.

The next morning, Vi again rose at dawn, but this time with that itchy feeling that meant she was worried about being late. She visited the cenote to bathe, made a mental note that she would need to either wash her clothes soon or buy another outfit as well as a towel, and headed for Savi's scrapyard. She didn't give Archex any orders or warnings on her way out—she just met his eyes and nodded. He'd been right, yesterday: She'd assumed the worst of him. Vi knew well enough that he was competent and intelligent, and she believed that he was also loyal and noble, and if a rancor ate him—well, then she'd know there was a rancor in the area.

She felt better today, at least. Armed with the med kit, Pook had worked his magic last night. Her neck was nearly functional now thanks to his care, although his bedside manner left much to be desired. Walking helped further loosen up her muscles, and she felt confident that she could do whatever work Savi's people would require of her. Her build didn't suggest that she was equipped for heavy lifting, but Salju had recommended her and Savi had accepted her, so surely she wouldn't just be carrying heavy fuel pods around with a bunch of Gamorreans.

The suns rose prettily over the stone walls of the junkyard, and the gates were thrown open, almost welcoming. Already bodies and machines moved around inside, with cranes swinging and welders welding. It reminded her a little of the Resistance airfield on D'Qar, and she felt a brief pang of loss. There was no way she could've built a facility that big and complex, even before all her supplies had been stolen. She'd have to figure out a way to report to Leia soon without having the call traced, but it could wait until she had reclaimed some of the Resistance's much-needed cargo and some good news.

As Vi scanned her new workplace, a woman waved from across the yard and hurried over when Vi waved back. "You must be Vi. Bright suns! I'm Ylena. Welcome to Savi and Sons."

Ylena was the complete opposite of what Vi had expected to find here. Not a Gamorrean or Besalisk or Trandoshan, the usual tough sort of muscle, Ylena was a slight human woman in her forties with pale skin and pink cheeks. Her head was covered in a scarf the soft green of lichen, and she wore a long leather vest over a scavenger's thick clothing and gloves. For all that she was dressed for rough work, there was a gentle air about the woman, and Vi couldn't figure out why someone like Ylena might've woken up one day and decided to work in a scrapyard.

"That's me. Bright suns to you, too, Ylena," Vi replied with a smile.

"Let me show you around the yard." Ylena began walking, and Vi caught up. "What kind of experience do you have? We always try to match people to work they will find fulfilling."

"Um, well." Vi had to think about it. She'd expected to be put immediately to work on the lowest rung, ripping rusted seats out of wrecked junkers, not thoughtfully interviewed by a calm but confident woman. "I have experience scouting, flying, doing maintenance. Never done any mechanic's work and can't run a blowtorch, but I'm a quick study." She paused; Vi hated admitting any sort of weakness. "Gotta be honest—I took some damage when my ship crashed, so I probably can't do a ton of heavy lifting just now."

Ylena laughed. "Heavy lifting isn't required. We have droids and cranes for that. Do you have sharp eyes?"

"I do."

"And your scouting—do you have any experience with expeditions?"

Vi chuckled, thinking back to her time on Parnassos—and other places still considered classified. "Oh, yes. I've been to plenty of inhospitable planets, looking for prizes large and small."

Ylena grinned. "Then I think I'll be selfish and keep you with me, among the Gatherers. I head the team that sorts through new acquisitions." She pointed to one corner of the junkyard, where old, rusted starhoppers and transports were piled near several cranes. It reminded Vi of tall birds standing over their nest. "That's where all the junked ships begin their processing. One team basically shakes them until anything small falls out. Promising ships are rebuilt over there." She pointed to another corner, where the ships sat up properly and a crew of humanoids hurried to and fro with tanks and toolkits. "Hopeless cases are torn apart over there." She pointed to the third corner, where the skeletons of ships were sadly tumbled together. "And over here is our domain."

Ylena stopped before a veritable mountain range of garbage. Not the smelly kind—not really. Just . . . so much stuff. Vi could see rusty metal, ripped tires, broken crates, a hairbrush, a cage that had once held some small animal. Several people of various species squatted or sat among the mounds of junk, wearing wide, conical hats and keeping up a pleasant conversation and exclaiming as they tossed items into wheeled baskets. One woman was in a hoverchair that looked like it had been cobbled together out of scraps—and souped up by Mubo, judging by its smooth controls.

"We sort through everything by hand, separating out small tech, personal items, artifacts, and other valuable objects from trash. The wheat from the chaff. And sometimes, every now and then, we find treasure."

Vi raised an eyebrow. "Treasure?"

Ylena inclined her head coyly. "Every now and then. We go through a scanner on the way home to make sure no one is trying to scam the boss. It doesn't happen often, though. Savi has this uncanny way of avoiding the bad eggs. Come on. Let's get you set up."

Ylena took Vi to a small shed where she was assigned a pair of sturdy leather gloves and a rolling cart fitted with a basket. She slid the gloves on and frowned.

"Do they not fit?" Ylena asked.

"Not like my old ones did. I had a great pair of gloves," Vi told her.

"But the people who ransacked my ship took everything. Just . . . everything."

Ylena put a hand on her shoulder and looked into her eyes more deeply than most strangers would. But it didn't make Vi feel uncomfortable—it made her feel seen, like she mattered.

"Sometimes the Force challenges us," the older woman said. "And we don't find out until later why we had to suffer. Every setback contains hidden blessings."

Vi's head jerked up. First Savi, and now Ylena. Outside of Leia's circles, most common folk thought the Force was just an old myth or a bunch of fairy-tale nonsense.

"Did you just say . . . the Force?"

Ylena had a knowing, impish look in her eye. "Just because a planet is far from the center of the galaxy doesn't mean everyone there is ignorant of the conflicts happening beyond and the forces that tie us all together."

"So you're a believer, then." And something about Ylena did remind Vi a bit of Leia, of her calm confidence and surety.

"Let's just say I know that all things happen for a reason. Maybe you were supposed to join us. Are you ready to see how salvaging suits you?"

Vi gave a confident nod and followed Ylena out into the yard. Friendly conversation was over, and her orientation began. She and Ylena pulled their carts to a promising section of the junk heap, and Ylena showed Vi how each day's area was assigned so that no part of the yard ever sat too long, risking damage to valuable finds. Vi went into learning mode, absorbing everything the older woman taught her about deciding what was dross, what held possibilities, and what might be considered treasure. Ylena kept mentioning artifacts, so often that Vi had to ask her, "What exactly do you mean by *artifacts*?"

Ylena considered her. "There are items of value from everyday life, things that can be sold secondhand to help others. There are sometimes items of great value, pieces of jewelry or recent tech that bring in plenty of spira. But sometimes, as you sift through the wreckage of time, you find objects of great power. Crystals, statues, artworks, even books." She gave Vi a significant look.

That earned a raised eyebrow. "Sounds like you're talking about Jedi artifacts."

A dimple played at the corner of Ylena's mouth. "Does it? There are many religions and many cultures in the galaxy, and each of them offers something sacred, some greater connection. We hope to preserve such items rather than see them pass from history."

Vi pursed her lips. "And, what? Sell them to the highest bidder?"

At that, Ylena snorted. "Oh, no. We also don't want to see such treasures pass into the wrong hands. If we merely wanted money, we could trade any antiquities to Dok-Ondar in the outpost. But Savi understands that there is honor in catching artifacts like pearls in his net and holding them safe from those who might abuse them. In saving them for the right person or moment in time."

"That's a lot of words to say, 'Just trust me.' "

"Then just trust me. More accurately, trust us. Such artifacts don't turn up every day, but it's important that you know what to look for. It's always better to err on the side of caution." Ylena held up a bobbing-head doll. "Even something as silly as this could be a hiding place for an object of value. If something looks like the kind of trash you would overlook but that could contain a kernel of power . . ." She shook the doll and grinned when it rattled. With a fierce motion, she popped its head off its neck, then sliced the neck off with a small knife she wore on a belt at her waist. When she dumped it upside down, all that came out were some rusted metal springs.

"No prize this time," Vi said for her.

Ylena nodded knowingly. "But once every thousand tries . . . there is. I assume you have a knife?"

Vi lifted her shawl to show the knife on her belt. Ylena didn't mention the blaster and tac baton.

"Good. We'll work side by side today as you get the hang of things. As time goes on, you can work alone or near others, if you're in the mood for conversation. Watch out for old Dotti—she doesn't have a mute button—or a filter. As you sort through your stack, toss the obvious garbage into the lane and sort the keepers into your basket. Every so often, a droid will come along and sweep up the trash."

"Got it."

Vi was soon absorbed in her work. She started out squatting, but when she noticed how Ylena would pick some piece of junk, an old chair or a child's riding toy, and sit on it as she moved through the pile, that strategy provided some relief. Some of it was easy to toss—the gutted tablets and old bottles and occasional moldering snack food still in its package. But even after her years of training and spying, every now and then she ran across some item she couldn't begin to identify. Ylena helped her with the more common objects and encouraged her to throw anything that looked old or valuable into her basket, just in case. When the suns were high in the sky and Vi was contemplating her need for a hat, a gong rang. Ylena stood and tilted her head toward the shed where they'd started out, and Vi followed her, pulling her cart along. There, they sorted their finds into bins, one for tech, one for valuable metals, one for antiques and curiosities, one for items of question, and the smallest one for possible artifacts and other items of historical or monetary significance.

"Savi sorts these bins himself," Ylena told Vi.

The rest of the Gatherers rolled their carts in, laughing and talking and bragging as they pawed through their finds. Various droids rushed out to collect the piles of refuse left in the lanes. The cranes ground to a halt and the sharp buzz of saws went silent, and Ylena pulled a large basket out of the shed and distributed wrapped packets. When Vi ripped hers open, she found a flatbread sandwich.

"Lunch is included?" she asked.

Ylena grinned. "Of course. I told you—Savi takes care of us. There's a water fountain by the restroom, if you get thirsty. If you bring your own canteen, you can fill it and keep it with you throughout the day. You're no good to us dehydrated."

Vi could've kicked herself for forgetting her canteen, but she had a lot to learn about the daily grind. Her sandwich was excellent and just the right amount of food to keep her working but not make her feel sleepy or full. She and Ylena were soon back in the fray with their emptied baskets, and the work became almost meditative. The fact that every single object required an evaluation and decision used up most of her mind so that, for what seemed like the first time in her life, she wasn't running a constant internal monologue about what needed to be done or berating herself for what had gone wrong. Time passed smoothly, interrupted only by Dotti's cackling laugh or a curious pipa bird landing on the junk pile in a flash of white feathers and long pink beak. When the gong sounded again, she looked up, startled. The breeze was cool, and the piles of junk cast long purple shadows.

"Are we done?" she asked. It was almost like waking from a dream.

Ylena nodded. "Well, we need to sort our baskets, but it won't take long. The suns take a while to set here, after all."

They pulled their carts back to the shed and repeated their sorting. Vi noticed that there were just two items in the artifact bin, and one of them almost reminded her of a lightsaber hilt—or a piece of one. She was about to ask when Ylena put a hand on her arm.

"We usually go into town for dinner and drinks to celebrate when someone new joins us," she said. "I should've asked you earlier if you wanted to go. It's up to you. I know you must be tired."

Vi looked around at Savi's Gatherers. They looked an unusually clean and pleasant crew for folk who worked in a junkyard. Everyone was smiling, and no one had hazed her or roughed her up or threatened her. It was . . . downright unsettling.

"Sure," she said.

In town, over drinks, she'd learn more about her co-workers, about Savi—and hopefully, about Black Spire Outpost itself.

Chapter Nine

IT WAS A PLEASANT WALK TO town along Savi's Path. Birds sang and flitted in the trees, and something about the area felt safe and protected, almost charmed. As Ylena had mentioned, they had to walk through a rudimentary scanner first to make sure no one was smuggling out anything, which they weren't—and they were all good-natured about the process.

Vi's co-workers seemed to be a cheerful, easy-going bunch. She counted ten humans, a Devaronian, a four-armed Xexto, and one quiet blue Narquois, although not everyone planned to join the group for dinner. No one stood out as the jerk everyone else barely tolerated. The gentle teasing and friendly roughhousing almost reminded her of the Resistance. As they talked and joked, she joined in, telling them a little about herself but not of her other work on the planet. She would save that for later this evening, after they were a few drinks in and once she had determined whether anyone might secretly be an old-fashioned Empire enthusiast or a First Order follower.

Without even discussing the decision, they passed right by Ronto Roasters and went to Docking Bay 7 Food and Cargo in the spaceport, where a surly Artiodac was the current operator of a weekly food freighter called Tuggs' Grub.

"Cookie is only here one week out of the month, but when he's here, we're here," Ylena told Vi. "He used to work at Maz Kanata's castle, if you can believe it. Best grub on the planet—for at least six days out of thirty."

Vi wasn't so sure that she wanted to eat food served out a window, but once she'd tasted the fried Endorian tip-yip, she decided she would be here for six days, too. Their group found a table with room for Roxi's hoverchair and sat, and Vi felt the knot behind her shoulders completely relax for the first time since they'd landed—well, crashed. She wasn't hiding, she wasn't suffering, she wasn't in trouble, she wasn't in charge. She was just . . . free.

The conversation stayed light as the stars rose, and Vi sighed and enjoyed the nighttime beauty of Batuu. The stars were sharp here, the moons were big and soulful, and a light breeze brought the scent of night-blooming flowers. The lanterns danced, throwing triangles of light across the walls and floors, and music flittered out of the cantina. When everyone was done eating, that's exactly where they went.

Oga's cantina had been quiet when she and Salju visited during the slow part of a workday afternoon, but at night it was clearly the place to be in Black Spire Outpost. Laughter, shouts, and the clatter of full glasses beckoned, and the group had to stand around a table until a booth opened up. After a full day of sitting and squatting, Vi didn't really mind it so much. She appreciated the room's warm, cozy glow, and any time the conversation lagged, her eye landed on an interesting tap behind the bar or followed movement as some colorful scoundrel slipped into the shadows. She started with the drink Ylena suggested, a Dagobah Slug Slinger. Vi raised her glass and murmured, "Now and till the spire!" with everyone else, and the night began in earnest.

Soon she found herself not acting as a spy and outsider but . . . actually participating in the conversation, genuinely laughing at the jokes. That separation was part of being a spy—always being outside of things, always listening, always watching. Whatever a spy appeared to be doing in public was generally an act to hide what they were *really* doing. And, yes, Vi was always listening for the words *Resis-*

tance and *First Order,* but mostly she was laughing at the antics of Roxi's tree-goat, which kept inexplicably ending up on top of her neighbor's house and requiring a borrowed crane to be retrieved.

Vi didn't have much money, but she wanted to be well liked by her co-workers, and she knew she was going to be on the planet for quite some time, so she went to the bar to buy the next round. When she came back bearing the tray herself, they'd taken over a corner booth and waved her over cheerfully. It was nice—they seemed to like her. The *actual* her. When they asked her where she was from, she even opened up enough to tell them true stories about getting in trouble back on Chaaktil with her brother Baako.

"So how'd you end up here?" Dotti finally asked. "Offworlders bring the best stories. Whatever you're running from, we won't turn you in!" The old woman had drunk more than anyone at the table and had her dark eyes trained on Vi like a bird hunting for berries.

Vi looked around at their faces—Ylena, Dotti, Roxi, Danjo, Lin, Madi Ro, Uz, Da-zorai, Fenda. It was time, she realized. Time to test the waters. Maybe time to start recruiting.

She put her drink down and leaned in.

"I lost friends in the Hosnian Cataclysm. Saw some action. Barely escaped the First Order myself. So I went looking for a place just like this."

Dotti nodded knowingly. "A place to hide. You chose wise, young'un. No troubles come to Batuu! The First Order—ha!"

"But what if they did come?" Vi pressed. "What would happen then?"

Ylena looked amused as she sipped her drink, but everyone else just looked befuddled.

"Why would anyone come to Batuu? It's not important," Roxi finally said.

"Maybe that's exactly *why* it's important," Vi answered, passion rising unbidden in her words. "People can hide here . . . but so can ships. So can movements. It's a good place to take shelter. And to plan. To rebuild. To recruit."

"You're talking about the Resistance," Roxi confirmed, her voice low.

In answer, Vi sat back, sipped her drink, and winked.

It was as if a little ripple went through the group. They looked to one another and to Ylena as if unsure how to go on, as if this information made them uncomfortable. Except for old Dotti, who scoffed.

"Resistance, Rebels, Republic, Senate. The First Order, and the Empire before 'em. All that gobbledygook has always happened far away. Their little scuffles are no problem of ours. This is the forgotten edge of the galaxy, child! Don't fill their heads with nonsense."

"It's all real," Vi said, her tone firm. "The Resistance, and the First Order. If you'd seen the things I've seen, things that happened on planets just as remote as yours, you would have no choice but to take it seriously. One day, you'll have to—I promise you."

Flapping a hand, Dotti finished her beer and burped before saying, "Lived here my whole life, and it's never been a bother. I didn't get this old worrying about other people's fights."

"But the First Order—" Vi began.

"Villains, of course, if they exist," Dotti interrupted, "but they're as far off as the Resistance to the likes of us. And if they did come, I'd probably just do whatever they asked. Never pays, fighting bullies."

"Glad Batuu's not worth wanting," Roxi added. "No point in robbing someone who isn't rich, is there?"

"I'll drink to that!" Dotti shouted, waving at the bartender for her next drink.

Vi ground her teeth. It was impossible to make any headway with someone like Dotti squatting on your efforts, so certain that her own view was the only correct one even though she'd never experienced the greater galaxy herself. So she tried another tack.

"So maybe you're not worried about the First Order, but have you thought about the benefits of joining the Resistance? Getting off-planet, seeing new places, learning how to—"

"Benefits can't be that good if you took a second job as a scrapper," Dotti said, and then she burst out laughing, and everyone else joined in. Vi could only sit there, helpless and annoyed, marinating in her own failure. She'd crashed the ship, she'd lost their cargo, and now her first recruitment effort had turned into a joke.

"And what if your very presence here brings them?" Lin said, his eyes wide. "What if they didn't even think about us before, but then they heard the Resistance was here, and they punished us for it?"

"Mm, yes." Dotti nodded sagely as if she'd thought of it. "What if *you're* the problem?" She followed that up with a cackle, and the rest joined in with nervous laughter.

"This is a fight of good and evil." Ylena's voice was quiet but strong, and Dotti stopped laughing. "And evil is always the problem. We believe in good, and we do our work quietly. But I assure you: Anyone who works for Savi is against the First Order, as we were against the Empire before it."

"But do you believe Batuu is worth fighting for?" Vi asked, stabbing the table with a finger for emphasis. "Because I do. And General Organa does, too. That's why she sent me here."

Much to her surprise, her fellow Gatherers . . . didn't seem surprised or impressed by this knowledge.

"To work at the junkyard?" Dotti asked before cackling and rocking back again. "Not much of a general!"

"What's she like?" Roxi asked. "She always seemed kind, on the holos."

"And smart," Da-zorai added with a nod of approval.

Vi was glad that something of Leia's work had reached the planet. "Kind, perhaps, but strong. Smart and wise. She sent me here to recruit for the Resistance. I arrived with a transport ship full of cargo that was meant to build our command location—but that cargo was stolen when my transport crashed. So that's what I'm working toward, that's why I'm at the scrapyard. I need to buy it all back. And find people willing to become a part of something great."

The Gatherers sipped their drinks and looked to Ylena like they were uncertain how to continue the conversation. Ylena smiled her warm smile and put a hand on Vi's shoulder.

"Everything happens for a reason, as the Force wills it. Perhaps Vi was meant to join us here."

That kind of answer wasn't very helpful. "I'm not here to focus on philosophy. I'm here to build a facility so the Resistance has a place where we can hide from the First Order and continue planning our defense against tyranny. We're trying to stop what happened to the Hosnian system from ever happening again. We need resources, and, more important, we need people."

Dotti snorted White Wampa Ale out her nose. "If the Resistance general is so smart, why did she send you here to ask the likes of us for help? I can't build anything but a bar tab!"

Vi struggled not to reveal her frustration. "General Organa believes that anyone can be a hero. Everyone has something to contribute, a special gift to share with the galaxy. The Resistance is built on people, on hope. It's about standing up to oppression, doing what's right, and helping others. Scrappers are valuable, just as valuable as pilots and officers. The First Order doesn't believe that, but we do. Anyone here could ignite that spark and help light the way to victory."

The Gatherers considered her words, and Dotti left for the bar, but Ylena's smile was gentle and a little sad. "What you must understand about Black Spire Outpost is that no one here is rich. No one can leave their job to come work for you for free, no matter how good the cause. We have our own reasons for doing things. We have our own balance to maintain. There is more under the surface than you can see from two days among us."

Vi shook her head and sipped her drink. They didn't understand. If the First Order came here, they would take over *everything*. Destroy businesses, raze homes to the ground, kill people, take whatever resources they wanted. If they came to Batuu, there would be no balance. The knot was back between her shoulders, and her jaw was clenched again. Spying was easy compared with this—with facing willful ignorance and stubborn naïveté.

"Let's hope you're all right and I'm wrong," she said softly. "Let's hope you're free to maintain that balance."

"The world naturally shifts to accommodate imbalance," Ylena said with an apologetic shrug that the others echoed. "It's not always comfortable, but that is life. Discomfort helps us grow."

Vi put her head in her hands. It wasn't as if she'd thought that one whispered speech in a bar would sway these people to her side, but . . . like most people who had never experienced war or tragedy, they just didn't get it.

"The discomfort of being executed by stormtroopers won't help anyone grow," she muttered, slumping down and sucking up her drink until her tongue went numb.

The scrappers watched her for a few moments as if watching a pot that was on the edge of boiling over, but when she didn't rouse again, they built back up to their usual cheerful chatter. Lin kept glancing at her nervously and whispering to Fenda. Dotti came back with a new drink, and she and Ylena had their heads together and were whispering, and Vi felt like she'd lost any goodwill she'd begun to build. She'd made her pitch, they hadn't bought it, and now she was just the weird, paranoid new person trying to shake things up. At least they didn't shun her or order her away. Ylena bought the next round and brought Vi another drink, trying to include her in the conversation again, and Vi realized Ylena had to be one of the kindest people she'd ever met.

"General Organa would like you," she said, and Ylena's already rosy cheeks glowed.

"Is it true that she used the Force to fly back to her ship after an explosion?" Ylena asked, quietly enough that the others couldn't hear. "We heard rumors, but then again, so much of what we hear is rumors."

Vi looked at her sharply. "I was to understand that incident wasn't public knowledge," she said carefully. "Where did you hear it?"

Ylena ducked her head. "I can't quite remember. Someone Savi knows offplanet."

"Then it's true, yeah. I wasn't there, but we spoke about it."

Vi didn't just tell Ylena this secret because she'd had a few drinks. It was mainly because she wanted to regain trust, and if the woman already believed it, what was the harm? She would use any means necessary to get the locals on her side. If telling tales of the glamorous Princess Leia's exciting exploits was the key to winning them over, then that's what they'd get.

"All these years," Ylena mused, her eyes far off. "All these years she

had access to the Force and never used it. She could've swayed the
Senate but wasn't willing to use cheap tricks when she believed in
diplomacy and freedom. That's a strong woman and a good leader,
right there. And yet, in her time of greatest hardship, when it bene-
fited not only her own needs but the greater good, she reached deep
inside and claimed that connection that had always waited, dormant,
for her call."

"I hadn't thought of it that way," Vi said, rolling the idea around in
her head.

She'd been glad that Leia had survived the destruction of the *Rad-
dus,* of course. And devastated to learn of Vice Admiral Holdo's sacrifice. But she had assumed that Leia's Force power had been activated
by her desperation. She had never even considered that all this time,
as a princess and a senator and a general, Leia had actively chosen
not to use such a valuable advantage. The general was a master strat-
egist who used every piece on the dejarik board. Usually. So this
choice, if it had been a choice, as Ylena suggested, must've been a
moment of great and important truth for a woman who had already
earned Vi's respect and loyalty tenfold, a moment she had been prepared to wait her entire life before reaching.

Vi looked at her hands, at their scars, at those two fingers that still
tingled, partly numb. She just felt so powerless. Maybe her moment
of need wasn't quite as dire as Leia's had been, maybe she wasn't
floating out in space, on the verge of death, but she was definitely in
a dark place without a clear path. Her cargo was out of reach, her collaborator was challenging, and her own task seemed insurmount-
able. Her first attempt at recruitment had ended in a round of public
laughter. Everything had gone wrong. She felt lost and unsure, which
was not her usual state.

If she reached deep inside herself, what would she find? Not the
Force, of course. But there was something there—an iron core. Determination. Tenacity. Stubborn persistence. She'd gotten herself out
of that First Order interrogation chair, after all. She just had to live
through one moment, and then the next, and then the next.

She just had to keep going—until she had a better hand.

When Vi looked down at her drink, she saw that she'd drunk it all, which she hadn't intended to do. She went to the bar for water to help her sober up, and as she waited, she scanned the room for possible allies . . . and possible enemies. Like any cantina, it hosted a motley crew of humanoids that ranged from cozy knots of humans in local gear slumped over cheap ale to shady, shifty-eyed collections of pirates and smugglers whispering and passing things under tables, to pilots and flyboys laughing a little too loud to impress the unimpressable Twi'lek women in a corner.

When she'd returned to the table with her water, Vi felt a prickle up the back of her neck, that familiar and hateful jolt that every spy feels the moment they've been identified. She easily found the source: a snub-nosed, moss-gray face in the corner, his bright black eyes lingering to make sure she knew she'd been caught out. He was an unusual-looking fellow, but Vi had an excellent memory for species, and it rose up from her training: Karkarodon. From Karkaris. And a particularly beefy specimen.

If the galaxy's biggest human and hungriest shark had an ugly baby, it would grow up to be this guy. And for all that he didn't look like the most intelligent fish in the school, he'd still been the one to identify her in the crowd. His stare was blank and alien and feral, and his wrapped hands were the size of shaak roasts. His nose was blunt and his sharp teeth glimmered in the low light. While she watched him back, showing her own power by not looking away, he lifted a tankard of something thick and red and took a long drink that left what passed for his lips coated in what appeared to be blood.

The ruffians around him hadn't so much as looked her way. They were the more usual sort of thug—big humans, the smaller man from Smuggler's Alley, a Gamorrean, a Talpini, and an older Wookiee who laughed a growling laugh and honestly looked a bit unhinged. If Vi had to wager a guess, she would've bet these were Oga's minions.

The Karkarodon finally turned to smack the Wookiee in the shoulder, and Vi gasped a breath, unaware that she'd been holding it in as long as she'd been locked in the staring contest. If one could even have a staring contest with a species that didn't actually have eyelids and therefore couldn't blink.

"Ylena," she murmured out of the side of her mouth. "Over there, in the far corner. Do you know those people?"

Ylena glanced up as she sipped her drink, and Vi began to wonder if the woman had had some spy training of her own, so subtle was the gesture.

"Rusko," Ylena confirmed, her lips twitching with disgust.

"Oga's men."

"Except for N'arrghela. The Wookiee is female. And you don't want to mess with her. I once saw her rip the arm off a Besalisk. You'll want to avoid the lot of them, if you value your limbs." In punctuation, Ylena loudly slurped the last of her drink from her straw. "We have an early day tomorrow. Dotti will stay here all night and be no worse off, but I'm ready to turn in." She gently smacked her forehead before continuing. "And I regret to say that when I invited you along, I didn't consider your safety after dark. Are you based far from here? My apartment isn't large, but you are welcome to sleep on my couch."

Vi patted the blaster at her hip. "I'm heavily armed, well trained, and unafraid. Nighttime is my favorite time. But I appreciate the kindness. After my confession earlier, I wasn't so sure I was still welcome."

Ylena put a hand on Vi's arm, and the weight was comforting. "You should always feel free to speak your truth. Just because you're ready to speak doesn't mean others are eager to hear it. Like I said— we're a simple folk, and many are not ready to absorb the reality of what you have to say."

"When the First Order arrives, it will be too late."

"Then that will be our own trial to suffer."

Ylena stood, and Vi followed suit. Dotti and Roxi stayed in place, shoulder-to-shoulder as they laughed and continued to drink. When Ylena waved, everyone smiled and waved in return.

"May the spires keep you, friends," Ylena said.

"And you!" they called back.

Vi's glass of water and the sobering glare of the Karkarodon had helped her regain sobriety, and even if she was still a little tipsy, she was trained to be lethal in that state. She was following Ylena toward the cantina door when she realized that nature had called and the outdoors held only bushes.

"I'm going to hit the restroom before I leave," she said. "Thanks for being so friendly today."

"Of course! We're glad you've joined us. I can tell you're going to fit in fine. Savi always knows."

Vi nodded in agreement. "May the spires keep you, Ylena."

Ylena turned and clasped Vi's forearm. Vi had no choice but to return the gesture, their forearms lying warmly alongside. It was an odd sort of leavetaking that reminded her more of how warriors tested each other, a closed circle of trust.

"And you," Ylena answered. The grin she gave Vi was a new one, almost cocky.

Ylena unclasped her arm and left, but Vi had marked the bathroom earlier and headed in that direction. As with every cantina ever, a dark hall was the only route to relief, and Vi's hand subtly strayed under her orange shawl to the tactical baton on her hip. She was glad to see that the restroom was clean and in good repair, definitely better than a patch of ferns full of who knew what sort of specialized Batuuan bloodsucking brain slugs. She came out of the stall and washed her hands, staring at her face in the dull mirror and noting that her eyes were red and her lips were cracked.

"Crashes and menial labor do not agree with me," she murmured.

"Good point."

A crescent moon of teeth appeared in the mirror right behind her—Rusko. Of course. Before she could spin and shoot him through his rubbery heart, he pinned her arms to her sides with cold, clammy hands and dragged her back into the stall.

Chapter Ten

IT WAS ALMOST A RELIEF, WATCHING Vi disappear into the forest on her way to work. Archex could finally sigh heavily and dramatically and stop guarding his expression and posture. He was a ball of nerves around her, and it took energy he didn't have, holding up all those walls.

He'd always had a respect for Vi Moradi, even when she'd cleverly twisted him like a knife back on the *Absolution*. She had grit and determination and a sense of humor that seemed to attack sideways, surprising him even in the darkest of moods. And he would even venture to say he liked her now, and that he felt it was part of his duty to protect her, even if that was physically impossible. Sometimes, when he watched her in quiet moments, when she didn't know he was watching, he felt . . . tender? It was so muddled and strange, feelings he'd never had before. But he wasn't ready to let her in, wasn't ready to show her the pulverized mush of what had once been a hardened core of belief deep in his soul.

All that work on Cerea . . . hadn't helped him at all.

He wasn't sure why he was here, what he was meant to do. Just the thought of the First Order made bile rise in his throat, so he tried to forget and ignore it, most of the time. Of course, that didn't mean he was rushing into the open arms of the Resistance. For all their talk of freedom, they hadn't offered him much of it personally. He'd had no choice regarding Cerea and no choice regarding Batuu, nor in the babysitter who seemed carefully selected to dredge up old, unwanted memories and new, confusing, conflicting feelings.

"Lieutenant Moradi is gone," Pook noted. "Would you like your extra painkillers?"

"You wouldn't be so smug if you could feel pain," Archex shot back, hobbling toward the droid for the extra pills he took whenever Vi wasn't around. "Cut in half, and you felt nothing. Lucky."

"Oh, yes." Pook's voice dripped sarcasm. "Lucky is definitely the word I'd use for my current predicament. I assure you, the torture of my continued existence far exceeds the paltry jangling of your simple human nervous system."

"Then power down and let me suffer in peace."

"That would benefit us both. It is my duty to remind you that Lieutenant Moradi has requested that you not venture too far from the camp."

Archex snorted. "Like I even could if I wanted to."

"You know, your healing might progress with marked improvement if you took better care of your psyche and didn't push yourself so hard. Your adrenal glands must be shriveled husks. Perhaps you could use this time to relax. The human body requires downtime, too."

He hated it, when Pook stopped complaining and started . . . well, *caring* wasn't exactly the word. But sometimes, when Vi was gone, it was as if Pook dropped his melancholy front and actively tried to do his job, putting his major focus on Archex. Which Archex resisted.

"Here's a little hint, Pook. No sentient being ever relaxed because someone repeatedly commanded them to relax."

"Then find something to do. It's not really my problem. Goodbye."

That was better. Snippy Pook was something Archex could deal with, and it was even better when the droid went offline.

Finally, he was alone. Vi was gone, Pook was pretty much asleep, and Archex could get on with the exercise protocol he'd been follow-

ing every day of his adult life—when he wasn't strapped down in a
Resistance medbay. Counting reps of sit-ups, push-ups, and pull-ups
was as close as he got to the meditation they'd pushed on him in
Cerea. When he had completed his workout, he was indeed calmer,
his mind clearer. He bathed at the cenote and tried not to bristle at
the feeling of dressing in the same filthy clothing, just as he had as a
child on Jakku.

Over the past twenty years, he'd taken so much for granted among
the First Order. Waking up in a comfortable bed. Enjoying a hot
shower with the proper accoutrements. Shaving with sharp razors.
Putting on a crisp, perfectly folded, freshly cleaned uniform. The
wilds of the Batuu forest made everything in him revolt. He hated the
chaos, the quiet, the sunlight, the feeling as if he were always being
watched, even though it was mostly by a curious pair of feathered
reptiles Pook had identified as lahiroo.

But most of all, he just needed something to do. Some way to be
useful. That was the greatest thing he'd lost—not the First Order itself, but his own personal sense of order, the solid knowledge that he
served a greater purpose.

They'd sent him here to help build things, but there was nothing to
build. He'd been told he could run the comms, but there were no
comms. He'd been commanded to support Vi, but she was the most
self-sufficient person he'd ever met. And now, after all their setbacks,
he couldn't hobble half a mile to work at the junk heap beside her—
she wouldn't even let him try.

He stumped out into the forest in a direction he hadn't yet scouted
and was pleased to find several tarine bushes. If he built drying
racks—using what, he wasn't sure—they could have tea. He didn't
like tea, but at the very least it felt like he was producing something.
He rolled the leaves into careful tubes and stuffed them in his pockets. Foraging on Batuu wasn't easy; there were so many unfamiliar
plants and no helpful guide for what was safe to eat. He'd been so
pleased to find the cenote, but he hadn't yet found running water
they could fish. The forest creatures were unusually shy, and he
couldn't bring himself to shoot the soulful-eyed dugar dugar or

gently trilling lahiroo, no matter how hungry he was. If they'd landed on a desert planet, he would've been indispensable. As it was, he was returning home with nothing but pockets filled with bitter, wilted leaves.

As if waking up from a dream, he realized that he was leaning against one of the gigantic trees, his face wet with tears and his knuckles scraped from punching the bark. He lost time, sometimes—not much, but just enough to remind him that his mind was just as fractured as his body. Turning his back to the tree, he slid down to sit, his legs straight out in front of him. His good leg wore the tracker that reminded him that he was a prisoner, and his bad leg—well, he wanted to punch it, but that only made things worse. As Major Kalonia had warned him from the very start, there were some things even the most advanced medicine couldn't fix. And because of the exact placement of Phasma's blade, they couldn't amputate the damn thing.

Phasma—no. He wouldn't think about her.

Wouldn't think about all his mistakes, all stemming from the moment his men yanked Vi out of that starhopper, dumping her ridiculous knitting on the floor of the *Absolution*. He'd been so determined to take down his rival, had seen Phasma as the rot in the heart of something great.

If only he'd left well enough alone.

He'd still be Captain Cardinal, still have respect and comfort and a purpose.

He would never have known his entire life was a lie.

Maybe it would've been better that way, even if now he knew the real mistake was buying into the First Order's fiction. His life had been easier, then, but he'd been part of something monstrous. Hosnian Prime had closed that door for him, forever.

But there was a certain cloying attraction to his old life, an exhausting nostalgia. If things had gone differently, he wouldn't be here. He wouldn't be *this*.

It was maddening. There or here, then or now, it all ended badly.

He could only deal with so much failure at once.

His hands were in the leaf litter now, curled into fists as if he could tear up the forest floor. But when he opened his fingers, he found nothing but needles and rich, black dirt. Not that he could do anything with dirt. He was no farmer. He had no skills on a planet like Batuu.

But these needles—he could weave them into baskets. Very nice baskets, actually, even if they weren't the silky, slender porlash needles back on Cerea. Then he'd have something to carry his meager foraged finds. But the very thought made him grind his teeth. The weaving was meditative, sure, but it also brought back the songs and poems and essays his Cerean guides had read in chiming monotone as he and his fellow prisoners—no, *students*—worked. He couldn't handle that. Letting go, living in the now, being one with the universe.

Garbage thoughts for contented people who weren't currently suffering.

He dropped the leaf litter and picked up a small log, turning it over in his hands. Maybe he wasn't willing to weave baskets and be bombarded with flashbacks of enforced Cerean peacefulness, but he did have one skill that wouldn't be hampered by his current injuries. Taking out his knife, he began to clean off the bark and get to the creamy wood inside.

Whittling had kept him alive as a boy on Jakku. Maybe it would keep him alive on Batuu now. If nothing else, it would give him something to do. Thinking back to one of their first conversations on the doomed transport, he almost smiled. He'd told Vi that there was no time to whittle on the Star Destroyer, but as Vi had told him, the Resistance would let him whittle wherever he wanted to.

This, at least, was making something. And it was perhaps the only aspect of his life that no one else controlled.

Chapter Eleven

Vi OPENED HER MOUTH TO SHOUT, but moist, fishy breath made her curl away as Rusko said, "Scream all you want. Nobody cares. And by the way: Oga wants to see you."

Twisting her head, Vi looked back to see where they were headed. A perfectly concealed door in the wall at the back of the stall was now open, and whatever lay beyond it was dark as pitch. Considering Rusko was operating on Oga's orders, it would be better for Vi to act cowed and confused instead of like a trained spy who could turn this monster into chum in half a minute. She struggled like someone who didn't know how to get out of his clumsy hold, and he just held her tighter. Good—let him think she was helpless.

For Vi Moradi, this kidnapping was actually an opportunity.

Vi was looking forward to meeting the mysterious gangster in charge of her new town—and to gathering intel on her minions and lair. She continued her ruse, twisting and pushing against Rusko's grip, testing his strength while secretly feeling for where he had weapons concealed. The way he held his blaster in the very arm now wrapped around her waist suggested kidnapping wasn't his usual job.

The temperature changed as Rusko dragged Vi through the door and slammed it shut. They were in a hallway carved from the same material as the rest of the outpost, with walls and floor of the same porous, creamy stone. It was cool here, and a damp breeze blew in from somewhere far off along with the plink of water, suggesting perhaps another cenote or spring. Someone had installed lanterns far overhead to light the way down the hall, and that was the direction they were headed.

"Stop wiggling, bait," Rusko growled. His teeth ground together like razor blades near her cheek. "Or I'll accidentally bite off your ear. It's not like you need both of 'em."

Vi wanted to inform him that she would be happy to stop struggling if he would just carry her in a reasonable manner instead of juggling her like she was a greased puffer pig, but instead she let her breathing speed up almost to a pant and whimpered, "Who are you? What do you want?"

"Already told you what was wanted. I don't repeat myself."

He carried her through another arched door and into a room with much better lighting. It resembled a throne room, with a tall, wide chair hewn from the rock and draped in cushions and blankets. On it sat—well, a shaggy tooka-cat, splayed out in sleep. Vi gave a wiggle and scanned the rest of the room as best she could. She noted a desk and a woven carpet, worn but finely crafted. Movement by the door caught her eye as N'arrghela ducked inside, cradling her bowcaster. Behind the Wookiee came Oga Garra.

The crafty Blutopian's eyes were but tiny dimples on either side of her leathery gray head, and she regarded Vi thoughtfully as she sat at a desk in the corner, plucked a piece of clamfruit from a waiting bowl, and peeled it, releasing an unpleasantly briny scent.

"You understand Huttese?" Oga asked—in Huttese. Her voice was like claws on a slate.

"*Tagwa*," Vi answered, her voice small, as if she were frightened.

Oga's pink-tinged mouth tentacles shuddered. "Your accent's garbage," she continued. "So if you understand Huttese and I understand Basic, let's do each other a favor and speak our native tongues. My protocol droid is a pain in the rump."

Vi nodded meekly, because that's what a simple scrapper would do. "Okay."

"Where are you from?" Oga sucked up the clamfruit pulp, and Vi struggled not to grimace; it sounded like an angry squid circling a toilet bowl.

"Chaaktil."

"More recently."

"Cerea. I was moving a shipment—"

Oga tossed the clamfruit rind at her, effectively shutting her up.

"I know you're with the Resistance," Oga said.

Vi didn't answer immediately because that's what a scared person would do—they'd be frozen or in shock.

"I . . . I . . ." she started.

"Put her down, Rus." Oga reached for another clamfruit. "Nobody can talk near those teeth."

Vi was ready when he dropped her, but she stumbled anyway, using the moment to scan the area. Her own teeth ground together with rage when she saw some of her stolen cargo piled in a corner— the most sophisticated tech they'd brought. Generators, nav machines, and her long-range comm—the one she would've used to contact Leia to let her know that the mission was off to a good start.

By the time she stood, she'd already recomposed her face to show fear and shock instead of fury. Nice girls didn't get dragged out of bathrooms by sentient sharks, after all.

"I don't know what you're—"

"Say it," Oga pressed. "You're Resistance. You were seen in the market wearing a jacket with a starbird crest two days ago, before you covered it up. Don't tell me you just found it during your travels."

Vi straightened the shawl she'd bought to hide that very symbol and stepped forward to meet Oga's eyes. The gangster was not the sort of person who would abide fools. But she also wasn't going to appreciate arrogance or sarcasm.

Fine. If she wanted a straight shooter, she would get a straight shooter.

"I'm with the Resistance," Vi confirmed. "And yeah, I earned this jacket."

Oga nodded and thoughtfully sucked up another clamfruit.

"Raaaawgh," N'arrghela groaned.

"No, you can't pull off her arms," Oga said. "Patience. Do you have any idea how hard it is to get blood out of that rug? Honestly."

Oga stood, picked up a small dish of something blue and gelatinous, and walked over to Vi, which made life even more uncomfortable. Instead of a rock and a hard place, Vi was stuck between a shark and a squid-thing, underground, and her allies and friends had no idea that anything was even slightly wrong.

"Why did you come to my planet?" Oga asked between messy slurps of her snack.

Vi kept her face neutral, even when pearls of goop sprayed her cheek.

"I'm supposed to build an encampment here," she finally said.

There was no point in lying about it, Vi reasoned. If Oga hadn't guessed already by her cargo and her jacket, she would discover the truth soon enough when Vi started building and recruiting. Dotti was probably singing about it upstairs. And even if Vi had chosen to keep her secret tonight instead of telling her co-workers, recruitment involved telling prospective recruits who you were and what you were doing, so it's not like she could've hidden her activities from the cunning and well-informed gangster for long, anyway.

"A Resistance encampment? On Batuu? Why? This place has no strategic value."

Vi exhaled. Time to put her cards on the table.

"The two things the Resistance needs most right now are bolt-holes and new blood. A place like this with a busy spaceport and folk looking to get lost—that's mighty attractive."

Oga squelched a wheezing sigh and moved a step closer. She had a powerful, animal musk about her with a tinge of the sea, and Vi wondered what she and Rusko liked about this relatively dry stone-and-forest ecosystem, so far from their own watery planets.

"They got a lot of money, the Resistance?"

Vi shrugged. "More for ships, fuel, rations, and other goods than for ransom, if that's what you're asking. I'm nobody special."

"Of course not," Oga agreed. "Or else they wouldn't have sent you here." She held up the small glass dish that had held her snack and inspected it closely before slurping up a few bits of fizzing goo. "Look here: I don't believe in the Resistance. They've got powerful enemies. And I don't want powerful enemies, so I can't have offworlders calling down trouble."

She crushed the glass dish between her fingers. The juice stung Vi's eyes, but she didn't flinch.

"I get rid of trouble, Vi Moradi, and it doesn't come back. That's why I'm the one in charge. So you can stay here as long as you have spira to spend, but you don't want to get on my bad side."

Vi stepped closer, chin up. "You know the First Order is *all* bad side, right?"

Oga laughed, and it sounded like a clogged drain. "I like people who bring me money, and if the First Order is as powerful as I hear, they might just do that. So far, you've only brought me annoyance and a pittance in exchange for some yarn. Guess who I like better?"

With a sigh, Vi swiped the clamfruit juice and blue spatters off her face. She was definitely going to have to wash her clothes now. "The only reason you're still in charge here is that the First Order hasn't decided to take it away from you. That's what they do—they show up and take. They destroy. Land, buildings, weapons, lives. That's what the Resistance is trying to stop."

When Oga's thick, rubbery fingers patted her face, it took everything Vi had not to slap her hand away. "I don't need you to fight my battles for me, little scrapper. I do fine."

Vi snorted. "Sure you do. Sending your muscle to steal from unconscious visitors who just survived a crash is a brilliant strategy."

Rusko roared and stepped forward, but Oga stopped him with a look.

"You're brave, I'll give you that," she said, and her long fingers stroked what might've been called a chin. "And maybe a little stupid. I might have a job for you."

Vi's eyes flashed at Rusko and N'arrghela. "If it's joining your crew, the answer is no."

Oga laughed a gargling laugh and slapped the Karkarodon on the shoulder. He didn't budge. "That wasn't the offer. They'd spend days picking bits of you out of their teeth. But let's say I recently came into possession of some cargo that might be of use to you."

Vi made a wrap-it-up gesture. These games were so time consuming.

"Yes, I would like my cargo back. What do you want?"

"There's this ancient Batuuan artifact. Dok-Ondar's been looking for it, but he's cleaned out most of the valuables in the ruins and still can't find it. I'd love to have it in hand before he does. Got a buyer all lined up, and then I wouldn't need to give Old Dok his cut. I want you to find it for me."

Vi's look was skeptical. "Why trust a stranger like me when you could send anyone?"

Rusko growled, N'arrghela screeched, and Oga held up a hand to silence them.

"I did. I sent *several* anyones. Some of 'em I actually liked. They didn't come back, and now none of my people are willing to try again. The ancients left their traps, see, and then Dok-Ondar didn't clean 'em up. But you're small, expendable, and probably trained for this sort of thing. Sneaking around, getting past traps. We don't know much about the civilization that used to live here, but we know they left behind a lot of ways to kill people, once you get deep into their world. And we know they hid their most valuable belongings where nobody could see 'em. Scrap of what we found says 'shining in the dark.'"

"So it's underground," Vi said.

"Looks like it."

"And do you have a map?"

Oga shook her head like Vi was a fool. "Old Batuuan people didn't leave maps, girl. The ruins are a maze of caverns and tunnels, and I reckon the prize is still in there somewhere. And if it ain't, well, then it's down another hole."

"Sounds cozy," was what Vi actually said, but she was thinking about how this assignment could have a major payoff. Not only could she get on Oga's good side and earn back some of her cargo, but if everyone else here was frightened of the ruins and Vi could survive them—and map them—maybe the Resistance could use them. Crait was never far from her mind, where an old cave had been the only thing that had saved the Resistance from total annihilation at the hands of the First Order.

"So you'll do it?"

Vi put a hand on her hip and grinned. "Let's set the ground rules. One: If I retrieve this artifact, I get my cargo back."

Oga nodded once. "What's left of it."

"Two: Considering I'm planning to stick around and I hear you own or control just about everything here, I'd like permission to temporarily use the ruins as part of the Resistance command post."

The Blutopian put her head on the side. "I don't really care what happens at the ruins unless someone is turning a profit, at which point I'll want my cut. But I can ignore some activity if it benefits me, eh?"

"We won't be turning a profit, and I think we'll definitely benefit you. The Resistance has fleets that need fuel. Troops that need food and clothes and weapons—and trips to the cantina. It's not like anybody else is using the ruins. And when we leave, they're all cleaned out of scary traps and ready for you."

Oga ambled to the bowl of clamfruit, pacing and slurping as she thought about it. Rusko grumbled about his cut of the cargo, and N'arrghela ran her fingers up and down her bowcaster, crooning at it. Vi suddenly noticed the Talpini squatting motionless in the corner of the room, his broad lips turned down and his bright-blue eyes unblinking; he might've been carved of stone except for the flicker of light on his eyes. The tooka-cat woke up, shook itself, hopped to the floor, and pawed at Oga's legs hopefully until she tossed down a bruised and stinky fruit.

"Fine," she finally said. "But remember: You don't own the land. And if anything's missing from the cargo you claim is yours, that's none of my business. I'm doing you a favor. Even if you succeed, you still owe me. Everyone does." Oga held out a leathery gray hand dripping with clamfruit juice, and Vi reached out to shake it. In careful Huttese, squeezing the bones of Vi's hand, Oga intoned, *"Du bargon Oga es du bargon macroon tee-tocky."*

A deal with Oga is a deal for life.

"Mendee-ya jah-jee bargon," Vi responded in Huttese, using her proper accent this time. *We have a deal.*

Oga nodded and the tentacles around her mouth curled up. "Come to the cantina on your day off. Rusko will show you where to go."

"But what is it? What am I looking for?"

"The ancients loved nature, especially water and stars," Oga said with a rubbery shrug. "Strange folk. Their greatest artifacts glow or shimmer. Might be a gemstone statue of a god, might be a piece of jewelry, might be a crystal. You'll know it when you see it."

Vi nodded. "And when I have the artifact in hand?"

"Bring it back here, and don't put it in any hand other than mine if you want to live, much less collect. Don't you get it, girl? As long as you're in Black Spire Outpost, this cantina is the center of your world."

Oga nodded with finality and turned her attention to the clamfruit, and Rusko shoved Vi's shoulder hard enough to make her stumble.

"She's one of us now, Rus. Don't damage the goods," the Blutopian called over her shoulder.

"I don't work for you," Vi called sharply. "I work for General Organa."

At that, Oga laughed so hard that the tooka fluffed up and ran away. It was a sound that might've shattered glass.

"That's not how things work here. You're far away from this gen-

eral of yours, and you're doing a job for me, and you live in *my* outpost on *my* rock, so, yeah, you work for me. Everyone in Black Spire
does, whether they know it or not. You're one of us." Oga turned back
around, and her face did something horrible that might've been
called a smile, somewhere in the galaxy. "Besides, the alternative to
being one of us is being an offworlder, and you never want to be seen
as an offworlder, an outsider, a stranger. We charge extra for that.
Welcome to Black Spire Outpost."

She went back to her clamfruit, and Rusko shoved Vi, and Vi
started walking. She was completely sober now, and without the buzz
of the alcohol, her back hurt from scrapping, and she'd been gone far
longer than she'd meant to be. But at least she was returning to her
camp with hope. All she had to do was defy death in a place that had
already claimed the lives of several people Oga actually trusted. That
couldn't be too hard—her minions appeared to have been chosen for
their muscles, teeth, and unhinged natures, not their cleverness,
training, or subtlety.

"Oh, and little rebel?" Oga called right as Vi was about to step back
into the hallway, because much like generals giving bad news, that
was always when tough gangsters chose to drive the knife of their
rule home.

Vi stopped.

"Yeah?"

"I can't stop you from talking in the cantina, but if I hear you're
bothering other customers, I'll have N'arrghela rip out your tongue,
and maybe a few teeth."

Vi shook her head but did not turn around. "Anybody ever tell you
you're a real benevolent despot?"

Oga's caustic laugh made her wince as it bounced off the stone.
"All the time, girl. All the time."

Rusko marched her back down the hall, through the darkness, and
up to a wall. His heavy hand pressed down on her shoulder to indicate she should wait. He put an eye to a tiny crack in the wall, opened
the door into the bathroom stall, and shoved Vi through.

"This here's a one-way door," he said, low and deadly. "Don't tell anybody, or we'll know who told. And maybe we'll let N'arrghela pull off one of your arms anyway."

"I'm one of you now, remember?" Vi said, turning around to give him her best unimpressed look.

"Not to me, you're not. And not to Oga, neither, unless and until you deliver that artifact."

Rusko slammed the door, leaving Vi alone in the bathroom. She exited the stall and went directly to the mirror, where she did her best to scrub the clamfruit juice and specks of blue slime off her face.

Black Spire Outpost, she was learning, could be a very messy place. She'd thought it would be easy, coming here and selecting a site and building a tidy headquarters. She'd thought the task beneath her. But the experience so far had been rife with chaos and uncertainty. It was startling, being so far from the Resistance and hearing someone respond to General Organa's name not with respect or hatred but with crude, mocking laughter.

Right now, she and Archex and Pook represented the sum total of the Resistance presence on Batuu, and they had almost nothing. Without resources and credits, it was hard just to scrape by in the galaxy, much less build something lasting. If she could pull off this job for Oga, they'd have a place to stay, and maybe even the beginnings of a headquarters.

At least now, they had hope.

Chapter Twelve

THE WALK BACK TO CAMP FELT a lot longer at night, and all Vi could smell was clamfruit juice. She'd learned much at the cantina and wished she could talk it over with the general. But no—not until she got their long-range comm back. And she wasn't even sure if that equipment was included in Oga's deal. For all she knew, she could risk life and limb to get a sacred pet rock in the ruins and receive nothing but a box of bolts in return.

That was the annoying thing about gangsters—everything was always on their terms.

The stars were beautiful here, at least, and the scurryings in the forest didn't sound dangerous. A dugar dugar, a slender, deerlike creature with long, silky fur the color of mushrooms, watched her for a moment before springing madly away, and night birds cooed and burbled to one another across the canopy. Vi hadn't asked exactly where the ruins were, but she hoped they were closer to the outpost, as the camp they'd made where their ship had just so happened to crash was too far away to be convenient. The protected caverns would serve many purposes, but the Resistance would benefit from a smaller setup near town where ships could land and take off quickly. That would also be valuable if the First Order showed up—maybe they would focus their fire on the smaller spot and ignore the more hidden and protected command center.

Fire flickered between stark black tree trunks as she approached their camp. Archex was slumped against a log, asleep with his arms crossed and his legs stretched out in front of him. Had he tried to wait up for her? The poor guy. There were purple hollows under his eyes, suggesting he was in pain and not getting enough rest, or maybe he'd been pushing himself too hard. A bird carcass had blackened on a spit over the fire, but Oga's clamfruit had dried up any appetite Vi might've had for a late-night snack.

She put a hand on Archex's shoulder and murmured, "I'm back."

He startled awake, his eyes wide, and jerked as if about to execute some well-programmed defensive movement that was beyond his body's current abilities.

"She's back," Pook echoed mournfully. "And thus does my torment continue."

"You could've told me sooner!" Archex barked, grimacing as he pulled himself to standing and rubbed feeling back into his leg. He cleared his throat and tried to look as if he hadn't been caught in a moment of complete vulnerability and wasn't a total mess. "How was work?"

"Functional and not nearly as bad as I'd expected. It's not going to pay well, but I'll definitely have a good chance at salvaging some scrap to help build out our site. There was this one old turret that looked like it would be useful."

"You were treated well?"

Vi smiled fondly at his drive to protect her. Even when Captain Cardinal had been in the middle of threatening and interrogating her back on the *Absolution,* he'd still felt responsible for . . . well, maybe not her health and safety, but he'd brought her food and water, which is more than what most victims received from their torturers. After all, he'd spent years looking after children, so it was natural that he would consider the needs of those in his charge. And now Archex was concerned that her new boss might mistreat her. He was also probably feeling guilty that he couldn't work in town and pull his own weight, she reasoned.

"I was treated surprisingly well. The scrappers are like a family, and the man who owns the salvage yard is . . ." How to describe Savi? "He's got this tranquility to him. Almost spiritual. Not at all the kind of person I'd imagine running that sort of business. He even supplies lunch for his workers. I'll get you a sandwich next time we're in town."

But then Archex's face went . . . stern. Almost like a disappointed father. "Then why were you out so late?"

Vi sat on her sleeping bag, which Archex had arranged for her by the fire. She took off her wig, fluffed her hair, and tugged off her boots and socks, then kindly shoved her feet home in the bag before Archex had to smell them. It had been a long day.

"The scrappers invited me out to the cantina, so I went. I wanted to get to know them, be liked, find out about this place and whether I might have any chance of recruiting them."

"And?"

Vi settled down and told him everything. His reactions were almost comical—outrage at Rusko's ham-handed kidnapping attempt and fury with how Oga had treated Vi.

"Been a long time since you lived in a lawless city, hasn't it?" she said.

Archex exhaled a long sigh and went silent for a moment before saying, "I've never lived in a city. Or at least, not as a citizen. More as a junk rat. Never been part of an actual community."

"But surely there was a boss in your . . . where you lived as a kid? Because any place with more than twenty sentient beings gathered together in this galaxy has either a boss or a government. And the governments are growing increasingly rare."

She could sense him fighting internally. Leia had told Vi that part of his deprogramming was about teaching Archex that the first voice he heard in his head was what he'd been taught by the First Order, by their propaganda and whatever they'd drilled into him for the past twenty years. But if he went quiet and listened hard, there would often be a second voice that was closer to his real feelings, closer to the heart of who he truly was.

"It's not right, a place like this being lorded over by a boss, by some random bully," he finally growled. Then he took a deep breath. "But that's their choice. People who don't like it can live elsewhere, pick a place with more order." His head fell forward. "And either way, no one can stop what happened to the Hosnian system. Not a boss, not a government. There's never going to be a perfect sense of order." He looked up. "Does this Oga seem like a good leader to you?"

Vi considered it carefully, as he had considered his words. "She's fairer than plenty of others I've met. Genuinely cares about this place. Not sure if she cares about the people as individuals or if it's more like . . . they're valuable animals in her care. But she's fiercely protective of them, at least. And Black Spire Outpost is prospering, even if its ruler is a little unsavory. I didn't see anybody starving or begging or sick. You ever seen a cantina with rules by the front door?" Before he could answer, she smoothly continued. "Never mind. You've never been to a cantina."

Stiffly, he said, "Not recreationally, no, unless you count the officers' mess on the *Absolution*." Then, softly, "What's it like?"

Vi's eyes blinked closed, and she nestled down into her sleeping bag. "I'll take you there soon," she promised. "For now, let's just sleep. I've got a lot of scrapping to do tomorrow."

He settled down, too, trying to hide his grimace. "And I'll be scouting for mushrooms and berries and doing my exercises. I found some tarine bushes today and gathered leaves for tea."

"Tea's nice," Vi murmured, which was a lie. She hated tarine tea.

She had to find something for him to do, fast. He was a man who needed a job. Without one, he would only continue to wither away. And she'd forgotten to buy the pot, spices, and oil she'd promised, too.

Leia had called her a leader. But Vi was beginning to think that for once Leia was wrong.

The next morning, Vi repeated her ritual: She woke up at first dawn, washed at the cenote, and was soon sitting on a box as she sorted through Savi's junk. The scrappers didn't mention her recruitment effort at the cantina and neither did Vi, although she noticed that Lin and Fenda kept their distance. She wanted to get comfortable with her fellow Gatherers again, so she avoided bringing up anything about the Resistance or the galaxy beyond Batuu. She also didn't mention her upcoming job for Oga and all that was riding on it. She did inquire about her day off, though, as she didn't want to wait too long. After all, Oga could always send someone else, and then Vi's cargo would get sold out from under her.

As they worked, Ylena told her some of the town gossip, like how Mubo had a crush on Bina, the fiercely independent Amani who lovingly ran the Creature Stall, or how Zabaka the Toydarian toymaker all but worshipped Oga, or how Hiro the Hutt was the reason Oga didn't allow monkey-lizards in her cantina.

"And watch out for Dok-Ondar," Ylena said quietly. "The Ithorian who runs the antiquities shop. He's been here longer than Oga, and he's ruthless. If you get on his bad side, what the locals call the Doklist, your days are numbered."

"You don't think any of my cargo would be in his shop?" Vi asked her.

Ylena shook her head. "Not unless it's old and esoteric and strange. He likes things that are rare and valuable."

Vi put two and two together. "So you're in competition with him," she said softly.

Ylena gave her a sharp look. "You see through to the quick of things, don't you? Yes, you could say Dok and Savi have similar interests, although Dok is more focused on black-market treasures and Savi is looking for historical objects of religious or spiritual value. It's almost a gentleman's game between them. Much respect. But such things aren't generally known outside these walls."

Sometime after lunch, Vi found something curious—a sort of strange box that looked like it was made of crystal.

"I assume this goes in the artifact bin?" she asked Ylena, enjoying the solid heft of the thing in her hands. It looked artisan-made and old, and something about it was just very pleasing.

Ylena looked up as she had countless other times when Vi wasn't sure whether to save or toss something—it was all part of the learning curve, and Ylena had been very patient. But this time, she gasped and put a hand to her chest.

"May I?" she asked.

Vi put the object into her hands and would've sworn it gave a soft pulse of . . . well, not light. Maybe a glow.

"What is it?"

Ylena's smile held an answering glow. "I'm not sure, but Savi will be glad to see it. And we'll be sure to let him know it was you who found it. Where was it?"

"Over here in this old trunk. Looks like it got shipwrecked maybe. And a little bit burned." Vi pointed to the object in question. She'd expected to find some old toothpaste and maybe some moth-eaten clothes within, but all she'd found was the multisided crystal, tucked into a nest of dried grass.

Ylena handed the object to Vi as if it were a delicate egg and explored every atom of the trunk, pulling out all the grass and running her fingers over the wood and hinges.

"Beautiful," she murmured. "Ancient. All handmade. See the hammer marks on the clasp?"

"Definitely seems old."

Vi stood and stretched and admired the chest, which didn't hold the same allure for her. She'd never been the sort to attach to antiques. She enjoyed the look and touch of bespoke items or handmade things like the shawls in Arta's shop or her own admittedly hideous knitted hat, but an old trunk? Not her style. The Resistance was beleaguered by old junk. Still, Ylena seemed delighted, which in turn made Vi happy. They lifted the trunk onto Ylena's cart and rolled it over to the sorting bins. Ylena took the crystalline object into the shed and returned without it—and locked the door behind her with a key Vi hadn't noticed before, which hung on a cord around her neck.

The next morning, when Vi arrived at work, Ylena was smiling that dimpled smile.

"Savi was glad for the artifact you found yesterday," she told Vi. "It's very valuable indeed."

Vi knew well enough that as a scrapper, she had no hold over the objects she found—everything here belonged to Savi. But it was always a nice feeling, knowing the boss was happy with her service.

She nodded. "I'm glad."

"He thought you might find this useful." Ylena gestured to a large—and very familiar—crate.

Vi knelt and unbuckled it to reveal neat coils of power cables. She swallowed down a lump in her throat. "This isn't salvage," she said.

"Well, some things end up in the right hands at the right time. We Gatherers take care of one another."

Vi closed the case and stood. "Can I hug you? Because I don't know if you know how much this means to me. To the Resistance."

Ylena held out her arms, and Vi briefly relished the human contact. Ylena felt almost like a mother figure, for all that she was only maybe ten years older than Vi. The woman smelled like the scrapyard, but also like herbs and flowers. Vi was suddenly aware that her only bathing experiences since crash-landing on Batuu had been with nothing but water. As soon as she'd received her pay, she would need to buy some personal care basics to avoid running everyone off before she could get around to recruiting them.

They stepped back and got to work, and that night, Ylena let Vi borrow her work cart to tow the power cords back to camp. Vi recognized that it was a kindness—and a test. The next day was her day off. She could use the cart as needed—but she was expected to return it in good working condition on the next workday.

Vi's step was sprightly as she neared camp well before dark, pulling a case of valuable cables that they would need to power their facility, once they had one. She'd worried that Oga's minions would sell them separately or otherwise make them harder to track, but here they were, all tidy and accounted for. Archex was pleased but just as confused about . . . well, just society in general.

"This Savi just gave them to you? Thousands of credits' worth of power cords? Just like that?"

Vi shrugged. "I didn't even have to ask. The case was just there, like a gift. Whatever that artifact I found yesterday was, it must've been very important. And valuable. Oh, and I got paid." She held up a credit chip. "So tomorrow, I'll be running Oga's errand, but I can pick up a few basics in town, if you need anything besides the cooking supplies?"

"I'm fine," he said, and she almost laughed at his stoic frown.

"Well, I bet you'd be better with some soap and deodorant, and maybe a shaving kit. You're getting a bit scruffy."

Archex rubbed his stubble and ran a hand through his hair. "Okay, yeah, I wouldn't complain about that. The cenote is better than nothing, but . . . let's just say I got accustomed to having a private shower on a Star Destroyer."

"I do not have scent receptors, but I am certain you are both one step away from acquiring a skin disease," Pook observed. With nothing to do and no power droid to charge him, Pook spent most of his time turned off, but Vi wasn't surprised to see that he had chosen to wake himself up just to insult them in the most woeful way possible.

"Chin up, Pook. I'm going to fetch this ancient Batuu artifact, get on Oga's good side, and win back our supplies. And maybe even find a better spot for our facility. I have a good feeling about this."

"I don't have a chin," the droid said. "Nor do I have feelings. Good night." His lights went out as he powered down.

"Till the spire," Vi responded, realizing that she was starting to use the local jargon without having to think about it. And she was starting to crave Cookie's food again, too. "Oh! And after my trip, I'll bring you one of those sandwiches."

Archex looked up, and it took her a minute to read his expression. Was it . . . wounded?

No. Reproachful.

"Oh, no. You ran out of food today, didn't you?"

His smile was sad. "I ate what was left over from yesterday. Couldn't shoot any birds. I guess I already got all the dumb ones in our area, or maybe the smart ones spread the word. The mushrooms melted off the spit, and roots are no good without spices or a pot to cook them in, and the berry bushes are picked clean, and the tea leaves have to dry. My leg hurt too much to wander too far, so . . . it was a hungry day. I'll survive. I've done worse." He gave her a brave smile . . . but then his stomach growled.

Vi stood, testing her own pain and energy levels, which weren't too bad—not as bad as listening to his stomach grumble all night and beating herself up over it. "Looks like I'm headed into town, then," she said. "It's my job to keep you fed, and I messed up. Should take about an hour." Ignoring her exhaustion, she gave him a nod and started walking.

"Sir?"

Vi stopped. "Yeah?"

"Requesting permission to come with."

When she turned to look at him, he'd pushed himself off the transport and was doing his best to stand tall and look capable and strong. To be fair, he was mostly pulling it off, for all that she knew that if she kicked his bad leg he would topple over in obscene amounts of pain.

"It's a twenty-minute walk. Your leg and lung won't thank you. There's clambering."

A sort of desperation flashed in his eyes. "I'm going crazy out here, alone with my thoughts. Nothing to do, alone. It's too quiet. Please. Let me try."

Vi considered it. He was accustomed to being surrounded by thousands of people in a Star Destroyer, and now here he was, resigned to a quiet forest. He didn't even have calm Cerean soul guides and interpretive dance to rail against. No wonder it was driving him mad. As much as his leg hurt, the pain would be worth it to him, if it meant something to do besides wait. She sighed and jerked her chin at the path to town. "Come on, then."

She slowed her walk to keep pace with him, and in turn he sped up, although it left him breathing heavily and nearly staggering. At first, they were silent, but Vi could tell Archex wanted to talk.

"You got anything in particular you want to do in town?" she asked.

"Well, I . . ." He trailed off before pulling something out of his cargo pocket. When Vi slowed to look, she saw two small carvings: a convor and a frog dog. They were charming and well made with personalities all their own. "You said there was a toy shop, right? Do you think whoever runs it might have a use for this sort of thing?"

Vi stopped to give him her full attention and considered the figurines. "Salju said the toy shop was run by a Toydarian named Zabaka. I haven't been in to meet her, but we can ask."

Archex shoved the toys back in his pocket and began walking again, brisk but with a limp. She matched his pace and struggled for something to say. He was so earnest but so naïve. So broken but trying so hard. She didn't want to patronize him, but she sensed that any sort of compliment or acknowledgment would bring his walls up. So she did what a spy did best: She got sneaky.

"Where'd you learn to carve?"

He seemed confused by the question at first. "What? Oh. On Jakku. I carved umbo nuts to sell as beads. There's no shortage of wood here. I just . . ." He sighed. "I have to do something. Feel like I'm contributing."

Vi stopped, turned, and put her hands on his shoulders, looking directly into his eyes to drive her point home. "Your worth is not measured by what you produce. You understand that, right? Leia sent you here to support me and the eventual recruitment facility, and you can't do that until there's a facility. You're doing exactly what I need you to do, right now. I'm not asking for anything more. I'm glad you're here."

His deep hazel eyes seemed to soften and melt, and his eyelashes swept down and his lips parted as he leaned in, and—

Vi released his shoulders and stepped back.

"Archex, what are you doing?"

He swallowed hard, eyes darting everywhere but at her in his confusion and embarrassment. "Oh, I . . . I mean, I thought that . . ."

"Were you trying to kiss me?"

He squeezed his eyes shut like a child trying to hide. "No. Yes. Maybe?"

Vi tried not to laugh. Dr. Kalonia had told her this might happen as whatever feelings the First Order had suppressed in him naturally arose over time. His confusion was only natural.

"Then I'll go ahead and let you in on a little secret: I'm not into it."

He grimaced. "Yeah, why would you be? After what I did to you. I can't believe I even tried to . . . It just felt like—I'm so sorry—"

She interrupted him before he could dig himself into a hole. "Look. We work together. We're partners. I care about you, but not like that."

She'd never cared for anyone like that, men or women, never had such urges, but he didn't need to know that now. She shrugged almost comically, put her hands in her pockets, and started walking again as if nothing awkward had happened. After a moment, Archex joined her.

"But when you touched me and looked into my eyes, I felt—"

"A connection."

"Yeah." The poor guy sounded so confused, and Vi felt bad that she was the only person around to explain it to him.

"People have those all the time. They have relationships. We're wired for touch. It's not always about kissing. Sometimes it is. This time it wasn't. But if you hit on anybody in town, I won't take it personally. I'll even be your wingmate." She tossed him a grin. "Look, just know that I'm your friend, and I'm here for you. Not romantically or physically, but for pretty much anything else. You can count on me. Okay?"

Archex sighed heavily. "Okay. Yeah. Sorry. Thanks."

Now Vi couldn't help chuckling. "Well, at least we've reached peak awkwardness now, right? So everything should be smooth from here on out."

"I'll tell you after I've seen town."

They'd reached the archway by then, and Vi enjoyed introducing Archex to Black Spire Outpost. Already it felt familiar and friendly, and their earlier miscommunication was soon forgotten. Archex was truly enthusiastic about the food at Tuggs' Grub and had a spirited conversation with Cookie himself about spices, which he later hunted down in the market to use on the wild game he hoped to serve up back at camp. He sold his carvings to Zabaka at the toy shop for almost nothing but was bursting with pride at earning his own money for the first time—especially since the busy Toydarian told him she'd buy anything else he carved of similar quality. He haggled with an old woman for a heavy cooking pot, and she tossed in a carved spoon for free. For a while there, he seemed almost happy.

When they stopped in at the cantina, she bought him a Jedi Mind Trick and watched with increasing amusement as he got tipsy and tried to sweet-talk the waitress. She didn't have the heart to tell him that it was a waitress's job to be nice to the drunk guy making a fool of himself at the bar, but she did slip the server a few credits for her trouble. As for Vi, she only drank a spicy Blurggfire, all too aware that if she wanted to live long enough to find and deliver the artifact to Oga tomorrow she'd need to be at her best.

"I like this place," Archex said, slurring a little as they walked back toward their camp, the moons glowing above and bathing the forest in silken blue light. "Th'outpost. Things don't hurt as much here."

"That's the alcohol," Vi reminded him. "It numbs the pain."

He shook his head. "No. I think it's the freedom."

Vi didn't argue. For a former First Order trooper and true believer, it was a major epiphany. Let him think what he wanted. It was good to see him healing—and to see his beliefs organically aligning with the Resistance.

Whether he knew it or not, Captain Cardinal was truly becoming Archex.

He was becoming . . . himself.

Chapter Thirteen

ON THE *PENUMBRA*, A FIRST ORDER STAR DESTROYER

LIEUTENANT WULFGAR KATH WAS OFF DUTY and in the gym when his comlink chimed. He finished his set before acknowledging it.

"Kath."

The answering voice was clipped, curt, and in no way friendly. "This is General Hux. We have received a tip that there may be a Resistance spy at Black Spire Outpost on the planet Batuu. The *Penumbra* is currently the closest First Order ship to that sector. You are therefore commanded to take a squad of twenty troopers, find the spy, and bring her directly to the *Finalizer*."

Kath stroked his beard contemplatively. "You said *her*. Is this a known combatant?"

"We suspect it is Starling."

Kath carefully hid his sudden interest. "The one who turned and kidnapped Cardinal."

He could almost hear Hux's sneer across the light-years. "Do not say that traitor's name to me again."

"Yes, sir. Is there anything else, sir?"

Hux exhaled, a measured *hmm*. "If the Resistance has business on Batuu, we need to know what it is. Any planet that gives aid to our enemies must be punished. Find the spy and learn what you can of Batuu's strategic importance. You are to leave immediately. Hux out."

The comlink went silent, and Kath reached for his towel. He cleaned off the bench press with the same measured patience and exactitude he applied to everything. It was an odd hour, and he had the officers' gym to himself, so he took his time as he considered this new assignment.

He hadn't been off-ship in years, not since he'd worn the number CD-0828 and gone on the requisite training missions alongside his old friend CD-0922. Captain Cardinal. They'd parted as young men but had met here and there over the years, always with a fond pat on the shoulder or a stiff nod, depending on who else was around. When he'd heard the news—that Cardinal was either kidnapped, dead, or defected—he hadn't believed it. But when the footage from Cardinal's personal droid had revealed an interrogation gone wrong and a man who'd been broken—who'd allowed himself to soften and weaken and break—then Kath had had no choice but to believe.

He hated nothing so much as a traitor, except maybe a coward. To him, Cardinal was both. It would be a pleasure to hunt and hurt the spy who had first sown doubt in his mind.

Although he knew Hux wanted results, and fast, Kath also knew that Hux was a man who understood appearances and the importance of doing things correctly. As he sat in the sauna, he considered the soldiers on the *Penumbra* who could be spared and who would do well on a rough planet on the edge of the galaxy, who wouldn't be wooed by the cantina or grow tenderhearted toward the local population. After Cardinal's fall, Hux had subtly tweaked the nightly programming to heighten a sense of duty and loyalty, and although he was not the commander of this vessel, the soldiers here knew that Kath would settle for nothing less than perfection. The *Penumbra*'s troopers, and Kath's chosen troopers, would never fail him.

After his shower, he packed a case and dressed in his officer's blacks. He was a thickset, muscular man, almost two meters tall with a barrel chest and pale skin spattered with freckles. He combed back his thick auburn hair, trimmed and oiled his bushy but meticulously maintained beard, and made certain his hat sat perfectly. Then he made his calls, ordering his chosen soldiers to meet him in the hangar at the beginning of the next shift. Ten men, ten women, all of them solid and experienced with no marks for misbehavior or cowardice. He put in the proper datawork for their transport, their weaponry, their rations, their codes. Every detail, flawlessly arranged.

Being chosen to lead this mission was a great opportunity for any officer hoping to work his way up the ranks. Thanks to a personal indiscretion in his past, Kath had lost some clout and was anxious to regain his footing. He had no doubts that he would succeed. Not only because Hux had given him clear orders, but also because he was a hunter who relished the thrill of the chase. He wanted revenge on Starling for what she'd done. And if it turned out that Cardinal had defected to the Resistance, Kath would take great joy in torturing the man slowly as proper punishment for turning his back on the First Order.

But there was a dark side to this assignment as well. Kath knew the destiny that awaited First Order officers who failed, and the executioner's vibro-ax was just as threatening as Vader's Force choke had once been among the officers of the Empire. Worse yet, if the assignment had caught the attention of the Supreme Leader . . .

Well.

Either he came back with the spy, or he didn't come back.

They landed on Batuu in the morning and eschewed the spaceport for a quiet clearing in the ancient forest. According to Kath's research, the First Order had never before shown interest in this backwater planet, so they had no way of knowing how the locals would react to their presence. On some of the more primitive worlds, the townspeople threw rocks at the troopers as if they were demons, and Kath wasn't in the mood to gun down half the outpost if they could be won over to his side. His squad would march into town with adequate pomp and weapons in hand, but the locals didn't need to know where they were based. Their massive transport, an MHU-6e Mobile Habitation Unit designed for temporary planetary occupation, was equipped with the necessary bunks, mess, armory, medbay, and supplies, so they should require very little from the outpost itself.

The moment the MHU touched down, Kath informed his soldiers of their assigned jobs, sending troopers to scout the area, scan for resources, and maintain watch over the clearing. What he'd seen so far suggested the planet was a useless relic taken over by vegetation, the sort of place too shriveled up and poor to be of much benefit to the First Order. No industries, no mines, no prison systems, no orphanages, no shipyards, nothing they actually needed. Just a crusty old junkyard full of refuse and a town cobbled together of slightly nicer refuse.

Personally, Kath rankled at such waste, to see a planet with breathable air and livable environments abandoned to languish and play host to parasites like simple farmers, shopkeepers, and filthy smugglers. Kath adored the orderly world of a Star Destroyer, the sharp lines and planes of architecture and the way doors slid silently and effortlessly closed, which meant he found the disarray of such wilderness insufferable, sneering at the way it was allowed to grow unchecked. The First Order had found him living in the slums on a desert moon in the Unknown Regions as a boy, and he'd never seen real nature until his first assignment onplanet. Consequently, trees made him uncomfortable.

When he'd determined that everything was exactly as it should be, Kath and four of his stormtroopers loaded into their landspeeder and took off for Black Spire Outpost. As they approached the jagged and aesthetically egregious structures, he made mental notes about the town, from its haphazard nature to the various natural landmarks along the way. As soon as they were among what must've passed for the outer limits of the outpost, people began to stare and whisper. They weren't a cosmopolitan folk, and they had unstudied manners and rough clothes that looked handcrafted of natural materials. When Kath saw another landspeeder parked at a filling station that looked like it also operated as a mechanic bay, he directed his pilot to park there.

"Bright suns," a young woman in a blue tunic and goggles said as she approached.

"That's close enough," Kath barked.

She stopped, both hands up. "No offense meant. I'm Salju, and this is my filling station. Do you need fuel?"

Kath stepped out of his speeder and looked down at the girl, noting her worn boots and grease-stained cheek and filing her away as a simpleton. "I need information."

Salju put her hands on her hips and nodded. She looked wary. That was normal enough, though; the First Order could be terrifying, when they had to be, and all his soldiers carried blasters.

"I'll try to help," the girl said.

"I need to know who's in charge here."

Salju smiled, a little impish, which Kath didn't like. "That would be Oga Garra. She runs the cantina and the spaceport and a lot more besides. If you want to see her, you'll need to ask at the bar. If you continue through the market, you can't miss it. She's a private sort, though, so you may need to deal with her second in command, a Karkarodon named Rusko."

Kath snorted. "Oh, she'll see me."

Salju inclined her head. "As you say. May the spires keep you."

Kath returned to his seat in the speeder. "They definitely will not."

They had no problem finding the cantina, and Kath regretted the necessity of entering a place so rife with unsavory characters. He would have to polish his boots the moment they returned to their camp. He left one soldier in the speeder and instructed the other three to march before him with the same precision they would've exhibited when lining up for a speech from General Hux.

"Just because the ground is uneven does not mean you may falter," he reminded them. "You represent the First Order, and I'm certain you can imagine how the Supreme Leader would expect you to carry yourselves."

There were rules posted just inside the cantina, which he didn't bother to read. If he broke a rule, they were welcome to attempt to throw him out and see if the wall still stood afterward.

Kath signaled for his troopers to halt and strode toward the bar, where a curious old woman watched him, one eyebrow approaching long, golden bangs that had to be a wig.

"Bright suns," she said, almost a question.

"Where is Oga Garra?" he asked.

She shrugged. "Only the ancients know."

He put a hand on his blaster. "Let me be more specific. I will see Oga Garra now."

"That's not mine to decide," she shot back, unafraid. "But I'll let someone know."

The old woman disappeared, and after a few moments a new barkeep approached him, a younger woman who might've been pretty if he cared about such things, which he didn't.

"Get you a drink, sir?"

He lifted a lip in disgust at such a thought. "I'm on duty."

The woman smiled a practiced sort of smile. "Well, come back when you're not. We've got over twenty—"

"No."

That single word, spoken so coldly, shut the girl right up, and she went off to find some greasy glasses to polish elsewhere.

Soon a burly Karkarodon in leather armor swaggered out from a dark hall and looked Kath up and down. Kath sized him up in turn and experienced the strange feeling of knowing he wasn't the largest guy around. That didn't happen to him often, in the First Order.

"Heard you want to see Oga," the Karkarodon said.

"You must be Rusko. So let me tell you how it goes. I'm Lieutenant Wulfgar Kath of the First Order, and I have been sent here by General Armitage Hux himself. My men have enough firepower to kill everyone in this town and enough ordnance to leave nothing but rubble behind. So don't play the local tough-guy business with me, because I'm tougher. And don't act like you're some sort of gatekeeper. Because I destroy gates."

Rusko laughed, a horrible scraping sound, and rubbed thick, sandpapery knuckles over what passed for his chin.

"I like you, Kath. Come along, and I'll take you to Oga—but only you. And maybe don't play so hard with her, eh? She's used to being in charge."

He turned to walk down the hall, and Kath signaled his men to stay—and stay alert—before he followed.

"Let's do each other a courtesy, Rusko. You try not to tell me my business and I'll try not to beat you to death."

"I was just offering some friendly advice to an offworlder. We do things different in BSO." The Karkarodon unlocked a hidden door and led Kath down another dark hall and up to a closed door. "But suit yourself. Just remember: You're real far away from the people who care about you, both on the planet and especially down here. The walls, floor, and ceiling are solid stone. Nobody in the cantina would hear a blaster bolt, much less your screams." He unlocked the door and waved a goodbye as he backed away. "May you have the better hand!"

"Insufferable colloquialisms," Kath muttered to himself as he stepped inside and waited for his eyes to adjust. At the other end of the room, a Blutopian sat at a desk surrounded by tablets and holographic screens. She didn't look up as he entered, but she did pluck a stone snail from a large clay bowl and crunch into it noisily before sucking out its soft bits with a slurping wriggle of the pink tentacles around her mouth.

"Figured you'd show up sooner or later," she rumbled in Huttese, her voice like a serrated blade on a ship's metal hull. Kath knew just enough Huttese to get by, and he had to assume she had the same understanding of Basic, even if her mouthparts would have trouble speaking it.

"I am Lieutenant Wulfgar Kath of the First Order, and—"

"Doesn't matter."

Wulfgar's eyes nearly bugged out of his head. "Excuse me?"

Oga looked up from her screens, the low light gleaming off her tiny black eyes. "It doesn't matter what your name is. I know why you're here, and I know what you want."

Kath crossed his arms. "Do you now?"

"The Resistance woman."

He nodded slowly. "The Resistance woman. Tell me where she is, and you will be rewarded handsomely. The First Order is always anxious for allies and can ensure ongoing peace for your planet."

Oga snorted, and snail slime flew across her desk. "Oh, I'm not your ally. I'll tell you the same thing I told her when she stood right where you're standing and tried to convince me to join her cause: The only things I care about are Black Spire Outpost and my interests here."

"You'll very much care about it when our Star Destroyers arrive and rain down—"

"I don't respond well to threats, and I wasn't done."

Something about her grating voice and the guttural nature of Huttese actually had the power to interrupt him, and Kath wasn't accustomed to being interrupted by anyone who wasn't a direct superior. He didn't like it.

"Oga, let's make an agreement. You don't interrupt me, and I won't kill you."

Oga sighed like he was a troublesome child. She crunched into another snail, sucked at it thoughtfully, and tossed the shell on the floor, where a shaggy tooka-cat pounced on it and proudly carried it back into the shadows.

"I was going to help you, *pateesa*, but if you'd rather keep threatening me, I won't. I have twenty ways to kill you in this chamber, any of which I can set into motion before you can draw your blaster. So let's just talk like equals."

"I have no equals outside of the First Order," he said, carefully enunciating each word.

"This is why I don't often leave this room," Oga muttered to herself. Her hand hovered over the snails for a moment, but then she stood and braced herself against the desk to look him in the eye. Even across the dark room, there was a piercing, predatory nature to her stare, and Kath forced himself to remain still, hands clasped stiffly behind his back, and listen.

"See, there's this artifact I want," Oga said. "And if you bring it back to me, I'll tell you everything you want to know about Starling, including her real name."

Chapter Fourteen

BATUU

Vi ARRIVED AT THE CANTINA SO early the next morning that the doors were still closed. As she contemplated knocking, a Wookiee's groan echoed from the balcony across the street and a familiar if unwelcome form stomped down the stairs and stood before her.

"No Rusko?" Vi asked N'arrghela.

In response, the Wookiee shook her head and scratched her armpit, then began walking. Vi didn't need to speak Shyriiwook to understand that this was her guide, so she simply followed N'argghela through Black Spire Outpost, waving at Salju as she passed the fuel station. Once beyond the outpost proper, the cantankerous Wookiee led her along Savi's Path, past the scrapyard and toward some natural rock formations out among the spires. Although it was quite close to town, Vi hadn't been to this part of Batuu before. The area around her camp felt quiet and old and resigned, as if nature had firmly swallowed up any sign of the trappings of civilization. But here, there were interesting shapes integrated into the landscape, carved into and cut out of the mountain crags, and she wondered why the outpost had been built separately from what had obviously once been a settlement. It all looked quite intentional but . . . ancient. Forgotten.

So these were the ruins she'd bet on—the dangerous caverns that she hoped to turn into a Resistance refuge.

"Hurrghn graaaahl," N'arrghela growled, pointing at a deeply shadowed part of the forest that felt both mysterious and a little sacred.

"That's where I'm supposed to go, huh? Doesn't look like much of an entrance. I just walk in and the artifact jumps out at me?" Vi asked.

She didn't know if N'arrghela understood Basic, and she cursed Oga for her lack of forethought in the communications department. If Oga wanted her to succeed, this sort of information was obviously pretty important. If she could retrieve the artifact, she should have enough of her cargo back to begin actually building the command location and getting her mission back on track. If only she spoke more Shyriiwook.

The Wookiee screeched a laugh and walked her hairy fingers through the air as if down the path before forcefully flattening out her hand. "Urrrghrl grrrow grrr nerrgh."

"So you're saying that everyone who's walked this particular path under these particular trees has not come back?" In punctuation, Vi walked her own fingers through the air, then rolled up her eyes and stuck out her tongue to simulate a nasty death.

N'arrghela crossed her arms and nodded, her eyes sparkling with an evil delight.

"Well, I plan on coming back. You gonna be waiting?" She tapped her wrist.

A headshake.

The Wookiee motioned toward the forest, flapping her hand in a shooing gesture. "Granerrgh grawwwwwr."

"Yeah, until the spires and all that to you, too."

After N'arrghela had walked off back toward town, Vi took a moment to check over her person and make sure she was ready for everything—or as ready as she could be, considering most of her belongings had been stolen. Under her orange wrap, she had two blasters and her tactical baton, and she carried a walking staff she'd made from a broken metal bar in her crashed transport. She'd thought about bringing Pook, but without a power source, he was heavily drained already. At least this way, she didn't have to listen to him complain about how the cave affected his sensors.

Part of her was annoyed to be under the thumb of an unfair gangster who'd sent her into danger with little information and no supplies, but most of her was grateful for something to do to earn her goods back faster than months of slow work at the scrapyard would. And, if she was honest, this mission was a lot more fun than the one Leia had given her. Vi Moradi had chosen to become a spy for a very specific reason.

She needed a little danger in her life.

As soon as she stepped under the forest canopy, the temperature dropped, and the sounds changed. Batuu suddenly seemed to transform into a very different planet. It didn't feel scary or threatening. It felt holy somehow, as if the land still listened attentively, holding its breath. Everything else might've been abandoned, but the spirit of this place remained, serene and noble. And perilous. She drew her blaster and paid close attention to the sounds of the forest. The birds were all singing happily high above, but Vi didn't think it was the wild animals or living people that were going to be the problem.

This place—it was just too beautiful to die here.

As she continued, creeping deeper and deeper into the forest through a sort of natural path weaving among the lush trees, she noticed that the landscaping around the rock formations in the clearing up ahead looked more planful. Flat stone pavers nestled here and there among the grass. A hollowed-out, petrified tree was surrounded by these pavers, as if it was part of a park or otherwise important somehow. Vi couldn't tell if the ancients had carved architectural features out of the stone or if they'd actually constructed the rock formations themselves, but a grand overhang merged seamlessly into the mountain. The sound of dripping water called her forth, and she found a cenote similar to the one near her camp, the cool, clear runoff from a small waterfall captured by flowing pools surrounded by rocks. Sunlight shone down through holes in the canopy, dappling the clearing with golden sunbeams and stripes of indigo shade.

The only thing that wasn't lovely was a corpse, and it definitely wasn't ancient.

The moment Vi saw it, she stopped in place and looked more carefully. It appeared to be a female Trandoshan in bounty hunter gear, relatively fresh without any odor or visible decay. The body lay by the blue pool, curled up and frozen in place, the hands in fists and the face puckered up. The overall impression was one of pain and constriction. The Trandoshan's weapons were still in their holsters, suggesting there had been no attack or altercation, nor were there any wounds or blood that she could see. Whatever had killed Oga's underling had most likely been in that beautiful pool.

Vi crept toward the corpse, staying low and hunting for trip wires as she avoided the pavers and stepped around stones that might've been pressure-sensitive triggers. Up close, she smelled something a little flowery, a little sour, and when she looked in the pool, it confirmed her suspicions. Sparkling rocks lined the edges of the pool, and among them glowed golden jewelry and a sprinkle of old coins. Flickering among these treasures, almost invisible, were the gently waving tentacles of glass anemones—or something like them. The freshwater creatures were highly venomous, and anyone reaching into the pool for some quick plunder would end up just like this Trandoshan—stung with powerful poison sacs and violently convulsing to death as they bit off their own tongue. This species seemed a bit different from those she'd seen on Naboo, and someone who hadn't traveled widely and studied up on natural poisons probably wouldn't even notice them.

Vi swiftly looted the Trandoshan's body, glad to take possession of the night-vision goggles and grappling gun, plus pocket the credits and spira she found. She also took the nice wrist comlink and nicer blaster. Surely Oga would want her to have the best chance possible of surviving this mission? Vi wished she'd asked Oga exactly how many people she'd sent here so she could anticipate how many corpses she was going to find on her way to the artifact. Then again, more corpses meant more supplies and credits, so even that dark cloud had a silver lining.

At least now she knew that whoever had once lived here at the ruins was subtle and clever—and didn't like greed. If someone reached into the center of the cenote to drink, they would be unharmed. Only if they tried to snatch the treasure among the nearly invisible anemones would they die.

She was closer to the rock structures now. Ancient, crumbling stairs were cut into the stone, while the remains of carved patterns decorated the walls. A curving path around the cenote led into the darkness of the caves, and Vi took a last, deep breath of the soft, warm air before heading in that direction. In her experience, pitch-black darkness full of traps was never as serene as a garden. The path led into the windowless depths of a chamber with moist, clammy air, and Vi stopped just outside the doorway. Niches and troughs cut into the walls suggested that perhaps water had been stored here, long ago. The remains of ancient vases littered the floor, the pottery broken and jagged. Among them, a dark shape huddled on the ground. Not an urn—another corpse. She slipped on her newfound night-vision goggles, which smelled vaguely of unwashed Trandoshan, and everything shifted into shades of red and black.

These were the remains of a human man, and he looked like he would've fit right in on Oga's team, with a long, greasy leather duster and a blaster slung over his shoulder. It took Vi a moment to find his head, as it had been severed from his body and had rolled away.

From her crouch in the door, it was easy enough to see the mechanisms at play, for all that they were carefully hidden. The stone pavers on the floor were in a circular pattern, and the dead man had clearly stepped on the wrong stone, which had triggered . . . well, something concealed in the patterns carved in the stone walls at just the right height. Due to the damp cold of the cave, the cut wasn't a clean one she could analyze. She was curious if it was just lucky that this man had been the right height; what if N'arrghela had stepped on that stone? Or the Talpini? The dead man seemed of average height for humans, though, so perhaps the people who had built this place had been of similar stature.

After scanning all the patterns in the chamber, she crept out to the edge of the pavers and used her metal staff to tap at stones until she felt one give. It barely took any pressure at all before a solid sheet of water sprayed at high velocity in a glimmering black arc, right at skull height for Vi. Nothing happened lower down. The water disappeared into a ridge in the stone, and Vi took note that the ancients really did have a way with water, to make it behave like a blade. She spent some time tapping every stone in the floor and even prodding some of the patterns on the walls. Nothing else happened, so she took the man's comlink, and sidled around the edge of the chamber and through the tall doorway on the other side.

The next room looked like perhaps food had been stored, butchered, and cooked there, with carved tables still showing the marks of knives. Shallow bowls had been hacked into the rock, worn smooth and stained dark, perhaps by mineral-rich liquid or ground spices. Or blood. A water trough like the one in the last room suggested the ancients had known well enough that cleanliness was important to food preparation.

There was one body in the room, and it was curled against the wall, a shriveled Weequay. The floor was rough here with no specific stones that could be activated, but Vi noted several odd, globular shapes growing from the rough stone. Remembering the anemones in the cenote, she put two and two together.

"Some kind of poisonous puffball, probably," she murmured to herself, a habit she'd gained whenever she was alone and using her brain to keep her alive. It seemed that each of Oga's minions only got one step beyond their predecessor before triggering a trap. Staying low, she took the Weequay's comlink and carefully sidled across the room, staying as far away from the puffball clusters as possible.

Vi paused in the next doorway, taking stock of the chamber beyond. This one had clearly been used for kitchen storage—an old pantry. Clusters of black twigs hung here and there from wooden racks set in the walls, the remains of dead roots gathered by the ancients. Some of the supports had broken, leaving racks fallen at odd angles like broken marionettes. The scent of rot rode the air, and Vi noted old bins filled with blackened soil—compost, maybe. She didn't see any of the telltale stones or wall designs that signaled pressure-sensitive death machines, but that didn't mean she felt safe. Every section of the ruins so far had included a hidden danger, and she just had to figure out what nasty sort of surprise the ancients had left behind here.

Whatever it was, it had rendered the requisite corpse nothing but a skeleton. There were no clothes or organic materials left, but a collection of metal gadgets still adorned the bones, including the comlink Vi was all too happy to collect.

With her metal staff, she poked the floors and walls and reached out to jab the nearest hanging rack, but it merely creaked and swung from its broken rod. Tapping the staff before her, she crouch-walked across the room, which reminded her all too much of her mother's story of cave witches on Chaaktil, ferocious viragos who gathered poisonous herbs and shapeshifted into chaakbats and cast spells on children who ventured into their underground lairs.

The first sign of trouble was a rustle in the soil-filled bins across the room. Vi froze and spun around, focusing on the dark corner. Every hair on her arms stood at attention as the old black soil shifted, filling the air with the scent of death as glowing, blobby forms burrowed up, making the dirt churn and splatter to the ground.

What were these—these maggots? They were bright red in her night vision, as big as a fist, with too many legs and fat, bulbous bodies and no eyes, and they plopped out of the bins onto the ground and scurried toward her. First just a few, and then dozens. Their mouths opened to reveal thick pincers dripping with juice.

"Giant mutant cave maggots that crave flesh? Are you kidding me?" Vi murmured, jogging low toward the next doorway with the maggot-things wobbling along behind her. As the first one got close, she speared it with her staff, and it died shrieking and dripping goo that hissed as it hit the stone.

The room beyond was smaller, and Vi wasn't willing to run in there blindly, so she pulled her blaster with her free hand and started shooting the maggoty things, which exploded and sprayed acidic ichor. The ones that got too close got speared with the staff in her left hand as she shot maggot after maggot with her right hand. Her ears rang and the cave smelled like rot and fire and tangy ozone, but she didn't stop until her goggles detected no more glow.

So much for the sacred calm she'd felt outside.

No wonder Oga's idiots kept dying here.

The ancient ruins were a creepy death carnival, and she was only three chambers in.

If she lived through the experience, she was going to have a lot of work to do, making this place safe for the Resistance.

Taking a deep breath, she reholstered her blaster and turned to the new room. This one was a shrine, with a semicircular altar in the center, surrounded by niches cut into the walls. Vi could imagine little statues in each niche, an audience of gods—or whatever the ancients had worshipped. But when they'd left, they'd taken their statues with them, leaving her alone in a chamber now empty of purpose.

There was no corpse.

"Doesn't mean it's safe," she muttered, looking more carefully. In one of the niches, there was a tiny statue of a starmark, carved of dark, shiny rock. She'd almost missed it, but now it called to her. Was this Oga's artifact?

Or was it another trap?

With her staff fully extended, she reached out and tried to swipe the statue onto the ground. It was about the size of her palm and should've easily been swept out of its niche, but instead it merely tipped over.

"Oh, kriff."

At first, nothing happened, but then Vi smelled something sickly sweet.

Some sort of gas.

A wall of stone began to fall in the doorway nearest her, another one across the chamber—an attempt to seal her in the room. But she wasn't in the room yet. She was still standing just outside, and she needed to get into the room beyond, if she wanted to find that artifact.

She held her breath, ran through the shrine, and skidded under the closing door and into the next chamber, which was actually a long, narrow tunnel. That sickly-sweet smell followed her, and she considered how nice it would be to lie down and take a nap. Just a gentle nap on the soft, pillowy floor of the cave. A brief nap. Just a little one.

"No," she barked, expelling the poisoned air from her lungs.

She held her breath and waved her metal staff ahead of her as she wound her way through the tunnel. These ancients—they must've been a thin folk, if this hallway had seemed like a good idea. She'd have to laser these stalactites and stalagmites out of the way when she took possession of the ruins for the Resistance.

At least nothing tried to kill her in the hallway, except for the seeping gas, and she soon stood at the entrance to a sizable storage room. Niches and benches cut into the walls were filled with old pots and crusted mud, but Vi wasn't thinking about the ancients and their strange ways—she could only think about how useful this room would be to the Resistance. Finally, a safe place, deep in the ruins, where no one could ever steal her cargo again without facing severe danger. This is where they would store their munitions. This would be their real treasure.

"But I'm sure it's not safe, either," she murmured.

She didn't see any stone patterns on the floor, walls, or ceiling. In fact, the only odd thing about the room was the collection of pots sunk in dried clay.

"Here we go."

Half hiding in the hall outside the doorway, Vi reached around the wall with her metal staff and poked at the nearest pot, half buried in hardened mud.

Poke, poke.

Nothing happened, so she jabbed harder.

Still nothing.

As hard as she could, Vi jammed the staff into the pot, and the pot exploded. She ducked back behind her wall as dust and smoke filled the room. Seconds later, there was another explosion. And then another and another. She crouched down, hands over her head—as if that would help if the ruins were going to fall down around her.

And yet she was quite sure that wasn't going to happen. These ancients—they'd known what they were doing. Whatever they'd rigged up was to hurt interlopers, thieves—not damage the existing structure. These dangers had been arranged to wound the greedy. Try to loot the pots, and you died—if you were dumb. As the string of vessels around the room exploded, Vi waited, hands crammed over her ears. When silence fell, she waited even longer as the dust dissipated. Finally, several moments later, she looked inside.

Most of the pots were broken now, their shards littering the room, sharp as razors. Still she crouched and waved her metal staff before her, but the room's damage was done. Anyone who'd been standing in here would've been dead. But the pots, at least, appeared to be a one-shot danger. She made it across the room safely, clay shards crunching under her boots as she carefully avoided the remaining pots.

The next room had that same clammy moisture as the first room but was much larger. It had once been a bathing area, judging by an ancient bathtub, old water stains, and spigots carefully placed at intervals. Several pillars were arranged with what had once been grandeur but now just looked sad and crumbling.

As Vi scouted around the space with her goggles, hunting for the traps she knew were hidden somewhere, she realized that something about this room was bothering her. Of course complex bathing rituals went along with everything else she'd seen of the ancients—they understood cleanliness, they were meticulous, they admired artistry. And yet . . .

"Heat!" she said, loud enough to hear the echo bounce around the stone. "Can't have baths or steam without heat. So how did they heat it?" There were faucets set in the stone walls, so it stood to reason that there must've been pipes behind them to bring in the hot water. And she was willing to bet that the bathing tub carved from the rock would have a drain in the bottom.

Edging around the wall, she tapped here and there with her staff. When she'd made it safely to the ancient tub, she tapped around the inside and outside of the curving basin until she was satisfied that it was safe—at least from the sorts of dangers she'd faced so far. Much to her confusion, there was no drain.

It made no sense.

"Can't believe I'm doing this," she said, staying low as she stepped into the tub.

"I can't either," said a new voice.

Vi looked up, blaster already drawn and aimed.

"I am Lieutenant Wulfgar Kath of the First Order, and you're under arrest. Starling."

Against all odds, there stood a First Order officer in his dress blacks wearing night-vision goggles of his own. He had his blaster pointed, too, as did the two stormtroopers on either side of him. How had they gotten through that tunnel? And the closed-off shrine?

Didn't matter.

Vi widened her stance and started shooting.

So did they.

A blaster bolt seared her forearm, but before she could really process the pain or even grasp what was going on, the floor fell out from underneath her, and she plummeted into the darkness.

Chapter Fifteen

JUST LIKE THAT, THE RESISTANCE SPY had evaded his grasp.

Again.

Kath's teeth ground. It had been so polite of her to spring every trap and kill every cave maggot. And then, right when he'd cornered her, the blasted fool had . . . escaped?

No. She deserved no credit.

She was simply falling into another trap.

"Go. Check the mechanism," he told his troopers.

Without a word, they hurried across the room, blasters drawn, to investigate the basin in which Starling had been standing when she'd disappeared.

It was her—he knew that now. Perhaps he couldn't see all of her face with the goggles blocking it, but he recognized the shape of her, the petite stature, the wiry nature, the twitchy movements. This was the spy who'd slipped past him in trooper armor that didn't fit. This was his prey.

"She's gone, sir," one of the troopers said, fear in every syllable, as it should be.

"Gone where?" he barked.

"It must be a trapdoor," the other trooper said. "But there is no visible trigger."

"It's obviously weight," Kath said tiredly. "So one of you anchor yourself with a grappling gun and then stand where she stood and see what happens."

The troopers looked at each other, shared some understanding, and the lower-ranking one reluctantly shot his grappling gun at the stone ceiling over the basin, hooked the gun to his utility belt, and stepped into the carved tub. He stood there, holding his blaster, for about ten seconds before disappearing. The other trooper watched and nodded.

"Yes, sir. A trapdoor. Must be rigged for weight and timing."

Kath hurried across the room and inspected the grappling wire caught tight in an invisible seam before deploying his own grappling gun, and climbed into the tub, his blaster likewise at the ready.

"I expect you to follow in precisely thirty seconds," he told the remaining trooper.

Standing on what felt like solid stone, he gently bent his knees and steeled himself for the fall, one index finger ready on the grappling gun's brake and the other on his blaster's trigger.

Below him, somewhere, Starling waited.

And she would leave these caves in his custody.

Chapter Sixteen

THE MOMENT VI BEGAN FALLING, SHE bent her knees and prepared to hit stone.

Instead, she hit water, dropping her metal staff.

The pool was cold, but not freezing, and just deep enough to cushion her fall without causing her to lose her blaster or scramble to swim. She cast around for her staff, but it had sunk to the bottom, and even though she felt around with her boot, she didn't find it.

The shallow basin of water was in a room clearly created by a cunning people. There were forges, bellows, pipes in and out, everything necessary to provide water to the rest of the ruins, for washing vegetables and powering the baths and steam rooms overhead. No ladder up, though. Only a door to a new room on this level. She was thigh-deep in the water and already slogging toward the lip of the pool to crawl out.

And that's when something tightened around her leg.

Vi's pulse shot through the roof as her leg was tugged from down below, and she looked up at the seemingly solid ceiling, knowing that she wouldn't be alone much longer. If she lived through whatever creature was trying to kill her down here, she'd still have to deal with Kath and his soldiers.

She looked down, but the water was black, completely opaque. Her metal staff was lost, but she still had her blaster, so she shot and shot and shot at the water, just beyond her leg, aiming for whatever creature was trying to pull her close. It let go, and her calf burned as she slogged away from it and toward the basin's edge. Something began to swirl and churn in the water, but she ignored it and ran with all her might, and it was like running in a dream, like fighting through syrupy ink, until finally she dragged herself up and out of the pool.

At least the creature hadn't gnawed on her or left lesions—her leg wasn't even harmed. And that was the first good news she'd had down here.

"Batuu is cursed," she grumbled.

She adjusted her night-vision goggles as she approached the grandly arched doorway to the next chamber. This room was ... different somehow. It pulsed, as if it had a heartbeat. As if there was something alive within, something powerful. She didn't have much time before the First Order soldiers figured out how to make the trapdoor work, and she didn't have her staff, so she extended her tactical baton and felt around as best she could, tapping the stones before her as she gazed into the chamber's depths.

The room was empty—almost. It was another shrine, similar to the humble chamber up above, but somehow more ... alive.

Vi pushed up her goggles to see it with her own eyes. The curving walls were decorated with glowing stars, and Vi couldn't tell if they were gems set into the dark stone or perhaps images painted with glowing lichen. Unfamiliar constellations swirled, galaxies and suns glowing gently and tiny planets and moons seeming to dance in orbit.

She felt it before she saw it—the artifact.

The same glowing blue as the stars on the wall, it lay in a perfect circle on a stone altar in the center of the room.

A necklace, crafted of ethereal gems that burned with blue fire.

It called to her and yet also repelled her.

This thing, this ancient artifact that pulsed with power—Savi probably would've traded her an entire ship for it.

But it belonged to Oga.

She paused a moment to savor the experience, knowing that she was the first being to view this hidden room, to witness this wonder since the ancients had passed from time. And then, in the room behind her: a heavy splash.

A stormtrooper.

She had to hurry.

"Screw it," she murmured, and she darted into the room, snatched the necklace off its pedestal, and went into a controlled roll toward the next arched doorway.

She felt air move overhead and flattened herself against the ground. *Thunk thunk thunk.*

Behind her, armor fell to the ground with a clatter and a soft, robotic gasp.

When she pulled up her goggles and looked back, she couldn't see the mechanism or weapon at play, only the stormtrooper on the ground, sliced into pieces inside their armor as if the betaplast was as soft as nerf butter.

In the room with the basin, another splash.

She looked ahead, but this new chamber was a dead end. Not only that, but it was empty. No niches, no tables, no altars. Just a peculiar grouping of ropes, vines, cords, and chains dangling from a circular hole in the ceiling.

Thanks, ancients.

Vi slipped the necklace over her head and tucked it under her top. The jewels were uncomfortably warm, like eggs snatched from under a sleeping hen. She could only hope it wasn't dangerous, but there was no time to test it. She groped around with her tactical baton and hunted for trigger-sensitive stones before running for the ropes. There were dozens of them, a thick and interwoven tangle, each one different in weight and feel. Looking up past the ropes, she saw the faintest glimmer of light.

"Stop right there!"

She gave Kath only the briefest of glances as she pondered this new puzzle.

One of the ropes would allow her to climb out of the lower caves and back toward ground level. The rest, she was sure, would attempt to kill her in a variety of fun ways.

Splash.

One more trooper, fallen into the pool.

At least this one screamed, splashed, thrashed, and went silent the moment after he landed in the dark water.

Thanks, water monster, Vi thought.

She looked up again, but there was no way to tell which rope meant salvation and which ones promised doom.

"I've been waiting a long time for this," Kath said.

It was almost funny—there were so many dangers in the ruins that he didn't even seem like the worst one, just now.

"You don't even care that both of your soldiers are dead?" she asked him to buy some time.

"That's their purpose." She could hear his sneer.

She didn't like him.

Of course, she didn't like anyone in the First Order, but this guy was a special kind of scum. And he also needed her alive or he would've already shot her.

She looked up again as she felt around on her belt.

"Put your hands behind your head—"

Without really looking at him, she thumbed the thermal detonator and tossed it at Kath, interrupting him as she pulled her grappling gun and shot it through the ropes and into the ceiling of the higher cavern up above. The hook stuck, and she swiftly attached the gun to her belt.

The heavy thump of fabric on stone told her Kath had chosen to save himself over pursuing her, and she let the grappling line zip her upward, brushing the ropes and chains out of the way as she hurtled up through the ceiling and, hopefully, toward safety.

Behind her, below her: an explosion.

Thanks, thermal detonator. Good riddance to bad First Order rubbish.

And thanks to the ancients for building caves that could withstand explosions—and proving it to her in the storage room with all those pots.

As soon as she was through the hole and in the higher level of the cave, Vi swung to the ground and finally stood again on the floor. When she pressed a button, the grappling hook disengaged from the ceiling and retracted into her gun, which she hung on her belt again. Looking around the chamber, she wasn't sure where she was compared to where she'd come into the ruins, but she was up here and Kath was down below and possibly in many small chunks.

Not that it mattered all that much.

Even if Kath was dead, there were still stormtroopers on the planet, and the First Order knew she was here. Her entire mission was compromised.

She'd taken it hard, crash-landing on Batuu and losing all their cargo. But now, knowing her enemy had cornered her, she felt true hopelessness. Someone had turned her in. And if there was one thing she knew about the First Order, it was that they were unrelenting. They would burn the planet to the ground just to keep the Resistance from planting a flag on it.

Sure, she had Oga's artifact, but she couldn't build anything on Batuu as long as the First Order was here. Even if she'd managed to end Kath and both his men down there, more stormtroopers would be waiting somewhere nearby, and she had to get rid of them, too. And then the First Order would come looking for them.

"We're screwed," she murmured to the darkness.

And yet . . . she couldn't quite believe it.

She was Vi Moradi, and Vi Moradi didn't give up.

She hadn't given up on Chaaktil, and she hadn't given up on the *Absolution*, and she wasn't about to give up now.

There was no way she would just lie down and let the First Order take over.

Not only because her general had given her an order, and not only because the Resistance was depending on her, but also because the people of Batuu had been kind and generous, and she wasn't going to let them suffer. Lin had been right—Vi had brought the enemy to their doorstep. And that meant it was her job to kick them right back out again.

But first she had to get out of the ruins.

Without her staff, she couldn't feel around for traps, but at least she still had her night goggles and tactical baton. She was in a massive chamber filled with neatly carved niches just the right size for large, thin people to sleep in. She'd remember this room when she came back to clear out all the traps and armor-clad remains, because she'd decided that she would continue her mission despite every setback that had been thrown her way. From here on out, she would move forward with the ironclad belief that she was going to succeed. She would get rid of the First Order and build a Resistance refuge, and that was that.

There was light up ahead beyond a set of massive open doors. The floor looked like solid rock, but she lightly ran her fingers over it just to be sure. Before she crawled toward the light, she waved her blaster in front of her, making sure there were no more hidden triggers. With painful slowness, knowing there was a slim possibility that Kath or more stormtroopers were still on her trail or waiting somewhere nearby, she felt her way along the cave floor until finally she could pull down her goggles and wait for her eyes to adjust to the natural sunlight. The blurry green came into focus, showing her the forest beyond. After her descent into the caves, the tall trees and jagged spires felt like coming home.

She cocked her head and looked more carefully. Just outside the ruins, there was a large clearing free of trees, spires, and rocks, a field big enough to accommodate several ships while shielding them from prying eyes beyond. The more Vi looked around, the more she realized that she'd been wise to include this land in her deal with Oga; it was perfect for what the Resistance needed. They could park ships outside and bring their equipment inside, shielding it from scouts and enemies. All she had to do was live through this mission, get back to town, and then find a way to eliminate every trap left behind so her people didn't get decapitated or eaten by screaming maggots. Oh! And get rid of the First Order.

Easy peasy.

She smiled—too soon.

Zip! Bang!

Vi turned, whipped on her goggles, and saw the hook from another grappling gun imbed in the cave ceiling above the oubliette.

How . . . was Kath even alive? How had he survived a thermal detonator?

It didn't matter how.

He was still coming. She had to hurry.

There was no more time for carefully creeping along, testing every stone. She'd have to hope the ancient Batuuans had been more interested in protecting their treasures than in covering their exits. Vi stood and ran into the clearing outside. When she felt the tiny sting in her calf and saw two more insect-sized darts skitter along the ground, she knew she was soon to be just one more of Oga's corpses.

Chapter Seventeen

VI YANKED OUT THE DART AND clutched it tightly, hoping that if she made it back, Pook could analyze its poison and heal her. On second thought, she picked up the other two darts, which still ostensibly contained their full doses, and snapped all three of them into an empty specimen case in one of her cargo pockets. With no way to know how quickly the toxin in the darts would work, Vi put all her energy into running away from the spot where Kath might eventually emerge.

She understood the ecosystem here now and was glad for the lack of undergrowth, for the forest floor puffy with old leaves and the tall, curling ferns that would bounce away without revealing her passage. As long as Kath wasn't a master tracker, and supposing he had taken as much damage as she had, he shouldn't be able to pursue her. Taking into account where she thought she was in relation to the outpost, she adjusted her course and jogged toward help. Even though she knew that running would only make the poison spread more quickly, she also knew that she'd rather die under the Batuu suns than get taken prisoner by Kath—and his superiors. Certain death versus painful interrogation where she might betray the Resistance, followed by—plot twist—certain death? No contest.

She got out of sight range of the stone ruins, and for the length of that run, she thought that perhaps the poison had dried up over the eons, or maybe it hadn't gotten through her cargo pants, or maybe it only affected the ancients, whoever they were. Maybe she'd gotten lucky for once on this cursed planet. But then the world started to go blurry, and everything took on a purplish tint. The spires rose up like winged gray mynocks the size of X-wings, and the ground buckled and rippled and tore beneath her feet, or perhaps it only felt that way.

Her heart kicked up like a steelpecker hammering on metal, and she licked her parched lips and started muttering, "Gotta keep going. Gotta get back home. Can't let Leia down. When she was out there floating, she didn't stop hoping. She opened her eyes. I just gotta keep my eyes open. One foot in front of the other, like I told Cardinal. Archex. He needs me. Resistance needs me. Batuu needs me. Still need both feet. Pook would like it too much if I died. Gotta keep going, gotta keep pestering that sad-sack droid."

Vi blinked and stumbled and tumbled, and then she was on her back, blinded by the light. She put up a hand to shield her eyes, but everything had gone white. She felt around the ground, but her hands were numb now, too. Did she even have fingertips? Or fingers? When she tried to speak, her tongue was dry and hard as a stone, too big for her mouth. At least the blaster burn on her arm didn't hurt, nor did her neck. What a relief.

"Gotta tell Baako," she whispered. "Tell Baako I love him."

She closed her eyes again and stopped flailing, just calmly settled down and let her limbs fall to the ground. Everything went still, and even the riot of birdsong stopped. It felt like she was in a sensory deprivation tank, like she was floating, like she was waiting to be born. The sky beckoned, and she reached out with her arms, and her fingers spread out, shooting rays of sunlight. Across the galaxy, she felt Baako on Pantora with his husband she still hadn't met, saw him look up at the sky and smile, then frown. She felt for Leia, wherever she was, keeping the Resistance alive, and Leia stopped speaking to Poe and shook her head as if scolding Vi for interrupting. She felt Archex in the forest, sitting on a log, carving a dugar-dugar from a bit of wood, and he cocked his head and stared hard into the fire as if listening for a song that wasn't playing, his forehead scrunched down in confusion.

In that moment, she felt hundreds of lives everywhere, interlaced like the fibers in the yarn of one of her hats, connected in a complex, living circle. She was suffused with love and light, trapped in unending brightness, and it was, she figured, a finer place to die than in the noxious belly of a First Order ship.

And then, something warm and wet slapped over her cheek.

"What's that, Waba?" an unfamiliar voice said. "Not another corpse. Don't lick it."

"Not a corpse," Vi tried to say, but her lips were quickly becoming as stiff and hard as her tongue.

"You're alive? Oh, by the spires. That's never happened before!"

Soon she felt fire-hot hands touching her face, rubbing her fingers roughly, and finally picking her up like a baby. She was cold as stone now while everything else was still burning white. She swung like a child in a swing, and from far away, she was aware that she was being carried. The voice murmured to her constantly, urging her to stay alive, to keep breathing—and also urging someone else to come along and stop licking her boots.

Time meant nothing, and then suddenly it did. Everything was pitch-black now, which was a welcome change. She was lying on something soft that smelled warmly of animals and hay, and someone was pouring something hot down her throat. It burned, and her tongue was boiling, and her teeth were so sensitive, but every time she tried to pull away, strong hands brought her face back around. She pinned her lips.

"By the spires, you must drink! Drink or die!"

Vi opened her mouth to say she'd take death, but they just poured more of the foul brew down her now easily accessible throat. A tingling started up in her toes, which she hadn't felt in some time, and began to spread up her legs. Firm hands were kneading her bare foot, but when she opened her mouth to apologize for the stench, yet more hot drink surged between her lips. When she could finally feel her hands, she held them up in front of her mouth and said, "Let a body breathe."

Whoever had been holding her foot released it and crowed in victory. Vi realized she'd been hearing two voices, one belonging to a robust-sounding young man, and the other to an old woman. But when she opened her eyes, everything was still dark.

"Am . . . am I blind?" she rasped.

The old woman cackled madly. "No, child. We've wrapped your eyes. Your pupils were so dilated they were like big black saucers. Give it a little time yet, just in case. The poison's still in your blood."

Something wet and warm snuffled around Vi's foot, and she pulled it back, but gently.

"Waba! Stop that! It's rude to lick a stranger's feet." That was the young man's voice, and she heard the sounds of a curious animal being reluctantly dragged away. "Sorry about that. He's, uh, into smells."

"Nothing smells as bad as I do right now, most likely," Vi said, trying to get her voice working again. Her throat and nose were dry and sore.

"Well, you very nearly died, at which point you would've smelled a lot worse!" The old woman cackled again.

"Grana, she's a guest!" the man said, sounding scandalized by the old woman's behavior.

"If she doesn't like a little fun, she can go die in someone else's home, then."

Vi reached up and felt around her face, finding a piece of soft woven cloth over her eyes. She pulled it back just a little, and although the world outside seemed awfully bright, it was no longer blinding. The light was warm and golden, and after a few moments of furious blinking, she was able to remove the cloth and see again, for all that it was blurry.

She was in a small, cozy room with polished stone floors, hanging metal lamps, and walls covered in colorful cloth like the shawls in Arta's shop. By her feet sat an old, withered woman with a sprightly manner and glittering eyes nestled amid a lifetime of warm, brown wrinkles. Her white hair was in a puff on top of her head, and she wore a long yellow tunic over soft leggings.

"There, now. Told you she would live," she said triumphantly.

"You did not, Grana. You swore she was going to die."

The hulking form in the corner was the male voice she'd heard, and he was every gram the milk-fed farm boy, with giant shoulders and arms and a round belly. His face was a shade lighter than the old woman's, his curly brown hair bleached from the suns. He was holding a very excited but strange animal, sort of like a pet-sized happabore with a huge snuffling snout that was busily working to escape his clutches, its four tiny trotters swimming enthusiastically in the air as it strained toward Vi. The boy—no, he was a man. But with a baby face and razor-burnt pink cheeks. Ah—he was embarrassed. Probably because his rude granny was betting against Vi living and his pet piglet wanted nothing more than to lick her feet, dead or alive.

"Thank you for saving me," Vi said, as they were all watching her as if she were a droid just coming back online.

"Dolin found you out by the ruins. You look like you got hit with Gambuu darts. Lucky you were wearing thick pants and the poison was older than me, or you'd be boar food," the old woman said with a knowing wink.

"Very lucky," Vi agreed. She turned to the man—Dolin. "Did you see anyone else in the area? Possibly a man in all black, following me?"

Dolin's eyebrows drew down. "No, no one. Is he your friend? Do I need to go back and find him?"

Vi barked a laugh and shook her head—or tried to. It made her want to pass out. She almost mentioned that she hoped Kath would die out there, but she didn't think these gentle country folk were accustomed to the bloody war raging elsewhere in the galaxy. "No. Please don't go help him. If you see him, run away. He's dangerous. He's hunting me."

The old woman rocked back, slapping her thin leg. "And the story grows! A near-death experience in the ruins, and you were being chased? What'd you do?" She scooted her stool closer, eyes bright as a bird's. "Is he your husband? Did you scorn him? Or steal his wife? Was it a crime of the heart?"

Vi rubbed her eyes. "He's with the First Order, and he wants to capture me."

"The First Order?" Dolin asked, stepping forward even as the porcine creature gyrated in his arms, anxious to return to Vi's stinky feet. "I heard they weren't even real. Just people wearing old Imperial costumes to frighten children."

At that, Vi sat forward and pinned him with a dizzy but firm glare. "The First Order is very real. They blew up the Galactic Senate on Hosnian Prime. They blew up *the entire Hosnian system.* I lost friends in the cataclysm. I saw the rubble left behind. And if they're on this planet now, you're going to want to stay out of their way. Believe me—I know."

"If the First Order is real, they would never come here," the old woman said knowingly, shaking her head for emphasis. Her earlier good mood had fled. "There's nothing here they want. We're a quiet place. Mind our own business. Not like those rich planets. Not like Coruscant." Her nose wrinkled up as she said it

Vi closed her eyes, her head in her hands. "That's what everyone always believes. *It won't happen to us. We don't look for trouble. We're not doing anything wrong. We're not important enough.* That's what the skittermouse says to itself as the ebon hawk glides overhead, right up until it feels the chill of shadow and bite of talons. Well, I tell you now that there's a Star Destroyer floating somewhere overhead, but you won't see its shadow until it's too late."

When Vi looked up, the old woman's eyes were narrowed in suspicion. "And you said they're chasing you. So *if* they exist, and *if* they're here, you're saying they're here because of *you*?"

Vi's face was still a little numb, but she felt the hot flush of shame nevertheless. "It's a lot more complex than that."

Dolin put down his pig and stepped near, just behind his granny. The pig-thing shuffled across the floor and pressed its snout against Vi's hand, and she absentmindedly stroked the stiff bristles on its head, making it snort in ecstasy.

"So you're sure they're here?" Dolin asked. "Not just one guy who probably already died in the ruins but the . . . the soldiers?"

"Stormtroopers," Vi supplied. "If he's here, they're here. At least two of them died in the ruins—but there will be more nearby."

"Well, why do they want you?"

Vi settled back. She was exhausted in body and mind. This mission—it wasn't supposed to be this hard. It should've been almost like being on leave. Construct the supplied facility, make friendly contacts among the locals, contact Leia and let her know that her best spy had, as usual, come through. But here Vi was, lost in the forest with these poor naïve farmers, pretty sure she'd almost died—and with the enemy at the gates.

"Do you really think it matters?" she said, rubbing her eyes tiredly. "You can't stop them. No one on this planet believes in the Resistance, and until people start believing and taking action, the First Order will just keep showing up, taking resources, and killing anyone who gets in their way."

Grana looked far off, thoughtful, but Dolin squatted by Vi, scratching his pig and staring at her with so much earnestness that it hurt her heart. "Have you met the Resistance?"

He said it with awe, and that was something Vi could work with. She nodded, very serious. "I have."

"What's it like?"

Vi struggled to keep her face straight. What did he think the Resistance was?

"The Resistance is a group of individuals who have joined together to fight the tyranny of the First Order. We're led by General Leia Organa—"

"Princess Leia," Dolin breathed, looking dreamy.

"Princess Leia," Vi agreed. "We have a fleet and we're gathering allies every day. There's a woman named Rey among us, and she has Force abilities. Luke Skywalker trained her."

Dolin gasped. "The Force—it's real? Lightsabers are real? *Luke Skywalker is real?*"

Vi's head dropped. "Skywalker is with the Force now, but he turned the tide. His legacy lives on."

"Nothing but stories," Grana snapped. "Might as well believe in the Snarlok."

Dolin looked wounded. "But you told me the Snarlok was real! And that if I didn't weed the garden fast enough, it would run me through with horns of bone and eat me!"

"Do you mean the Naklor?" Vi asked, remembering Salju's tale.

"No, the Snarlok," Dolin corrected her. "A fearsome monster that built a black spire out of the corpses of naughty children."

"Look, we're getting off topic. It's all real," Vi assured them, giving Grana a hard look. "Not the Snarlok thing, probably, but the Force, the Jedi. Luke and Leia. I've seen the Force in action. Rey helped kill Supreme Leader Snoke of the First Order, and she's going to help us destroy them once and for all."

Grana snorted and waved a hand. "Sell it somewhere else."

Vi ground her teeth together. Here she was again, failing at her most basic charge.

Recruit warm bodies. Help rebuild the Resistance.

It was infuriating, telling people the complete truth and always watching them deny it or turn away from it when Vi herself had to live it. She was a spy, not an orator or even a person who inspired warm fuzzies. How was she supposed to turn their hearts? She sighed and looked down. The pig-thing had its trotters on her knee now and was crooning at her as she scratched behind its ears.

"So who's this guy?"

"Truffleboar," Dolin said, edging closer. "His name is Waba. He can sniff out truffles, and he can also find the gruffin herd when they wander too far or go into hiding to calve." He leaned even farther forward. "Do you have Force powers? Are you a Jedi? Watch! I can move things with my mind."

He stretched out a beefy hand toward a stack of kindling by the crackling fire, but after several moments of him groaning and nothing happening, Grana smacked his hand and said, "Stop that. Don't get involved. You're a gruffin herder, a grain farmer, a proud son of Batuu. You shouldn't need anything more." She hobbled over and poked Vi in the chest. "And you! If I'd known you were only going to stuff more silly stories in the boy's head, I wouldn't have saved you!"

Vi looked around the room. Everything in it was handmade, and much of it was worn and threadbare. The only visible tech was an ancient analog radio with a bent antenna. "I get it." She nodded at Grana. "Keeping your head down is a good way to stay safe. You avoid trouble. A bigger force like the First Order shows up, and you know that if you take sides, you might get noticed, in the bad way." She leaned forward, even though it hurt, and poked the old woman in the chest, far more gently. "But if you keep letting bullies bully other people, eventually they run out of other people."

"And what would you know, hm? Fancy smuggler, scooting around the galaxy in a ship somebody else paid for. Little people like us are tied to the land, to the crops and the animals. We have history here. A responsibility. We care for our own." Grana sat back down on her footstool, thin arms crossed and eyes daring Vi to disrespect her elders. "It got me this far."

Vi stood and tested her faculties. Her calf was swollen where the dart had struck, but it felt good enough to walk—hopefully. The blaster burn on her arm was going puffy, but that couldn't be helped just now; if she asked Grana for more medicine, the old woman would probably poison her just to shut her up. Her sight was back, and she definitely felt less dead, but that didn't mean she felt good. She slipped her fingers under her tunic and touched the necklace there, heavy and warm. She had to get it to Oga quickly. Something about the artifact felt wrong, like it didn't belong to her and it was all too aware of that fact.

"Here's what I know, Granny," she said, abandoning all pleasantry and cajolery to show the pain under the mask she always wore. "I grew up on Chaaktil. One day, we were in the market, just buying bread and fruit for dinner. Some stormtroopers came through. Old-school Empire guys. They shot some locals to make their point. Just rounded up a random group of people. My father was one of them.

He died on his knees with his hands behind his head. I had to hold my little brother back from running into the blasterfire. I was five. After that, they razed our hydroponic gardens and set our homes on fire for good measure. So don't you dare tell me that keeping your head down is a foolproof method for growing old." She took a couple of limping steps. "Now, which way is the outpost? Because if I'm going to spend breath trying to find good people willing to fight for their way of life and for freedom all across the galaxy, I'm going to at least talk to more than two people and a pig."

Grana harrumphed, but Dolin's open mouth closed with a snap.

"They burned your gardens?" he asked.

"To the sand. And it wasn't just our own personal garden—it was the community garden. The entire city depended on that harvest. Just like the Empire, the First Order doesn't care about the people, much less the land and beasts that sustain them. People with no hope, with no homes or food, are weaker and easier to control."

Dolin's jaw firmed up and his eyebrows struggled down, and he finally stood, puffing out his chest.

"I want to help," he said.

"No!" Grana barked. "Your place is here. Tend to your beasts, sow your seeds, care for your elders! That is our way!"

Dolin hooked a thumb at Vi. "Sounds like the First Order wants to put a stop to our way. If they're here, then I want to help fight them. I don't have a lot of experience with weapons outside of hunting and butchering, but I'm smarter than I look." The truffleboar capered around him, snorting excitedly, his trotters clicking on the floor. "Waba's in, too."

In that moment, Vi felt as if a heavy weight had fallen from her shoulders. There was this tender point in time when you felt a heart twist open and a new possibility flood in, and it was happening now. One poor man's yes was the finest sound in the galaxy. She grinned.

"Great. Let's go. If you can help me get back to the outpost, I'll collect my cargo, and you can join us at our temporary camp."

"There's more of you?"

"He means girls," the old woman grumbled. "Girl-crazy, he is."

"I only know nine girls my age!" Dolin wailed. "And I'm related to six of them!"

Vi tried not to laugh. "I just got here, and there have been setbacks, but I promise you that the galaxy outside of your farm has plenty of women of all species, as does the Resistance."

Dolin grinned. "Let me pack a bag."

He hurried off with Waba on his heels, and Grana stood and stalked toward Vi. "You can't take my grandson away from me," she said, her voice low and ugly. "He's never been off the settlement. He knows nothing of the outpost and what's beyond it. He's weak. Tender. Foolish. It'll destroy him. And what's more, I need him. He runs the farm. He has duties."

Vi faced her. "I'm not taking him away from you—he's choosing to leave, as most children do. He's an adult. He can do what he wants."

"He's not an adult!" Grana screeched. "He's only twenty-five!"

Vi shook her head. "I try not to judge other cultures, but . . ."

Before she could complete the thought, Grana lunged forward. Vi's training kicked in and she jumped back, clasped the old woman's arm, and slid the knife from her withered fingers.

"Aren't healers supposed to do no harm?" Vi said, holding up the sharp stone blade.

"Just because I healed you doesn't mean I'm a healer. I took no oaths."

"I can see that."

The tiny old woman drew herself up as tall as she could and stuck out her hand.

"Return my knife and get out of my house."

Vi walked to the door, knife in hand. "Once I'm out of throwing range, I'll drop it. I don't trust you, Grana."

Grana's nose wrinkled up. "And I don't trust you. I always told the boy: Offworlders are trouble."

"Trust me on this: Offworlders are going to save your life—and your animals and farm. Maybe even your planet."

Vi moved aside the blanket covering the doorway and squinted against the afternoon light, which felt a thousand times brighter than it should have. So easy to forget she'd recently been dying of poison. Poison left behind by an ancient, forgotten civilization that really, really didn't want people among their ruins. It would be good, having Dolin around. Maybe he knew how to disengage and clean out the traps so the caverns could be made habitable.

"May the spires keep you," she called back to Grana.

"Oh, go sit on a spire and twirl," Grana replied.

Vi let the blanket fall back in place, blocking the old woman's rude hand gesture. Once outside, she saw a new side of Batuu. Squat, round homes made of stone and dried clay were widely spaced in an immense clearing ringed by the huge trees and spires. Fields of grain waved in the breeze, careful lines of vegetables sprouted inside nicely kept fences, fruit trees and bushes flourished, and herds of woolly beasts milled about in pastures, grazing and making a soft whuffling *gruff* noise as little girls and boys watched over them, half asleep and cradling shepherd's crooks. Farther away, a blue river twinkled among the green, and beyond it, a larger settlement spread out, big enough to make this one look quaint and rustic. She couldn't tell where she was in relation to the ruins or the outpost, but they were far enough out that it felt as quiet as the forest where she and Archex had made their camp.

This picturesque settlement was just the sort of place the First Order would destroy without a second thought, a place with nothing they wanted but everything they hated. To them, destroying all these lives, all this work, would carry no more importance than an anthill, smeared by the foot of a careless child.

The blanket moved aside, and Dolin stepped out with a bag slung over his shoulder. "I'm ready. Want to take my crankbike?"

"I don't know what that is, but if it means I don't have to walk, sure."

When he pulled the rough brown tarp off a bulky shape leaning against the hut, Vi had to admit she was surprised. A crankbike looked like it had begun life as a swoop bike, but had then been added to over the years, just like the outpost itself. It had huge back tires with struts, smaller front tires, and a surprising number of spikes.

Tires had gone out of fashion as tech spread throughout the galaxy, and now it made sense, all the tires she'd seen in Savi's scrapyard.

The seat was big enough for Dolin, and a small box on the back gave Vi a place to perch. Waba rode in a sidecar, and Vi couldn't help imagining what it would've been like if Dolin had invited a local girl to go out for a ride and given his pet pig the place of honor while leaving her to cling to the box. He handed Vi a helmet with goggles, and they were soon zooming through the forest, the bike drowning out all other sounds. It would've been a few hours' walk back to her camp, by her count, but on the crankbike it was only half an hour or so. The kid was fast and had remarkable instincts and reaction time—if all went well, maybe the Resistance pilots could teach him how to fly something significantly bigger.

As they pulled into camp, Archex stood, his blaster in one hand. The crankbike was pretty loud, after all. As soon as it rumbled to a stop and Vi took off her helmet, Archex relaxed, taking a deep breath and sitting back down on his log.

"That appears to be a pig," Pook noted.

"Sharp as ever, Pook," Vi said, smiling despite herself at the way a too-smart droid could still sound like a little kid. "Archex, this is Dolin. Dolin, this is Archex." Dolin placed the truffleboar on the ground, and Vi added, "And that's Waba."

"And they are . . . ?" Archex asked.

Vi grinned. "Our first recruits."

While Vi went for the medpacs and painkillers, Dolin wandered around the sparse camp, inspecting first their crashed transport and then Pook. The droid inspected him in turn, and when Waba came to smell him, Vi had to say, "Pook, do not kick that pig."

Pook put his foot down. "I was merely inspecting him. With my foot."

"Well, if you boys are cozy, I need to head into town and give Oga her prize," Vi said.

Dolin looked at her in alarm. "But you almost died!"

Vi shrugged and met Archex's eyes. "Yeah, that happens a lot. Nothing that can't be fixed. I feel better already." When he seemed unconvinced, she rolled up her pant leg to show Dolin the dart wound, which was already healing. "You're going to love modern medicine."

"At least let me carry you to town on the bike."

Vi considered it. The thing was big and loud, and Dolin hadn't been to the outpost before and would probably attract attention as he gaped and asked questions she could barely answer herself. Her leg was still swollen and aching, and her arm was beginning to itch as the medpac did its work. But she had to get the necklace to Oga before something worse happened. Once that was accomplished and she had her cargo in hand, she could turn her attention back to her real problem: the First Order.

"Maybe you could drop me off on the outskirts," she finally said. "I don't want you anywhere near Oga's place, and I don't want anyone to see me with you. Now that the First Order is here, they'll be on the lookout for me."

Archex bolted up again. "The First Order is here?"

Vi sighed heavily. "Yeah. Surprise! There was an officer in the ruins with me. I think Oga might've sent him after me as a joke, or possibly a backup plan. He had two stormtroopers with him, but you know he wouldn't be here without more of them."

"Let me go," Archex said, voice husky with emotion.

Vi walked over and pushed him back down to sitting on his log. It was all too easy, and she briefly felt shame and guilt for doing it to him, but she had to get her point across, and for something this important, words weren't enough. "That leg can't hold you up in a fighting stance. It might never be able to, Kalonia said. You can't fight one trooper, much less a squad or platoon. And if anyone recognizes you, things will get personal fast. So you have to stay here and protect the camp." He looked like he was going to argue, so she barked, "And that's an order!" As she climbed back up on the bike behind Dolin and rammed on her helmet, she added, "And also, please watch the truffleboar."

They shrieked out of the clearing before Archex could complain. Vi didn't look back. She didn't want to see the hurt and rage on his face—and she also didn't want him to see how much it scared her, the thought of what would happen to him if the First Order discovered their turncoat captain.

The crankbike was too loud for talking, but it was a peaceful kind of noise, and the late afternoon was pretty under the canopy. When Black Spire Outpost came into view, she tapped Dolin on the shoulder, and he stopped and waited for her to climb down. She pointed at the ground, hoping he understood that she wanted him to stay there. He nodded, and she kept her helmet on as she walked toward the arched entranceway of the outpost.

The goggles and helmet were a common enough look, but she knew it would stand out to anyone looking for a spy. She put the helmet under her arm as she ducked into Dok-Ondar's Den of Antiquities to see if he might have something more natural, the sort of mask a being might wear constantly instead of removing it for social situations. The shop was immediately compelling, with a carved stone mural showing an ancient battle that included lightsabers. On the other side of the mural she discovered a tall and curious chamber filled with fascinating artifacts, objects, and actual paper books. Everywhere she looked, something drew her eye. On a high mezzanine, she noticed a variety of ceremonial headdresses and masks, on another tall wall she goggled at taxidermied beasts with menacing teeth, including a terrifying Nexu, a bug-eyed Kod'yok, and a shaggy white snow monster. A special tank housed a baby sarlacc, its revealed belly glowing under the sand. One object in particular looked promising until she realized it was a Kaleesh mask, which would only make her stand out more. Ithorian weather chimes dangled from a chandelier of interlocking circles, adding shifting shadows and an esoteric grandeur to the space.

"Can I help you?" asked an older human woman in tattered robes, smiling the smile of someone who knows just how effectively interesting objects can sell themselves.

"I need a mask," Vi told her, as if this was a perfectly normal thing to request. "Something that will filter air and disguise my appearance from the neck up. I got in some trouble with another smuggler, and, you know." She smiled a crooked smile. The fewer details, the better, when you were telling lies.

The woman's mouth quirked up. "You know, I think we have just the thing, and you can be assured all our transactions are discreet. Follow me."

As the woman moved around the cavernous interior filled with nooks and crannies, the hair rose up the back of Vi's neck, that old spy's intuition. Someone was staring at her. She flicked her eyes at a dianoga's tank and saw the reflection of a tall Ithorian in robes watching her from the mezzanine.

So that was Dok-Ondar. It was better if she didn't speak to him directly or even acknowledge that she had noticed the crafty collector of black-market goods.

"Here we are!" the woman said, reappearing as if by magic. "An Ubese helmet. Filters air, adjusts for light quality. It's older and a little small, but it should help you blend in. We see enough of them in the spaceport that it won't stand out."

Vi set down Dolin's crankbike helmet, and the saleswoman put the Ubese helmet in her hands. She inspected the inside of it briefly for blood or other unpleasantry before pulling it on. Her immediate feeling was one of claustrophobia, but as she adjusted to the way it filtered sound and light, she realized it was actually a perfect choice. No one asked an Ubese to remove their helmet. Vi didn't even know what an unmasked Ubese looked like.

"How much?" she said through the helmet, appreciating how it masked her voice as well, making it unclear whether she was male or female, old or young.

The woman cheerfully named a price so high that Vi had to stop herself from laughing, and Vi took off the helmet and held it out.

"I can't afford that, but I appreciate your time," she said.

"No one can afford it," the woman conceded, but the Ithorian standing on the mezzanine said something in his deep, throaty language.

The woman listened respectfully and inclined her head. "Dok-Ondar recognizes your need and asks if you have anything of value to trade," she said out loud, and then, more quietly, "I would not disappoint him, if you are able."

Vi was too well trained to touch the necklace she owed Oga, but she did reach into her pocket and pull out the case containing the darts—two that had failed to hit her and one that had. Was it a smart move, giving ancient and intriguing poisons to a shadowy and powerful character who ran the black market in Black Spire Outpost?

Probably not.

But it was better than getting on his Doklist. Dok had plenty of untraceable ways to kill people already, from what she'd heard around town, so it's not like the darts were without precedent.

"Gambuu darts, they're called," she said, handing the woman the case.

The woman smiled and hurried up to the mezzanine. She and Dok went into a room, and soon she returned empty-handed while the Ithorian lingered at the railing up above.

"Dok-Ondar says you are welcome anytime, and he hopes you enjoy your acquisition from his collection. It is an even trade for the darts. He'd like to know how you found them?"

Vi didn't have long to come up with the right lie, so she went with one that was at least adjacent to the truth. "I found one on a body in the forest. A Trandoshan hunter. The other two were near the corpse."

Dok gave a weary sigh and rumbled something that didn't sound too much like a death threat.

"Dok-Ondar says that should you find any more such antiquities to trade, he has information that may help you," the woman translated.

Vi put on her new disguise and enjoyed the voice that was nothing like her own. "I will take that under consideration. Good trade."

Helmet on and still carrying Dolin's crankbike helmet under her arm, Vi scanned the market outside for First Order troops and, seeing none, headed out. It was time to visit Oga.

Chapter Eighteen

VI WAS ALREADY EXHAUSTED AND COULD feel the painkillers wearing off as she stepped into the cantina. She knew it was ridiculous to keep pushing herself after her time in the ruins, but she didn't want to possess the necklace for a single moment longer than she had to. She understood well enough now that things on Batuu could be taken away in a flash and fortunes could change in a heartbeat. Walking around most worlds, she felt safe and competent, but Batuu just kept surprising her . . . or maybe it was that she'd arrived here beat up and hadn't had the time, energy, or resources to heal properly and rise above. When you were in pain and falling behind, everything was a struggle.

She went straight to the shady corner where Oga's minions dominated their usual table. Rusko wasn't there, but N'arrghela was.

"Tell Oga I have what she wants," Vi said, her voice filtered through the Ubese mask and coming out flat and round like a robotic frog.

N'arrghela looked her up and down and must've done the math on Vi's size and the orange Black Spire wrap she'd been wearing this morning when they'd parted ways, or perhaps the Wookiee knew her scent. She nodded, pushed out of the booth, and disappeared down the dark hallway, leaving just Vi and the Talpini, who hadn't been introduced to her by name.

"How's it going?" Vi said, trying to be friendly.

The Talpini's head canted to the side just slightly, his wide frown firmly in place and his blank blue eyes staring at her and through her. It was like talking to a scary statue.

"I don't think we've met. I'm Vi."

The Talpini said nothing.

"Good talk."

Fortunately, N'arrghela roared for her from the hallway just then, and Vi gave the Talpini a little wave and followed the Wookiee down the hall and through a different door into Oga's office. This route, Vi noted, was much more pleasant than being dragged past a toilet. Oga was at her desk, petting the same unkempt tooka-cat when Vi stepped into her lair.

"*Coona tee-tocky malia?*" Oga began, her focus not wavering from the holos around her desk.

"What took me so long was trying real hard not to die," Vi replied.

Oga looked up, annoyed. "Take that helmet off. You sound like a frog-dog with indigestion."

Vi glanced around the room to make certain they were alone. Now that she had to assume Oga had sent Lieutenant Kath into the ruins after her, she didn't trust the gangster to keep her identity safe. With the helmet off, she was surprised to realize that the air down here actually tasted fresher through the mask's filters. Without it, she could smell Oga's damp musk plus the bowl of clamfruit that still sat on her desk, right beside a juicy pile of snail shells.

"Well?"

Vi slipped the necklace out from under her tunic and over her head and held it out for Oga's inspection. After all this time, it was still warmer than her body temperature, and it had never stopped glowing. Oga tapped a rubbery finger on her desk, and Vi laid the artifact down, just so, glad to be rid of it.

"This is it, huh?"

"Nearly died five times fetching it, so I hope so."

"What is this thing?" Oga asked, poking the necklace around and lifting the large crystals one by one. "What powers it?"

"I'm an errand girl, not an archaeologist. You told me to bring it, so I brought it."

Oga focused on her, the Blutopian's mouth tentacles curling hungrily. "What else did you find? Anything else of value? Multiple artifacts?"

Vi sighed. She knew that word of what she'd given Dok would get back to Oga, so she might as well be honest. Black Spire Outpost was a place where someone was always watching. She vastly preferred the anonymous nature of big-city life.

"It was the only artifact that wasn't a weapon. There were corpses aplenty, but nothing of value that could be carried out. The necklace was on a pedestal in a very ornamental room and seemed like it might be related to worship. On my way out, I triggered some toxic darts, which I brought back with me and had to trade to Dok-Ondar."

Oga slammed her hands on the table and stood. "Had to? You don't have to do anything but what I tell you to do! And now he knows you were at the ruins, which means he knows I made other arrangements to collect the artifact. I'm your boss, not him!"

"That sounds great here in your personal office, but it's not always true out there in the real world." Vi rubbed the skin between her eyebrows. "I've heard of his Doklist. I figured a few darts would keep me on his good side, and if you wanted the darts, you could go threaten him instead of me. Gambuu darts, they're called. If I find any more when we're cleaning out the ruins, they're yours."

Oga sat back down, her mouthparts twitching. "Ah, yes. Now it all makes sense. You needed a disguise, so you went to see Dok, and that gossiping old gibberer knew what you were about and had you by the tentacles."

"Ah, yes. Now it all makes sense," Vi echoed. "You sent that First Order womp rat after me into the ruins, and now that he's seen me, I have to hide my face because every time I come into town I'll be in jeopardy." She crossed her arms and glared, daring Oga to deny it. "I didn't go shopping for an expensive mask for fun, you know."

But the Blutopian just raised a sloping shoulder. "If you want a job done and everyone else has failed to do it, might as well send in two expendable and annoying offworlders. The hope being that one of you would get the prize and the other would disappear. Look at it this way: I gave you the chance to kill your enemy. If you didn't take it, that's your own fault."

There was a twisted sort of logic to it, if you were a crime boss who sat in the center of her web and didn't go out into the world and get her hands dirty. Make two enemies compete, give them the possibility of killing each other, and minimize your own future problems. Vi had to admire Oga—but she didn't have to like her.

"Well, I guess you did tell me from the start that you weren't taking sides," she said.

"I don't care about you, equally," Oga said with a rasping chuckle.

"Then let me have my cargo, and I'll get out of your way and take it back to my murderous ruins and start setting up shop." Vi cocked her head. "If he did live, you're not gonna tell him we're out there, right?"

Oga pulled up some screens on her desk and clicked around before answering. "No. You did what I asked, and I honor my deals. I won't tell him about either of your two camps. But he's got a squad of armored soldiers, and you know they'll be looking for you. I doubt you can hide for long."

"Yeah, me too."

Luckily the area around the outpost was wild and wide, and maybe it was a good thing that Kath had experienced the ruins himself and wouldn't be eager to return anytime soon. Vi herself didn't want to go back, and they were part of her prize. At least if he did show up, she would have the advantage of cover. She had to get the caverns cleaned out quickly and her goods moved inside and hopefully recruit more people to help—and to guard their supplies. With each hurdle she crossed in this mission, five new ones popped up. They weren't supposed to crash. They weren't supposed to get robbed. The First Order shouldn't be here.

"Say, Oga . . ."

The Blutopian looked up in annoyance. "Why aren't you gone yet?"

"When Kath was down here, as I'm sure he was, did he happen to mention what brought him here, to Batuu?"

"Of course he did," Oga said, as if Vi were an idiot. "It was you. He's looking for you. What else could he possibly want here?"

Vi ignored that question. "So someone tipped the First Order off. Any idea who that might've been?"

Oga turned off her screens and gave Vi a cold stare. "It wasn't me. And you know it wasn't me because if it was, I wouldn't have sent him out to find the artifact. I would've let him sit right here with me, and when you returned, bedraggled and triumphant, I would've given you right over to him and collected a reward. If I'm going to stab you, at least I'll stab you in the front."

Vi held up her hands. "I can appreciate that. Let's skip the stabbing. I'd still like to know if I have an enemy on Batuu."

With a husky sigh, Oga pulled her screens back up. "You don't need an enemy. You just need someone who's more desperate for money than they are for friends. It could've been anyone." She picked up a clamfruit. "We done here? Rusko'll have all your cargo loaded up, what's left of it. Go on."

Vi didn't like being dismissed by anyone of a lower rank than general, but she'd seen how Oga had treated Dhoran and didn't want to be on the other end of the boss's blaster. She gave a nod of respect, put her Ubese mask back on, and followed N'arrghela back out into the cantina. She walked right by Ylena, Dotti, and Roxi having an ale, but they didn't even look up. The disguise worked, at least—they hadn't recognized her. Still, she'd need to buy a new wrap that wasn't connected to Vi Moradi. Someone in this very cantina—perhaps even someone here at this very moment—might've been the one to use a long-range comm to call the First Order with a tip about a certain Resistance spy trying to recruit for her cause.

Surely it wasn't Ylena or the other Gatherers? They'd accepted her, they were warm and welcoming, and they were already beginning to feel like family. And it couldn't be Savi. Goodness shone out of him like a laser beam. Maybe it was Rusko or N'arrghela or the Talpini, or maybe Salju or Mubo or Arta . . . but no. She couldn't consider any of them. She had training in reading people, after all, and some were just good eggs, and the bad eggs in Oga's crew would've been under strict orders. Dok-Ondar was a definite possibility, though. Or any random smuggler who'd overhead her private conversation or seen the starbird on her jacket before she'd bought her wrap. At least everyone she noted around the cantina couldn't see her eyes under the mask, couldn't see her mouth twisting up in a silent snarl as she sought the snitch who had only made her mission all the harder.

Didn't these people know that Vi's entire life was dedicated to helping them? To keeping them safe? But instead, someone had called down the very villain Vi was working so hard to save them from. The irony did not escape her.

Outside the cantina door, Rusko waited in a junky landspeeder, one burly arm thrown over the back of the seat. The floating trailer behind the speeder carried a load covered by crusty old tarps. Vi tried to guess which shapes corresponded to the cargo she'd lost, but Rusko growled, "Stop counting and get in unless you want to walk."

So she got in and put the crankbike helmet by her side, sitting as far away from Rusko as possible, which wasn't very far, as he was big and the speeder was built for humans, not giant sharks. They zoomed through the market, and as they neared the archway, she asked him to stop. Dolin sat on his bike where she'd left him, looking conspicuously innocent. Vi would've bet any amount of money that he'd ventured into the outpost, at least a little bit, just to satisfy his curiosity.

"Would you mind following us?" she asked, lifting her helmet to show him her face.

"What? Yeah, sure. I think." He had that twitchy look folks got when they couldn't believe they hadn't gotten caught. That was fine—the Resistance wasn't his Grana, after all.

"We're headed back to the ruins to start setting up the base."

He nodded and pulled on his helmet, cranking up the bike to follow them. As they neared the ruins, however, he pulled his crankbike in front of Rusko's speeder and angled in a slightly different direction, waving for them to follow.

"What's this gruffherder doing?" Rusko asked, slowing down as Dolin's path forked.

"He lives out here. He knows the ruins. So he must be leading us in either a more direct route or a less deadly one."

"You trust him?"

Vi wanted to say, *More than I trust you*, but she really didn't trust Rusko and didn't want to make him mad, so she just said, "In this particular area, yes."

Grumbling to himself, Rusko followed the crankbike, and Dolin led them off the path and deeper into the forest. As far as Vi could tell, they were headed in the right direction, and Rusko didn't complain again. Soon she saw the rock formations rising up ahead, and her skin prickled when she thought about all that she'd faced here just a few short hours ago. If not for Dolin's truffleboar, she might be just one more corpse.

"This is as far as I'll go," Rusko said, stopping the speeder inconveniently far away from the clearing around the entrance to the ruins.

"But Dolin's up there and unharmed. He's waving at us, and it's not the wave of a man full of darts and assaulted by ancient spirits. Can't you just pull up a little closer?"

The Karkarodon turned his body this way and that, his version of shaking his head. "No way. I'm not dying out here. I don't mess with the ancients. Trailer's yours anyway, so just float it to wherever you want. I did my part of the job. Like I said: You're not one of us."

He unhitched the cargo and sped off toward the outpost without another word. Dolin lumbered over and helped Vi direct the floating pallet toward the entrance that led into the maze of stone caverns.

As they pushed, she asked, "So I forgot to ask—how much do you know about these ruins? Because you knew enough to save me."

Dolin sighed and blushed and wouldn't quite meet her eyes. "I know a lot, but Grana said that it had to be kept a secret, that the ancients left things this way for a purpose. That anyone who came here to steal deserved what they got."

"Then why did you save me?"

He cocked his head at her and shrugged. "Because you were running away from the ruins, not going into them. I figured you were lost, and you were definitely hurt. I just have a soft spot for hurt things."

Okay, so technically she'd been running away from the ruins after stealing from them, but Vi hadn't told him about the necklace. She felt bad for that lie of omission, but she needed him on her team. And what's more, she liked him. He was a great recruit for the Resistance, and it might even help him grow beyond his own expectations. She wanted him to meet the pilots, test up, and see what he could do. He would never be another Poe Dameron—no one but Poe was Poe—but the Resistance could use all the steady, bighearted people it could get.

"Well, how do you think the ancients would feel about sharing space with a plucky group of goodhearted rebel fighters led by a princess and determined to save the galaxy?"

He paused to give it real thought; it was clearly important to him, and he was figuring it out as they went along. "You know, I think the ancients would want to do the right thing. We don't know much about them, but . . . do you feel it? Out here, around the ruins . . . it's so peaceful. It feels holy. I think they were wise and kind, and I think they loved nature, and I think they would understand the need to protect Batuu and our way of life. Grana would disagree with me doing that personally, but . . ."

"Sometimes the older generation resists change?" Vi supplied.

"I guess so."

"And sometimes they're afraid of losing the younger generation and being left alone. I imagine it's hard, when you've got no one else to turn to. You would do anything to keep those you love near."

"But that's not fair," Dolin argued. "The younger generation has a right to go out and discover their destiny. They can't stay home hunting truffles and herding gruffins until they're old, too. Sometimes we just . . . want more."

"I agree with you," Vi said softly. "My mother didn't want me to leave home, but here I am. And now I'm supposed to build a command center, so let's see how much of my cargo the boss of Black Spire has returned."

They settled the pallet over an open patch of grass, and Vi went around untying the tarp. Dolin helped her tug it off, and she let it fall to the ground. Oga had indeed been generous, and most of the Resistance gear was here.

But the one important thing that was missing?

All the communication equipment, including their long-range comm.

They still couldn't get word to Leia.

The Resistance had no idea the First Order was here, and that Vi and her people were in peril.

Chapter Nineteen

THE NEXT DAY, DESPITE THE FACT that she'd recently been poisoned and that the enemy had arrived planetside, Vi still went to work for Savi. She'd made the commitment, they still needed the money, and she had a feeling that the old scrapper and his junkyard would some-how prove to be a great help to the Resistance. Although she longed to slip away, find Kath's base, and destroy it, she also knew that such a brash action would only serve to convince the First Order that she was actually here and that Batuu was worth investigating. So she had to stick to the standard spy protocol: lie low, act normal, and strate-gize.

While she was gone, Dolin was to hook the empty trailer up to his crankbike and haul Archex and Pook from the transport camp over to the ruins, where the droid would charge up using their returned power droids and begin unloading all the cargo while Dolin focused on disabling the defenses inside the cave system. As for Archex, Vi assigned him the task of deciding how to organize and set up their new facility. He needed something to do, desperately. Carving wooden convorees for the toy shop wasn't going to fill the hole in his soul. The man needed a purpose.

Out at the scrapyard, Vi chose a spot a little away from the other

Gatherers. She was painfully aware that someone in town had alerted the First Order to her presence, and even if she told herself it was impossible, it very well could've been one of her smiling, happy co-workers. Ylena sat near her again, but Vi would've bet anything that Ylena wasn't the problem. She, like Savi, seemed to have an almost spiritual calm about her, as if she glowed from within and radiated tranquility.

When the others were working elsewhere, Vi lowered her voice and said, "Ylena, do you think one of the other scrappers might've turned me in to the First Order? There's an officer in town looking for me, and he knows who I am."

Ylena's mouth turned down. "I've heard that troopers were making trouble in the market. Their officer was seen going into the cantina. But I promise you it wasn't one of us. I know we like to gossip, but no one here possesses the avarice to call down such trouble on our home just for money. As I think you've seen, Savi doesn't hire people like that."

"But he hired me," Vi argued. "A complete stranger from offworld, one who already had a chip on her shoulder. I look like a trouble-maker."

At that, Ylena dimpled. "There are people who stir the pot for personal gain, and then there are people who cause trouble because they have a higher calling. Savi can tell the difference. We all can. You have the gleam."

Looking up from the old, tarnished medal in her hand, Vi raised an eyebrow. "The gleam?"

"That's what we call it when the Force has taken a shine to someone. The gleam. It's a little like an aura, but . . . it doesn't lie. And you have it. That's why Savi took you on so readily."

Vi stood as she dropped the medal in her basket. She glanced around the junkyard at all of Savi's workers, cheerfully going about their business. Dotti laughed as she sorted, Roxi settled her hoverchair in a more promising section, people worked cranes and directed droids and cut apart the husks of broken ships.

"All the people here have this . . . gleam?"

Ylena nodded, her eyes twinkling with a sort of pride and a lot of love. "Oh, yes. We're a family. You never see any of us fighting, stealing, anything like that. Savi doesn't hire anyone until he's met them himself and taken their measure." She leaned closer. "He had an old friend named Lor San Tekka, and Lor once met Luke Skywalker. Savi and Lor grew up together, and they bonded over a belief that the Force needed a little help to stay balanced. Savi came here so that he could continue his work in peace. We may not be able to join the Resistance, but we are with you in spirit."

Vi untangled some rotting power cords while she thought about Ylena's speech—and what Savi had told her, too. She'd gotten a job at the junkyard to make money and buy scrap cheap, and now it was sounding like she'd stumbled onto a . . . Force cult? She needed to know more, but she also recognized that saying the wrong thing could close Ylena off.

"So this Lor—he was friends with Luke Skywalker?" she asked, hoping to draw out some more information. "Before Luke left?"

Ylena looked stricken and had to turn away as she struggled to maintain her composure. "I don't know if a Jedi Master really has friends. But Lor knew him. He and Savi kept in touch. Lor spent his last days in a spiritual village on Jakku, knowing that he was to serve a greater purpose."

"A spiritual village?" Vi pressed.

Ylena wiped her eyes and turned back to the pile of scrap before her, pulling out an old synthleather jacket and dusting it off, considering whether it might be saved. "Do you ever feel as if you were meant to serve a great purpose, Vi? That you have a role to play somewhere that you can't yet fathom?"

Vi tossed the now untangled cords into her basket. "I'm already playing my role. Serving the Resistance is a great purpose."

"To be sure." Ylena nodded in a knowing, motherly way. "But sometimes, it's like a puzzle. You can see the pieces and guess at what they will reveal, but until all the pieces come together and you step back, you will never truly understand how one small part might fit into the whole. Sometimes, you must sit, and wait, and gather pieces to see the entire picture."

Sitting and gathering pieces—that was a sentiment Vi felt deeply, just now.

They worked in companionable silence for a while, as often happened at the junkyard. What Ylena said made sense, and yet there was something underneath her words, something she was hinting at that Vi didn't yet understand. But Vi knew enough about interrogation to recognize that Ylena was being purposeful with her clues and that asking too much or too aggressively would only drive the woman to silence. For now, Vi was willing to be content with the knowledge that no one here had turned her in, and that in their own way they supported the Resistance, or at least that they fought against evil. For some reason she couldn't quite put a finger on, she was certain it was true.

She looked around at each of the Gatherers but saw no gleam about them. They just seemed like normal people doing a normal job and trying to make the best of it. They were happy, healthy enough, and in good spirits, and that was better than many people throughout the galaxy. Whoever Savi really was and whatever he truly believed, he definitely knew how to manage his workers.

After lunch, Vi and Ylena were sorting through the guts of a rusty transport, and Vi was disappointed to see that its comm array was completely busted. She'd been hoping to find something salvageable that she could buy off Savi for the price of scrap, but by the time most ships made it to this part of Savi's scrapyard, they'd already been torn apart and had various creatures nesting in their controls.

"You look sad," Ylena observed.

Vi decided to repay Ylena's earlier honesty with a truth of her own instead of hiding her feelings as a spy truly should. "Oga returned most of my cargo but not my comm array." She ran a finger over the ancient buttons. "So I can't contact my general. She doesn't know about our setbacks or that the First Order has found us. But if I go into town and pay to use someone else's equipment, they'll know the

codes that can be used to find the Resistance, and that kind of information is clearly dangerous here when I don't know who my enemies
are, or at least who would sell me and my cause down the river."

Ylena thought about it for a moment and said, "There are many
people in town who can be trusted. Not like the Gatherers here in the
scrapyard, but good people."

"More troublesome is that even if someone didn't betray us, the
First Order could take control of their equipment and punish them
for helping me. I need my own gear back, or a way to buy something
similar we can keep out at the base."

Ylena sorted junk for several moments before responding. Vi liked
that about her—she didn't just say whatever came into her head but
took it seriously and endeavored to give the best answer she could. It
was an unusual trait and took some getting used to.

"I can speak with Savi, and we can be on the lookout for something suitable. That sort of thing is hard to come by here, and most of
our scrap buys have already had any valuable tech torn out, as you
can see. Oga controls all the bigger purchases, and anything her crew
salvages comes to us at her discretion." She waved her hands at the
scrapyard. "Let's just say we're never going to find a new, usable
comm array here. Have you been into town to see what's on offer and
how much it will cost?"

"I tried Smuggler's Alley once and was disappointed, and I haven't
looked again. I've been pretty busy. We still need to tune up the personal short-range comms we found in the . . ." Vi trailed off. She
wasn't sure she wanted Ylena to know she'd looted all the bodies of
Oga's minions she'd found in the caves. "Returned cargo."

Vi opened an old canteen that had an odd rattle and poured two
small crystals out into her palm. They landed, cold, against her skin.

Ylena gasped. "May I?" she asked, holding out her hands with an
odd reverence.

Vi dumped the crystals into Ylena's palm, and the older woman
held them up to the light, studying each one in turn. "Do you know
what these are?"

"No. Never was much into jewelry."

Ylena chuckled. "Oh, these aren't jewelry. They're kyber crystals."

"Now, why does that sound familiar?"

Standing, Ylena cracked her back and motioned for Vi to join her. Vi stood, cracking her back as well, and followed Ylena toward the hut. Oddly, Ylena didn't pull her basket along or encourage Vi to bring hers. Ylena had eyes only for the crystals, which were clear and faceted. They were pretty, to be sure, but didn't seem special in any way. Vi had been in caves filled with crystals, and these specimens were each smaller than her finger.

"Kyber crystals are sacred to the Jedi," Ylena explained. "They have a way of focusing the Force. They're used to power lightsabers."

Vi chewed on the inside of her cheek a moment. "You keep using the present tense, but I thought that except for Rey, the Jedi have disappeared?"

"Perhaps," Ylena said with a half smile. "Then they're what *once* powered lightsabers. These crystals are very rare. They grow in only a few places around the galaxy." She stopped and glanced back toward the spot where they'd left their baskets. "And you found them in that old canteen. How strange! I wonder how they got there."

Vi could only shrug. They were crystals. Without Jedi or light-sabers, they likely had no value, except perhaps to a collector like Dok-Ondar or for some everyday industrial use. But something told her that whatever Savi wanted with such objects, he wouldn't put them into the hands of someone who would use them for the wrong reason.

"Another rare find. Like I said: The Force has taken a shine to you," Ylena said with a smile.

That kind of sentiment made Vi feel squirmy, like a little kid caught in a lie. "I'm not Force-sensitive. I'm a nobody from Chaaktil. I've been near General Organa, and you can definitely feel the power radiating from her. But I'm not like that."

Ylena stopped, both of the crystals cupped in one hand. She placed the other hand on Vi's shoulder and beamed at her. "The Force is all around us," she said. "You don't have to be sensitive to it to attract it, to be part of it. We're all part of it. Some people are just . . . well, think of it like a butterfly landing on you. That doesn't mean you're a flower. It just means that you smell sweet. It's a good thing." She squeezed Vi's shoulder and walked on, and Vi followed, feeling amused and almost pleased. Ylena sounded a little crazy, but it was a comforting thought. After spending all her time with Archex and Pook, it was nice to be liked.

"So what will you do with the crystals?" she asked, changing the subject to something more concrete.

"That's for Savi to decide." Ylena unlocked the hut door, went inside, came back out, and locked the door behind herself. "He'll know what to do. He always does." Her eyes went bright. "And he'll probably give you a bonus for bringing him something so valuable. It's a good find. Perhaps that will help you buy the equipment you need."

That lifted Vi's heart. "Hopefully."

Vi didn't find any more crystals or valuable artifacts that day, but it stuck with her, what Ylena had said about the Force favoring people. She'd often had an intense gut feeling about people, like the one she'd had about Archex, even as he'd done his best to torture information out of her. Under the hard, First Order shell, he'd been a good egg. She felt the same way about Ylena and Savi. She'd seen it in Finn and Rose and Poe. Even with Dolin, she'd known almost immediately that he was truly a good person. Now, if she could just find some more Batuu locals with that kind of hero's heart who were willing to join her cause.

After work, she walked into town with Ylena, who lived in a warren of apartments Savi owned around his storefront and workshop. Dotti and Roxi lived there, too, sharing a ground-level apartment with an extra-wide door for Roxi's hoverchair. Vi could almost imagine herself living here in another life. The Trilon wishing tree made the area pretty and bright, and the building was well kept, with gardens outside.

Vi didn't have long to do her errands before the bulk of the shops closed for the evening, and she had to get food for Archex and Dolin, too. That was part of running a command center: feeding the troops. And as she already knew, they could hold a lot of food. Sure, her returned cargo held nonperishable foodstuffs, but that would be saved for a time of greater need. As new people joined their cause, she would need to either hire a cook or come up with an agreement like Savi had for his workers' daily flatbreads, at least until they could get a garden growing and start keepings beasts. Lucky that she had a farm boy on hand to help with that. It was pleasant, dreaming of a busy encampment, of the day when she could focus on that part of her job instead of worrying about the First Order troops who'd be looking to destroy everything she'd fought for.

Ylena and the other scrappers retired to their apartments, waving their goodbyes, and Vi considered where to look for comm equipment. It would be expensive, and she didn't want to get ripped off. Not sure where to start, she stopped in at Mubo's Droid Depot.

"Not having trouble with that PK-Ultra, I hope?" the Utai called, clambering down from a high shelf as soon as he saw her. "He looks like the sort who would pull out a wire to get some sympathy on a slow day."

Vi had to laugh at that. "He probably would. A few too many programs running for one hard drive. But no, I'm here for something else. Where do you think I could get a fair deal on some long-range comm equipment?"

Mubo stroked his missing chin. "Gol might have some," he said. "He usually sets up shop outside the market and Merchant Row, just a makeshift stall on the outskirts. It'll be pricey, though. Of course, it's all pricey here because we're so far off from the rest of the galaxy. But I'd trust him more than that pawnshop in Smuggler's Alley. I take it you're settling in, then?"

Vi nodded. "Trying to."

"Say, have you heard that the First Order arrived? Angry guy in black and a bunch of soldiers, look just like the Empire's old stormtroopers. I saw some once, on Tatooine. Dangerous folk. One tried to kick me!"

Ah, yes. Mubo didn't know who Vi *really* was, did he?

And—drat. She'd walked into town without her Ubese helmet. Most specifically, she'd left for work without it and then just continued on in kind. There were so many concerns in her head that her mind felt like a sieve, and she'd definitely let something big slip past.

Living her life as Vi Moradi and living life as a wanted spy had never overlapped like this before. She'd accidentally and foolishly fallen into the trap of believing she was just a normal person, living a normal life. She glanced around Mubo's shop and pointed at a big pair of welder's goggles.

"How much for those goggles?"

Mubo picked them up and inspected them. "Not much? Cracked, and I don't even know where they came from."

Vi handed him a few spira and pulled her shawl up over her head, wrapping it so that only her eyes were exposed and putting on the goggles over it. She'd seen plenty of locals dressed this way, especially when the suns were proving especially hot. Mubo waved her away, shouting, "Till the spires!" as if it was perfectly normal for someone to come into his shop and leave hiding under a shawl and greasy old goggles. Then again, being such an eccentric person himself, perhaps he didn't hold it against other people when they acted strangely.

Vi followed the droid tech's directions to the outskirts of the market, where a disorganized jumble of wares was strewn out on tarps and woven blankets and old tables and displayed from carts and wheelbarrows. She briefly longed for the neat rows and boxes of Coruscant's shops, but then she dashed that thought aside. She'd left such places behind on purpose. She wanted to feel like she was a part of a greater cause, and she wanted adventure, and if she had to dig a little more deeply to find what she needed among the scrap, so be it. As she waded through twisted cables and moved monitors and keyboards aside, a small and squeaky voice asked, "Bright suns! Might I help you?"

When Vi looked down, she found a Chadra-Fan standing there, hands clasped earnestly and black eyes bright and shiny. She—at least Vi thought the batlike alien was a she, based on her belted purple tunic and pretty bead necklace—was short like all of her species and covered in soft gray fur with big ears and four nostrils. She seemed very eager to help—but also nervous or possibly frightened. Her big ears twitched backward, and Vi looked over the Chadra-Fan's head and noticed a youngish man behind a table, arms crossed, watching their interaction closely. She immediately disliked him.

"Thank you," Vi told the Chadra-Fan with a warm smile. "I'm interested in buying some long-range comm equipment."

The Chadra-Fan nodded vigorously. "We do have a few things. Not much—we're quite far out from the main markets, but I've been fixing up a relatively new unit with only a few little dings and glitches—"

"Blast it, Kriki!" the man said, storming around his table to stand far too close to Vi as he pushed the diminutive Chadra-Fan aside. "There's nothing wrong with that unit, m'lady! Fully functional and the best on the planet." His eyes flicked to the Chadra-Fan, who flattened her ears. "Only the ancients know why I even hired her. Taking a job from a proper human and not even doing it well."

His voice was loud and booming, and the Chadra-Fan—Kriki— flinched and tried to make herself as small as possible. It had to hurt her sensitive ears—it was definitely hurting Vi's ears.

"Sorry, Master Gol!" Kriki whimpered. "I didn't mean to—that is, I was only trying to be honest—she'd see the dings herself soon enough—"

The man's hands went into fists, and Vi drew herself up tall and stepped between Gol and his worker.

"I know you weren't thinking about hitting her," Vi said.

"If I did, I would be well within my rights," he shot back. "Look, I can see that you're new around here, so maybe you haven't learned to keep your nose out of other people's business yet, but—"

"Oh, and you're going to tell me where to put my nose? That should be fun," she said, fighting her instinct to pull back her wrap and show him her blaster.

"Reprimanding a paid employee is my business," he shot back.

"But when a paid employee visibly recoils from you, it suggests that you're a very bad businessman," Vi finished for him.

The man's jaw worked, and he finally grunted and made a shooing gesture. "Get out. You can't have the comm at any price. This is my shop, and I'll not be lectured by my customers, much less offworlders who don't understand how things are done here."

Vi looked longingly at exactly the equipment she needed but

wouldn't debase herself or her morals by kowtowing to this brute. "Good trade," she said sourly, meaning exactly the opposite.

As she turned and walked back the way she'd come, she heard a squeak of terror and the slap of flesh on fur. "How dare you, you filthy little mongrel?" Gol shouted.

Vi stopped. She turned around slowly. As she saw Kriki cowering and Gol looming over her, his hand drawn back for another slap, she knew she couldn't just walk away. This was why the Resistance was so important to her, on a personal level: She couldn't stand a bully.

She drew her tactical baton. "If you want to hit her again, you'll have to go through me," she said, low and deadly.

Gol's shoulders tensed, and he turned to face her, his features twisted with disgust and rage. It was a look she'd seen a hundred times on dozens of planets: the loathing of someone who's accustomed to being in charge momentarily realizing that they're not calling the shots.

"Oh, and what? You're going to beat me? Oga Garra will hear about this."

"You say that like I care."

He snorted and looked like he would've spit on the floor if he weren't surrounded by his own goods. "You're not going to hurt me. I know all about you—I can see right through your pathetic disguise. Rebel trash. People in the market talk, you know. Some of us think it would be better if the First Order got rid of you."

Vi sighed deeply and rolled her eyes. "It's so funny how you keep lecturing me as if you can't even comprehend not being the one with the power," she said. "As if I couldn't beat the actual crap out of you in a fight. And, yes, I'm well aware that some of you would rather kiss the First Order's tight, black-clad behind than stand up for your way of life, but that hasn't stopped me from doing what's right so far. So my next question is for Kriki: How would you like to work for someone who treats you like a person?"

The Chadra-Fan lowered her arms, her mouth open in shock. "Work for you? Doing what?"

"Duties are negotiable. I can promise room, board, and the chance to do good work for a boss who believes in you and an organization

that's fighting against guys like this. And no one will ever talk down
to you or strike you, or they'll answer to me."

Kriki looked from Gol to Vi, eyes darting back and forth as she
thought about it.

"How dare you even consider—" Gol began.

"I accept." Kriki scurried over to Gol's table and slung a crocheted
bag over her shoulder. "And I'll take my back pay now, please, Mr. Gol."

Vi tapped her baton on a nearby droid casing. "If you owe her,
you'd better make good."

She was a second from pulling her blaster and shooting the ground
at his feet to get him moving when he lumbered over to the table and
tossed some spira on the old wood.

"You won't get a good reference from me," he warned.

"As if you ever would've given me a good reference anyway," Kriki
said. Her earlier crouch and timidity were gone, replaced by a jaunty
step and broad grin.

"You're going to regret this. Both of you." Gol pointed to Kriki.
"You, because I treated you well and you're going to find out that the
rest of the world is cruel. And you." He pointed at Vi. "Because I'm
going to tell everyone I know that you're bad for Black Spire. I can't
wait to see what that First Order officer will pay me for this intel."

"I'd be doing the galaxy a favor if I shot you," Vi said, slamming her
tactical baton back in its holster and showing him her blaster. "But
that's not how good people operate. I help the Resistance because freedom matters to me, even when it's freedom to let slimy little mynocks
like you spread their hate. C'mon, Kriki. If you're ready?"

Kriki nodded. "Ready for anything!"

Vi gave Gol one last nod. "Till the spire," she said, mentally adding, *falls on you, crushing all your bones to mush.* She turned her back
on him and walked away, and Kriki followed her.

"We should probably run," the Chadra-Fan said apologetically.
"He'll make good on that promise. If he doesn't have a comm channel open for the First Order already—"

Proving her point, Gol screamed, "Oi, First Order! Here's that Resistance spy you're looking for!"

Chapter Twenty

AT LEAST KRIKI WASN'T THE SORT to say *I told you so.* She just murmured, "Follow me!" and darted down an alley. Vi pulled her wrap more firmly over her face and followed. They were soon out of sight of Gol's shop, but she could still hear his shouting. Kriki seemed to know the small spaces around the market well, and she led Vi through shops, out back doors, past garbage yards, and even through a private home with a lovely courtyard with its own sparkling blue fountain and an angry Toydarian who shook her fist and shouted, "Hey! Get out of here, you!"

Vi realized she had no idea where they were, as she'd only seen the fronts of the businesses so far and had never ventured into the less public spaces of the outpost. If it turned out that Kriki was less than scrupulous or fell more in line with her ex-boss's morals, Vi knew the Chadra-Fan could've easily led her directly to the First Order for a tidy reward. And yet she knew in her heart of hearts that Kriki was a good person—she'd felt it, the moment she'd met her. So she kept following and didn't ask any questions, just ducked or froze or ran, as she was directed.

Finally, Kriki stopped in a shadowy spot under a balcony, hidden by a rug vendor's hanging wares.

"We're out of range and safe here," Kriki said. "But I guess I should've asked: Where are we going?"

Vi pulled up her goggles and recalled her original mental tally of errands. "Well, I guess we won't be shopping for long-range comm equipment tonight, so that's off the list. If circumstances were better, I'd pick up another one of these shawls from Arta in a different color, plus enough food to feed you, me, and two hungry human men. And I'd hoped for some nice-smelling soap and a brush. But I imagine Gol brought the stormtroopers running, so I can't be seen here tonight. Guess I'll have to stink and let my wig get tangled."

Kriki grinned and puffed out her chest. "I can do all that. Probably get better prices than you, too. Anything I need to know about food preferences, boss?"

Vi fluffed her bangs, which were suffering under the goggles and making her forehead sweat. The afternoon had quickly gone off the rails, and now she inexplicably had an employee despite the fact that she barely had enough money to keep Archex and Dolin fed. At least she hadn't promised Kriki pay. No one in the Resistance got paid—at least not in credits. How much did Chadra-Fan eat anyway? It couldn't be more than the boys did.

Vi held out a handful of spira and smiled. "No real preferences, although we're all pretty big on meat, so I wouldn't go in for too much Ithorian Garden Loaf. Just remember that I'm cut off from the Resistance just now, and I'm short on credits, so everything we do . . ."

"Has to be frugal. I'm great at frugal. I'm the frugalest!" With a wink, Kriki shimmied up a wooden post and disappeared.

It was a longer wait than Vi would've liked, and more than once she wondered if she'd guessed wrong about Kriki and her new employee had taken her hard-won spira and split. A spy's job was to see through masks and disguises, but she hadn't had much experience with Chadra-Fan and didn't know how to read their expressions. What would Ylena say about Kriki? she wondered. Did Kriki have that "gleam" Ylena had mentioned? She didn't even know if her new recruit was any good with tech. She'd said she was fixing up a comm unit for Gol, but maybe she meant she was polishing it or scraping old gunk out of the keyboard.

Amazing, how doubt could creep in if a person was left alone in a dark place for long enough. Vi decided that if Kriki didn't come back—or worse, betrayed her—she would just sell all her cargo and use the credits to buy passage for Archex, Pook, and herself back to a busy Mid Rim world where she could contact Leia and apologize before disappearing in a cloud of shame. Somehow, having her trust demolished like that would be the straw that broke the ronto's back. She could keep pushing here despite the impossible odds as long as she had people she trusted, people she could believe in who also believed in her, but she was almost looking for a sign that she should give up on Black Spire and move on. Everything had gone wrong.

And, yes, the First Order showing up could've been that sign—for someone else, maybe. But to Vi, that was just a reminder of why she had to keep going.

A soft thump drew Vi's thoughts back to the present, and her hand went immediately to her blaster.

"I think you're going to be pleased," Kriki said with a little trill in her voice. "All the vendors are glad to get rid of the ugly and bruised fruit and veg this late at night, and Arta had just priced some resell tunics. I think the green will really bring out your eyes. The soap is made with hand-grown Batuuan jasmine and the vibrobrush should be perfect for your wig." Kriki put a rough, heavy sack into Vi's hands. "Oh, and your change is in there, too."

It was so dark now that Vi couldn't see well, but she figured that whatever Kriki had brought, it would do. Just knowing that she would smell better tomorrow immeasurably improved her mood. "Green works," she said. "All that works. Thank you! Now, can you get us out to the ancient ruins without being seen?"

"The ruins? You mean the old post? I've heard tales that it's haunted."

Vi nodded, pleased. "Good. Let's hope those tales are still making the rounds. They're not haunted, they're just booby-trapped, and we're working on that part."

Again she followed Kriki through the dark, clinging to the shadows around buildings and darting around hanging laundry and crumbling walls. Kriki knew a way out of the outpost besides the main gateway, and Vi would have to remember this route in the daytime. They didn't see Kath or any of his stormtroopers, and no one they passed seemed to even register their existence. The moons were fat and full, and it was easy enough to see as Kriki navigated the forest on the way to Savi's Path, stopping every now and then to check her route, ears and nostrils twitching.

They arrived at the cenote without incident. There was no fire outside, and at first Vi was alarmed, thinking that the men might've come to harm in the caves. But then she heard the metallic thunk of Pook's feet, followed by the heavy crash of stone hitting the ground.

"I have had it with stalactites and stalagmites," the droid said. "Honestly. How many colloid deposits does one extensive underground cavern system need?"

"Hey, Pook!" Vi called.

His flat black face swiveled to face her. "Oh. It's you."

"Rising moons to you, too. Where are Archex and Dolin?"

"Archex is within, building a fire in a natural chimney in one of the caverns. Dolin returned home to fetch bedding. Apparently humans do not enjoy sleeping on shelves of solid rock. Is that a Chadra-Fan?"

"Yes. This is Kriki. She's one of us now."

"One of us?" Kriki asked, her ears flattening a little with worry.

Vi winced. "Oh. Maybe I didn't make that part clear. We're with the Resistance. I'm recruiting for the cause, and we're building our Batuu headquarters here. That's what I was offering you. Not so much a job as a . . . calling. I'm sorry if I misled you."

Kriki was frozen, ears and nose twitching furiously. Vi recognized this as a sign that the Chadra-Fan was thinking hard, so she bumbled on, feeling like she might've royally mucked up again.

"You're certainly free to return to the outpost, if you'd prefer. And if so, I apologize for destroying your relationship with your former boss. I just can't stand a bully, and—"

"Okay."

"Okay?"

"I mean, as long as you meant what you said about room and board. Oga charged too much for her apartments, and my room was barely a closet, and the neighbors were awfully loud." She turned this way and that, eyes blinking bright. "I like it out here. It's quiet."

"It won't be quiet once the fleet starts using it as a waypoint," Vi warned. "Ships coming and going, the pound of boots, dozens of people talking at once during meetings."

Kriki looked down. "You said no one would hit me or yell at me. You were kind to me. That's not something I've seen much since leaving Chad. I wanted adventure, but no one seems to take me seriously."

"It is probably because you are diminutive and furry, and you have a high voice," Pook observed. "These traits combine to trick the human mind into thinking you are a child or a pet because humans are of lesser intellect."

"I mean, rude!" Kriki squeaked. "The part about me, I mean."

Vi shot the droid a dirty look. "Okay, so maybe that's all a little true. But I take you seriously, Kriki, and the Resistance will take you seriously. Everyone has something valuable to contribute in the fight against the First Order."

Kriki looked down and fidgeted with the main bead on her necklace, a rough gray rock. "And . . . well, I don't like to talk about it, but my sister Reelka was on Hosnian Prime when it . . . when . . ." She hiccuped a sob and turned away.

"I'm so sorry," Vi said gently. "I had friends there, too. Once you've seen the damage the First Order can do, it's hard to go back to normal life, knowing that you could always be a heartbeat away from another tragedy. The Resistance has become my family, and I hope it'll feel that way for you, too."

She had more to say on the topic, but her stomach grumbled loudly, and Kriki turned back around, wiped her eyes, and giggled.

Vi did, too. "Enough speeches. Let's go eat. I'm beat."

Pook led them into the ruins, under the overhang and along the same route through the caves that Vi had taken when she'd come here to find Oga's artifact, and Vi wasn't a bit ashamed that she flinched when they entered the first chamber.

"Dolin and Archex have removed every trap," Pook said. "With a great deal of my help, I might add. Hence the dents in my chassis and the large pile of unnecessary stones outside."

She was pleased to see that a string of lights had been added to the cavern hallway, and as Pook stumped ahead, she likewise approved of the way their cargo had already been distributed among the various rooms in a logical manner. Pook had even used their vibrosaw to cut passages between some of the rooms, giving them more routes in and out so they wouldn't feel trapped. She'd hoped to bring home a long-range comm, or at least secure one that Pook could retrieve later, but she was beginning to think that having Kriki around was going to be more useful than anticipated—maybe even better than a long-range comm. Finally, they had someone on their team who could navigate the outpost and get good deals, not to mention someone that other people consistently underestimated. What's more, Vi just liked her plucky attitude.

"So this is the old outpost," the Chadra-Fan said in awe. "I've been in BSO for five years and heard so many stories about this place. Looks like they were all wrong, unless I somehow missed the vengeful ghosts."

"Ghosts do not exist," Pook said. "And don't get me started on the Force. Ridiculous tomfoolery."

"Oh, Ylena's gonna love you," Vi murmured.

Pook stopped in front of the next open doorway, and there was Archex, feeding twigs to a fire in a wide fireplace carved from the stone in the room that had once held the screaming maggots. It smelled noticeably better without them and their foul bin of rotten soil. Archex looked up and did a double take when he saw Kriki.

"Kriki, this is Archex. Archex, this is Kriki."

Kriki bobbed her head. "Rising moons, Archex!"

Archex flicked his eyes at Vi in question. "You too."

"Kriki is joining us," Vi said.

Archex looked like he wanted to know more details—of course he did. He was accustomed to being a leader, and even way out here on the edge of the galaxy, he would be thinking about building and leading teams. Fortunately, just then they heard the roar of Dolin's crankbike, and soon they were all helping him carry heavy sacks of wool into the big chamber that had the rudimentary bunks hacked out of the walls.

"It's not much, and it's not been felted," he apologized. "But I reckon gruffin wool is softer than stone. Grana didn't want to let me leave again, I can tell you that much!" He blushed a little and looked away. "Said you were a devil woman, seducing me away." He brightened. "But I brought some eggs and jerky, so there's that." He spotted Kriki, and his jaw dropped. "What's that?"

Kriki bristled, her fur puffing up and her teeth bared. "What's that? Did you mean *who's* that? I'm a who, not a what!"

Dolin's eyes flew wide, and he blushed an even brighter red. "Oh, by the spires. I'm so sorry! I've never met a person like you."

"You've never seen a Chadra-Fan before?"

He looked down. "I've never met anyone who wasn't human. Never saw the outpost until today—and just a bit of it, I swear! The matriarchs of our settlement tell us that even the Surabat vicinity is too modern. Grana said it was dangerous, outside the valley."

The idea of an insular community that shunned tech and the greater galaxy was fascinating, but Vi was putting the pieces together and had questions. "If you haven't been to town before today, and you can't go to the filling station, then how do you get fuel for your crankbike?"

He looked at her like she was dim. "Brew it from grain, of course. Our settlement doesn't need anything from the town. We were here first." He extended a hand to Kriki, and she slipped her much smaller hand into it and held her own in the handshake. "Nice to meet you. I'm Dolin. Sorry if I've offended. I'm still learning."

"I'm Kriki. And I suppose it's okay. Probably best not to call anyone a 'what' if they look like they might be sentient, though. There are stranger beings than me in the galaxy."

"Yeah, just wait until the Resistance stops by and you meet Fossil,"

Vi said. "She's a Martigrade, and . . . well . . . I think you're going to be surprised."

For a moment, the four of them just stood there, until Pook said, "Well, my programming suggests that this is sufficiently awkward. Give me a job to perform, I beg you."

Vi looked around the room, which was very familiar, as it resembled Oga's lair behind the cantina, with the same sort of stone cut into the same sorts of shapes. She wondered what the ancients had been like, if they'd been human or a species that did best underground. Perhaps as they explored further into the ruins, they'd find clues. But for now, it was nighttime, she was hungry and exhausted, and she had to keep reminding herself that for the first time, she was the boss in charge of other people and had to think of them first.

"Okay. So we need water. Pook, go assess if the waterfall is potable, and if so, let's gather all the bottles and canteens and fill them. From the waterfall, though—the cenote is full of poisonous anemones."

"Poisonous what?" Dolin asked, jaw dropped again.

Vi wiped a hand through the air. "Don't worry about it. Just don't stick your hand in there unless you want to die. Probably should've mentioned that earlier. Now, Kriki brought food—I've no idea what. Archex, think you can put those spices to work?"

He grinned. "I'll get the oil heated."

"There's roots and fungi, and I bought kaadu ribs from the butcher!" Kriki piped up. "But I had 'em double-boxed so they wouldn't attract predators."

Vi smiled—and drooled a little. "Thank goodness. Now we also need to set up the beds—probably all in here, since it's where the fire and light are. We can work out better barracks later, once we find and unpack the cots. Eat, drink, sleep—"

"I set up the portable restroom from the cargo haul for you," Pook said tiredly. "As I believe you will require it after eating and drinking. For all my many burdens, at least I don't possess any sphincters."

"Thanks, and yuck. So let's all . . . do that."

Pook went out to test the water, and Kriki trailed behind with bottles, since she could navigate the darkness easily. Dolin worked on turning his wool into bedding. Archex pulled Kriki's food haul from the big sack, cut up the fungi, and set the tubers to roast in the fire. Soon they'd all dined on kaadu ribs, tubers, spiced fungi, and fresh fruit, had their fill of water, and claimed their own little niches to sleep in, nestled in warm gruffin wool. Talk was a little odd still, but they were trying. Vi went to sleep feeling as if the Resistance shelter was finally on track.

All was well until she woke up to screams.

Chapter Twenty-One

"VI! HELP!"

Vi bolted upright, whipping her blaster from under the rough pillow of gruffin wool. The fire had died down, and they'd turned off the lights, making the room as black as the wrong side of a sarlacc.

"Kriki? Where are you? What's wrong?"

"In the corner. Something's trying to eat Archex!"

Vi got into a crouch and blinked rapidly, hoping for the tiniest bit of light and finding nothing but pure darkness. If Pook had been there, he could've helped, but she'd sent him outside with a power droid to recharge and guard the cave entrance. Never had she thought the threat might come from within.

"What is it? What's that? I can't see!" Dolin shouted.

Vi fumbled with the pack by her side and pulled out her infrared goggles. She slipped them on, and there in the corner in shades of red and black she saw a nightmare come to life. A giant glistening snake was wrapped tightly around Archex, who'd gone floppy. Tiny Kriki was trying to pry the creature away. As Vi watched, Kriki sank her teeth into the thing, but it didn't budge. Vi couldn't even see its face.

Blaster in hand, she jogged across the room, put the muzzle to the creature's clammy skin, aimed away from Archex and Kriki, and pulled the trigger. The blast was muffled, but the creature didn't drop away—it just squeezed tighter. She tried again and again, hitting it in different spots, but the thing felt like it was all muscle. It was as big around as her waist, and she couldn't find a head, but she did see tiny arms and legs. She dropped the blaster and felt around until her fingertips landed on something feathery and wet. Gills, maybe? She rammed her fingers into them, and the thing hissed and flailed but didn't let go. Poor Kriki was still tugging and biting and shrieking, some of her sounds so high-pitched that they made the hairs inside Vi's ears quiver.

"Hold on," Vi said. She ran out into the hall and screamed, "Pook! Hurry! We need the lights on!"

"Oh, bother," came the mournful call from the courtyard. "I'm not done charging."

"Can I help?" Dolin asked. "What can I do?"

"Working on it," Vi said. She hurried to the fire and poked around in the ashes with a stick, finding one of the tubers left over from dinner. Using the knife on her belt, she stabbed the red-hot root vegetable and carefully carried it over to the beast. Hoping for the best, she shoved the tuber against the wet, slimy flesh. It sizzled the moment it struck, and a sick scent like burning fish assailed Vi's nose.

A high shriek filled the air, and the worm-thing writhed and loosened, dropping Archex to the ground. Vi stabbed harder, letting her knife go through the tuber and into the beast, pinning the hot root to it.

"Archex?" Vi called, reaching over to pat his still cheek. "Come on, buddy. It's just a little snake. Wake up."

She was momentarily blinded as the lights along the ceiling buzzed to life, filling the room with cool blue light. The worm-thing screamed all the harder and uncoiled completely, writhing on the floor, its tiny arms and legs scrabbling uselessly in the air and its skin turning an angry pink, as if even the scant amount of light burned it.

Dolin picked up an ax—where had that come from?—and said, "You want it dead, boss?"

"Do you know what it is?"

"I know it's no good."

"Then sure, kill it."

Dolin planted his feet and hefted the ax. He didn't look like a soft, innocent farm boy just now—he looked like a competent, murderous brute. "Stand back," he warned, motioning Kriki away with a jerk of his head. She scuttled away, panting, violet blood dripping down her chin.

With four mighty thunks, Dolin chopped the worm-thing in two, and after a few long seconds of screaming, flailing, and juicy spattering, it fell still in two massive pieces. Vi scrambled over it and knelt by Archex. He was waxen and pale and cold, and she slapped his cheeks and rubbed his hands with hers and said things ranging from, "Come on, Emergency Brake! Wake up! Don't let the worm win!" to a more aggressive, "I swear that if you don't wake up right now, I'm going to send you back to Cerea for another month of healthful stretching and drum circles!"

"He's too cold," Kriki said. "But I can hear his heart beating. Did you know he only has one?"

Vi's laugh sounded more like a sob, even to her. "Yeah, that's a human thing. Let's get him over by the fire. Dolin, can you build up the fire. Kriki, where'd we put my orange tunic?"

Dolin had a fire going more quickly than Vi could've accomplished it, and Kriki helped wrap Archex up as tight as a baby in swaddling, and Pook began moving boxes and eventually produced a temperature control device that helped warm up the chill room.

"Just another design failure of your species," he grumbled. "I'll be over here, sensibly regulating my own temperature."

It was a long night, waiting for Archex to wake up. No one could sleep now, not only because they were worried about Archex and hyped up on adrenaline, but also because they didn't know if there were more cave worms lying in wait. They pulled crates around the fire and sat, taking some comfort in the light and warmth. Dolin got fidgety, and he used his energy to untangle the snakelike creature and lay it out on the floor. Uncurled, it was at least five meters long and seemed part amphibian and part worm, with a pale-blue segmented body burned pink here and there, feathery gills, and those tiny, clammy hands and feet that seemed mostly vestigial. Its mouth had no teeth, but that hadn't stopped it from brutalizing Archex. He had deep bruises on his chest from where its lips had clamped around him.

"It came in from the hall," Kriki said after disappearing for a bit. "There's a bigger room down that way with a waterfall and pool, and there are wavy marks in the sand around the water."

"We need doors," Vi said. "The kind that close. Maybe Savi has some scrap I can buy cheap. And Pook's first priority tomorrow will be to find the security equipment packed among the cargo crates and set up the cams and sensors, focusing on the cave worm's suspected entrance and the perimeter of the base. These ruins are perfect for what we need, aside from the giant strangling cave newts."

"That's not a very catchy name."

They all turned to Archex, who hadn't moved, but whose eyes were now open and bloodshot. He looked as shaky as his voice had sounded.

Vi beamed. "Well, since it nearly killed you, you're welcome to name it."

"Call it Hux, then," he said with a light cough. "The Hux Worm. That's fitting. It's dead, right? Please tell me it's dead. Or did you recruit it? I swear, the Resistance will take anyone."

Kriki squeaked a laugh, and Vi walked over to Archex and stared down at him. "It's very dead—didn't even pass the job interview. You should see Dolin with an ax, though. He and Kriki saved your life." She turned to the Chadra-Fan. "How'd you know what was happening? I didn't hear a thing."

Kriki shrugged. "I only sleep a couple of hours a day. I was in the other room working on a generator when I heard it. Big ears, you know. Came running, and tried to stop it, but . . . well, I guess my teeth are just little tickles to something that big. It tasted awful, though."

Vi handed her a water bottle. "That was very brave of you. I can't imagine trying to take down something that size without a weapon."

"I don't have a weapon."

"Do you want one?"

Kriki's nose wiggled as she considered it. "You'd have to teach me how to use it. But I think I'd like to learn."

"I could teach her," Archex said.

Vi hid her delighted grin. It was the perfect job for him—teaching new recruits how to shoot.

"That would be helpful—her and Dolin both. Unless you know how to shoot, Dolin?"

Dolin shook his head. "I can hunt with a bow and arrows or a spear or ax, but blasters are forbidden, back home. I do want to learn, though."

Vi nodded. This was good. Archex clearly wasn't aware of how much value he brought to the Resistance, how just knowing he was here, knowing she wasn't alone had been a huge boon and comfort to Vi ever since they'd crashed on Batuu. He'd found the cenote at the last camp, cooked food, and carved his toys for spira and even produced several useful baskets, for all that he seemed ashamed of them. Of all the things the First Order had taught him, perhaps the cruelest lesson was that he wasn't useful unless he was overproducing, unless he was constantly doing work and getting grades and being measured. Vi didn't know how she could go on without him here, and yet he still wasn't satisfied with his contribution.

Maybe this was the key to giving him purpose: reprising his role as a mentor and instructor. Teaching Dolin and Kriki about blasters and fighting would give him confidence and pull his attention away from his pain, and they would all need to be ready if the First Order found them.

But something was bothering Vi, something Kriki had said earlier. "Wait. Kriki, did you say you were working on a generator?"

The Chadra-Fan ducked her head. "I hope that's okay. I wanted to be useful, and it's strange to sit in a room with three sleeping people, doing nothing. So much breathing and twitching! So I figured we would need more generators as we got more equipment going. The first two I found were in good shape, but the third one must've gotten damaged in your crash. I was tuning it up."

"So you *are* a mechanic," Vi confirmed.

Kriki smiled and looked down shyly. "Nothing that special. A tinkerer, of sorts. I know how things work, and I like taking them apart, cleaning them up, and trying to improve them. Gol hated that, just wanted me to work as fast as possible, make things functional enough to sell. But I like knowing something can work more efficiently or with greater reliability. Why would someone choose mediocrity?"

"Because Gol was a fool."

"Yeah, well, he's not the first. People can come up with some ugly nicknames for those who don't look or think like them."

"The First Order doesn't generally take on nonhumans," Archex said. He pushed himself up to sitting. "They say it's because the armor is made to fit only a certain body type."

"That's because nobody likes to say the word *xenophobia* out loud," Vi said bitterly. "It's easy to forget that humans built the Death Stars and Starkiller Base. A human gave the order that destroyed the Hosnian system. Those people don't represent all humans, but they definitely don't make us look like the galaxy's best bet."

Kriki held up her necklace, the gray bead in the center between her long fingers. "This is a piece of it. Of Hosnian Prime, I mean, or some part of the system. Or maybe it's just a normal rock and I was swindled, but I don't really care. I keep it with me always to remember my sister. It's hard when there's nothing left of those you love."

Archex was carefully silent on this topic, as the new recruits didn't know about his past, but Dolin pulled back his sleeve to show a leather cuff with hair woven into it in intricate patterns. "I carry this for my parents. They were trying to save the gruffins before a hurricane. Grana kept me in the house and . . . they didn't come back."

"I never knew my parents," Archex said. "I grew up in an orphanage on Jakku, was sold to a mining operation, and managed to escape."

"And then what?" Dolin asked.

Vi was curious to see how Archex would handle the question. He wasn't much of a liar, but she also suspected he wasn't ready to tell everyone about his time with the First Order.

Archex sighed. "And then I fell in with a bad crowd, did some things I'm ashamed of. And now I'm trying to make up for it."

Vi smiled at him. "You're doing the right thing," she said, then looked around at all her crew, meeting each person's eyes. They looked exhausted to a one. "All of you. But now you need to get to sleep. I've got to get to the scrapyard on time in the morning if I want to buy that long-range comm. And more kaadu ribs."

"Do you think . . . I could work there, too?" Dolin asked. "Help make some spira?"

He sounded so sincere, so earnest, that Vi wanted to hug him. "We can always ask Ylena and Savi. The more the merrier."

"And I can maybe work with you at the scrapyard during the day and stay up at night to get the tech running," Kriki said.

"And I can help organize the armory and teach everyone to shoot," Archex added.

Pook sighed. "And I will endeavor to put up with you all."

Vi stood and yawned. "It's a plan, then. Good night. Sleep tight. Don't let the cave worms bite."

"Again," Archex added.

Laughter rang in the cave for the first time, and to Vi, it sounded like success.

Chapter Twenty-Two

THE NEXT DAY, WHEN VI SET out to walk Savi's Path, Kriki and Dolin walked with her. She'd barely had time to bathe in the recently installed shower, but at least most of her smelled like flowers, and thanks to Kriki's vibrobrush, her wig looked good as new. She was almost starting to feel like herself again. Dolin smelled of the same soap, although he'd later complained about the feeble lather and offered to teach Vi how to make a superior bar from gruffin fat and ashes. Ylena of course had to zip into town in a landspeeder to introduce Dolin and Kriki to Savi, but they soon returned with a smiling Dolin and purring Kriki, who had both won the old scrapper's approval and were ready to work. Despite her lack of sleep due to last night's excitement, the day went by quickly and Vi was content.

When Ylena and the other Gatherers headed off to the cantina after work a few days later, Vi, Kriki, and Dolin just naturally followed along. The walk was pleasant, and Vi had to hide her grin as Dolin trailed after Ylena looking lovestruck. The way Ylena stopped to adjust her boot to let him catch up suggested that she, too, felt something there. Kriki nudged Vi with her elbow, pointed, and gave a squeaky little giggle.

It was a pretty evening with a beautiful sunset, and as Vi walked

the old path through the ancient forest toward a town cobbled together of cast-outs and love, she realized that this place was starting
to feel like home. She hadn't felt that tug since Chaaktil, and even
then Chaaktil was too wrapped up in pain and anxiety for her to ever
consider settling there or going back. Whenever she thought about
visiting, she again saw her father kneeling, the white-clad troopers
behind him a row of identical blank masks and blasters.

But Batuu was beautiful and strange, old and new, magical and yet
natural. She even loved the funny little pipa birds with their long
pink beaks that trailed behind the scrappers, hoping for some kindness in the form of crumbs. When the gate to the Land Port came
into view, Vi pulled down her goggles and pulled up her new green
shawl to cover her face. She'd thought about bringing her Ubese helmet this morning, but that would've made a scene among the scrappers and cantina regulars. Oga had promised Vi she'd be safe in the
cantina, and for now the wrap and goggles would have to do. She'd
use the helmet the next time she was here on her own business.

As always, the cantina was a little slow when they arrived, as some
bosses weren't as generous with quitting time as Savi was. Two Bith
were quietly playing jazz in the corner as a pretty Zeltron woman
crooned into a mike. Vi greeted old Nanz at the bar and ordered a Jet
Juice, Kriki sipped at a Bespin Fizz, and Dolin happily slurped his
Gamorrean ale, claiming he'd finally found something better than
the sour beer they made back home.

Over in his usual corner, his broad arms spread over the top of his
booth, Rusko gave Vi a nod of respect while N'arrghela cleaned a
knife with her teeth—or cleaned her teeth with the knife. It was hard
to tell. The Talpini, as usual, just stared, but Vi was getting used to
that.

She was getting used to everything here. The ruins were coming
along, she was well on her way to purchasing some bigger pieces
from Savi, and Kriki had her BSO contacts on the lookout for a long-
range comm. Vi's main problem right now was the presence of Kath
and his troopers, and she planned on using her next day off to scout
for their encampment. And she was also troubled that she only had

two recruits so far—maybe two and a half, considering Ylena's constant but subtle support. It would've been easier to repel the First Order if she had some soldiers of her own.

"Bloody wonk!" a loud voice cried.

Everyone glanced at the cantina door, where a small group of exhausted-looking offworlders was hobbling in—well, except the one who was swaggering in ahead of them. The others wore the usual sensible mix of leather, armor, and stained cloth in forgettable shades of brown and black, but the fellow leading them had a taste for the flamboyant.

The man in question was tall and rail-thin, with long purple hair tied back in a loose ponytail and smudges of kohl around piercing eyes. His ripped black leather pants fit like he'd been sewn into them and thrown into a sartorially minded sarlacc, but the flawless midnight-blue shimmersilk blazer draped over them looked like he'd just bought it from a lower-level Coruscant dive five minutes ago. His loose white blouse and brightly patterned scarf were the last combination Vi would personally want to wear in a fight, but the matte-black blaster on his hip suggested he handled most of his killing from several meters away.

"Barkeep! An entire bottle of Corellian wine!" he called, facing away from the bar, his elbows on the scarred wood as he leaned back, surveying the room.

"We don't have that, I'm afraid," Nanz said, but instead of giving him the usual glare as he glanced back with a rakish grin, she batted her eyes a little. "What's your next favorite poison?"

He turned to face her, leaned in, and winked. "You tell me, missus. If you and I were to go find us a nice corner and down a few, what would you choose?"

"The Toniray wine is nice," she said, raising her eyebrows almost suggestively. "If you like to feel a bit dizzy and posh before you forget everything."

"Then Toniray it is, and five glasses." He slid his creds across the bar with one long, elegant, beringed finger and said, "And keep the rest for yourself, eh?"

Vi would not have thought the grouchy old woman could simper like that, but simper she did. With more swiftness than she showed serving anyone else, she brought down a dusty bottle and a stack of glasses, and the mysterious figure jerked his chin at his companions, took a jaunty step, and stopped abruptly. All the tables had been claimed by regulars who'd had the good sense to get here early.

All of which only seemed to make the newcomer louder.

"Bloody sort of port this is, with only one bar and not a single seat!" he boomed.

His voice was utterly lovely, commanding and loud and clear and just deep enough. If Vi had a voice like that, she would've done radio for a living like the outpost's local hero Palob Godalhi, whose smooth crooning could be heard from pretty much every corner of the outpost, day and night, if one listened hard enough. But here this new, suave smuggler was, howling about a backwater bar, surprised that no one would immediately bolt up and make room for his shenanigans. Pretty much all the locals were laughing at him now, grateful to have something new and interesting to watch.

"C'mon, Zade," one of his friends said, standing by a hightop. "This'll do. We've been sitting all day, anyway. Just bring the drink and stop fussing."

"Well, of course I'm going to fuss! After a long day of hauling, a man just wants a little elbow room. And possibly a corkscrew." With a sulky and resentful glance around the cantina, he clanked his bottle and glasses down, pulled the stopper out with his teeth, and poured.

"To chaos!" he shouted, glass held aloft. As far as Vi could see, every person in the cantina was watching him, whether outright or covertly. Many of them had dropped jaws, and some were whispering.

"Sure," one of his friends said, with far less enthusiasm and some amount of embarrassment. "Uh, chaos." They all clinked their glasses and drank, and the ringleader—Zade—was soon smacking his lips and pouring himself a second glass.

As his companions focused on their drinks and Zade stopped talking and started gulping, the cantina's chatter returned to normal.

"He's a fancy lad," Dotti said. "We don't get that kind here very often. He could be a holostar, couldn't he? Or a musician? I dated a musician once, when I was young." Her face became dreamy. "Nice lips on a musician."

"He's definitely interesting," Ylena said, head cocked as she considered the man. "There's something about him. He has a certain gleam."

That got Vi's attention. "A gleam?"

Ylena gave her a knowing smile and nodded.

As the night drew on, Vi watched the man and caught snatches of the tales he told. Rather than sticking to his own table, he made the rounds like a benevolent prince deigning to visit his underlings. He was loud and enthusiastic, though, and didn't seem cruel or bullying, which supported what Ylena had said. This Zade definitely didn't have the feel of a hero, but sometimes the Force knew best, and it always worked in mysterious ways.

Eventually, the stranger made it to their table, but instead of standing at the edge of it and greeting them, he leapt atop it, strode in a wobbling sort of way across the liquor-sticky wood, and slid into the space between Dotti and Da-zorai. "And who's this pretty young thing?" he murmured.

"Your next girlfriend, if you play it right," Dotti trilled, shimmying a little.

"He's a bit much," Dolin whispered. He was sitting between Dotti and Ylena and had blushed bright red as soon as Dotti began wiggling. Vi didn't blame him; Dotti could've been his grandmother, and Zade had her under his spell.

"I've never seen anyone with this kind of charisma," Vi whispered so only Ylena and Kriki could hear. "I imagine he could rob her blind and she'd thank him for it."

"I'm not a thief, my mysterious friend," he said, louder. "Although I could be. Got good ears, though. Good hands, too. Most of me, honestly, is pretty good."

Vi leaned over, feeling a bit caught out. "I didn't say you were a thief," she shot back. "Just that you could be one."

"And I might thank you, if you picked the right pocket," Dotti added.

"By the stars," Kriki said. "She's gone all twitterpated."

The man leaned in, one elbow on the table, and held up a drink— Dolin's drink, if Vi was right. "I do have that effect," he purred. "I'm Zade Kalliday, by the way. If you need something smuggled, I'm your man. Of course, you would need to steal it first. I'm more of a transport fellow, you know. Getting things from point A to point B with a bit of zigging and zagging in between. My ship's the *Midnight Blade,* and she can outrun anything you please." His smile twisted up a bit. "Usually. Having a spot of local trouble at the moment, but I would definitely give you a deal if you paid first."

"Do you have a long-range comm?" Vi asked, making sure not to look too anxious.

He gave an eye roll. "Naturally. It *is* a ship. Unfortunately, however, it's a bit, er, impounded just now. This Oga Garra is quite the character, isn't she?"

Vi sighed. Of course it couldn't be that easy, just traipsing onto a charismatic stranger's ship and making her calls outside of Oga's jurisdiction.

"Let me know when you've got her back in your clutches, and I'll gladly pay for a few moments of privacy with your comm," she told him.

He caught her eyes across the table, and even though she was exempt from twitterpation, she recognized the power of his appeal. His eyes were like falling down a waterfall.

"Oh, I'll let you know. And give you privacy."

The way he said it was like a caress, and Vi shook her head; he'd seen nothing but her eyes and hands, and he was still flirting with her. "Sell it somewhere else," she said, using the same intonation as Dolin's grandmother and making the farm boy snort. "I need a comm, but that's all."

After giving Vi a nod that suggested he thought she was lying, Zade kissed Dotti's hand and made her giggle. Without another word, he jumped back up onto the table, tiptoed around the empty glasses, hopped dramatically to the ground, toasted them, and tossed back his drink.

"Hey, that was mine!" Dolin shouted, but Zade had already disappeared into the crowd.

"I heard him talking to his friends earlier," Kriki told Vi as the Gatherers all enthused over their new friend. "He owes Oga tons of credits. Hasn't paid his docking fee in years, so he was supposed to do a job for her to get even, but he got boarded and lost the cargo, and now she's furious."

"Then how is he paying for drinks?" Vi asked.

Kriki shrugged. "That's not the sort of thing he'd talk about, I think. But I would definitely check your pockets. People who shout about not being thieves are often just telling you that they're actually thieves."

Vi doubted that even the most talented and charismatic thief could steal from her tightly zipped pockets with three bodies between them, but she checked anyway. Was it possible for someone to have what Ylena called a "gleam" and still be dishonest? Although she chatted with Kriki and Ylena and the rest all night, her eyes casually followed Zade around the bar. The man oozed charisma and goodwill. Everyone loved him. Even Rusko patted the guy on the back, for all that it made Zade snort blue liquor out his nose.

For once, Vi didn't leave early—she stayed as long as the other Gatherers. When Ylena got up, Dolin gallantly offered to walk her home, and Kriki asked to join them. Dolin almost managed not to look disappointed to have a tiny, furry chaperone with flawless hearing. But Vi just waved them off with a smile and kept her seat, a little away from Dotti and Roxi, who were both in their cups and slumped on the table.

The cantina was still active, full to the brim with smugglers and visitors who didn't have to wake at dawn or risk the fury of their employers. There was a difference in the noise level and energy of the place with the most responsible of the two-ale locals gone for the night. The music got harder, the shouts got louder, and a few fools even got dragged out the door by Rusko for fighting, as it was expressly forbidden by Oga's posted rules. At least no one got a limb ripped off, although N'arrghela certainly looked like she was waiting for the opportunity.

"They're bastards!"

Zade's voice rang out, and the clamor of the cantina quieted down a bit. "Trust me, mate: You don't want to join up wif 'em. The First Order, they call themselves? Ha! There's nothing orderly about them. They're thieves. Bullies. Monsters. Took my whole cargo for no reason. I had the proper codes, had my documentation, was flying in the normal space lanes. But they boarded me, saw the value of what was in my hold, and stole it." A space had cleared around him in the center of the cantina, and he spread his arms and twirled. "And here I am. Hopelessly stuck. Because of the First Order."

"That's just your opinion," someone said. "They pay good."

Zade rounded on the smuggler in question, a squat, bald man, and stuck a finger in his face. "Ha! They pay well as long as you have something they want and it's easier to pay you a few credits than just take what they want and kill you and do the requisite datawork. Did you see what happened to Hosnian? A whole system, gone, just like that." He snapped his fingers, and the room went silent, watching, riveted.

"You can't fight something that big," someone else said, and Zade slipped over to stand in front of her.

"Oh, like a lowly little spikeworm can't take down a fully grown ronto? I assure you: There's always a way to fight something big, especially when many small people band together. Or work separately with shared intent and lots of explosives."

Vi felt a lift in her heart, watching him work the crowd. He was right on every point, and the people were caught in his spell. The few times Vi had tried to recruit people here, they'd been resistant and grouchy, but when Zade spoke, their faces were open and friendly. Of course, Vi had been trying to sway the hearts of the locals, who were fiercely loyal to Black Spire Outpost and hoped to just ignore the conflicts of the rest of the galaxy in favor of balance back home. And Zade, it seemed, was leaning on the smugglers, like him, who knew full well what was happening out there and who had perhaps been victims of the First Order themselves. Still, watching Zade talk . . .

well, it definitely gave her ideas. For a moment, she almost considered that he might be with the Resistance himself.

"You shouldn't be saying things like that," old Nanz shouted over
the din. "There's an officer in town, and he brought his bucketheads,
and if you cause too much of a ruckus, you'll wake up missing your
pretty head!"

Zade grinned at her and patted his hair as if checking that his head
was still attached, but Vi noticed that he did wobble a little. The man
had to be soused, but he hid it well. And he was probably accustomed
to being pickled.

"Right you are, lass! It shouldn't be illegal to speak badly of one's
government, but then again, they're not quite a government, are
they? We had one, once. We had a Senate. It wasn't always fair and it
was a wee bit corrupt, but we had it. And then what happened?" He
held up his hands, miming an explosion, and Vi winced. "Kaboom!
And now the First Order thinks it can govern, just because it wants
to? Well, I didn't vote for it!"

"You can't vote! You're wanted in two systems!" one of the smugglers shouted, and the room broke out in raucous, drunken laughter.
In response, Zade grinned and bowed as if conceding the point.

"All I'm saying is: Don't trust 'em. Don't let that officer dig his vile
toes into your sand and set up shop. Don't let him think he can just
come here and rough up your people. Don't make him feel welcome.
Don't take his credits."

"I'll take anybody's credits!" another smuggler yelled.

"Then buy me a drink, my good woman, and let's discuss something a little less nauseating. Hutts, perhaps?"

"Hey!" a young Hutt shouted from his corner. "That's offensive!"

But Zade had already been enveloped by his fans, and he had a
drink in each hand, and he was toasting to the health of his fine new
friends. Vi stopped drinking but kept on watching quietly from the
shadows. When he finally staggered out of the cantina alone, she
slipped away and followed him.

Chapter Twenty-Three

ALTHOUGH HE'D LOOKED QUITE FUNCTIONAL IN the cantina when still surrounded by a sea of people equally inebriated, out in the alleys Zade was a complete mess. It was soon apparent that he was lost—or maybe, with his ship impounded, he simply had no place to go. He drunkenly lurched to a closed apartment door, pulled out a small datapad to hack the code, and cursed at the door when it refused to open. Vi was just about to go chat him up when she heard the familiar clatter of armor.

Two stormtroopers came around a corner, blasters in hand. Vi had heard that Kath had his soldiers doing late-night patrols, but she'd thus far easily avoided them. Now she melted back into the shadows, carefully drawing her scarf up to hide her face and tucking it under her goggles so it wouldn't come loose.

Zade wobbled to the right, his shoulder fetching up against a wall. He crossed one boot over the other, crossed his arms, and said, "Can't even enjoy a nice walk without tyranny clumping along to ruin a perfectly pleasant evening."

Vi silently smacked her forehead. No way was he a spy, much less Resistance, if he was saying something that suicidal.

The troopers, who had previously been marching past him, gave each other a look and turned as one, their grips tightening on their blasters.

"Is there a problem?" one asked, a woman.

"Yeah, there is. I don't like my corner of the galaxy getting all mucked up by murderers and dictators. You have no justerfiction— jurbaliction—" He paused and belched. "Jurisdiction here. Can't go around roughing people up."

The other stormtrooper stepped closer, letting his blaster press into Zade's belly, a feeling Vi knew all too well. "Yes, we can. Who's going to stop us? Your precious Republic? Bad news, space scum— it's gone. The First Order is here to bring order, which means that disintegrating someone like you is a public service."

Zade's eyebrow went up, and his mouth opened to say something both clever and outrageously stupid, probably the sort of thing that would get him shot. So Vi did a thing she definitely shouldn't have done: She checked to see that they were alone in the alley, pulled out her own blaster, and shot both of the stormtroopers in the narrow, unarmored space between their helmets and back plates. They both collapsed forward, forcing Zade to step sideways, wincing as if they were leaking on his expensive boots.

"Hello? My savior? Or possibly my wish come true?" Zade said, squinting toward where Vi hid. He stepped around the fallen troopers. "I'm not hallucinating, am I?"

Vi looked up and down the alley again before bolting out and tugging off the troopers' helmets to make sure they were both out of commission. Taking one of the helmets—and both of their blasters— she stood and asked, "You need a place to sleep?"

Zade looked her up and down. "Are you going to shoot me if I say no?"

"I'm not going to shoot you, but I will know you're lying. We should leave before someone notices these troopers are missing. Come on. We'll talk on the way. Until we get out of town, do me a favor and shut up."

"That's not how I like to—"

"I said shut up."

Vi handed him one of the blasters and jerked her chin toward the fastest way out of town. After disabling the tracker within, she slipped the helmet under her wrap and started jogging, carrying the other blaster in her other hand. What Zade did couldn't really be called jogging as he was mostly still drunk, but he followed her well enough in a lolloping sort of flailing stagger. Vi stuck to the shady parts of the thoroughfare, as Kriki had shown her, on alert for anyone to cause a ruckus about the troopers they'd left behind. But it was beyond late and all reasonable people were home and asleep. Luckily, the sort of people who were still awake were also the sort of people who didn't blink twice at random blasterfire and looted bodies.

She breathed a sigh of relief when they'd crossed under the archway and were headed out into the wilds. Beyond exhausted and pretty sick of carrying a heavy helmet, she couldn't wait to get to camp. When Zade stopped, she spun around and whispered, "What do you think you're doing?"

He held up a finger, swooped his scarf out of the way, vomited up at least a liter of alcohol, wiped off his mouth with the back of his hand, and said, "Getting rid of excess baggage. Feel better already. Do you have any water, wherever it is you're taking me? I'm assuming you didn't drag me all the way out here for some strange sort of ritual murder, but I'm not holding my breath."

She rolled her eyes. "If I wanted you dead, you'd already be dead."

"I got that idea by watching you commit murder, actually."

Vi looked toward the outpost, which was still dark and silent.

"Look, I heard you talking in the cantina. Sounded like you might be sympathetic to the Resistance."

"The Resistance." He said it like it was a very fancy sort of party to which he hadn't been invited. "I heard most of that got wiped out."

Vi shrugged and started walking again. He'd either follow now or he wouldn't, and either way it was out of her hands. When she heard his boots crunching along behind her, she smiled to herself.

"Most of the Resistance did get wiped out by the First Order, but that's the tricky thing about doing what's right and fighting the good fight: People just keep doing it no matter what."

He hummed a musical sigh. "And judging by the fact that you killed those troopers and claimed their bucket and haven't yet issued me a citation, I'm led to assume you're one of those people?"

"Well now, that depends." Vi looked back over her shoulder. "You never said if you were sympathetic or not. Plenty of people talk the talk, but it's harder to walk the walk."

"I hate walking."

She laughed. He was quick; she'd give him that. "We have ships for that."

"I suppose this Resistance of yours sounds fun," he finally said, "by which I mean it doesn't, and it might actually be a lot of work."

Vi shrugged. "Like most jobs, it has its ups and downs. One thing we could really use is help recruiting. Bringing in some locals, maybe catching the attention of folk just passing through. And you seem like a fellow who'd like to stick it to the First Order."

Zade was walking beside her, his step more certain now that he'd gotten rid of the liquor. He chuckled low, and Vi assumed it was the sort of sound that made most women swoon. It did not work on her.

"I would like to stick it to the First Order, but I know that guerrilla groups rarely pay well, and I like being paid. I especially like being paid so that I can get my ship back and not get stuck on mangy planets like this one."

Vi nodded; it was a start. "Money is tight, it's true. But we have the beginnings of a refuge nearby, plus food, water, and camaraderie with like-minded people. If we're successful here and you helped, General Organa would pay you. And since your job would mainly be to hang out in the cantina and win people over to our cause while drinking on our creds and living in our barracks, it's not like you'd be going out of your way as long as your ship is still grounded."

"And does the Resistance mind if its members gamble and smuggle to supplement their income until the princess ponies up? Because I'm not sure if you know this, but my ship—"

"Is impounded, and you owe Oga. You said so multiple times."

"I owe Oga, big time." He paused. "That's fun to say. Owe Oga. Owe Oga. Oh no, oh my, I owe Oga outrageously."

Vi burst out laughing. "Are you still drunk, or are you just this way?"

"Yes."

They walked in silence for a moment, and Vi wondered how close it was to dawn. Her adrenaline was still up from shooting the troopers, and she wasn't yet sure if she regretted that action. She could've tried to talk them out of killing Zade, or even pulled her tac baton and bonked them both hard enough to render them unconscious while she and Zade escaped. Killing them would only serve to make Kath angry. *Angrier.* And if anyone had seen it happen and could identify Vi as the killer . . .

Well, it was unlikely Kath could possibly want to capture her even more than he did now. It would be better if she stayed out of the outpost completely, or at least paid more attention to bringing her helmet along. It was fortunate that one angry lieutenant and whatever troops he'd brought could only search so many places on the planet at once.

As they approached the ruins, Zade tensed. That was good—he'd seemed a fool outside the cantina, but at least he was alert for danger.

"This is our camp," Vi told him. "The beginnings of our command center. The locals are scared of the ancient ruins, so we've cleaned them out and taken over. Just don't try to steal or drink from the cenote. It's full of poisonous anemones."

"That seems safe."

"It's safe for the people who know not to steal or drink from the cenote."

He stopped, his voice oddly soft as he said, "I never asked, but why did you save the bucket? Wretched thing."

Vi stopped, too, and held up the white helmet in both hands. "I'd like to say it's a souvenir, but I just know this sort of thing can come in handy. It has a comlink built in, for one thing. We lost a lot of our cargo on the way in—to Oga, so we have a common antagonist there—and now we're patching together what we have from what we can scavenge, win, or buy on the cheap. Now that I think about it, I wish I would've had you carry the other one."

His lips wrinkled up in disgust. "Nah. Probably would've yarked in it."

Which made Vi think about how Archex might react to it. "Yeah, you're not the only one who feels that way."

"What's your name, by the way? I'm sure you already know mine. Saw you watching me in the bar, just mistook one kind of interest for another."

It still felt strange to give her real name, but Vi felt it—Ylena was right about him.

"I'm Vi," she said. "Now come on. The crew'll be asleep, but we've got empty bunks."

Zade regained his old swagger, expecting a crowd as he followed her in. "Excellent. That's ever so much better than falling asleep under the table in the cantina and waking up with that Talpini fellow staring at me like a lurid gargoyle."

"He's creepy, isn't he?"

"Beyond."

They were under the lights now, which were dimmed for sleeping, and Vi held a finger to her lips. She wasn't sure if Zade could actually be silenced, but for the moment, at least, it worked. She showed him to an unclaimed niche in the wall, and without asking for padding or a blanket, he flopped into it, saluted her, and instantly began snoring with one long leg dangling to the ground.

"Welcome to the Resistance," she whispered.

She stashed the helmet among the cargo and fell into her own bunk, fully clothed, exhausted for the second night in a row and aching from skull to knees. What she needed was a day off, a medpac, and an audiodrama to listen to while she knitted. But what she was going to get, she knew, was another early morning and long day followed by a night of leadership.

"I don't know how Leia does it," she murmured to herself as she fell asleep.

That peace, of course, was not to last.

Vi startled upright when Archex barked, "Who are you?"

She was groggy and barely awake, and she had maybe thirty more minutes to sleep until Pook's morning alarm, but she scrambled to her feet to find Archex looming over Zade. The newcomer simply sprawled out of his niche in the rock, elbows out and booted feet crossed. Even when deeply hung over, he definitely had no shortage of moxie.

Zade opened his mouth, but Vi interrupted him before he said something regrettable. "This is Zade. He's our new recruit."

Archex looked Zade up and down, his arms crossed and his eyebrows drawn down. Dolin woke up and wandered over, too, his hair sticking up and his face creased from the pillow he'd brought from home.

"It's that guy from the cantina," Dolin said. "The loud one."

"That's me," Zade agreed. "The loud one. And you're the big one."

"I mean, that's fair. Welcome." Dolin went back to his bed, rolled over, and pulled up his blankets. It was a relief, Vi thought, to have someone easygoing and open and reasonable like Dolin around. Archex, on the other hand, was like a live wire, always on the alert, always waiting for the other shoe to drop, seeing danger around every corner. And why wouldn't he? He'd experienced enough trauma and betrayal in his life that it was a wonder he could function at all.

"Zade, this is Archex. I found Zade in the cantina last night, convincing pretty much everyone that the First Order is terrible. Archex is my second in command, and he's in charge of training, weapons, security, and chow."

Vi hadn't spoken Archex's jobs out loud before, and she hoped it would be the balm that helped him not immediately simmer with rage over Zade, who was almost exactly the opposite sort of person. Archex was moral, noble, hardworking, exacting, and hard on himself. Zade, on the other hand, appeared amoral, lackadaisical, disrespectful, and cocky—at least, that was what Vi had seen of him in just a few hours of his acquaintance. There was a chance the two men might get along, but . . .

Well, they were still in a staring contest, weren't they? The more amused Zade looked, the more annoyed Archex looked.

"Somebody blink so we can have breakfast," Vi said, rubbing her eyes. "I've got to get to work."

"Ah, work," Zade said, stretching luxuriously. "My least favorite word. I mean, it's not so bad when I'm zooming about on autopilot with a hold full of bounty, but something tells me no one on this planet knows how to get hard-earned sweat out of shimmersilk, you know? I mean, who would I even ask?" He brushed at a spot on his sleeve that he definitely had not cared about last night.

"Hmph. Shimmersilk. Who would even wear it in the first place?" Archex shook his head in disgust and left.

Zade transferred his mischievous grin to Vi. "He's a laugh riot, that one. I bet he really loves to let his hair down by brushing his teeth with his other hand and folding his socks a new way."

Vi sighed. "We each bring our own unique gifts to the Resistance. You can't do his job and he can't do yours. Don't get too far under his skin, though—he's had a rough year."

Zade sat up, his feet smacking on the floor. "I noticed the limp."

"The damage goes deep. You'll be here together for most of the day. Try not to antagonize him too much."

Scratching the stubble that had appeared overnight, Zade said, "You're asking for compassion at this hour? Woman, I can barely offer you sanity." When she gave him a hard look, he sighed. "Yes, fine. I'll try not to poke the gundark—but considering the hours of my work, I hope he understands that sleeping in until lunch isn't in-dolence. It's self-care."

Vi gave him a nod and headed to the bathroom, hoping that Zade would just sleep through the afternoon and the problem would can-cel itself out. Pook had finally uncovered the crate containing her clothes, and it was eye-rollingly wonderful, wearing a clean pair of pants. Once she was presentable, she found Archex at a makeshift table he'd instructed Pook to set up, one of their old transport's doors balanced over some empty cargo crates.

"What are you doing?" she asked him, as he appeared to be doing nothing, which was his least favorite thing to do.

"Dreaming of caf and trying to stop myself from shaking some sense into that space hobo you brought home."

Vi could sympathize with both desires but could only indulge one. "If you promise not to break him, I'll send Kriki into town after work today for caf and some more meat. After all, a leader can't lead without feed."

Archex looked at her strangely. "Who told you that?"

"I did, after my team leader ran out of food after Crait. The Resistance has had some lean days. At least you guys always had nutrient paste and amphetamine-drugged water."

He tipped his head in concession at that. "The officers' mess did have good caf, though. Speaking of which . . ." Archex motioned her close, and Vi grabbed some fruit from a box on the table and sat on a crate beside him while she munched. "Do you know the name and rank of the officer that's on Batuu? We haven't had a chance to discuss it, with all the new kids around, but I can help with strategy if I know more."

Vi leaned in, too. "Lieutenant Wulfgar Kath. Big guy. Biggest First Order guy I've seen, actually."

Archex leaned back, and his microexpressions went from surprise, to rage, to craftiness. "Yeah, I know him. We came up together. We were friends for a while when we were young and new, but his ambitions got a bit out of hand there, at the end. He always had his sights set on rising up as an officer. Took down a fellow trooper in a particularly dirty way to gain our instructor's approval once. One of the most precise and particular people I've ever met. Almost fussy." He sighed. "This is not good. Kath is the worst sort of enemy. Unrelenting. He's not in it for pride or altruism; he's in it for Kath, for power, for control. Utterly obsessive."

The meiloorun in Vi's mouth went tasteless, and she swallowed the lump and threw the rest of the fruit in the compost bin. "That's not what I wanted to hear. I was hoping for an idiot."

"Kath is far from an idiot. No one who rises to lieutenant in the FO is."

"Good morning!" Kriki sang, bustling into the room carrying a box that hid her face.

Vi and Archex gave each other a look that said *This conversation isn't over* and schooled their expressions to avoid spreading their disquiet to the cheerful Chadra-Fan. Kriki set the box down on the table and beamed at them.

"I gathered up all the comlinks I could find and built a private channel for us. It's totally shielded, untraceable, and only unlocks at the code phrase." Her giggle was high-pitched—and diabolical. "Can you guess what it is? The code word?"

"Snoke's butt?" Vi guessed. Archex rolled his eyes at her immaturity.

"Oh, now I kinda wish it was! But it's actually—" Kriki made a high-pitched, sneezy sound that was a little like *snee-klee-pfix*, then laughed again. "It's perfect, right?"

Vi tried to repeat the sound, and Kriki's nostrils fluttered as she grimaced. "Oh, no, that's nothing like it. You'll never be able to access the channel."

After Vi tried a few more times and Archex chimed in as well, both of them sounding like they were having allergy problems, Kriki finally shook her head, her ears drooping. "I didn't know Chadra-Fan was so impossible for other species to speak. Should we just go with 'Snoke's butt,' then?"

"Why not something easy, like *hippoglace*," Vi suggested.

Kriki shrugged. "If that's what you want, but I think it's a real missed opportunity for group bonding." She reached into the box and pulled out all the wrist comlinks Vi had taken off the corpses of Oga's minions. "I can get them reprogrammed tonight after work, and then we should be able to communicate no matter where we are on Batuu."

"Thanks, Kriki. I don't know what we'd do without you," Vi said.

The Chadra-Fan fluffed up her fur and purred. "Eee! I didn't know how much I needed to hear that today."

"You're doing a good job, too, Archex," Vi added, giving him an earnest look.

But he didn't purr—or even smile. "It'll mean more when it's actually true. Don't patronize me." He stood with a groan and walked out of the kitchen.

"What's his problem?" Kriki asked.

Vi shook her head and said, "Everything. And the lack of caf's not helping."

Chapter Twenty-Four

THAT EVENING, VI WAS ON HER way to Ronto Roasters in her Ubese mask to pick up dinner for the base. She knew it would be best for her to stay at home as long as Kath was looking for her, but she also knew that no one else in her crew had been trained on gathering intel, and she needed to see how the First Order was operating in the outpost. She was feeling refreshed, as it had rained hard that afternoon, causing the scrappers to take refuge in the hut during the downpour. She'd napped for two hours as the other women gossiped and spun with drop spindles and crocheted—and sipped from a flask old Dotti kept on her hip. Now everything sparkled with raindrops. She had a spring in her step and a sense of rightness in her gut.

Things were finally going well—or at least better. Thanks to Kriki's short sleep cycle and genius way with tech, the caves were beginning to feel like an actual headquarters, and at this very moment the Chadra-Fan would be setting up their network of comms so they would finally be able to communicate from all over the outpost, a task far more valuable than fetching supper. Dolin had gone out to hunt truffles with Waba, which would bring in a little more cash and pacify the frachetty beast, who'd taken to wailing all day long while his master was gone, driving Archex to surliness and Pook to new depths of melancholy.

Vi was keeping to the shadows, enjoying one of Palob Godalhi's news breaks playing from a nearby radio, when she heard raised voices.

It was stormtroopers, their blasters pointed at a couple of old women weaving baskets and selling fruit and vegetables from their cart, altogether too close to the cantina for Vi's comfort. She quickly hid behind a column to watch. The Ubese mask amplified the sound of her own breathing and sweat dripped down the back of her neck. All around the market, vendors watched cautiously from their storefronts and shoppers hurried to safety.

"There was a murder last night," one of the troopers said. "Right here by the cantina. Two of our own were killed. Executed. What do you know about it?"

Vi knew these women—she had helped them pick up their spilled baskets once on a windy day, and she remembered that the one in the wide woven hat was named Jenda and her sister with the freckles was Oh-li. Jenda just shook her head sadly like it was a shame, and the trooper pulled his blaster and pointed it at her.

"We know nothing, nothing!" Oh-li cried, standing, her withered hands up and jingling with cheap wire bracelets and her toothless lips trembling. "We go to sleep early!"

The other trooper aimed his blaster at her, and she sat back down, her long dress billowing around her. It was a cruel display of the First Order's bullying, two armored soldiers aiming their weapons at frail and powerless old women, and it made Vi's blood boil.

"Do you know Vi Moradi?" the first trooper asked.

"Who?" Jenda asked.

"The Resistance spy."

Oh-li shook her head. "We don't sell pies."

The trooper's boot shot out, crushing the complex basket the woman had been weaving. The entire market seemed to go quiet at that crunch of straw and reed.

"There is a new woman in this town," the trooper barked, loud enough for all to hear. "She is a Resistance spy. She has dark-brown skin and may call herself Vi Moradi, Amaka Kottu, Evette Harlo, or Starling. She is an enemy of the First Order, and there is a large reward on her head. Now I'll ask you again." He pointed his blaster directly between Jenda's eyes.

"Do you know this woman?"

Jenda's lips quivered, and her eyes darted to her sister, who shook her head just the tiniest bit. Vi was overcome with gratitude for these brave women willing to stand up to troopers for her—or maybe for the Resistance. Was it because she'd helped them that day with a cheerful heart when no one else would? Because she'd stopped another time to offer them some water and compliment their basketry? Was it because she'd tried to fit in, unlike the space racers and smugglers who came, spent their coin, and left? She hadn't been here long, so it's not like she was one of them. Yet. Even if she felt like it, sometimes.

"I'm going to ask you one more time where I can find the Resistance spy. We know she's here."

"I'm just an old woman—"

The trooper whipped his blaster across Jenda's face. Blood spurted from her nose, and she doubled over, rocking and crying as her hat rolled away down the street. Oh-li put an arm around her and murmured to her, bracelets jingling. All around the market, people stared, but no one spoke up or stepped forward. They'd melted back into the shadows, behind columns, under awnings. No one did anything to help. No one picked up the hat or offered Jenda a rag. Some of them looked like they wanted to, rage burning in their eyes. And yet something held them back.

One more strike like that, and he'd kill the old woman.

"Tell me what I want to know or I'll have to ask your friend here," the trooper said. He drew back his blaster and let it hang in the air, on the cusp of striking Oh-li, and it felt as if the entire world went silent, waiting. Oh-li turned her face away, rheumy eyes squeezed shut.

Just as in that moment in the alley with Zade, Vi's will coalesced. What she was about to do? It wasn't the smart choice, and everything in her training told her to run away and hide, but Vi hadn't joined the

Resistance because she was the kind of person who could watch old women get beaten to death by bullies in the street. Unwilling visions of her father in the marketplace, of the executions, of white armor *just like this,* blasters *just like this*—there was no way she could walk away, even if it's what Leia would've ordered her to do.

She settled her Ubese mask more firmly, slipped on her black gloves, and wrapped her shawl up over her head before jogging over to the scene, shouting, "No! Please don't hurt them! They are innocent!"

As she got close, she made sure to trip on the women's baskets, sending them and the meilooruns and tubers inside scattering, directly into the stormtroopers' legs. They looked down, trying to sort out this new bumbling idiot, and Vi motioned for Jenda and Oh-li to hurry away. Jenda held her shawl to her streaming nose, and her eyes were flowing with tears, but she gave Vi a nod of thanks as Oh-li wrapped an arm around her and the sisters hobbled into the shadows and scurried into their apartment. Vi stayed there, using her body to mask the sisters' retreat, but the stormtroopers were quickly onto her scheme.

"Another troublemaker," the second stormtrooper said with a clipped accent. "This planet is full of scum."

Now the blaster was pointed at Vi's chest, and she was grateful for the jacket under her green wrap, which featured cleverly hidden pieces of plate armor. She trembled like a normal person would and held her gloved hands in the air.

"Please. They were innocent. So am I. No one here knows this spy," she said, her voice flat and strange through the mask.

Crack!

The swing was so fast that she didn't even see the blaster until it was bouncing off her helmet. Her skull rocked back, and everything went fuzzy and slow as stars exploded in her vision. This mask, uh. It wasn't padded. It wasn't meant to—

Crack!

"Remember anything yet?"

Her vision was flashing; the mask was damaged. When she drew in a breath, it felt like there was no oxygen left. She was starting to panic. Was the voice modulator broken? If she spoke, would he hear her true voice? Was the filter gone, too? Would she asphyxiate?

She couldn't speak, then. She couldn't call anyone, even if she'd had the comlinks Kriki was working on. The locals weren't going to step in—if they wouldn't stand up for two old women who'd lived out their entire lives in BSO, they wouldn't help the very person whose presence had drawn the enemy in the first place.

That meant Vi could either run or fight. With her vision limited, both options were risky. She'd have to play it by ear.

Vi wobbled and dropped to her hands and knees among the rolling baskets and bruised fruit. One stormtrooper had his blaster trained on her; the other held his weapon up to land the next strike. She couldn't see his face, but she would've bet that he was smiling, that he enjoyed the fact that his job let him punish rebellious trash in the street. She knelt and then began to stand, swiftly whipping out her own blaster and using it to strike the weapon pointed at her head out of the trooper's hands to skitter across the street. Before the other stormtrooper could react, she shot him in the black bodysuit revealed in the rift between the armor over his thigh and his torso.

But she wasn't fast enough, or maybe she was just a little bit concussed, as the other stormtrooper snatched his friend's blaster and smacked her mask so hard that it halfway flew off. He must've had orders not to shoot anyone who might be the wanted spy. Now she couldn't see at all. Her next shots went wide, ricocheting off the buildings and making the crowd gasp and rustle as it took cover. She heard the stormtrooper she'd shot fall to the ground, making animal groans and whimpers, but the one she hadn't managed to shoot knocked her blaster out of her hands and laid her out on her back with a forceful kick from one big boot.

"Let's see who's hiding under here," he said in that clipped accent.

The boot pressed into her solar plexus, making it impossible to breathe, and he reached down, grabbed her mask, and tossed it away.

The impersonal white-and-black helmet looked down on her, framed by the blinding suns.

"Well, if it isn't Vi Moradi," he said.

Chapter Twenty-Five

AS VI MARCHED THROUGH THE FOREST in binders, blindfolded, all she could think was, *At least that's one more stormtrooper dead.* In her years as a spy, she'd learned that in the moments when it felt like she couldn't go on, when she was moving step by step toward the bad thing and not yet away from it, it helped to think positively.

Sure, she could think about how she'd been captured by the First Order.

She could think about how none of her friends or fellow Resistance members knew that she'd been taken. How Leia didn't even know the FO had traced her to Batuu.

She could think about how there was no way to track her, and how she couldn't even find her way back to the Outpost if she managed to escape since the buckethead who had captured her had cleverly blindfolded her.

Or she could think about how she'd killed five troopers so far and if things went her way, she'd kill this one, too. And the rest of them.

And Kath.

And she'd find a way to do so without calling down the First Order's wrath on all of Batuu.

Her chance to do some damage would come soon, as that was

surely where she was being taken: directly to their camp. She would then have invaluable information . . . and no way to relay it to the Resistance. If she died out here, whatever she learned died with her, leaving Archex and her recruits all alone in hostile territory with no way to get in touch with Leia. At least Vi knew she wouldn't give up the location of her own headquarters or the Resistance fleet. She would die first. But her people—they would have no chance without her. Archex hadn't even begun to teach them how to handle a blaster yet. If Kath and his soldiers found the ruins, every single person there would die.

Vi knew they were getting close when she heard noises other than gentle birdsong and their own footsteps on the soft forest floor. Generators, armor clacking, machinery whirring. The First Order had their own mobile command center out here, and she couldn't wait to see it. The trooper's arm landed roughly across her chest, and she stopped.

"Well, well, well. What have we here?" a deep and familiar man's voice said.

"A bunch of brainwashed orphan kids in silly armor and their sadistic, sycophantic leader, who's probably wearing starched breeches as black as his heart," Vi answered.

A pleased chuckle. "Oh, this is going to be fun. Bring her into the transport. It's not outfitted with an interrogation chair, but I'm sure I can whip something up."

A blaster prodded her in the back, and Vi stumbled forward.

"Hello again, Wulfguts."

"Ugh. So childish. My name is Lieutenant Wulfgar Kath, and you may address me as Lieutenant. Or sir. I've been very anxious to find you after our meeting in that cave."

"I had hoped you would die there," Vi observed as she stumbled forward, unable to see, occasionally prodded or directed with the blaster's muzzle as Kath walked beside her, smelling of expensive cologne dominated by scents of leather and rotok wood.

"I'm so sorry to disappoint," he said lightly. "You've given us quite the chase through this rancid backwater pit. But I knew we'd eventually flush you out." She could imagine his sneer, just then, and she longed to wipe it off his face. "Let's hope we can get what we need today, and then we can raze this planet to the ground, like its dishonest inhabitants deserve. All this fresh air. I swear I've had indigestion for days."

Vi sighed loudly. "Great story. Can we get on with the torturing so I can go home?"

Kath's laugh was a gruff bark, and Vi's stomach went sour. She'd met enough bad guys by now to know what she was dealing with. Some villains, like Oga, were no-nonsense, and if you just did as they asked and stayed out of their way, they could be benevolent, or at least ignore you. They technically weren't even villains unless you got on their bad side. Some villains, like Archex had been as Captain Cardinal, were conflicted, and Vi could carefully twist the key inside them until something clicked open. Some villains were just straight-up evil—like anyone with the last name Hux.

But Kath—he seemed like the kind of villain who rode that fine line between reality and madness and hid it carefully under crisp pleats and hair product. She could almost picture him, neat as a pin, perfect posture, quite proper, all those obsessively built muscles contained in a starched black suit—until the beast underneath peeked out from a crack in amusement. Or rage. She would have to be very careful. If she pushed him too hard, he wouldn't stop hitting her until she was pulp—even if he had direct orders to keep her alive.

This kind of villain was a monster, tightly bound and barely leashed, even if he thought himself a gentleman.

"Ah, here we are. Sit her down, please."

The stormtrooper's gloved hands caught her shoulders, spun her around, and forced her down to sitting. From the feel of the cold metal, it was the usual sort of jump seat found on just about every transport in the galaxy. At least it wasn't another interrogation chair. When the harness seat belt clicked down over her head and was pulled too tight against her chest, she had to remember her training and focus on her breathing to avoid panicking. No matter how hard they pressed, she told herself, there was always enough space for one more breath.

Finally he whipped off her blindfold.

Kath was exactly as she remembered him—almost. In the cave, he'd been a shadow, a rough red shape in her night-vision goggles. In person, he was substantial—and scary. She'd never seen a First Order officer as big as him, and she'd assumed they had nutritional protocols and enforced calisthenics and brainwashing in place to make sure these guys could always fit in their armor or regulation black uniform. But Kath was built like a bear, tall, with a broad chest and muscular arms. His auburn beard was just as perfectly trimmed as she'd imagined, though, his hair neatly combed and gelled into submission, and his sideburns sharp.

A man this fastidious was bound to be unhinged, and it shone out of his eyes like black oil leaking from a brand-new landspeeder.

"I bet the First Order tailors hate you," Vi deadpanned.

His mouth twisted up in disgust. "What, do you think they're humans with feelings? That's why we have machines. They don't complain." He tapped a finger to his chin as if thinking and turned his back to her.

She took that moment to glance around the transport. It was a new sort of mobile habitat, bigger than anything she'd seen before and kitted out to carry several dozen troops, along with racks for their blasters, rifles, and axes. A lift suggested it had multiple levels, which meant it was probably fully stocked for extended occupation. The cockpit was sectioned off so she couldn't see it, but she could see the door, and she knew she could get it open—

The world exploded as Kath's fist rammed into her cheek, a solid left hook.

Vi's head bounced sideways, her vision going blurry. Two head shots in one day, less than a week after a bad concussion. That was not . . . not good.

"I think I like the interrogation chair better," she said with a slight slur. "But they didn't give you one of those, huh? Just this flying junk heap. You must be in trouble. Or not very important."

Kath's eyebrows drew down in anger right before he punched her again.

Vi went unconscious before she could consider how to insult him next.

Water splashed over her head, and Vi spluttered awake. Kath stood before her looking serious and inquisitive. For a big man, he'd shown flawless self-control. Neither hit had broken a bone or busted her skin, and she didn't think she'd been out for very long. He could keep doing this all day, and to some extent she could keep taking it. Even through the ringing in her ears, Vi was still taking note of every detail. He had a weak spot around his ego—he must've been in serious trouble with his higher-ups.

This mission—collecting a Resistance spy—was somehow personal.

As much as she wanted to keep metaphorically poking that rotten tooth, she had to space out these hits or she was going to go unconscious again, which meant it was in her best interest to avoid making him too mad just yet. She let her head hang, breathing heavily. It was an act, but not by much. He was welcome to take the lead, if he wished.

"Ready to let me speak?" he asked, right on cue.

She bobbed her head the minimum amount.

"Good. Now. Here is what I need to know, and you should be aware that I'm willing to push you to the very brink of human suffering to get this information. I require the locations of three things: your Resistance headquarters here on Batuu, Leia Organa with the remaining Resistance fleet, and the girl Rey. Would you care to make this an easy afternoon for us both and tell me any of the above so we can forgo spending any more time together than we must?"

Vi raised her head and looked up at him, blinking innocently. "Who's Rey?"

Kath sighed heavily and his fingers twitched like he wanted to hit her again but knew that his big, meaty fists were simply too damaging. Instead, he turned to a crisp black satchel sitting on another seat and withdrew a slender leather cylinder from its depths. He showed it to her and unrolled it over his hand, revealing a variety of unpleasant metal instruments that reminded Vi of things she'd found in Savi's junkyard, but cleaner.

Vi's face remained a mask, but inside she was screaming. At least in Cardinal's interrogation chair, she had felt a sliver of hope, had sensed that even in the dark, hidden belly of a Star Destroyer, she might find a way out. Back then, strapped down, she'd known he would have to leave her to return to his duties, or he'd make a mistake, or, as eventually happened, she'd manage to turn him and convince him to let her go.

But with Kath, she had no such hope. She could see no way out. This man could not be turned; he was a monster glad to live among other monsters. His commitment to exactitude would leave no room for error that would allow her to escape, and even if he left for a time, there were many more troopers between her and freedom—she still didn't know how many or how they might be dispersed. There were just so many variables.

Even worse, no one knew where she was. Her own people had no idea she was even in trouble. Her only option right now was every prisoner's sole option while under interrogation: to last as long as possible and hope that something better would happen down the road.

"Let's not waste time lying to each other. I know who you are, Starling. I know that you're the one who turned our upstanding Captain Cardinal into a childish idiot who deserved what he got. I remember when you pushed him past me on the hovergurney in the *Absolution*, and I noticed that your armor was an imperfect fit, but I didn't stop you."

Ah. So that was it. It *was* personal. Vi fought the urge to smile.

Kath withdrew one of the slender silver tools and leaned close, inserting the sharp, hooked point of it into the tender pink corner of her eye, letting the edge of it barely caress her eyeball.

Vi didn't dare move.

"I was reprimanded for that, when they watched the recordings," he said softly, almost regretfully. "I should've stopped you, they said.

I missed an aberration in the system. I was chastened by that rebuke and have only grown more punctilious. I never liked Cardinal, although I was happy to use him, and I wasn't surprised by his defection and stupidity. But I deeply resent that stain against my record. From you."

He tugged the instrument down, and Vi's entire world centered on that tiny, hot pinprick lodged in that tender, wet tissue.

Med droids could do many things, but fixing busted eyeballs wasn't one of them.

"I'd like to make you pay for that," he continued, "but I need information. So: You tell me where Leia and the Resistance fleet are hiding, and I'll remove this instrument before I tear your flesh."

Struggling to keep her breath steady, Vi murmured, "I'm just a minion. Do you know where Kylo Ren is right this moment? Which ship, which world? Probably not. So I don't know where Leia is, either."

Kath considered that a moment, turning his instrument a little this way and that and causing Vi's flesh to twitch and shiver with horror.

"That might be true. But I know you have a good idea where Leia Organa was *recently*." He sank the tip of the instrument deep into that fragile place between eye and skin with the reckless curiosity of a child reaching into a bag for sweets, and Vi fought to hold very, very still as tears and a thin trickle of blood wept down the edge of her nose.

"I haven't talked to Leia in weeks. I don't have a long-range comm. If you don't believe me, ask anyone in town and they'll tell you I've been trying to buy one. How could I know where she is now? Leaders don't tell their spies their important plans. They send us out with little chunks, with just the info we need to do our jobs. You have to know that."

He exhaled sadly and withdrew the instrument, and Vi looked down and blinked rapidly, unable to stop the bloody tears hurrying from the corner of her eye where he'd prodded her.

"And your headquarters here on Batuu?"

"I don't have a headquarters."

Vi's face flew sideways as he slapped her. This time, she tasted blood.

"I don't understand why you would lie. I *know* you have a facility here. Batuu is just the sort of gritty, useless planet that you rebels like to dig into like worms. Why else would you be here?"

"I needed to fuel up, took friendly fire, and crashed," she said weakly. "You can ask in town about that, too. I had no choice but to stay. My ship is a wreck, and I'm out of creds. Black Spire Outpost is a crossroads, anyway, isn't it? I'd be happy to leave. Just let me pack my bag."

He smiled, but there was nothing kind in the gesture. "Oh, you're not leaving this rock alive unless it's in my custody, Starling. And even if you die before I can get the info, rest assured I will find your people and destroy them."

Vi coughed, and blood dripped from her lips onto the dull gray metal between her feet. She'd spat blood onto Cardinal's shiny red boots once, but she suspected that spitting on the well-polished black boots of Lieutenant Wulfgar Kath would enrage him to the point of a total loss of control. She had to be far more careful here. This wasn't a give-and-take; it was a give and give and give and try not to infuriate. At least what she'd told him so far was true: She didn't know where Rey and Leia were exactly, and she didn't have a headquarters yet, technically. It didn't matter how much he tortured her and beat her, she would never have the intel he craved.

On the other hand, there were bonuses to a fool who'd gone over from man to animal, to letting the old lizard brain drive the speeder. It would definitely hurt, but if she could get him to hit her one more time . . .

She decided to change her strategy.

"I bet if you bring me back alive, they'll give you a promotion," she said, grinning up at him through bloodied teeth. "Bring me home like a big ol' shaak steak for Hux to sink his pointy little weasel teeth into. Bet he's got all sorts of fun torture toys. And that rascal Kylo Ren could probe my brain easy as a comb gliding through your greased-up beard. But you want to do it yourself, don't you? I bet you can't wait to blast off and let everybody on the FO channels know that you got a Resistance spy to spill all her secrets." She playacted a childish pout. "If you kill me, they probably won't throw you a parade."

Kath rolled his eyes and paced around to her other side. He made her feel like an animal in a zoo, and even if she couldn't reverse their positions, she at least wanted him to stop thinking and start feeling. If she could just get his amygdala to kick in, she'd have a better chance of changing her situation.

"So either you bring me in and get promoted . . . or you lose me and get . . . what's demotion like in the First Order? Do they just throw you out of an air lock or do they stop to behead you first? I bet they make you take off that jaunty hat before they turn on the vibro-ax." She smirked. "I bet it just kills you, knowing that I walked right past you in your own ship. I'm gonna walk right past you again, Wulfguts. Right out of here."

"You know, I've never personally spoken with someone from the Resistance," Kath said conversationally, his hands clasped behind his back as he considered her. "I've always wondered what made anyone sign up for a suicide mission like that. You can't fight the First Order, which is immediately obvious to anyone with eyes or a protocol droid who can run the odds. But now I begin to see." He leaned forward, and his eyes were as flat and dead as a swamp snake's. "You have this foolish hope, this childish instinct to rebel. To act out. And that's exactly what we're trying to crush all around the galaxy. You think you're special and clever, but you're just overly confident idiots willing to die for the most useless of reasons. Like kith-lemmings, falling off the cliff. But we are the cliff, you see. And we'll always be here. No matter how many of you die, we remain. Eventually, as places like Batuu realize that it's not worth fighting and your ranks diminish, there will be none of you left."

"Better a life of foolish hope than one of committed oppression," Vi said, unable to remain silent in the face of such an arrogant statement. "There will always be people willing to stand up to bullies like you."

Kath pulled back again and gazed toward the hatch. "Yes, well, the people of Batuu don't seem to share your point of view. They welcome us, take our coin, wish us bright suns and rising moons. Those that don't love us fear us. And those that fear us will know that *you're* the reason we're here. I can turn them against you. You may have gotten here before us, but you clearly didn't win their hearts completely."

"Yes, well, at least I don't go around beating up old women. Or sending my underlings to beat up old women while I sit around the transport licking my wounds because I'm on Daddy Hux's Naughty List."

Crack.

There it was, the punch she'd been fishing for.

Vi's head jerked sideways, and it was an odd feeling of relief mixed with pretty much everything terrible in the world. Her skull felt like a sack of puffballs, and she didn't even try to hold it up, just let it snap to the side and fall forward. She went totally limp against the restraints, and when Kath tried to rouse her, even going so far as to yank her face up by her hair, she gave no resistance and let her eyes roll back in her head.

"Blast," Kath growled. His boots stomped across the transport, and he rapped on the metal door. "Open up." Vi watched through her eyelashes and the veil of her bangs as the door to the cockpit slid open. A stormtrooper sat in the pilot's seat and turned to face Kath.

"General Hux requests an update, sir," the trooper told him. "He said you weren't responding to your personal comlink."

Kath glanced back at Vi, who was glad that her wig was pinned on tightly and helped hide her eyes. "She's weaker than she looks. Watch her while I return his comm."

The trooper stood and walked back to stand near Vi, arms crossed. Kath sat down in the pilot's chair and sighed heavily as he settled his hat and fixed his lapels. When he pulled out a small personal comlink from an inside pocket of his jacket, Vi's entire body went on alert.

If she could just get her hands on it . . .

"Lieutenant Wulfgar Kath for General Hux," Kath said crisply.

The answer was almost immediate.

"Hux here."

Vi had never encountered General Armitage Hux personally, for all that she knew about his father, Brendol Hux, and the fact that Armitage himself had conspired with Phasma to bring about the senior Hux's death. Armitage sounded like someone who didn't know how to smile and who would probably wear ironed swim trunks to the beach and drink only very dry red wine while he complained about how the ocean breezes destroyed his carefully gelled hair. The comlink most likely included a visual, but from where she was strapped in, head hanging low, Vi couldn't see it.

"Sir, I was told you wanted an update."

Hux's annoyed sigh was even more melodramatic than Kath's had been. "Yes, obviously I want an update. And?"

Kath glanced back to Vi, almost nervous, and licked his lips. "We're very close to having the Resistance spy in hand."

"Very close? You don't have her yet? It shouldn't be difficult. Batuu is a simple place."

"Yes, sir," Kath agreed. "Except it's also a vast, overgrown, and largely uninhabited world. Dense, extensive forests, complex and impenetrable cave structures. The spy could be hiding anywhere."

Hux sniffed. "Perhaps I have entrusted this duty to the wrong man."

Kath's meaty hand curled into a red fist against the tight leg of his breeches. "Absolutely not, sir. Believe me: I will capture the spy and deliver the information you've requested. I will not return until we know the location of the Resistance fleet and the girl, Rey."

Hux let the silence draw out for an appropriately chilly amount of time before saying, "No, you will not. Wulfgar, I do not need to impress upon you the importance of your mission. Not just to the First Order, but to your own future. As an officer, and as a breathing organism. Find the Batuuan Resistance headquarters and the spy hiding there, and all is forgiven. Fail, and . . . well, your troopers will have their orders. Hux out."

The channel went silent, and Kath stood. His upright bearing didn't change, but Vi could sense him panicking, imagine his eyes twitching back and forth and his heavy jaw working as he considered his next move. He couldn't hurt her too much, definitely couldn't kill her, but he needed the intel he thought she possessed at all costs—and he wanted to get it personally. Her chances of escape had plummeted with every word of that last speech from his superior officer.

Kath walked to stand beside the stormtrooper guarding Vi and considered his prisoner. "Still unconscious. Pathetic. Let's make her suffer a little. Put her facedown on the floor. Bind her wrists tightly behind her back and bind her legs at the ankles. Put something heavy on top of her. Allow no food, no water. I want her to feel what it is to be crushed and helpless," Kath said. "I want her to lose all hope. I want us to be the only promise of succor."

Vi forced herself to go limp as the trooper unbuckled her harness and dragged her roughly to a dark corner near the restroom, where he dropped her on her chest. She didn't move, didn't so much as whimper as he reached underneath her, unbound her arms, wrenched them behind her, and re-bound them tightly enough to make her shoulders burn. The real panic set in when he bound her legs and then placed something on her back—a full case of rations, if she had to guess. It was heavy enough to make him grunt, and it took everything she had not to groan as the weight settled down fully.

Her entire world focused on the points where her body was pressed between cold metal and heavy cargo. Her cheekbone, crushed against the floor. Her shoulders, on fire and pulled ever higher as the weight pushed down on her wrists. Her ribs, their points bruising her flesh, making her skin feel like the thinnest tissue. And her legs, bound together, giving her no room to adjust, no room to turn. Her lungs, burning with every scant breath. She did indeed feel crushed, but she never felt helpless.

It was part of her training, and it was just part of who she was. No matter how little space she was given, she could find a way to dwell there. As long as she had time, there was always a way out.

She just had to find it.

Chapter Twenty-Six

ARCHEX WAS CONTEMPLATING THROWING A SPANNER at Pook's back just for fun when he heard a gentle but insistent beeping.

"What's that?" he asked.

"Ask Kriki," Pook said, sounding bored as he installed more cables and stapled them to the ceiling. "Her ways are nonsensical. And perky. It's disturbing."

Kriki's head appeared in the door as if on cue. "Is that the perimeter alarm?"

"How should we know? You install things while we're asleep and then forget to tell us about them." But there was no real annoyance or cruelty in his words; Archex liked Kriki and admired her work—and her work ethic. She was a genius with tech, and with cobbling together the ancient and damaged goods the Resistance had given them. Thanks to her energetic tinkering all night, they now had electricity and dimmable lights in all the caves, plus a working kitchen. It was really starting to feel like a home, if living in dark caves could be considered homey. Even the power droids seemed friendlier.

Kriki scurried in and pointed at a dusty old screen, where a red dot was blinking. "This means someone has entered the cenote courtyard. So one of us with a weapon should go make sure they're friendly. Probably not me, though. Someone bigger. And meaner."

"You're getting better with your blaster," Archex insisted.

Kriki looked down, her nose wiggling. "Better, but not good."

"I can do it."

They both looked to a pile of canvas on the floor and were surprised to see it rustling. Zade popped up, his hair disheveled and his jaw covered in stubble. "Even hung over, I'm probably the best shot here." He stood, flicked some cobwebs and rock dust off his shimmersilk blazer, and swaggered out into the hallway.

Archex sighed. "Well, that takes care of that, then. Worst-case scenario, they shoot each other."

"But we need him!" Kriki argued.

Archex held up a hand and wobbled it. "Do we, though?"

"Yes! He's going to be a great recruiter. He just needs time. And he *is* a better shot. My aim is bad, and that's just with trees and rocks. I don't know what I'd do if I had to face off with a real stormtrooper. Probably just shriek and flail."

"Well, you can't blame yourself. When you haven't been involved in violence, you don't know how you're going to react. Fight, flight, and freeze are the three main responses, and if you're scared to fight, flight and freeze aren't that comforting. I used to train soldiers, and freeze is more common than you'd guess. These days, it might be my response, too." It hurt, every time Archex had to admit that he couldn't do something he was accustomed to doing. The painkillers helped, but nothing Kalonia or Pook could do could fix the mess Phasma's poison had made, rotting his lung and leg and spreading out into his bloodstream. "I know Vi and Ylena say Zade is a good guy, and you and Dolin like him, but . . . you've got to understand: The past ten years of my life were all about being stuck with people who had a bad attitude and poor work ethic and training them into being effective soldiers. But unlike them, I can't bend Zade to my will. He's like a wound that won't heal to me. An annoying one."

That was the most he'd told anyone other than Vi about his past, but he liked Kriki and wanted her to know that there was no shame in the way she felt, in her fear around violence. Maybe one day he would tell everyone about where he'd come from . . . and maybe not. He didn't want them to look at him like he was a monster.

"Yes, well, life is full of wounds that never heal, isn't it?" Kriki watched the screen, where another red light was moving swiftly toward the original one. "You know, I can get us each a tracker, just a little button you could pin on your clothing, and then the perimeter alarm would recognize our people." She grinned and nodded vigorously. "Yes. Yes! And then Waba wouldn't set it off, and—oh."

"What?"

"The dots are moving very quickly toward us, so either Zade is running away from a Batuuan braga bear or there's trouble."

Zade appeared in the doorway. His face was no longer a cool, charismatic mask. He looked terrified, his eyes wide and his breathing labored from more than the jog.

"It's trouble. Ylena just arrived. There was an altercation in the market—with stormtroopers. The First Order took Vi."

Chapter Twenty-Seven

AFTER ONLY A FEW MOMENTS CRUSHED between the heavy crate and the floor, Vi wished she were actually unconscious. Every breath, every minuscule movement was a fight. Playing at being unresponsive was nearly impossible. She couldn't writhe, couldn't wimper, couldn't even blow the bangs of her wig out of her eyes without alerting the trooper guarding her to the fact that she was, in fact, observing everything she could about the transport and the people in it.

From what she could learn in her lucid moments, Kath kept three troopers at the transport while the rest were sent out to hunt for the Resistance base, monitor and recruit in the outpost, or scan the wilderness for resources. The First Order tended to favor planets that already had factories and industries in place so they could merely take over the mines or refineries rather than go to the trouble of building mines and refineries of their own. That's how smaller planets like Batuu flew under their scanners: They were simply more work than they were worth.

But at the same time, even a primitive planet might offer easy pickings that the First Order could exploit. They were always on the lookout for certain ores and fuel sources, and Vi learned that Kylo Ren would look favorably on any scouting party that returned with Jedi or Sith artifacts when she heard Kath use his comlink to order his men to visit Dok-Ondar's Den of Antiquities and demand access to Dok's special collection—at blasterpoint, if necessary.

She made a mental note to talk to Ylena about warning Savi to hide his own Force-related artifacts for the day Kath or his troopers stopped by the scavenger's workshop.

Well, she would talk to Ylena about that if she ever saw Ylena again.

Which she would. She would get out of this situation.

Because even if Leia had sent her here to build a refuge for the Resistance, she was also carving out a haven for the people on Batuu who needed it, people like Kriki and Dolin. As much as she needed them, they needed her, too. She had to protect women like Jenda and Oh-li, keep the market safe for people just living their lives. That frail old woman had taken a blaster to the face for her, and Vi was determined to live long enough to repay that kindness. She'd made this mess, and she would fix it.

"Enough of waiting," Kath said. "She's never going to wake up, at this rate."

When Vi opened her eyes and squinted through her bangs, she saw the polished tips of his boots, mere centimeters away from her face. She tensed, waiting for a kick.

"Get this box off her and put her back in the chair."

Vi couldn't stop her sigh of relief as the weight of the cargo crate finally left her back. Gloved hands roughly grabbed under her arms and jerked her upright. She went instantly dizzy as the blood drained from her head. Her vision went red, and when she exhaled, she could feel every bruise down her front, the pain concentrating on the bones that had pressed against the metal floor, her ribs and hips and knees.

"Ah, good. You're awake," Kath said.

The trooper slammed her back in the seat, and her muscles and bones screamed at the sudden change of position. She pinned her lips and breathed through her nose, unwilling to show them how much it hurt her. The harness was pulled down tightly and clicked into place, cutting into her chest where it was puffed out from the hands clasped behind her back. She'd been tortured before, but never in so simplistic a manner. An interrogation chair was about mind games and riding out the shocks, but this was about an animal's contorted body screaming for relief as the human being's mind struggled to function.

"This is the worst hotel I've ever stayed at," she said, and she hated that it came out in gasps.

"Yes, well, you're not my favorite guest. Tell me what I want to know, and your life will become infinitely more comfortable. I'll unbind your wrists and legs, give you water."

Oh, by the stars. *Water.*

Vi would've wrestled a rathtar for some water.

At least when Cardinal had interrogated her, he'd kept her fed and hydrated. She'd recognized early on that whatever the First Order had hoped he would become, he still had empathy and nobility.

Not so Kath. With Kath, they had succeeded in expunging any heart he'd ever had.

Now she couldn't stop thinking about water, feeling the dry burn in her throat and the thick weight of her tongue. A human being, she knew, would die in a couple of days without water. She'd gone three days before, and it had hurt more at the beginning than at the end. Kath most likely knew this, too—and would soon use it as a more active part of the torture.

"Have anything to tell me?" he prompted.

Vi snorted. "What, do you think I suddenly got answers while I was unconscious? I still don't know where anything or anybody is. But I did have a dream that Daddy Hux was disappointed in you. Not gonna get the award for Best Toady this year, huh?"

Crack.

His slap was a harsh reminder that he was in charge—and that his relationship with Hux was as sore as a bad tooth. It did help wake her up, though. She felt groggy and stiff. Perhaps she had slept—there was no way to know. Time ran strangely when you were being tortured, but it couldn't have been a long time. Kath looked just as fastidious and exacting as ever.

He leaned in so close that she could see the pores on his nose and smell the cinnamon on his breath. "Perhaps three questions is a bit too much for you. You don't look very smart. If you were, you wouldn't be here. You wouldn't even be with the Resistance. So let's start small: Where is your base on Batuu?"

Vi tossed her bangs out of her eyes and licked her desiccated lips, for all the good it did. "We don't have one. This planet is strategically useless. You know that."

He pulled out his leather roll of instruments again and selected a scalpel, gently placing the blade on her eyelid in that tender place where the eyeball rested in its orbit inside the skull. She'd been tortured several times, but it was generally rough and loud, with big movements and broken bones and her body going rigid with electricity. This strange, soft torture wasn't something she'd ever fought before. She struggled not to move, knowing that the tiniest twitch could puncture her eyeball or leave a gaping hole in her eyelid.

"Where. Is. The. Base."

It wasn't a question this time—it was a command.

The blade pressed in, and a drop of blood rolled down her eyelid and caught in her lashes.

Vi's lips pressed together.

She could feel the line of the blade against her eyeball through the lid, and she realized that in all the pain she'd been through, this one felt the most intimate, the most invasive, the most personal, the most utterly inescapable.

"I—"

The blade hovered there, waiting, the tiniest push from slicing directly into her eyeball.

"Sir!"

Vi shuddered as the blade left her flesh. Kath growled and straightened his posture before addressing the stormtrooper who had just appeared, her blaster at the ready.

"What?" he barked.

"There's a local here. Says he wants to help us."

Kath threw the scalpel against the wall, and it plinked off the metal floor. "You interrupted me to tell me some local cretin wants to chat?" After moment of internal struggle for control, his voice went slow and deadly. "You think that's important enough to halt an interrogation? Are you a soldier of the First Order or a complete idiot?"

The stormtrooper didn't move, didn't reveal any reaction to this outburst. "He says he knows who shot CF-3363 and 3871 in the market, sir. He has one of their helmets."

With a heavy sigh, Kath turned his back on Vi. "Fine. Watch her. Don't take your eyes off her for a single second. I'll be back shortly. And don't speak to her."

The trooper took up position, standing as still as a statue.

"So your boss is a real piece of work, huh?" Vi said.

The trooper said nothing, didn't move.

"Just between us girls, how's the First Order treating you? Are they all like him?"

Not even a twitch.

"So it looks like the new programming protocols are working out well. You're practically a droid."

Nothing.

In fact, the stormtrooper was so dedicated to staring at Vi and not moving that she didn't turn around when a new figure appeared in the transport's open hatch, and Vi was well schooled enough not to give the trooper any reason to turn around, even though she immediately knew who had just joined them despite the goggles, hat, and orange Batuuan wrap.

She could tell by the limp.

It was Archex.

To think that he had actually stepped onto a First Order ship—

To save her. Of course.

The fool.

Not that she was about to complain.

Chapter Twenty-Eight

DOLIN SHIFTED FROM FOOT TO FOOT as he stood by the jagged stump of a spire deep in a part of the forest he'd never seen before. Waba strained against his harness, anxious to smell the small box Dolin had placed on the ground a dozen meters away, per Archex's orders.

"No, Waba," he said, pulling the truffleboar back. "It's not safe."

Archex had ordered him to wait for a signal before carrying out his part of the plan, and the farm boy had never been more nervous about anything in his life. Sure, he believed in the Resistance and was excited to join up if it would help preserve his planet, family, farm, and way of life. But working at Savi's and helping build a settlement was one thing, and what he was doing now—Sabotage? An act of war?—was another. If the First Order caught him, they would take him prisoner. Or kill him. What would they do to Waba, to Grana, to his community?

There was nothing he hated more than seeing the flora and fauna of Batuu suffering, so he'd chosen this spot carefully. No living trees would be harmed, no nests would suffer, no tall, ancient spires would topple. Just this old stump and some logs, maybe, things that were already dead.

Nighttime birdsong filled his ears, and as much as he wanted to push the button and be done with it, he couldn't help wincing at the knowledge of what he was about to do and how it would upset this little corner of his planet. The ancients had left their mark here, but the forest would be fine. Surely the ancients, or their gods, or their echoes, would understand that everything he did, he did for Batuu. Nature knew well enough how to heal, even after a heavy blow. Everything grew back richer after a fire, after all. But there was no way Batuu and its smaller communities would recover if the First Order razed the planet, so he would accept this small sacrifice to preserve the greater whole. Maybe one day, if they all lived, he'd come back and plant seedlings, do his part to help the land heal.

Far off, he heard a raised voice—Zade.

"Look, I'm just trying to do a public service!" he wailed melodramatically.

"Now," Archex whispered through the commlink on Dolin's wrist.

That was the signal.

"Come on, Waba. Hurry."

Tugging the hog's leash, he jogged back the way he'd come. When he could no longer see the box on the ground or the rocky stump, he pulled Waba behind a jagged rock formation, picked up the struggling creature, and tucked Waba's wide face into his shoulder.

"It's okay, pal," he assured him. "It'll be over soon."

Taking a deep breath and scrunching his eyes shut, Dolin pressed the button, and the world exploded.

Chapter Twenty-Nine

ZADE SHOOK THE WHITE STORMTROOPER HELMET at the tightly wound and all-too-familiar officer raising a manicured eyebrow at him—it was a heavy bastard of a helmet, too.

"That's right, a public service!" he wailed, letting his voice carry, per Archex's instructions, and hoping his racing emotions came across as the usual bellowing rage. "Just being a good citizen! And what do I get? Doubt and a definite lack of credits crossing my palm. What's the point of supporting the First Order if you don't respect or remunerate a man, eh?"

The two stormtroopers on either side of their officer shifted uncomfortably. Zade wondered whether it was because their armor was uncomfortable, because their leader was a rancid, puffed-up frog-dog, or because they didn't like thinking about their own mortality as they beheld the blood splattered up the back of the helmet's otherwise pure-white betaplast.

"Look here, you histrionic piece of space effluvium—" the officer began, and then it happened.

Boom!

The farm boy had actually gathered up his guts and detonated the ordnance. Of course he got the fun job. No one ever let Zade blow things up.

On purpose.

His job was to be loud in a different way.

"What the skrit—" he began, but the officer cut him off.

"You two go find out what that was," he barked.

The stormtroopers said, "Yes, sir," and jogged off in lockstep, holding their identical rifles in identical positions that made Zade's stomach turn with their precision.

"You." Kath pointed at Zade. "You look familiar."

Zade's heart cranked up. Perhaps dressing so well had its drawbacks. If this monster realized who he was, the situation would take a dark turn—and it was already pretty dark.

"I have a brother," he lied. "Famous musician. Always on the holos."

He'd never been so grateful that he'd re-dyed his hair before he'd come to Batuu, because that was possibly the only reason this officer didn't realize they'd met before.

"I don't care about your brother. Stand right here. And no more of that high-pitched caterwauling. No reward was offered for this information, and you've already given us said information, so we're not required to pay you. It's a simple concept."

"Me not getting paid is far from a simple concept," he said, his mouth running full-speed as his brain and heart tried to catch up. "You see, people who don't work for a tyrannical political movement require something called 'money' so that they can do something called 'live,' and I like to eat—and drink—rather a lot, so—"

The officer rubbed his eyes and held out his hand. "You will give me the helmet and leave, and in return, I won't have you executed for being annoying and maligning the First Order."

In the wake of the explosion, the forest had gone deathly still, and thus Zade, as someone who craved a crowd and recognized the moment when he no longer had one, realized that he and the black-clad officer were utterly alone.

"Yes, sir," he said, saluting with the helmet in hand.

The moment the officer exhaled and let his guard down, Zade swung the heavy helmet backhand in a 180-degree arc with all his might, bashing the bearlike officer right in his big, dumb skull.

"At least the 'yes, sir' counts toward the part where I promised to leave." Zade looked down at the man's hated face, relishing the odd numbness that zinged up and down his arm from the impact. "I can commit to that. The rest of that rot you can stuff into your hairy belly. I don't work for you. I don't take orders from you. And I sure as—"

The officer's eyes blinked open, and Zade screeched in surprise and lunged, swinging the helmet again and bashing the man directly in the forehead with it.

This time, the officer blessedly returned to unconsciousness, a very wise move on his part, as Zade's next plan involved kicks directly to the face with expensive pointy boots. There was very little in life he wanted as much as to cause this man grievous bodily harm. As far as he could tell, the officer wasn't even breathing. Maybe—

Right on cue, ever the spoilsport, Archex limped into view from behind one of the far-too-large-to-make-sense trees and awkwardly loped toward the transport wearing Vi's hideous orange wrap.

"Blaster ready?" Archex whispered.

"Always," Zade stage-whispered, because he wasn't particularly fond of real whispering. "But if I can just make sure he's dead first?"

He pulled his blaster, which he'd lovingly nicknamed Nadia, and aimed it at the officer's face.

Archex looked back at him, frustrated. "No. We need him. Interrogation, or at least as a hostage. Just watch the forest and make sure he doesn't wake up. Protect me. Got it?"

Zade twirled his finger in the air with a raised eyebrow and turned his back to the transport, spinning dramatically on one heel with his scarf swirling around with him. He hated doing what Archex told him to, especially when it was the opposite of what he longed to do. Archex was exactly the sort of person that made Zade's skin crawl. Hurrah for rules and order and duty! What if we never smiled or laughed again? Tra la!

It was enough to make Zade sick—or perhaps that was last night's alcohol intake, or the officer's face. He still couldn't see any breathing, so he would have to focus his thoughts on something else and hope the man was dead.

Zade couldn't hear what was happening in the overly large transport, but he was glad to find that no one appeared to be barreling into the clearing to attack him. Most of the troopers would be back in town berating children or off doing whatever they did in the forest instead of hanging around home base. Hopefully the two that had run off toward the explosion hadn't hurt Dolin or his hog, both of whom Zade quite liked.

These Resistance blokes were actually growing on him.

And as much as he hated it, he couldn't forget the debt he owed Vi. Zade knew, without a shadow of a doubt, that if she hadn't interfered, he would've drunkenly shot his mouth off at those troopers and ended up dead in the alley that night. His wounds were just too fresh. When he was drunk, it was easy to imagine the relief that might come with not existing, without feeling the pain of loss, for all that he hadn't yet shared his particular reason for hating the First Order with his new friends. But when he was sober, he wanted to live, and well. Death was terrifying, and if there was one thing Zade wanted, it was to keep being Zade.

And sometimes, deep in his cups, as he heard the cantina folk cheer as he preached against the First Order, he actually felt like one of them. Like he belonged. Like he had a family.

"Never had one of those before," he murmured to himself. "At least, not a good one. Strange. Possibly a future weak spot—caring about people. Didn't work out so well, last time I tried it. Best not to think about that right now. The bastard's dead, at least. I hope."

Still, when he heard blasterfire in the transport, he took great glee in defying Archex's order completely.

He turned back around and ran to help.

Chapter Thirty

VI HAD BEEN TRAINED TO NEVER reveal any secrets to the enemy—not through words or actions. But she was weak and starved and dehydrated and possibly concussed and definitely not at her best. Whatever microexpression showed on her face, the stormtrooper guarding her detected the intruder entering the transport, whirled around, and shot.

The blaster bolts zipped past Archex, singeing—was that Vi's old orange wrap? Archex returned fire, but he kept hitting the white betaplast, leaving black burns that failed to stop the trooper. At least his strikes kept her from effectively returning fire. Archex ran down the center aisle between rows of seats, shooting all the while, and tackled the soldier, taking her down to the floor. Both of their blasters skittered away as they grappled, their skills equally matched.

It was possible, Vi realized, that Archex had personally trained this woman in her youth, whoever she was.

Watching the fight while helplessly trapped in binders and a harness was painful, physically and emotionally. There was nothing she could do to help except remain silent and avoid drawing Archex's attention away from his foe. He would almost get the trooper into a lock, but then she'd wiggle out and try the same move on him.

"You," the trooper finally growled, having knocked off his goggles to reveal his face. "It'll be a joy to kill you, Cardinal."

"My name is Archex," he said, although it was clearly a struggle and his bad lung was making the fight twice as hard. "And I would expect no less from you, CF-9164. I trained you, so I know how you're programmed."

"To think: I once looked up to you. We all did. And you betrayed us."

"Only from a certain point of view."

Just watching them wrestle was exhausting, and Vi quickly realized that there was no way Archex could win. The stormtrooper had full armor and a helmet, had more weight on her side, and probably didn't have constant pain and chronic ailments. If only Vi had a little more room, she could get out of these binders, she could help, could grab a blaster and finish off the trooper, could—

"Oh, my. What a tussle!"

Much to her surprise, it was Zade, popping in the transport door and scurrying up the aisle, scarf fluttering behind him. He already had his blaster in hand, and as Archex strained against the trooper's gloved hands, his face turning a disturbing shade of puce as she strangled him, Zade aimed for the spare few centimeters of black body glove exposed over her knee and shot her.

She immediately let go of Archex as her body contorted in pain, and by the time she'd refocused, Archex had dragged himself out of range and Zade had the blaster aimed at her chest, not that a direct hit to her armor would do much damage. One of his fancy krayt-leather boots kicked a blaster over to Archex, who picked it up, still wheezing and panting as he leaned against the metal wall and aimed his weapon at a more useful patch of the trooper's black body glove. He didn't shoot her—yet—but the implication was there.

"My heroes," Vi said, the words low and dull, pulled rasping from her dry throat.

After a nod from Archex, Zade reholstered his blaster and hurried over to unbuckle the harness pinning Vi to her seat.

"Stop! My hands! You need to—"

She didn't get to finish. The moment the harness wasn't holding her up anymore, she fell helplessly forward, nose-diving toward the floor with her hands still bound behind her back. Zade barely caught her in time, and she spent a strange moment with her face buried in his neck, smelling sweat, alcohol, and plom bloom cologne before he managed to shift her to the floor on her side. It wasn't comfortable, but it was the only way to attack her binders. If she tried to stand up now, she'd fall over on bloodless legs. The businesslike way he handled her and released her binders suggested he'd had experience with being in this position, which piqued her curiosity. Thus far, no matter how drunk, Zade had never talked of his past. Soon she was sitting up against the wall, rubbing feeling into her hands. Her shoulders burned like a thousand fires, and her legs couldn't really straighten.

"Wait," Zade said as he stood up. Everyone else was on the floor, and he swayed a little, the brightest thing in the uniformly gray space.

"Wait for what?" Archex asked, annoyed.

In response, Zaid aimed his blaster at the trooper again and murmured, "Take off your helmet, love."

She did so, revealing a scowling golden-brown face with dark, upturned eyes and ink-black hair shaved on the sides.

It only took one shot, and she slumped against the wall, the light gone from her eyes.

Archex surged up angrily, or tried to. He winced and lowered himself back down, massaging his thigh.

"Why did you do that?" he barked.

Zade shrugged. "She was the enemy? She was just waiting for a chance to steal your blaster and do that to you? We didn't need her? I don't like witnesses? You wouldn't let me kill the officer? Take your pick. Or, better yet, get up and find our Mother Hen something to drink and possibly one of those magical stim-shots the bucketheads use to keep going even when a normal person would be sacked out. We need to get out of here."

Archex shook his head. "Can't stand yet. I could use a stim, too. Up the lift and in the back right corner, you should find a kitchen with water and a refrigeration unit. The stims will be in there in a red box."

Zade nodded and hurried to follow his directions.

Vi chucked her chin at Archex. "That was some real heroic stuff back there, Emergency Brake. You saved my carcass."

Archex gave her a wry grin, his forehead creased with pain. "Yeah, well, you're our Mother Hen. I hate pretty much everything that comes out of Zade's mouth, but that one was spot-on. I'm glad you finally have a nickname as bad as the ones you gave me."

Now it was Vi's turn to scowl. "Mother Hen? Don't you dare. I'm not some busy matron guarding chicks and building nests—" She burst out laughing, feeling every bruised rib. "Oh, no. I totally am. I'm a mother hen. I started out a sharp, deadly spy, and now I might as well be clucking around on Endor, waiting to become fried tip-yip."

They were both laughing like Kowakian monkey-lizards when Zade returned, holding two syringes and a canteen and scowling.

"What's so funny that it could make Mister Stifflip laugh?" he asked, annoyed. "I swear, the moment I do something responsible, he finally breaks character. Was it a binary joke? Did someone wear unmatched socks or part their hair in a ridiculous place?"

"Calm down. He was just making fun of me," Vi said. "Now hand over the goods. Mother Hen wants to feel like a person again instead of a human punching bag."

The water was heavenly if a bit metallic, and as always, she wondered what First Order cocktails she was ingesting with it. She didn't have to say anything, though—Archex also knew that the water was probably spiked, and he was always watching, always waiting for something to go wrong. She jabbed the stim in her thigh and pressed the plunger, and immediately her blood warmed and her pain ebbed as the stimulants flowed through her. Within moments, she was standing and bouncing on the balls of her feet.

"I could fight an acklay," she enthused. "This stuff is great!"

Archex dragged himself to standing and threw his own empty syringe on the floor. "First Order magic," he said, not wheezing for once. "We've got about an hour to get out of here before we return to normal, which for me means I'm done."

Vi picked up the trooper's fallen blaster—and her helmet. She glanced around the transport, her mind coming back into delicious focus. "Zade, go grab all the stims. If you see any dense foodstuffs or quality medpacs, grab them, too." He saluted and jogged off, and she continued taking inventory of the available resources. "I'm taking the helmet. Hell, I'm taking the armor. Wait. Where's Kath? He's got that long-range comlink I've been looking for."

Archex nodded. "Every officer has a personal holocomm. It will only work locally unless relayed off a nearby satellite or dish, so they must have a ship in orbit. If we're going to use Kath's comlink to contact the Resistance, we're going to need Kriki to scramble the code and make sure they can't trace it back to us—or out to the general."

"Got it. Can you get all their codes, whatever Kriki needs to make that happen? And, hey, if you can wipe out all their tech so they can't communicate locally, that would be great, too. I don't want any remaining troopers to be able to contact their superiors in the fleet and bring in reinforcements. I wish we had time to disconnect their entire comm system and take it back home, but we've got to get out of here before the scouts return. I'll put on my trooper costume and grab Kath's comlink. Let's hurry." Then she looked around at the glorious resources the transport contained and grinned. "Or we could steal it. It has everything we need."

Archex shook his head. "Kath's ship is different. It's voice-locked to Kath and perhaps two of his top soldiers. Maybe Kriki could get around that kind of lock, but they went to great trouble to ensure a grunt like me can't do it."

Vi sighed. Of course.

"Then back to the original plan."

Archex nodded and headed for the cockpit.

Vi's steps were light, her head clear as she disabled the helmet's tracker, stripped the dead trooper, and put on the armor. It wasn't impossible to accomplish, but it wasn't easy, either, and she wondered how fast Archex could do it. The fit wasn't ideal—the trooper was bigger than her in every direction—but it would work. Finished with his tasks in the cockpit, Archex passed by her on his way to grab supplies. His brow drew down as if he longed to help her arrange the armor like he'd once done for his juvenile pupils, but he gave her a reluctant nod of approval.

Vi bounded out of the transport and into the soft stillness of the Batuu forest. Night had fallen, but the transport's perimeter was flooded with artificial light. Lieutenant Wulfgar Kath lay on the ground beside a trooper helmet, unconscious, his breathing slow and shallow, a huge bruise blooming on his forehead. Vi's mouth twitched. Kath wasn't dead, and she could change that with a single shot. But interrogation worked both ways, and this burly brute would have tons of information the Resistance could use. She found the comlink in his jacket pocket and jogged back over to the transport.

"Is there a hovergurney in there? Or a speeder? I want to take Kath hostage."

Zade appeared, his arms loaded with boxes. "He's not dead?" he asked, sounding disappointed.

"No. Which is good. We can use him. About that speeder?"

Zade's face fell, and Vi could tell that it was more than simple sadness at the enemy's ongoing existence, but there was no time to probe more deeply.

He ran a hand through his hair and said, "We came over in a landspeeder. Borrowed it from Ylena and Savi, so it needs to be returned in good shape. I was informed quite firmly that I was not allowed to drive. Let me jog this over and zip right back, and we can carry the bastard to it in a jiff." Vi opened her mouth to remind him that he would *not* be driving when she heard someone outside shout, "Sir!"

"Guys, we've got company. We've got to go!" she said, her voice low.

Zade's eyebrows went up and he hurried to her, holding the boxes close. Archex emerged from the back of the transport wearing an armored breastplate and carrying a blaster and a med case.

"I'm going to go out there and stall them," Vi said. "I'll cover you guys. Wait until I shoot."

Vi yanked the helmet over her head and hurried to the transport hatch. The entire world looked different through the helmet, but there was no time to ponder all the readouts.

Seeing the two troopers squatting around Kath, she pointed away from the transport and pitched her voice to sound like the trooper whose armor she wore. "He was attacked. They went that way. Hurry!"

The troopers stood and pulled their blasters. It didn't matter what had tipped them off to her disguise—the jig was up. Without another word, Vi started shooting. She took down one trooper, but the other one shot back, and she felt the impact of a bolt on the armor over her shoulder, another against her belly. Archex and Zade exploded from the transport behind her, running in different directions, zigging and zagging, their arms full of stolen goods. When the remaining trooper's helmet and blaster pivoted in their direction, Vi landed a lucky shot, forcing him to drop his blaster and clutch his hand, blood dripping from his glove.

She gave one last, longing look at Lieutenant Wulfgar Kath and shot him in the chest before following Zade into the forest at a full run.

Chapter Thirty-One

THE STIMS, OF COURSE, WORE OFF before they returned to the ruins. It happened suddenly, like liquid draining from a hole drilled in a bucket. Vi was sitting in the back of Savi's speeder, taking inventory on their loot, bursting with energy and hope, her mind moving a kilometer a minute. And then all of a sudden, she deflated and felt every bruise, every abrasion, every place where the armor dug in, every slender cut where Kath had held a scalpel to thin and tender skin. She'd had him, finally had an advantage, and then she'd lost him. She'd have to settle for seeing him dead. It didn't make her feel any better, just now.

Nothing did. Nothing could. She felt empty and drained and broken.

Vi always had to remind herself: Trauma is traumatic. For all that she'd survived the ordeal and they'd accomplished much in the rescue mission, the truth was that she'd been tortured and was a complete wreck, physically and psychologically.

"Oh," Archex said, sad and surprised, and the speeder slowed down and jigged a little.

So his stims had likewise given out. Vi didn't envy him the return of his own pain, of the constant burn in his leg and the way his lung would never again draw a full breath. She would have to watch him around their box of stolen stims—for warriors left with decimated bodies, addiction was always waiting around the corner, any kind of numbness offering a welcome balm. She couldn't imagine Archex bellied up to Oga's bar like Zade, slurping down a dozen Fuzzy Tauntauns to lose himself in a drunken haze, but she could all too easily picture him alone in the recruitment post on a bad day, when the rain made his bones ache, standing over the stim stash and promising himself just one hour of blessed relief, just one quick nap without nightmares.

The spires knew she would've done it herself, just then.

They made it back to the ruins and found Kriki, Ylena, and Dolin anxiously waiting in a puddle of artificial light by the cenote.

"It worked?" Dolin asked, his features lifting. By his side, Waba snortled enthusiastically.

"It worked," Zade confirmed. "And we have bounty! And we killed people! Who very much deserved it!"

The speeder stopped, and Archex struggled to get out, nearly falling when his boots hit the ground. Vi would've helped him—but her condition was no better, and he would've just slapped her hands away. Dolin hurried forward and offered an arm, and Archex was so beat up that he actually took it.

Archex held out a datapad that Vi hadn't seen him steal. "Kriki, this should have all their codes, everything they have onplanet. It can also scan crates, hack droids and doors, and translate unknown languages. And I bugged the ship, so if it moves, we'll be able to find it. If it hits atmo, we'll know."

"Okay?" The Chadra-Fan looked a little uncertain as she stepped forward to take the tablet. "I mean, I don't have any experience with First Order tech, but . . ."

"You can do it. We believe in you. Just . . . use it to really mess 'em up, okay?" Vi said from the speeder; she was still working herself up to standing again. "The goal is to keep them from getting a message offplanet and letting their superiors know we killed their officer. And if you can make sure all their personal comms die, too, so they can't talk to each other using their helmets ever again, that would be great.

I know Archex did some work on their transport, but we need there to be no way to fix it. I've got a helmet, if you need to know the parameters."

Vi held out the helmet, and Kriki took it, taking pains not to show how the heavy weight challenged her. On second thought, Vi held out the comlink she'd lifted off Kath.

"And this holocomm is our golden convor egg. I need it set up so I can call General Organa but not have the codes recorded or intercepted by anyone, especially when it pings off the First Order ship in orbit."

"I can do that," Kriki said. She took the comlink, too, and looked down. "I'm sorry I couldn't participate in the rescue. I . . . that is . . . after losing my sister on Hosnian Prime, I just can't . . . the thought of . . . I'm just so . . ."

"Scared," Ylena said softly, a hand on Kriki's shoulder. "It's okay. Everyone has a role to play. We are not all fighters." She gave Vi a quiet, secretive smile. "And some of us wage our war elsewhere, with our heads and hearts instead of our hands. Your knowledge is a weapon, Kriki. No one could ask any more from you."

Vi returned Ylena's smile. "That's true, Kriki. None of us can do what you can. And Ylena, we owe you thanks for the speeder. And to Savi as well. Without it, I'm pretty sure Archex and I would be flat on our backs in the forest, crying. Or dead."

"Oh, I would've joined you," Zade said. "In the flat-on-your-back part, not the dead part."

"Did you kill everyone?" Dolin asked. "Is the First Order gone?"

Putting her boots on the ground and testing her ability to stand, Vi shook her head. "No. We got their officer, Kath, and two stormtroopers—I think. Shot the fingers off a third trooper, so unless he's ambidextrous, he probably won't be shooting at us again. Add those to the ones I took down in the market and in the ruins, and that's . . . uh . . ." Her head was spinning.

"Eight dead, one wounded," Kriki supplied.

"Nine down. And we still have no idea how many soldiers Kath ultimately brought with him." Vi sighed and flicked her eyes at Archex, hoping he would say something about what kind of numbers they could expect, but he just looked away.

Fine. So he wasn't ready to let the others know about his past yet. Vi would find him, later, to strategize. After they'd both gotten some rest. But first she had to play Mother Hen and get everything sorted.

"I doubt I'll be functional tomorrow. Ylena, can you please tell Savi that I'm sorry, but I won't be able to work for a couple of days?"

Ylena chuckled. "Oh, he already knows. And as you know, gathering—I mean, scrapping—is not that kind of job. Return to us when you're well in heart and mind. Work only half a day, if you need to, enjoying the company in the morning and then napping through the heat of the afternoon. We will always be there, when you're ready."

As with everything Ylena said, there were undercurrents that Vi could detect but not accurately decode. Ylena was always saying two things at once, it seemed. But the overall gist was that she could heal and work when she was ready without getting fired, which was a better deal than most employers offered.

"And can you take back the speeder before something happens to it? I already owe Savi too much and don't want to pay for any dings." She tossed a glance at Zade, who was admiring the controls, running a finger over the fuelboost button.

Ylena inclined her head. "I can. Dolin, do you want to ride with me and join the others at the cantina?"

Dolin fidgeted with Waba's leash. "That would, uh, that would be great!"

But Ylena cocked her head to the side. "Waba was the one who tracked Vi's path to the First Order transport, right?"

Dolin squatted down to scratch the hog's back, making him snort-purr with pleasure. "That's right! Old Waba can find anything, if you give him a sniff first."

"So if I let him sniff certain artifacts at the scrapyard, he might be able to find similar objects in the piles?"

"Probably." Dolin considered it. "Although we'd need to be careful that he didn't eat something unsafe or scratch his snout on rusted metal."

Ylena's face lit up with a smile. "Then perhaps you'll consider bringing him along tomorrow. If he can do what I think he can do and find what I think he can find, the artifacts uncovered might greatly accelerate your ability to buy large pieces of equipment for your facility."

"That's some pig," Vi said appreciatively. "Remind me to scratch him behind the ears when I can move again. Good luck, everybody. Good job. Thanks for saving my life. I'm gonna go into a coma now."

She wasn't sure how she made it back to her bunk, much less how she managed to get all the armor or her wig off, but she experienced a moment of utter ecstasy as she was finally wearing nothing but her underclothes and settled in under a blanket. After her years with the Resistance, it was hard to remember the last time she'd slept in a proper bed, which this rough stone niche definitely was not, but being horizontal and not in First Order binders was enough. At some point as she slept, Pook arrived and injected her with something or other, complaining all the while about the annoyances and multiple weaknesses of flesh and internal organs, but she just went back to sleep.

Time ceased to have meaning. The lights dimmed and rose, people came and went, Pook prodded her and scanned her and muttered. She drifted in and out of dreams. One time, she woke up screaming, and Kriki patted her hair gently and told her everything was going to be fine. Another time, she felt something cold and wet on her cheek and woke from a nightmare to find Waba licking away tears. But when Vi finally opened her eyes and sat up, feeling almost healed in body, if not mind, she knew one thing very clearly.

Despite whatever work Kriki had done to break down the First Order's communications on Batuu, the remaining troopers were eventually going to blast back out into space, return to their main ship, and let their leaders know exactly what had happened here.

And then Vi's worst premonitions would come true, and these good people would learn the might and power of the First Order.

They would be crushed, along with Leia's plans for the Resistance base.

Which meant it was Vi's job to stop that from happening.

Chapter Thirty-Two

"SIR? SIR!"

Lieutenant Wulfgar Kath tried to open his eyes, but the bright light only made his skull hurt worse. It was like the worst hangover of his life combined with heavy dehydration and a round of kickboxing in the gym. His head felt like a metal box full of ashes and wet towels, and even tiny movements were bad enough to make him wince and, to his great disappointment, whimper.

"He's alive."

Kath's troopers helped him sit up and hobble to the transport's medbay. He was not the sort of man who would allow himself to be undressed by his inferiors, so he lay there in full uniform, down to his shined black boots. He could actually see some spots and scuffs on them, which he found intolerable. But not nearly as intolerable as the story the troopers told him about how his prisoner had escaped.

He drifted in and out of consciousness for days and finally woke in a medcenter gown, his beard overgrown and his temper high. His second in command told him more bad news about how the Resistance had taken a cache of valuable supplies, a datapad full of First Order codes and plans, and their overall ability to communicate, whether long range or just across the outpost. Their helmets were basically useless now.

This was beyond a headache.

This was a *catastrophe.*

The only good news was that if General Hux called again, he would get nothing but dead air.

The bad news was that if that happened too many times, General Hux would send down another ship, and then Kath's mission and career would meet a short and violent end.

"It's a good thing you were wearing that armored vest, sir," the medical droid observed, checking Kath's vital signs. "Your chest is badly bruised, but nothing has been broken, and there's no hemorrhaging."

"Then fix me up and let me get back to business," Kath said coldly.

"You have a concussion, sir. A *very bad* concussion. Further blunt-force trauma would've left you with irreparable brain damage. You're going to be confused, dizzy, and incapacitated for several more days at least."

Kath sighed heavily, which hurt like hell. "Then fetch the stims and boosters. I can't believe you haven't already put them to use."

The med droid looked to the nearest trooper, Kath's second in command, CE-6675, who cleared his throat. "They've been stolen."

That hit home; Kath needed those supplies. "All of them?" Kath asked in disbelief. "Including the ones in cold storage?"

"All of them, sir. As well as many of our medical supplies."

Even with his brain muddled, Kath quickly put two and two together. "If they knew where to find them that quickly, then one of them must be ex–First Order. Considering Starling is here, I'd wager it's Cardinal. Did anyone see a man fitting his description?"

"Yes, sir." Kath carefully swung his head around to address a trooper sitting on another berth in the medbay, his hand wrapped in a bacta glove. He was young, in his twenties, and his face was a war of pain and shame. "It was Captain Cardinal. He ran off with the Resistance spy and a thin man in flamboyant clothes. They split up, and I was unable to catch them."

Kath took a deep and painful breath and felt the vein throbbing in his forehead. "You couldn't catch them? You're part of the most highly trained army in the galaxy, and *you couldn't catch any of them*?"

The trooper held up his hand. "They shot off two of my fingers, sir. I was unable to pull the trigger of my blaster. And as I was the only trooper in the immediate vicinity left alive, I felt it unwise to leave you unattended, lest there be other hostiles in the area."

"Your blood pressure is dangerously high, sir," the med droid noted, only fueling Kath's rage; he hated being told things that were obvious.

Still, Kath struggled to control his temper, breathing through his nose and quivering with rage. "If the situation were favorable, you would be severely punished, and this droid would be melted for scrap."

The med droid wisely and silently returned to his closet.

"But we're down to fourteen troopers—"

"Twelve, sir," CE-6675 corrected. "Two were killed in the escape."

Teeth grinding, Kath muttered, "Down to only twelve troopers. You're dropping off like flies. Maybe I should put you all in the brig and request reinforcements, considering the failure of this squad."

Not that he would do that—his troopers had no idea how much was riding on this mission for him—but he needed to motivate them somehow.

"Should we prepare to rendezvous with the *Penumbra,* sir?" CE-6675 asked. "They'll have a more advanced medbay and will be able to tend to your wounds better. With the supplies left on hand, I'm afraid there's little the med droid can do. He has recommended rest and rehydration." CE-6675 stepped back, hands behind his back in a show of deference that suggested he knew he'd overstepped his bounds.

"No. Absolutely not. I will not leave this planet until I have Starling in hand and have crushed whatever base the Resistance has built here and punished all their allies."

"But, sir—"

Kath picked up the canteen by his side and threw it at CE-6675 with all his might. The heavy container bounced off the trooper's betaplast armor and fell to the floor with a clunk. "I said no! Do not attempt to interrupt me again unless you want to be rebuked for insubordination, CE-6675. Just because I have a concussion doesn't mean you're free to opine on my strategy or the orders of my superiors. Remember your place."

The trooper stepped back, head bent in acknowledgment. "Yes, sir."

"Nothing has changed. Our mission remains the same. The troopers we lost were either weak or foolish, and good riddance. Those who are left must step up to the challenge and prove they are worthy soldiers of the First Order. Does anyone have a problem with that?"

"No, sir!" every stormtrooper in the area barked.

Kath tried nodding but found it made him want to vomit. "Good," he said. "Then here are your orders. Go into the outpost and rough up these yokels. Question them about the Resistance spy. Hurt them—in her name. Threaten their families. Make them reconsider their allegiance to our enemy. Show them the might of the First Order. Repay those who appear eager to help us find victory. We caught Starling last time because she stepped in to defend civilians."

Kath smiled and settled back into the pillows.

"Force her to do it again."

Chapter Thirty-Three

VI HAD NO IDEA WHAT DAY it was when she hobbled into the room they were using as a mess hall. It smelled of caf, and she found the carafe beside a stack of metal cups and poured herself a healing portion. Dolin and Kriki looked up from their places at the makeshift table and smiled, but Archex, as expected, only scowled.

"You shouldn't be out of bed yet," he said. "Pook estimated that at least two more days would be necessary for you to heal properly."

Vi rolled her eyes as she sat down heavily on a crate. "First of all, most of what bothers me won't ever heal, so I'm not holding my breath. Second, I feel pretty good and have work to do. Third." She put her hands on the table and cocked her head. "How long did Pook tell *you* to stay in bed?"

Archex cleared his throat and sipped his caf. "Uh," he said. "How about that local holo-chess team?"

Vi snorted, glad to see a tiny glimmer of his sense of humor returning. "That's what I thought. Somebody catch me up on what I've missed, in the outpost and around here, if you will."

"The sentient beings were vexing, I am filled with existential dread, and your broken rib is mostly healed," Pook said from a corner, where he appeared to be drilling holes in the rock just to make an annoying noise.

"Great, Pook. Good info. Next?"

Kriki puffed up her chest as she took a deep breath. "I was able to use the datapad to completely scramble their communications. Anytime they attempt to use their helmet comms, they'll be patched into Palob Godalhi's radio show." She giggled into her hands. "And I jammed the signal on their on-ship long-range comm, so there's no slicing out of that. I also reset and scrambled the comlink you found on the officer so you'll be able to use their ship as a relay to reach the general, but their scans will just show some interference as it pings. Oh! And as you've learned, I bought some fresh caf in the market."

That news made Vi grin so hard it hurt her bruised face. "Good job. Very, very good job. If I could pay you, I would pay you double. I'd say we're just a few dead troopers away from having the perfect setup."

"There's bad news, too," Archex began.

"Of course there is," Vi muttered. "Hit me."

Now Dolin spoke up. "The troopers have been spending more time in the outpost since the attack. They're roughing up shopkeepers who won't help them or who claim they know nothing about you or the Resistance. And the locals who want to help the First Order— those cowardly womp rats—the soldiers are giving them credits. Which means some people are starting to change their minds about you. About us." His head hung. "One of the soldiers hit Oh-li with his blaster. Broke her jaw. She and Jenda still wouldn't say anything."

Vi's heart seized up as she thought of how much suffering good people were willing to undergo in the pursuit of what was right. It was just like the First Order to figure out how to hurt her the most—by threatening innocent people. Of course, that was what they did best, anyway.

"Okay, so let's think about this. We've got the surviving stormtroopers, but no officer. These troopers—they're not paid to think, right?" She looked to Archex.

He snorted. "They're paid to do as they're told. Any instincts regarding creative thinking or rebellion against authority are pro-grammed out—or they wash out and get sent to the mines or factories. So if they have no leader, then the highest-ranking trooper will take over. If they can't contact their superior officers for further orders, they'll most likely get offplanet as soon as they can."

Vi looked up at him. "How much time before that happens?"

Archex shrugged. "Depends entirely on the trooper in charge. They could be making preparations right now, or they could have a tech with enough slicing skill to get the comms working. No offense, Kriki."

"Oh, no," Dolin muttered.

Everyone looked at him.

"One of the people who was saying nice stuff about the First Order was this skeezy slicer who hangs out at Oga's—Marin Anke. Bought a round at the bar last night and said everyone could thank the First Order. D'you think they might be using him to fix whatever Kriki broke?"

Vi leaned forward. "This changes things. We've got to make sure that ship doesn't get offplanet. If Hux and his cronies find out that not only am I here, but I killed their officer and the local populace is friendly to the Resistance . . ." She trailed off.

"They'll kill everyone," Archex continued for her. "They have no respect for people, for culture. Old, young, native, visiting, siding with the Resistance or the First Order or remaining neutral. They'll raze the outpost to the ground and forget it ever existed."

A dark silence spread around the room as the makeshift lights buzzed overhead. Vi looked to each person there—Archex, Kriki, Dolin. She even looked at Pook, for all that he had no eyes. Zade, she knew, was probably sleeping off whatever he'd drunk last night. This site was never meant to be a permanent thing—it was just a collection of cobbled-together tech where Resistance ships could land for a while, where volunteers could come together to help plan strategy or teach recruits how to shoot and fly and slice. For all that they'd chosen a space created and lived in by the ancients, now it was just the briefest rest stop in the wide galaxy.

And yet Vi was willing to die for it, for this team that had collected around her and for the people of Black Spire Outpost. Savi and Ylena and the Gatherers, doing what they could to fight evil and helping her, even when they didn't have to. Jenda and Oh-li, saying no even when they knew it would get them hurt. Salju trekking toward the crash not to loot it—but to make sure that if someone needed help, they would receive it.

These were good people, and this was their place.

And in a way, for now, it was Vi's place.

And that meant that it was up to her to save it.

She took a deep breath.

"Okay, so let's figure out how to make sure that ship never leaves Batuu."

Everyone nodded.

"Can we just blow up their ship?" Dolin asked.

Vi gave him a warm smile. "I wish it were that easy. If the ship just exploded onplanet, the suits up in space would know that someone here had taken decisive action against the First Order. At the very best, they'd send another officer and a larger squadron to investigate. At worst, they'd skip that step and go straight to setting everything on fire, just in case."

Kriki's nose fluttered. "So we can't kill their soldiers or blow up their ship, but we also can't let them leave?"

Archex nodded. "We need some way to send a message from the transport to the First Order saying that the Resistance spy was here but died in custody and that Batuu is not strategically useful. This place has to seem like it's not worth caring about."

"But it is!" Dolin nearly shouted.

Vi put a hand on his arm. "We know that, and you know that, but you don't want the First Order to know that."

"You know what you need?" said a new voice from the hallway.

Everyone looked up as Zade swanned into the room in a burgundy shimmersilk bathrobe.

"Well?" Vi prodded.

"Caf," he finished on his way to the percolator, pouring himself a cup and then pulling a face at the taste. "I take it back. You need better beans. This stuff tastes like it came out of the business end of a dewback."

Archex sighed heavily. "Do you have anything useful to contribute?"

Zade reclined on a stack of cargo crates to sip his drink. "The cantina is all riled up. There's a lot of talk about the First Order. Some folk think they're fabulous, that they're going to make this a lawful place with a real government instead of Oga and her muscle and her underhanded, gangster ways. Hmph. Fools." He took a sip. "Some folk—more than you'd think—have fond feelings for Vi and think the Resistance is the only way to go. They've seen what damage a few members of the First Order can accomplish, and they know that a larger force would leave nothing but rubble. With Savi and his scrappers on your side, they assume you must be doing good, fair work. Those who saw what you did, defending the old women, believe in you. Most folk think everything is in good balance on its own and that the First Order and Resistance are just mucking up a good thing and should go elsewhere and mind their own business."

"Would that we could," Vi said, rolling her eyes skyward. "Anything else?"

Zade held up a finger and gulped down the rest of his caf. Vi watched his stubble ripple as he swallowed and spent a moment considering who hated Zade more, Archex or Pook.

Finally finished, he set down his cup and smiled. "So I was listening to you bicker from the hall for a bit, and I believe the only way to solve this little imbroglio—yes, I know big words—is to let the First Order escape back into space."

"But if they—" Archex began.

"Wasn't done," Zade broke in. "We let them escape into space, and then we blow them up." He held up a finger again as he belched and Archex squirmed. "But before either of those things happen, we get Kriki on board, and she programs the ship to send a message the moment it hits space, reporting that the Resistance spy is dead and that Batuu is, as you put it, strategically useless. Let the message play, and then . . . boom. But here's the extra-tricky part." He leaned closer and stage-whispered, "Kriki also makes that explosion look like a malfunction. No enemy fire; just a bad motivator. Shipbuilders these days. Always cutting corners."

For a moment, the room went silent.

"Can you do that, Kriki?" Vi finally asked.

Kriki looked down, her claws clicking nervously. "Am I able? Yes, sure! I can do that. But . . . I'm not good under pressure. I get scared, and . . . it's like my brain feels all light and fluttery, and I get clumsy, and . . ." She sighed a squeaky sigh. "Even imagining what it would feel like, sneaking onto a First Order ship and waiting for one of the soldiers to find me and hurt me like they did Vi . . ." She trailed off, her teeth chattering. "I don't know if I can do it. I don't think I'm strong enough. I'm just too scared."

Vi reached out and put her hand over Kriki's much larger one. "You're strong," she said, hearing her voice break. She didn't often let others see this side of her emotions, but she was still feeling a bit fragile from the torture. "Don't let anyone ever tell you you're not enough. There is no such thing as 'enough.' There's just you, doing the best that you're able. I'm scared, too. I'm scared all the time. I wake up in the night, covered in sweat—"

"I've heard you whimper in your sleep," Kriki confessed. "I wondered why."

"I've been through some bad things." At that, Archex looked away, and Vi looked down. Her throat hurt, saying it. "People have hurt me. Most of the time, I manage to ignore it or hide it, but it's always there, lurking underneath. And what I've learned is that the only way out is through. That I have to feel the fear, acknowledge it, and do it anyway. Fear can't hurt you."

"But the First Order bloody well can!" Zade roared.

Vi gave him a quelling look and squeezed Kriki's hand. "They can," she agreed. "They can hurt you even if you just live your life, avoiding what scares you and minding your own business. Because that's what bullies do—they don't care if you're invested or not. But what we're trying to do will, hopefully, save this place, the entire planet, and everyone on it. And for me, that's a risk worth taking. When I jumped in front of Jenda and Oh-li in the marketplace, I was scared, and I knew there would be consequences. But I'm glad I did it. I don't think I could live with the person I'd be if I'd just watched that happen and walked away."

"So you're saying that if I don't do this, I'll regret it?" Kriki asked.

"Take it from somebody with a lot of regrets," Archex said, his voice gentle and his eyes more than a little wet. "You can live through fear and hurt, but when the First Order decides your home is in their way, you won't have regrets. You'll just be ashes. First the TIE fighters come through and strafe the city and every settlement. Then the transports land and the troops bring flamethrowers and blasters and laser axes. They scan for signs of life. They hunt down what they find. They leave nothing behind. Nothing."

He got up abruptly and left, and Vi's heart ached for him.

"That man," Zade said, watching Archex leave as he ate some stale popped grains, "has seen things. I still don't like him, but I begin to see why he's absolutely no fun."

"I'll go with you, Kriki," Dolin offered shyly. "I mean, maybe I'm not the best fighter or the smartest person we've got, but I can protect you. You don't have to go alone, if that's what you're worried about."

"You wouldn't be alone," Vi agreed. "You'd have all of us. And maybe some of the locals, if they knew how important it was?" She looked from Zade to Dolin.

Dolin nodded. "I can ask around the settlement. My people don't go to the outpost, but they do tune in to the local radio. Maybe it's been on the news—the people who've been hurt. I'll tell them what I've seen." His voice went softer. "I'll tell them what they did to you. Maybe they'll understand what's at stake."

"And I'll make the great sacrifice of a night in the cantina." Zade stood, a hand over his heart. "I will burden myself with local liquors and buy many rounds of said liquors—the cheap ones for them, of course, although I do enjoy that Toniray wine myself. Perhaps if we can rouse enough hearts around this attack, those remaining troopers will be too dazzled or harried by the hordes of locals with pitchforks to notice our wee friend working her magic." He waggled his fingers at Kriki, who wiggled hers in return; they had a chummy relationship like two small children, Vi had noticed.

"So everyone else will distract the troopers while I go on the ship and reprogram it, and then I'll get off the ship, and then what?" Kriki asked, still a little nervous but gaining confidence.

Vi smiled. "Then we retreat and let them leave, and when they hit orbit—"

"Boom!" Zade supplied.

"Boom," Vi agreed.

Kriki puffed out her chest and nodded. "I think I can do it. Boom."

Chapter Thirty-Four

LONG AFTER EVERYONE ELSE WAS ASLEEP, Kriki sat at the makeshift table surrounded by datapads. She'd gone into BSO to gather any info she could on First Order tech. Savi had given her an old collection of ship manuals, while Mubo had let her interrogate a KX-2 unit he was rebuilding. She'd considered stopping in at Dok-Ondar's Den of Antiquities, but despite the fact that he was a vegetarian, the ancient Ithorian made her feel like a prey animal and would likely sense her desperation and overcharge her accordingly if he even had anything useful. Although she knew her old employer Gol likely had some First Order tech among his wares, she'd gotten quite accustomed to not being berated and just assumed he would refuse to sell it to her at any price. No matter what Dolin and Zade said about the locals, it was clear that certain people in the outpost did not have pure hearts.

Normally, Kriki loved nothing more than having some new bit of tech to tinker with. She'd had great fun optimizing the old generators the Resistance had supplied, and she now had the lights set to glow and dim in time with the humans' natural rhythms. But that was tinkering and this was . . . well, life and death. If she messed up the tech, Batuu could get blown up just like Hosnian Prime. If she messed up her timing or bad luck struck, she could end up dead or in the custody of the First Order. She could be put in one of those interrogation chairs, be electrocuted, have her mind probed—

Kriki shivered. She wasn't big enough or strong enough to live through that, and she dreaded what they might pry from her thoughts. Vi was the strongest person she'd ever met, and Vi had barely escaped the First Order alive.

Not only that, but for all that Vi kept up a cheerful, caring, confident, competent front, she whimpered in her sleep all night, begging for release and help and muttering two names over and over again. Kath, whom Kriki knew, and someone else named Cardinal. If Kriki was nearby and heard Vi fussing, she would go sit by the human's side and pat her hand or stroke her hair back from her sweaty forehead until Vi's mouth relaxed into a smile and she went back to sleep. This nearly nightly routine was one of Kriki's many secrets. She slept for three hours in the afternoon after work, but other than that, she was awake and haunting the corridors in her own way, for such was the Chadra-Fan's biological imperative.

She'd seen Archex struggle in his sleep, too, although she was too shy to touch his face and would only pat his hand. He sometimes woke up around midnight and went outside or into the cave's smallest chamber to do stretching exercises and walk in circles, growling and grumbling strange, rhyming slogans to himself, trying to force his injured leg to heal through sheer stubbornness.

She'd watched Zade stumble in before dawn, drunk beyond belief and arguing with a ghost—someone named Valoss—about whether it was time to run again, whether it was ever worth it to fight, as Valoss had, and whether or not he'd repaid his debt to Vi yet.

And she'd silently followed gentle Dolin as he ventured deep into the caves to some ancient statues, kneeling on the hard rock and praying for strength, praying that his land and animals and family might remain safe, all while Waba lay at his feet, quiet for once as if even the hog sensed the presence of the old gods listening.

If the team had a weak link, Kriki was certain that she was it. And the only thing she could do to up her chances of success was to study these datapads, reading every manual and code list for First Order transports that she could get her hands on. From Archex's descriptions, she'd narrowed the bulky transport's model down to some sort of Sienar-Jaemus Mobile Habitation Unit and felt confident that given enough time, she could perform her duties and win the day.

The problem was that they might not have enough time, and that, as she'd confessed, she didn't perform well under pressure. She felt both of her hearts flutter when everyone at the table stared at her, and these weren't even scary strangers or enemies—they were her friends! Since leaving her sister Reelka and, before that, her nest, she'd never felt so welcome, so like a part of the group. In most places, she was treated as a lesser or an adorable walking pet, but Vi and the other Resistance members saw her as a real person, and one with much to contribute. She didn't want to let them down. She wanted to be liked. She wanted to help.

But above all else, she didn't want to die.

Chapter Thirty-Five

SINCE HE'D JOINED THE RESISTANCE—HIM! DOLIN! A member of the Resistance!—he'd stayed away from his community completely. Well, except for when he ran home to snatch up last year's gruffin wool and his favorite pillow, but that didn't really count.

He'd avoided returning not only because he wasn't sure what his friends and extended family would say about him using tech and cavorting with droids and aliens, but also because he didn't want to inadvertently lead the First Order back to his home. Now, on his crankbike, with the squat, round huts on the horizon and Waba snorting happily in the sidecar, he wasn't even sure he'd be welcomed back.

What he was doing—what he had done—went well beyond the usual boyish rebellion. Most young men where he was from tore up fields on their crankbikes or got involved with illegal podraces in the Galma vicinity.

Whereas Dolin had gotten himself involved in an intergalactic conflict.

He'd chosen a side, committed near blasphemy by letting offworlders into the ruins, and exploded the stump of a holy spire.

Even if no one else understood, he knew in his heart that it was the right thing to do. He'd stood before the old gods, made his gifts of golden lichen and black stones, and the caves had gone still, some noise chiming down the hallway. He'd taken that as a message from the ancients. Surely they wished to see their world safe, to have their native sons take up arms and protect their land and beasts?

The gods, perhaps, did.

But his own grandmother? Maybe not.

He pulled up outside the hut and stood before the door. It was the middle of the day, and Grana was usually napping at this time. But she must've heard his bike, loud as it was.

Did he call out or go in?

Oh, bosh it.

"Grana!" he called through the heavy rug over the door. "Bright suns!"

Waba tried to waddle in as he usually did, but Dolin held the hog back. If he wasn't welcome, then his pet surely wasn't, and he didn't have the heart to watch Grana chase Waba around with a broom today.

"Maybe they're bright and maybe they're not" came the reply, which was far from a welcome.

"It's bright where I stand."

"Sometimes we forget the suns, when we stand in darkness too long."

"But, Grana, didn't you once tell me that the suns are always shining? Even when clouds cover them, the suns are still there. They never stop bringing life to Batuu."

She had no answer to that.

Dolin couldn't stand it anymore—waiting outside his own hut, the place where he'd grown up, where he'd mourned his parents, where he'd become a man. He'd fixed this roof with his own hands, helped to weave the rugs, polished the furniture until he had blisters.

Grimacing, he pushed the thick fabric aside and walked in.

Grana glared up from her loom in annoyance; she looked exhausted and like she'd lost weight. "How dare you? In this settlement, we don't enter the homes of others unless we're invited."

Dolin stood up straight. "This is my home. I grew up here. I buried my parents here. I carved the chair you're sitting in and spun the yarn you're weaving with. Unless you toss out everything I made, then this is still my house, too." She rolled her eyes and looked back down at the loom, her shuttle zipping back and forth angrily. He paused for a moment, his frustration building, before saying, "Not that you could drag that chair outside yourself. I've done most of the work here for years, taken care of you. Carried you when you were sick. I guess if you really want to get rid of me, you'll just have to set fire to everything in this hut and start over."

Grana looked up, her mouth as puckered as a jitfruit. "You left. Nobody said you could come back."

"I'm a man grown. I don't need anyone's permission."

The old woman met his eyes, and what he saw there was chilling.

"Get out, or I'll start screaming."

She wasn't playing around.

She wasn't going to forgive him.

She was done with him.

Dolin took a deep breath. "Fine, then. I can see your heart has gone cold, and you are determined to die alone. But you might like to know that I have a job. That I'm useful. That I joined the Resistance, and they're glad to have me. And that even if you reject me, I will keep fighting for you. For you, and for our home and way of life. For the gruffins and the fields and the ancients. I've seen the First Order with my own eyes, seen them bully and shoot and kill. So know that even if you think I'm abandoning you, what I'm really doing is protecting you. Even if you don't want it. Or appreciate it."

He thought she might say something then, that there might be some tiny crack in her resolve that he could wiggle open until she held out her scrawny arms for a hug.

But she kept her mouth pinned, and so he nodded and said, "So be it then. May the Force be with you, Grana."

Dolin turned on his heel and left, Waba following him confusedly.

"There's no such thing as the Force!" Grana shouted after the curtain had closed behind him.

"Wrong again!" he shouted back.

Perhaps his own grandmother had rejected him, but there were others in the community who might be swayed. His friends and cousins, boys and men, girls and women who, like him, guarded the beasts and land or else railed against such strictures and worked on their bikes and sneaked out to Galma and Surabat and Peka. He would find the other young people, in ones and twos, where they always lurked.

And he would tell them his truth and deliver them to the Resistance, as many as would come.

Someone here had to believe him.

Chapter Thirty-Six

FOR ONCE, YLENA LEFT THE SCRAPYARD early, trusting that Dotti would keep everyone in order. While she walked Savi's Path to the outpost, she thought carefully about what to say, what to do. Something was coming, she knew. Something that would threaten all of Batuu. But this, perhaps, wasn't it.

Perhaps this was the beginning, the instigating factor.

They had to be careful, but they also had a job to do. A calling.

She passed by the Trilon wishing tree, smiling at her own contributions still waving in the wind, faded and worn. So many wishes, hopes, dreams, fears, oaths, promises, some going back decades and some only a few hours old. It was beautiful, the faith of the people of Black Spire. Stepping under the shade of the awning and up to the counter, she asked for Savi. It was more ceremonial, at this point, since she knew how to find Savi and was one of the few beings for whom his door was always open. But still, they were a people of ritual and respect, the Gatherers, and so she played her part.

Kimbe nodded and informed her that she could go on inside, and she inclined her head with thanks and ducked into the entryway of Savi's personal workshop. Very few people in the outpost knew what truly happened within. They saw the scrapyard and Savi's public showroom, where he sold their old goods and bought their scrap, but no one ever questioned what was stored in the bulk of the building or what Savi spent so much of his time doing with his collected junk. This hallway was mostly for storage and show, with a variety of old objects displayed on the walls. But if you went a little farther in . . .

Well, Savi's workshop was private for a reason.

It wasn't long before the old man walked over in his work apron, dusting his hands off before giving Ylena his full attention.

"It's happening," she told him. "This afternoon. The Resistance must make their move, for soon the First Order will leave and tell their superiors in the fleet what has happened here. We can't let that come to pass. The consequences could be dire."

Savi put a warm, wrinkled hand on her shoulder. "I know, child," he said. "I've been listening. The heated water must eventually boil. What is it you need?"

Ylena looked down. "I'm . . . not sure. I feel certain we must help Vi. That she is part of our destiny."

Savi's nod was knowing. "And we *have* helped her. More than she'll ever know."

"But what if it's not enough? Can't we give her one of the—"

"No." He cut her off firmly but kindly. "Just as we follow the Force but cannot access it, so is she bound by her limitations. The only weapons she'll bring to this fight are those she has discovered on her own."

"And our people?"

"We are not fighters. We serve a greater purpose. You know that, too."

Ylena's head hung. "I strongly feel that we are meant to play a greater role in this conflict between the Resistance and the First Order. Why else do we collect artifacts and ancient weapons? Why else do we learn all that we can from the legacy of the Jedi and the Sith if not to use it, as they would, to protect the balance?"

Savi sighed. "We are Gatherers, not Jedi. The flock, not the shepherds. We have no powers, no edict. We can only wait and watch and listen, not guide. We hold a candle but will not light any fuse. We do protect the balance, but not always by shifting the scales. This conflict is far from over. I'm certain we will play our part one day. But not today."

"I suppose Oga has also come to call on you," Ylena dared to venture.

A roguish smile. "She has. I have been forbidden from personally interfering with the escalating trouble between the Resistance and the First Order here at the outpost."

"As you say." She looked up, raising her chin; she'd heard the hidden truths between his words. "Then what if I wish to use my own money to purchase weapons. As a regular customer of the scrapyard?"

Savi's laugh boomed, and Batlizards fluttered in the room's dark corners, roused from their nests. "Then I would let you know that we have a great many old blasters that can be purchased at a very reasonable price. Tell Kimbe to load up the speeder."

Tears shone in Ylena's eyes. "Thank you, Savi."

"You're welcome, Ylena. Take care. And may the Force be with you."

She smiled. "It always is."

That's one of the first things he'd taught her, when she'd become one of his loyal Gatherers—you couldn't escape the inescapable. Perhaps she could not use the Force, but she could let the Force use her.

Chapter Thirty-Seven

ARCHEX HAD LIVED IN FIRST ORDER quarters for so long that being out of doors on a planet like Batuu made the permanently knotted muscle between his shoulders itch. Such a place was too big, too wild, too . . . disordered. Some might consider the twitter of birds and rustle of leaves calming, but his idea of calm had been forged among perfectly polished plastoid, flawlessly smooth metal, and squadrons of identical figures who moved as one. The most tranquil thing he could imagine was his own cabin back on the *Absolution*, right after he'd shined his armor, shaved his head and face, and taken a shower while the cleaning droids had visited—and all on a good day when everything went as planned with no surprises, no one was out of line, and no mechanical or technological malfunctions occurred.

He longed to do a good job, to serve a function, but the chaos and noise of the Resistance outpost made him uncomfortable. That's why he'd found a small room among the ruins that no one else seemed to care about, a place built of nothing but cold, clean stone where he could finally let all his masks drop and just . . . be.

Here, he could feel his pain. He could mutter to himself. He could catch his breath or rub the aching place under his ribs or beat on his leg with both fists or work through the fight combinations he'd taught tiny children so that they might one day graduate from his teachings and learn from Captain Phasma how to kill. He liked the symmetry of it—using the First Order's teachings to make himself stronger now so that he could beat them in turn—or help beat them. He wasn't very useful on his own, these days.

He was accustomed to being around thousands of people, yet four beings, a droid, and a pig nearly drove him mad. Even if his current companions were louder and less disciplined than anyone on a Star Destroyer, he still didn't want them to hear him muttering, to see the rituals he needed to complete in order to feel like himself. It was private, this connection to what he'd once been: a man in his prime, unhindered by wounds, powerful and confident and strong, certain of his place in the world. Not only that, but he'd been programmed to never show weakness, and no matter how firmly his Cerean metaphysical guides had tried to break those connections in his mind, still they lingered, just as firm and unyielding as they'd ever been. Archex had simply learned to hide certain parts of himself to make those around him feel more comfortable.

That was the hard thing about leaving the First Order: They forged you into a weapon, but a weapon was useless without hands to guide it. Archex actually missed the whispers in his bunk—the orders, propaganda, and First Order philosophy slogans pumped into his brain while he slept. When someone else told you how to think, you could free yourself from decisions and just do your job. There was an elegant, tidy simplicity to that kind of life.

And that was another thing he missed—having a clear position, clear duties. As Captain Cardinal, he'd known exactly where he stood in the pecking order—the First Order organizational chart was easily accessible. He knew who was below him and owed him deference and who was above him and deserved his respect. But here, they were all equals—no officers, really, no chain of command. Just Vi, doing her best to lead, and without recent orders from her own superiors. Perhaps she had a rank, but no one used it. She had natural leadership skills but no proper training, especially regarding how to command.

And that was what truly cut the most deeply: In all their preparations for the assault on the First Order transport, Vi had given him no orders. No one had even mentioned him.

They'd completely forgotten him.

Chapter Thirty-Eight

THE CANTINA HAD ALWAYS FELT LIKE home to Zade. Not this cantina, necessarily, but any cantina—the absolute reality of a cantina. It didn't matter if it was Oga's pub or any other bar on any other world. He'd practically grown up in a cantina. He had fallen asleep on ale-sticky leather booth seats as a boy on Tatooine as his mother and stepfather drank heavily to forget the harsh demands of life in the dunes, and he'd sneaked into the seediest establishments possible before he was twelve, posing as a Jawa to buy the cheapest booze available. Half the time it would work, and he'd get sauced and shout *"Utinni!"* all night to keep up the charade. The other half of the time, he'd get kicked outside in the dirt in his stolen brown robes, seething with rage, swearing that he would grow up and show them.

Show what to whom, though? He still hadn't figured that part out.

And now, to think he'd lucked into a job that combined his two greatest strengths: drinking and demanding attention. Not only that, but both activities were in the service of the Resistance. Zade had never been one for politics or labels before quite recently, but he hated the First Order now with the fire of a thousand suns.

The job should've been easy: Pick up a load of moogyyrko sap on Kashyyyk that would be refined into liquor later, party with the

Wookiees for a couple of days, deliver the loot to Oga Garra at Black Spire Outpost on Batuu, and all his previous fees and fines would be forgiven. Nothing special, nothing flashy, nothing he hadn't done a hundred times for a hundred different shady gangsters, and the deal had never gone awry in his hands. Honor among thieves and all that.

And it had gone fine—especially the partying-with-Wookiees bit—right up until the First Order hailed him, interrogated him about his cargo, used their tractor beam to suck his ship into their much larger ship, and stole every last barrel of sap. It had been such a businesslike theft, too, almost as if it had been a tax instead of outright thievery. A crisply dressed officer in all black had unapologetically explained that Zade was being "relieved" of his cargo, and that was it. No real explanation, no apology. They cleaned him out and let him leave.

Oh, and they killed his partner, Valoss, for trying to stop them.

Valoss had been his best mate since childhood, his navigator, his better half, the quiet and respectable side of their duo. And while Zade had accepted that sometimes the bigger fish caught and ate the smaller fish, Valoss had always had this obnoxious sense of right and wrong. The peculiar Devaronian just couldn't handle injustice—or the loss of creds she could send back home to her family.

And she picked exactly the wrong time to go from the strong and silent type to the strong and stupid type.

"This is illegal theft of privately owned goods," Valoss said reasonably.

"Pew," the officer responded unreasonably, speaking through his blaster.

Valoss fell to the floor, and the officer looked to Zade, his expression as flat and blank as the clean silver walls surrounding them. He didn't even look human in that moment—he was like a droid, expressionless and certain.

"Do you wish to register a complaint?" he asked.

Zade took a deep breath. "No, sir."

"Then you may go."

Zade was halfway back to the *Midnight Blade* before the officer reminded him to clean up his friend's corpse, and he learned just how much Valoss had grown as he dragged her body onto the ship they'd been piloting together for ten years. As soon as he was out of range of that tractor beam, he'd ejected Valoss into space among the stars she loved per her once-hypothetical wishes and started drinking. He'd had enough fuel to get to Batuu, but that was it. They'd run out of cash and had desperately needed Oga's promised delivery fee and clemency. And thus, when Zade landed without his cargo, his ship had been impounded by the minions of one furious Blutopian gangster. And here he was.

Ah, but now he had the chance to strike back at the heart of both the First Order and Oga Garra. Rusko had reprimanded him several times for speaking too loudly against the First Order in the cantina, but tonight—oh, tonight would be fun. Who cared if he got kicked out of the biggest cantina on the entire planet? Chances were good he would die in the fight, buying time for Kriki to reprogram that First Order ship. And if it didn't work, the cantina would be rubble, anyway, after the First Order razed the planet. The planet Zade was trapped on.

His luck, lately, had not been good. As they said around here, annoying as it was, he did not have the better hand.

Valoss had been the better hand, and look where that'd gotten her. Zade liked to think of her orbiting the planet now, a third moon.

He gulped the last of his Outer Rim and licked the salt off the edge of the glass. He straightened the knot on his scarf and shot his cuffs, for all that they were ratty and dusty now, not at all how he preferred them. Throwing his shoulders back, he turned and leaned against the bar as he had on his first night here, surveying the room.

It was the busiest time of night, when both early pippa birds and night starmarks were buzzed. A Sullustan quartet was playing live jazz, a lively number that kept everyone in a good mood. Rusko, thankfully, wasn't at his table, but N'arrghela and the Talpini were, just taking up space and staring down the clientele as the Wookiee picked her teeth with the bone from her Bloody Rancor.

Zade felt the tiniest thrill of stage fright. Sure, he'd been talking down the First Order for days, telling his own story and spreading the tales he'd heard of abuse in the market streets. He'd loudly described the bruises and cuts on Vi's face and how Oh-li had plucked one of Jenda's bloody teeth from the cobblestones. But tonight, he wouldn't just be stirring up discontent and reminding everyone how close they were to the galaxy's biggest bully. He wouldn't just be spinning yarns about how the First Order could show up out of the blue at any moment, like some childhood monster, and destroy someone's life, livelihood, and bone structure.

No, tonight, he would actually try to rile these people to action.

He was fully aware that just a few weeks ago, such a speech would've had zero effect on him personally. He would've sat in a shadowy booth, elbowed Valoss in the ribs, and said, *Would you look at this poor sap? If you stay in place, of course they're going to find you. That's why we keep moving.*

But now, he was staying in place. And he was going to fight.

He pushed away from the bar, just the right amount of tipsy to be charismatic, fearless, reckless, and boneless. He'd been watching the cantina door all night, but not a single stormtrooper had stuck their bucket into the business of the common man. Surely they had allies and toadies in the crowd, but he'd be watching for them—and gone before they could report on his activities here tonight. Yes, he was positively fizzing and high on life, but for once, he wasn't nearly as drunk as he looked.

"My friends!" he roared, so loud that the poor Sullustan musicians in back all left their song on awkward toots and blats. The cantina's chatter went quiet, the expectant silence punctuated with curious whispers.

"You all know me," he began with a delicate bow. "But perhaps you don't know my story. My name is Zade Kalliday, and my luck ran out when the First Order intercepted my ship while I was en route to deliver a load of liquor to our beloved proprietor, Oga Garra." He blew a kiss in the vague direction of the dark hallway where Vi said one of the secret doors to Oga's lair was hidden.

"Now my ship is impounded, my friend and navigator is dead, and I'm stuck here without a spira to my name."

"Then how'd you get the drinks?" some naughty heckler called out.

Zade winked at him. "Ask your mother," he quipped.

The crowd clapped and laughed appreciatively, warming up to him, and he stepped forward, for once letting pain show in his eyes. Tonight, he needed more than pizzazz—he needed vulnerability. He needed honesty. And he would deliver.

"Most of us live lives of quiet dignity. We toil, we reap, we drink, we die—with perhaps a few other pleasant pastimes in between. We instinctively shy away from pain, or else we'd all hop into the first pretty fire we ever saw. We move away from fear, from cruelty. And so it's easy to hear tales of the First Order and think—*but I live a good life, so surely that won't happen to me.* We tell ourselves that if we just keep our heads down and keep working, the monster won't see us. We toe the line, and we hope to be ignored by the beast at the gate."

He paused, the crowd held enraptured, and drank a shot sitting untouched and forgotten on a table.

"But, my friends, the beast has passed through the gate. The beast is on our planet. In our outpost. The beast has planted spies among your fellow drinkers tonight, possibly among your friends. And these spies think, *If I do as the beast asks, I alone will be immune to its hunger.* But they are wrong. The First Order doesn't care about any of you. Not a one."

He hopped up onto the bar. "Let me say that again: *The First Order doesn't care about you.* They only care about order—their version of it. It's right there in the name. They only care about leaving no one alive who wishes to stand up to them. They want your silence, your complacence, your fear. They want you to turn your head when you see old women beaten in the street while minding their own business. They want you to ignore citizens of the galaxy being shot point-blank or dragged off to secretive interrogations that leave them broken and scarred. The First Order does not ask for your vote or your consent; they want only your obedience and silence."

"Yeah!" a few voices shouted as fists banged on tables. A shadowy figure detached from the back of the cantina and fled into the night, and although Zade couldn't identify them, he knew his time was now ticking down.

"People of the spire, the line between minding your business and defending your freedom is thin as a razor blade. You can't tiptoe along it. You have to make that cut, draw that line in the sand, and believe that you can make a change. That your choices can leave a mark. That you can serve something better. There's a hero inside each of you, waiting for your moment of greatness."

Zade knelt by the ancient bartender and caressed her withered cheek.

"How much do you love this place, your home? Your planet? Your children and neighbors and friends? What are you willing to do to preserve that? Because believe me: The beast is here, and there is no more hiding."

He hopped down to the ground, meeting eyes one by one. "Take it from a guy who had to drag his best friend's corpse across the deck of a First Order ship, a guy who can't see that white armor without his hands shaking and his bowels going loose: I'm willing to do anything. That's what the Resistance is all about. And tomorrow when the spire's shadow is long, we fight. Come with me tonight, or take up your arms tomorrow. Every dead buckethead is one less monster at the gate."

At first, he was met with only silence, but he knew better than to say anything. He simply stood, open and aching and steely with resolve. Then someone in back started clapping, and someone else pounded their fist on the bar, and then they all began stomping under their tables, and finally, the applause built to a roar.

"To the Resistance!" Zade shouted, his fist in the air.

"You there. Stop!"

The room went eerily silent.

Zade's bowels did that pesky loosening thing the moment he heard the voice filtered through a stormtrooper's helmet as he sprinted past. There the metaphorical beast stood, in the cantina doorway, armor immaculate and blaster drawn. And Zade was just excited enough and drunk enough after that stolen gulp of liquor to whip out his blaster and shoot the trooper in the belly, always aiming for those black lines where armor ended and vulnerability could be found, if luck was on one's side. The trooper shot back, and blasterfire pinged off the bar. One particularly close shot hit one of the creature tanks, leaving a mark on the glass.

Zade kept pulling the trigger, and he hit something first. The trooper doubled over, bright-red blood spattering the white armor, and Zade charged him. The crowd opened up, making an aisle, hungry as always for a scene, and Zade picked up a big glass on his way and crashed it into the trooper's buckethead as he bolted past. He pinged off a few shots in close range and bolted out the door, zigging and zagging as he ran through the sleeping market. Behind him, he heard blasterfire and the crash of glass, but there was no telling what was happening, and he wasn't going to stick around to find out.

The excitement and exercise fizzed the liquor right out of his bloodstream, which meant he was sober enough to take a circuitous route home. It wouldn't do to lead the troopers back to their headquarters. As the running fell off to a gentle jog and then a loose walk, Zade wished he'd made a holo of that performance. It was flawless, from the opening to the meat of the message to the applause to the fortuitous arrival of that shiny-armored monster like a big white exclamation point. He'd seen it in the eyes of the locals—they'd felt his passion, absorbed his message. Hadn't they?

Or maybe they were just a bunch of drunks in a nowhere backwater outpost on a nowhere backwater planet, desperate for anything more entertaining than betting on holo-chess. Maybe they would've applauded anything. Maybe they still believed that if they just kept their heads down and feigned ignorance, the beast at the door would give up and go away. He hoped that they would make the right decision, that he'd played some small part in helping the Resistance turn the tide. He hoped he'd done enough to satisfy the life debt he owed Vi. He was sick of heartache, sick of worry, sick of hating himself for being the only one still alive when Valoss was obviously the best of them.

He realized, suddenly, that he was bleeding. The bastard had grazed his shoulder, making a right mess of his shimmersilk blazer.

Not that it mattered.

He fully planned on dying tomorrow.

It would be easier, that way. For everyone.

Chapter Thirty-Nine

THE STOLEN COMLINK NESTLED SAFELY in Vi's pocket. To think: Such a small thing could be the difference between success and failure. For her, and for what was left of the First Order forces on Batuu. For all that her time here had been riddled with bad luck, finding Kriki was a godsend. And Zade and Dolin and Ylena, too. Maybe what Ylena had told her held true: The Force was always watching.

Carefully, slowly, groaning all the while, she clambered up the outside of the ruins, hoping for privacy and trying to get a little closer to the sky when she made her call. She could only use the comlink once, Kriki had informed her, as one ping off the First Order ship could be seen as a glitch or interference, while a second ping would be instantly suspect. And she wouldn't have much time before they investigated the ongoing connection. This had to work, and quickly.

It had to.

Vi pushed the button, triggering Kriki's scramble sequence as she opened the channel. "Magpie for General Organa."

She spoke a secret code, her voice rusty with feeling and hope. A long moment later, a bleary blue hologram appeared—Leia in night robes, hair down, seated at a rough desk, supporting her chin with a hand like she might fall over at any moment. "Magpie. Good to hear from you. You made it."

Leia sounded as beat up and exhausted as Vi felt, but Vi felt a rush of warmth, seeing her leader, knowing that wherever she was, whatever was happening, Leia was still up and working, burning like a candle, keeping the Resistance going as if through sheer force of will.

"We made it, but with a lot of caveats. We don't have much time—I'm using stolen First Order tech. We crashed and much of our cargo was stolen by a local gangster, but we're in the process of earning it back. The First Order is here looking for me. An officer, Lieutenant Wulfgar Kath, with a transport full of troopers. We took down Kath and at least eight troopers, but we don't know how many are left. We have a plan to get rid of them all and convince the FO that this planet is useless, but it's dicey, and if you can send more people and supplies—"

"We can't spare more people and supplies. I'm sorry, Magpie, but you're on your own. I have faith in you."

"I'm injured and we have almost nothing—" Vi's voice broke.

"Almost nothing is still something. You're a leader, Vi. You're brave and smart and strong, and you understand people. Whatever resources you have, I know you'll find a way. Your kind of dedication and commitment is the reason the Resistance is still here. You have my complete trust."

The connection wavered, and Vi knew her window was closing.

"That's all the time we have. Hope I can live up to your trust, General, but the odds are not good."

Leia smiled a sad little smile. "Never tell me the odds. And even if you did, I'd still bet on you. Good luck, and may the Force be with you."

The moment the general's holo disappeared, Vi felt cold and alone, as if she could sense every empty bit of space between her and the Resistance, the living breathing people on the other end of that transmission. Somehow, it always felt like it was safer where Leia was, even if it also seemed like she was forever in the thick of danger. In contrast, Batuu felt so desolate and far away. As if Leia were the warm heart of everything.

In that moment, Vi had a realization: That was what she'd become to her own small contingent of rebels, why they jokingly called her Mother Hen. She was the warm, life-giving sun around which they orbited. She held them together, encouraged them, made them feel useful, gave them purpose. She took a deep breath and firmed up her chin. Rising from where she'd wedged herself into the stone, she felt every injury, the pulls in her shoulders and the bruises on her face and the tenderness over her ribs.

It might seem impossible, but like Leia, she would keep going.

For her people.

For her general.

For the Resistance.

And for the galaxy.

A rough, underfunded, understaffed refuge on a backwater planet, after all, might one day be what turned the tide against the First Order.

It was up to her to ignite that spark.

Chapter Forty

AS MUCH AS HE DISLIKED THE outpost itself, Lieutenant Wulfgar Kath wanted to see for himself the progress his troops were making. They still hadn't found Vi Moradi, and one of his soldiers had taken injuries when following a tip to Oga's cantina last night, where a known malcontent had been openly fomenting rebellion among the local populace. That left him with only eleven functional stormtroopers, one of whom had a damaged trigger finger. He still had probe droids canvassing the forest, but thus far they'd only found a bashed-in transport with a pair of lahiroo nesting inside.

By Kath's reckoning, he had only a handful of days before General Hux decided to stop sending fruitless comms and start sending down a new officer with explicit instructions regarding relieving Kath of duty and possibly his head. Therefore, Kath needed to complete his mission, immediately. Never mind that everything about this trip to Batuu had gone jogan-shaped up until now. He would find Vi Moradi, and he would destroy the Resistance base, and then he'd return to the *Penumbra* and give the general the good news himself. Success was the only option he would entertain; that strategy had served him well up until now.

He sat up perfectly straight in the speeder, and from the moment they zipped into the marketplace, he could tell a definite difference. Those citizens performing vital, useful duties continued to do so quietly, their eyes downcast respectfully, while the most distasteful of the population silently melted into the shadows or slipped through doors, trying to avoid detection. Old women didn't sully the avenues with their fetid handicrafts, and small children didn't chase one another around the trees and shout unnecessarily and get underfoot. The streets were cleaner and more orderly already—a good start.

As he stepped out of the speeder and strolled through town, meeting every eye and gazing into every shop, some folk offered him food or drink, which he of course turned down. Even if poisoning on purpose or by accident hadn't been a constant possibility in a place this primitive, it would be vulgar for a man of his office to eat in public, and his troopers of course were never to remove their helmets. And besides, all the local foods looked rampant with sugar, salt, and spices. He vastly preferred his bland First Order rations.

As a last resort, his soldiers had found stims and boosters for him in town, and the bruise on his chest was fading. His headaches had mostly receded, but the walk in the hot, bright suns definitely cost him. Back on the *Penumbra,* such negligible injuries would've been healed easily in the medbay, but here, on the frontier edge of the galaxy, his physical frustrations stubbornly lingered. The fresh, pollen-filled air didn't help.

"Bright suns, sir!" a young man said, giving something like a salute from where he stood amid piles of refuse.

Kath scowled as his soldiers stepped in front of him, blasters drawn.

"Move along," one said.

"But I have, uh, intel," the man said, fumbling for the right word. "On the Resistance."

Kath waved the two stormtroopers away and stepped forward, hoping the unkempt young man wouldn't try to touch him. He clasped his hands behind his back.

"Well, what is it?"

"My name is Gol, sir. I run Gol's Tech Bay, right here. If you should need any tech while you're onplanet." He laughed nervously and waved at his garbage.

Kath sighed and made a go-on gesture.

"I think my former employee may have joined the Resistance."

"What's your point, Gol?"

"Well, I mean, uh. I heard you paid for valuable intel?"

Kath stepped forward, forcing Gol to step back. "We do pay for *valuable* intel, yes. I'm looking for Resistance spy Vi Moradi or any evidence of a Resistance base here on Batuu. Tattling on your ex-employee isn't useful to me."

"But she could lead you right to them! The Resistance, I mean. And Vi."

Kath ground his teeth. This is why the First Order was needed: People were just so unimaginably stupid. And greedy. And weak. No wonder they couldn't self-govern.

"CD-5502, take down a description and search the outpost for this supposed Resistance sympathizer." He looked to Gol, hoping his true disgust showed in his eyes. "*If* we should find your ex-employee and *if* she should lead us to either Vi Moradi or the Resistance base, you will be compensated."

Gol stepped forward. "How much are we talking?"

Kath wanted to say, *I'll let you live,* but instead he merely said, "Enough."

Chapter Forty-One

THE NEXT MORNING, VI SAT AT the mess hall table, hands wrapped around her mug, her caf gone cold. The corridors were heavy with that sort of grim, oppressive sense of expectation that always hung around right before a fight against an unbeatable enemy. Vi had slept poorly, and she wasn't the only one. Kriki had been up all night studying an array of datapads and manuals. Vi knew that the Chadra-Fan stayed up all night *every* night, and yet Kriki looked exhausted and frail this morning, her eyes blinking overmuch and her nose flickering and her breathing fast.

Archex had deep-purple smudges under his eyes and was rubbing his leg more than usual. Vi didn't remark on it, but Kriki had told her in confidence that she'd followed him to a quiet chamber one night and watched him secretly practice fighting and stretching as if, with enough willpower and struggle, he might be returned to full health. No matter how often Pook told him that there was no chance of miraculous healing, thanks to Phasma's poison blade, still Archex held out hope—which was one of the things Vi liked best about him. But just now, as she worried about the coming fight, she would've felt better if Archex had looked well rested and capable of carrying on with the Resistance refuge, should something tragic happen to the rest of them.

Dolin had been gloomy ever since he'd returned from his futile visit home yesterday. The Batuuan farm boy had resisted any efforts at conversation about what he'd found there, but Vi had no choice but to assume they couldn't count on support from the agrarian communities beyond the outpost. Her heart went out to him—his grandmother must've rejected him, or at least given him an earful. If Vi's own brother, Baako, ever found out what she did with her time, she'd get a good chewing-out, too. It was hard to make a more traditional family understand that one's passions lay elsewhere, that not all lives were meant to be lived in safety and comfort, and that some paths led off the farm. At least Dolin had Waba, the hog contentedly snuffling up the leftover breakfast on a plate at his master's feet.

And then there was Zade. He was usually the last one awake, and many mornings Vi didn't even see him before she left for the scrapyard. But this morning, she wouldn't be going to sort through piles of discarded junk, hunting for treasure, joking companionably with her friends. And Zade wasn't sleeping in his bunk, contorted into strange, lanky shapes as he snored and mumbled in his sleep to someone named Valoss. No one had yet asked him about this mysterious figure, but judging by the way he often had tear tracks on his cheeks when he rolled in to breakfast, Vi had to assume that Valoss was dead, or at least permanently out of the picture.

No, this morning, Zade sat among them—slumped, really. His usual wry and carefree humor was conspicuously absent. He hunched over his caf, his knee jiggling madly under the table. There was a blackened blaster mark on his shimmersilk jacket showing a white bandage underneath, but he was ignoring it, so everyone else did, too. He hadn't spoken yet, which was unusual. He hadn't even made fun of Archex, which told Vi that Zade, too, was worried about what was to come.

Finally, she couldn't stand the tense silence any longer.

"Anybody have anything to report?" she asked, aiming for friendly confidence and landing somewhere around chipper anxiety.

"As I have no real duties, I have nothing to report," Archex said, his face tight. "But if you can give me some way to be useful—"

"You are useful," she told him for the millionth time. "Being here, running things, training people, cooking, carving, knowing what's going on. All of that is invaluable. And saving me from death by First Order torture was also a job well done. Full marks, now and forever."

He sighed and put his head in his hands. "But you've given me nothing to do to help you today, on this mission. It's driving me mad!"

"You know full well why you can't be there. It's beyond personal. And you know that you can't . . . that you're . . ."

"Yes. I'm broken. Thank you for the reminder."

"You're no more broken than I am!" she barked, at her wit's end. "But we need you here." *In case we don't make it,* she wanted to say but didn't. *Someone has to keep trying to build a refuge here if I die.* "Now does anyone have anything positive to report?"

"I've been studying all night," Kriki said. "I think . . . I think I can do it. I've downloaded every First Order code or manual I could find into my datapad, so it shouldn't take longer than fifteen minutes. Been practicing the keystrokes. Trying to eliminate mistakes."

Vi smiled encouragingly. "Well done. I know you can do it."

"I can try," Kriki said weakly. "But I need to double-check something." She bolted up and scurried out of the room, hugging her datapad to her chest.

For a moment, the only sounds were chewing, sipping, and the gentle snuffling of the truffleboar hunting for scraps under the table.

"I got shot for the first time last night," Zade said, breaking the silence. "I didn't like it."

Vi tipped her head. "Welcome to the club. You get used to it."

"Just a minor graze," Pook observed. "As long as he keeps it clean, he's unlikely to die of sepsis."

Zade threw his spoon at the droid and muttered, "How cheerful!"

The spoon splattered breakfast meal on Pook's screen, and Pook moaned, "You are a study in the grotesque," and everyone laughed. It was a pleasant moment of relieved tension . . . that didn't last.

"The good news is that I got shot while shooting a trooper," Zade continued. "I didn't stick around to see if he expired because I had to run. I'm guessing, at the very least, he's in the medbay today. I believe I got him in the groinal area, and blood was involved. Bit of a planning error in the armor construction there."

"If the troopers want to be able to walk or run, they need that articulation," Archex said, looking beyond exhausted. "Believe me: First Order scientists have tried everything. Seal up those vulnerable rifts and they might as well be frozen in carbonite. It's hard enough to move as it is."

"And how would you know?" Zade shot back. "Look, mate, I know you're desperate for something to do, but acting like a kriffing expert about everything is not a hobby."

Archex snorted. "Don't tell me my business. You don't know me."

Zade leaned back, sneering. "And why would I want to? Got a stick up your rear, don't you? Rules this and caution that. Thinking that way never gets nothing done. Sit at home while the rest of us go out and work, then call me lazy. How would you know anything? Probably faking that limp so you don't have to risk your biscuit."

Archex stood, his box seat squealing over the stone floor. "Fine. You want to know the truth? Then let me tell you, because I'm sick of your disrespect and dismissal, and I'm sick of being ashamed of my past."

Vi's eyes widened in alarm and she shook her head at him, the tiniest movement. Now was not the time to sow distrust in their little group. The truth could wait. Surely he knew that.

But he kept on anyway.

"I know how their armor works because I used to be one of them. A First Order stormtrooper. Then a captain. The Resistance kidnapped me, and I informally defected."

"You were one of them?" Dolin asked, his voice half wonder and half horror.

Archex put his shoulders back and one by one met everyone's eyes. Vi could see the war inside him, the programming fighting the integrity, the self-disgust fighting the pride. "From the time the First

Order rescued—no. *Abducted* me as a child, yes. I was one of them. *Was.* But now I'm with the Resistance."

Zade looked to Vi. "And you knew this?"

Vi settled back, echoing Archex's confidence and challenge. "Of course I knew. I'm the one who kidnapped him from that Star Destroyer. I'm the one who brought him to Batuu. I'm his partner."

"And you trust him?"

Vi nodded, slowly. "With my life."

"He's Cardinal, isn't he?" When Vi looked up, Kriki hovered in the doorway, half cowering behind the stone as if Archex might suddenly rise up and strike her. "When you call out in the night, begging Captain Cardinal to stop. That's him, isn't it?"

Vi sighed heavily. "It is. He tortured me. On the *Absolution*. And then he let me escape. And then, when Captain Phasma had nearly killed him, I rescued him. So now you know our history. But you also need to know that Archex has given the Resistance invaluable knowledge on all echelons of First Order training, propaganda, programming, weapons, philosophy, even the interiors of their ships and their strategies. Without question, his scales are balanced. General Leia Organa herself handpicked him for this mission. And if I can forgive him his past and move on, you should able to do so as well."

"Was he still with them when they were building Starkiller Base? And during the Hosnian attack?" Kriki asked, her voice tiny.

Archex sat down again, collapsing into himself, his head in his hands. "I was in the First Order while they were building the weapon, but I had no idea. The First Order's intel is on a need-to-know basis. They don't tell the troopers until a plan has become a victory, and even then the reporting is heavily biased. At the time, I had been brainwashed to believe the New Republic was evil and dangerous." He pounded the table with his fist, once, with meaning. "I promise you, Kriki: I had no part in Starkiller Base. I was on the *Absolution* for over a decade and never saw outside her walls. I didn't build the weapon, I didn't aim it, I didn't push the button. I didn't even know it existed."

"But you cheered when it happened, didn't you?"

Archex's head dropped. "No. By then, I was a prisoner of the Resistance, and seeing that footage is part of what brought me here. It was unfathomable. It was evil." He looked up and met her eyes. "But if not for Vi, I would've cheered with the rest of them. Because I was programmed to do so. Because I was brainwashed and chemically controlled."

Dolin pointed at the stolen stormtrooper helmet and armor neatly piled among the rest of their cargo crates. "So you wore one of those?"

"I was fitted with my first armor as a child. Wearing it became more comfortable than not. It was my life."

"What was it like? Wearing it every day?" The way Dolin asked it wasn't admiring; it was more like a child asking about an animal carcass they'd found in the road, horrified and morbidly fascinated.

"It felt like belonging," Archex told him, his voice raw with emotion. "You know who you are, in that armor."

Archex gazed around the room sadly. He looked more broken than ever, without their trust. Without their friendship. It was like losing his armor, all over again. Everyone was closed off now—arms crossed, eyes hard. Kriki was sniffling, trying not to cry in front of them but unable to leave.

"It was easier," Archex said softly. "When I wore the armor, people trusted me, looked up to me. I was given clear orders. I knew who I was and how to serve a purpose. This?" He gestured around the chaotic jumble of goods in the ancient cave, at the distrustful faces around the table. "This is a lot harder."

No one said anything, and Archex got up and left.

"Why didn't you tell us?" Zade asked, looking at Vi, angry, his wet eyes betraying the hardness in his voice.

She shrugged. "It's not mine to tell."

"We trusted you!"

"You trusted us both," Vi said. "And you found us worthy of your trust. That doesn't have to change. Archex is the same man he was yesterday. He's the same man he was when he rescued me from Kath's interrogation. He's the same man he was when he tried to kill Captain Phasma. Given the chance, he would step between any one of you and an enemy and gladly take the hit."

"You can't know that," Zade spat. "Programming is programming."

Vi cocked her head. "So you don't believe people can change?"

Zade sighed and shrugged, leaning back as if trying to reclaim his carelessness. "Not enough to sleep next to the once-enemy with blasters and blades scattered all around us."

Vi looked to Dolin. "Do you feel the same way?"

Dolin hunched down a little. "Ylena told me Archex could be trusted, and I trust Ylena, and I trust you, so . . . I want to trust him? But it's hard."

Nodding along, Vi felt twenty years older. "It *is* hard. But sometimes, it's worth it."

"I have calculated the odds of Archex betraying the Resistance," Pook said conversationally. "If anyone wants to know."

Vi stood.

"Shove those odds up your can, Pook. We have a job to do. It happens today. Everyone has a role to play. I can only urge you to place your trust in Archex, as I have, or at the very least, to place your trust in me and in the plan we made together. Because if we fail today . . ."

"We all lose," Dolin finished for her.

"No," Kriki said softly. "We all die."

Chapter Forty-Two

THE MORNING . . . HAD NOT GONE WELL. And Vi wasn't sure how to fix things.

Any camaraderie or cohesion they'd had was gone. They haunted the ruins, drifting aimlessly from room to room in the semi-darkness. Kriki studied datapads and muttered to herself. Zade tried to find something alcoholic to drink, then tried to discover where Vi had hidden the stims, then spent the rest of the day sulking in conspicuous places. Dolin worked on his crankbike, making minor upgrades and talking to Waba as if the hog were responding—and quite argumentative. Archex simply disappeared. Vi looked for him—but not too hard.

He was right—he didn't have a real function for this afternoon's raid on the First Order transport. His job was to stay behind and carry on their work for the Resistance if things went wrong. His job was simply to stay away and stay alive. If the worst happened and the stormtroopers managed to capture or kill Vi, at least they would go away and hopefully leave Batuu in peace.

So what would happen, Vi thought, if she just turned herself in?

What if she just ignored their risky plan and gave herself up?

Would the troopers—and the First Order's leadership—assume the supposed Resistance base would wither away without her? Would they stop looking? Would Archex be able to carry on, perhaps with Ylena's help and maybe Kriki and Dolin's eventual trust, if they lived through it? She knew that Zade would be gone the moment Archex was in charge and his liquor budget dried up. And considering he'd openly shot a stormtrooper last night, part of Zade's sulk surely focused on the fact that as long as there was a First Order presence on the planet, he couldn't go back to the only well-stocked watering hole on Batuu. The troopers would be on the lookout for him there, now—or have a toady just waiting to run off and tattle. So that was at least one recruit gone. Which would most likely make Kriki and Dolin lose faith and drift back to their safer, more predictable lives.

Vi was the glue that held them together, and without their Mother Hen, this Resistance refuge was doomed.

And then she considered what would happen if she just gave up completely, sold everything they had, and used the credits to buy passage offplanet for her entire team. She might return to the general a failure, but there was still something she could do for the Resistance, still hope for her recruits. They could find meaningful work and help to turn the tide alongside the fleet.

But then what would happen to Batuu? To Savi and Ylena and Jenda and Oh-li and Salju?

She knew the answer to that. Eventually, General Hux would discover that she'd killed his officer and escaped his grasp, and he would retaliate by blasting Black Spire Outpost to rubble.

So that answered that question.

Self-sacrifice wouldn't work, and running away wouldn't work.

The only way forward was a complete commitment to success. This group needed her. The Resistance needed her. Batuu needed her.

They would follow the plan, together.

Either she'd die today, or she'd succeed.

They had everything they needed to triumph. Like General Organa had told her regarding building the refuge here from seemingly nothing, she just had to make it work.

Chapter Forty-Three

DOLIN WAS SITTING BY THE CENOTE with Waba when Ylena showed up around lunchtime. She was carrying take-out boxes from Ronto Roasters, and both Dolin and his hog looked up with pleasure.

"Thought you might need some strength today," she said, handing him one box and gracefully sinking to the grass beside him to open the other. When Waba snuffled close, she laughed and scratched the bristly head and produced a handful of Kat Saka's plain grains, Waba's current favorite treat.

They ate companionably for a little while, enjoying the chime of the waterfall tinkling into the pool below and flowing into the cenote. Dolin often came out here to sit and relax and think about things. Back home—or back at Grana's house, he should say now, since it wasn't really home if you weren't welcome there—he'd had plenty of time to enjoy nature, falling asleep against a haystack as the gruffins grazed or riding his crankbike out into a new patch of forest that he'd never seen before as Waba hunted for treasure. He was amazed that no one else among the Resistance recruits seemed to enjoy being outside, but he was glad to learn that Ylena did.

"Did you give Savi my apologies?" he asked, once he'd wiped his mouth on a napkin. "For not working today?"

"Of course. He knows how important it is, what's happening. He has no choice but to stand outside the conflict if he wishes to stay in the outpost and not end up in Oga's bad graces, but he's aware of . . . the value of the Resistance, let's say. He also believes you're a good worker, and he'll be glad to have you back at the scrapyard."

Dolin didn't consider himself a smart man, but he understood well enough what she was saying: If Vi's gambit failed and their cause was lost—and if Dolin lived through it—he still had a job, a way to survive in the outpost.

"I appreciate that. I guess there's always his apartment block."

Ylena sipped her Batuubucha tea and nodded. "Yes. Savi always takes care of his Gatherers."

"I'm glad you're not coming with us," he confessed. "I wouldn't want you to get hurt."

She patted his upper arm, and his skin went all over with goose bumps. "Don't worry. Everything will happen as it must."

"That's . . . not very comforting."

"The Force will guide you."

"But how do you know?"

Ylena gave her mysterious little shrug. "I just have faith."

He snorted. "Faith."

He used to have faith. Faith that his parents would live forever, and after that, that his grandmother would take care of him. And look where that had gotten him.

Ylena put down the remains of her flatbread and settled closer to him, leaning into his side, her head against his shoulder. He went very still, terrified to move. It was like watching dugar-dugar in the forest, creeping close and barely breathing, hoping for just another few precious seconds of knowing the unknowable.

"I can feel that you're hurting, and I know you went back to the settlement to visit your grandmother and try to recruit for the Resistance. I can only assume that your trip didn't go so well. But you must remember that people fear change. You come from a place where new things are not only feared but actively ignored and pushed away. Where strangers are repelled and advances in technology and education are snubbed. It's easy to live in a bubble without examining your biases. It's hard to change minds and hearts when the people are so determined to remain in the dark." She squeezed his arm. "But there's hope. There's *you*. You saw something that made you open to experience, and now you've got a destiny. You're doing something great for the galaxy, playing your part in a larger story. And your grandmother might not be able to see it, but I do, and I'm proud of you."

Filled with a daring he'd never yet experienced, knowing that despite her faith in the Force, her faith in him, it might all end soon, he put his arm around her. When she relaxed against him, it was like starmarks singing at night, a great shivering crescendo in his heart. He put his lips to her temple and murmured, "The galaxy is so much bigger than I'd ever imagined. I don't want to lose it now." And then, more softly, "I don't want to lose you."

Ylena turned her face up to his, her eyes full of smiles and sunshine and trust and, yes, so much faith.

"You won't," she said, firm and true, and then she kissed him.

Chapter Forty-Four

THE WALK TO THE FIRST ORDER'S mobile habitat felt like a walk to the gallows—and yet also like stepping into the cockpit of a podracer. Vi knew her people were nearby, ready to play their roles, and yet she walked alone, out front, the bait in an intricate trap with many moving parts—and many potential downfalls. She didn't stim up beforehand because her adversaries weren't supposed to expect a fight. She just kept her eyes down on a junky old metal detector Ylena had borrowed for her from Savi, a piece of equipment his scrappers often used when out in the forest, looking for ancient artifacts or crash sites.

It was almost time.

Her throat was dry as she moved the scanner over the springy ground, close enough to the transport's new resting place that if she stepped on a twig and a trooper was standing outside, they might hear it. She could see little flashes of the two-story monstrosity through the trees, the outside a dull-gray camouflage. Thanks to Archex's tracker, it hadn't been hard to find.

"Mother Hen, in position," she said into her comlink.

With her heart pounding in her ears, she edged closer and closer to the clearing made when the massive transport had broken through the treetops, creating its own landing pad on the forest floor. She hadn't yet seen signs of any troopers patrolling outside, but she knew that most of them were either searching the outpost for her or carrying similar scanners as they hunted Batuu's forests for her secret Resistance headquarters. With Kath gone, there might be only one or two soldiers sticking around to guard the mobile base. And hopefully, thanks to the absence of a commanding officer, they would be sloppy.

"Devastatingly Handsome Space Hobo, in position," came Zade's voice through her own comlink, and Vi was able to breathe again.

That meant that Zade and his blasters were sneaking up behind the transport from the other side, along with Kriki and her datapad. Dolin would be somewhere nearby with his bow and arrows and all the blasters they'd stolen off dead stormtroopers.

And that was it.

Archex and Pook had remained in the ruins. If this gambit failed and Vi died today, they could only hope that the First Order would believe that the Resistance on Batuu died with her. On a useless planet with no comm system and no officer, they would most likely return to the fleet. With this transport and its troopers gone, Archex could continue building the Resistance facility with Pook's help. Even if none of the outpost locals were willing to join the cause, even if Zade and Kriki and Dolin left, at least there would be a refuge where Resistance ships could land, fuel up, and wait for orders. It was one more hidey-hole in a universe that increasingly felt too small, thanks to the First Order's aggressive presence.

Vi found it gratifying, knowing that her work would go on without her. Even if she failed, she didn't fail completely.

She hadn't told anyone else, but she had one more card up her sleeve: that same poison tooth that had been her comfort while Cardinal tortured her in the bilges of the *Absolution*. Just running her tongue over it was calming—the ultimate ejector seat. If Kath had pushed her just a little further with his instruments, she might've considered it—but she hadn't reached that line. She'd decided that she would never give up Resistance intel to the First Order, no matter what. Even if Kath's troopers managed to drag her back to Kylo Ren's interrogation chair, she still had a way out.

That little rebellion would always remain the ultimate *Screw you* to anyone who sought to control her.

She stretched, cracking her back and feeling every bruise, every cut, every tender wound from her last visit to this transport. Pook could've continued to accelerate her healing in their makeshift med-bay, but instead, she still wore the marks of Kath's fists on her face. This was all part of the plan: These stormtroopers needed to see her as weak, damaged, foolish. Without resources. Without friends.

"I'm in position, too," Dolin whispered through the comlink. "Uh, Farm Boy, that is."

And that meant that it was finally, really, truly time to act.

"Gah!" Vi shouted, tripping over a branch and letting her scanner crash on the ground.

It wasn't the greatest war cry ever heard, but as she slowly pulled herself to standing, groaning and clutching her bruised rib, she heard the exact sound she was hoping for yet dreaded: armor clacking as boots ran, right for her.

"You there!" a woman's clipped tones called with that familiar robotic flatness of a stormtrooper helmet's speakers.

Vi looked up and feigned panic, spinning as if to run.

"Stop! Hands on your head!"

She let her hands shake as they slowly rose in the air.

"What's wrong? What did I do?" she asked

Gloved hands jerked her arms behind her back and slapped on binders.

"Did I do something wrong? I'm just hunting for scrap—"

"We know who you are, Resistance scum." The woman's tone dripped scorn.

A second trooper moved in front of her, blaster at the ready.

"Now turn around and march," the woman said.

Vi sighed heavily as she turned around.

"Look, I'm not who you think I am—"

Crack.

The blaster split her lip open and might've knocked a tooth loose. Apparently her new gray wrap and natural hair were as clumsy a disguise as she'd hoped. They really weren't playing around.

"Don't open your mouth. Don't speak. Walk."

A blaster prodded her in the back, and she had a momentary flashback to Cardinal marching her through the corridors of the *Absolution*. She wandered if Archex ever thought about her time in his interrogation chair under the watchful eye of his floating droid Iris, if he felt guilty about it or considered himself a completely new person, someone free from the shackles of his past. Thanks to Kriki, he now knew that she still had nightmares about him, that she hadn't gotten over it. Those moments were buried in her soul, probably permanently, and she never knew when they would rise, unbidden, from the dark.

And now she was going back to that same place, again, putting herself willingly into the enemy's hands.

Because that was her job.

The blaster prodded harder—that was going to leave a bruise.

"Walk!" the male trooper barked as the woman led the way.

"Lieutenant Kath will be most pleased to see you," she said, smug.

Vi's blood ran cold.

Kath isn't dead?

And it was too late to tell her people.

All she could do was stay alive and hope.

Chapter Forty-Five

KRIKI HUNCHED UNDER HER TUNIC, THE datapad clutched tightly against her chest. She hated being near the First Order transport; the area around it just felt . . . wrong. Even the birds could sense it and had stopped singing. The scent of burnt metal hung in the air, and high overhead in the canopy, the branches and leaves were cruelly shorn, leaving an empty hole where life should've thrived.

Zade stood beside her, his energy as tightly wound as a spring. He'd tried tapping his foot once, but she'd gently elbowed him—it would be the highest tragedy for the entire mission to go jogan-shaped because of one nervous human's inability to control his extremities. She limited her own panic to blinking and fluttering all four of her nostrils. Both of her hearts were pounding, though, and the whole ordeal would probably take a year off her life, if she lived through it at all.

Still, she told herself, it was worth the risk.

She couldn't let Batuu die, as Hosnian Prime had. This place was her chosen home, and these were her chosen friends, and the Resistance needed every snippet of hope it could get. She was glad to play her part. It was an honor, being able to contribute to something so important. For months now, Gol had told her she was useless, annoying, weak—and she had almost begun to believe it. But her time with Vi and the others had been like rain watering shriveled plants. She'd bloomed, her fur had fluffed up, she'd woken from every sleep cycle eager to return to her work. It was a blessing, to find what a body was good at and a way to use those skills to help the galaxy.

All she had to do was reprogram a ship.

No big deal.

She had the skills, the knowledge, and the downloaded plans. It was harder to fix up a grumbling generator than it was to program a silly old ship. And a First Order ship, at that! One of the most up-to-date, technologically savvy machines in the galaxy! Why, it would practically program itself!

"D'you need to pee?" Zade muttered. "I always feel like I need to pee when I'm nervous."

"You drink a lot more than I do," Kriki whispered back. "Now hush."

"Yes, exactly. Hush. We need to wait for Mother Hen to get all the nasty soldiers out of their lovely ship."

When his boot started jiggling again, Kriki gently, politely, firmly stepped on it and held it down.

Soon she heard Vi mumble something, out in the forest, and two troopers ran off in that direction. It was time! Time to do her job! Kriki swallowed hard, trying to slow her breathing so she wouldn't get light-headed.

It was easy. Just machines. She was good with machines.

But she was very, very bad with . . . well, pressure. With fear. With dread.

When Gol had hit her, she'd frozen, ducked and cowered, never fought back.

She simply hadn't known how to.

And despite Archex's patient teachings, she still didn't.

And that meant that the only thing standing between her and death was Zade, and Zade was . . . well, not the most dependable person she'd ever met. Sure, she liked him, and he seemed committed, but he didn't seem as confident as usual, which only made her more nervous.

"Sir, we found her," said a woman's clipped voice on the other side of the transport.

"Excellent," a man responded, his voice unmarred by a stormtrooper mask. "General Hux will be most pleased."

Beside her, Zade had gone completely still, and when she looked up at his face for reassurance, he'd also gone very pale. In Kriki's estimation, that was probably a bad sign in a furless humanoid. They weren't supposed to change color.

"What is it?" she asked.

"It's Kath," he said, voice low. "The lieutenant Vi shot is still alive."

"So?"

He exhaled shakily. "So this isn't going to be as simple as we'd planned."

Kriki's ears drooped. She was beginning to think that this time, they didn't have the better hand.

Chapter Forty-Six

VI BLINKED ONCE AND LET REALITY wash over her like a wave.

Because, as it turned out, reality had changed.

She'd killed Lieutenant Wulfgar Kath. She was sure of it. She'd shot him in the chest at point-blank range. And yet here he was, very much alive, even if he was holding himself in a way that suggested nearly dying had hurt a bit.

"Starling," he said with pleased wonderment, like someone discovering a new species of bird for the first time. "Also known as Resistance spy Vi Moradi. Here we are again."

"Well, technically, you moved your mobile torture house, so we're a few klicks to the west," she said through mangled lips. "But otherwise, sure."

"I'm going to enjoy continuing our interrogation." And then Vi saw Kath's smile for the first time and realized he was probably a sociopath, which changed things. In addition to the two troopers who'd brought her in, four more troopers emerged from the transport, as well as her old friend Gol and two more unsavory sorts from the outpost, including, to her great surprise, Rusko.

Fantastic. Now they had an audience of people who actually hated her.

Which . . . was perhaps something she could use.

"Sure, we could do that interrogation thing again." She cleared her throat, feeling blood collecting on the back of her tongue. "Or you could prove to your buckethead buddies and local do-boys here that you can actually beat a woman who's not tied up. What do you say, Wulfguts? A little one-on-one fistfight? Because I bet you lost face when I shot you and escaped. I bet your soldiers have questioned your leadership, or at least whispered about you while you were asleep." She smiled sweetly. "Unless you're scared to fight a little bitty busted-up thing like me."

Kath sneered and began to speak, and Vi spat a big wad of blood on his crisply creased uniform.

In response, he punched her in the gut, making her double over. She barely stayed on her feet, the breath driven from her lungs. He was definitely strong, but she'd already known that. She just had to do the same thing she'd done with Cardinal, drawing out the torture for as long as possible. Somewhere in the forest beyond, Kriki would be waiting to sneak into the transport and do her magic. But first, Vi had to get every single trooper out here and focused on watching her die.

"I don't have to prove anything to you," Kath said, nose in the air.

"Me, no. But Gol and Rusko and their friends are going to go back to the outpost and tell people you were too scared to fight me one-on-one. That you had someone else put me in binders. Where's the First Order's might? Do they know you got sent down here as punishment, that all the good lieutenants get to stay in fancy digs on Star Destroyers and keep their hands clean? Want me to tell them what got you sent down here?"

Slam.

Another gut punch. At least he telegraphed, so Vi was able to tighten her core before his fist hit. And luckily, he wasn't hitting her face this time. Concussions were bad, but two concussions in the same week were really, really bad. Or was it three? She couldn't remember.

"Wulfguts here saw me on a Star Destroyer and let me go," she taunted. "You hear that, Rusko? I walked right past this bootlicking coward and kidnapped one of his men, and he didn't even notice. He just let me continue on my merry way."

Whump.

The punch thunked her in the chest, and Vi swore she felt her heart stutter as she stumbled back.

That one was gonna bruise.

"Oh, the scary girl! With her hands behind her back!" She grinned at Gol with bloody teeth. "This 'officer' can only hit me when I'm restrained. I bet you wouldn't be too scared to unbind me and take me on in a fair fight, huh? Bet you're still mad at me for stealing the underpaid servant who did all your work for you."

"I'm not scared of you," Gol yelled, and Vi could hear in his voice that he was—but he was also furious.

The others could sense it, too. The outpost regulars crossed their arms and looked from Gol to Kath. Rusko and the other guy were big, rough types, and they were adding up what they thought of the First Order and the Resistance in terms of attitude, right now. If stringy little Gol was willing to fight her but big, burly Kath wasn't . . . well, that said something.

"Fine," Kath said coldly. "Troopers. Recruits. Make a circle. Blasters drawn. Unbind her. Might as well loosen her up for interrogation." He then did something Vi would not have anticipated: He took off his First Order coat, revealing a white undershirt. Carefully folding his coat, he walked back to the transport and returned with empty arms and neither hat nor blaster. Another trooper trailed behind him, this one with his hand bandaged, and Vi almost smiled, hoping that this meant the transport was now empty.

"This," Kath said carefully, "is off the record."

A trooper stepped behind Vi and unbound her wrists. Her arms sprang apart and flopped forward, bloodless. It would be several minutes before she would be able to land even the most pathetic punch.

"Off the record," she echoed, hopping around, shaking her head and wiggling her arms. "Okay, fun. I like off the record." She looked around at the buckets and everyday monsters moving in to form a predator's circle around the two fighters. She did not look at the transport, hoping to see some sign that Zade and Kriki had found a way aboard. If there was a hatch on the other side, they might already be at work. If the open hatch was the only way in, though, they were doomed. Half of the circle would see anyone attempting to sneak in. There were eleven hostiles watching the fight, and within the circle Kath was shadowboxing, moving with a disturbing swiftness and lightness for a man of his size. Vi had hoped he would be slow and ponderous and careful, but it turned out that beneath the fastidious façade lurked a bare-knuckle brawler.

Despite what Ylena had told her, the Force did not seem to be with her today.

"You understand that I'm going to beat you to a pulp and then interrogate you anyway," Kath said, advancing toward her, his hands held in boxing position.

Vi considered her options and went with the Echani arts, which might give her some small advantage against a much larger opponent. Head shots would be smart, thanks to the beating Zade had given his skull. And of course she'd shot Kath in the chest recently, and even considering whatever hidden armor had saved his life, he would surely have bruising.

They danced in a circle, and Vi wished they could circle forever, that there was some way to keep everyone's attention occupied while she avoided getting pummeled. The crash, and her trip into the ruins, and then the last beating—well, she wasn't getting any younger, and their medbay supplies were limited, even with what they'd regained from Oga and stolen from the First Order transport. No matter what happened, it was going to hurt.

Kath barged forward with a wicked cross, and Vi dodged and followed it up with a kick, which he caught neatly on his shin. Vi felt the hit reverberate up her bones; he was built like a bantha! She would need to go for pressure points, then, and especially try to get inside his guard and hit his sternum or head. She went for a jab, but he batted her hand away and landed a powerful left hook, catching her in the ribs.

It was like being electrocuted, being on the receiving end of his punches. Vi was usually fast, but she was not at her best. She staggered back to the tune of robotized laughter and Rusko's foul, grating cackle. That rib was bruised, possibly broken again. She sucked in a breath and noted Kath's pleased grin before surprising him with a running tackle. Darting under his ill-timed punch, she got right up against his chest and stabbed two fingers into the pressure point closest to where she'd shot him.

And right into the armor that had prevented her bolt from killing him the first time around.

Should've gone with a head shot.

Kath shoved her away, hard, and she twisted and stumbled to the ground, catching herself on hands and knees. When his big boot came in for a kick, she rolled away, but when she hit the edge of the circle, a stormtrooper kicked her back in, right in the gut. She staggered up, staying low.

"This going the way you thought it would, Starling?" Kath taunted, bouncing lightly on the balls of his feet and shaking his carefully gelled hair, making it flop out of place. "You think I don't know Echani? You think I'd walk around an enemy planet without armor? You think I'm so foolish that I don't know that this entire fight is a diversion?"

Right on cue, a stormtrooper appeared in the transport hatch, nudging Zade out with a blaster.

"Sorry, darling," Zade called sadly. "They apparently frown on having their ships stolen. And here I thought it was a government that served the people."

Vi let the dismay show on her face—which wasn't hard. With Zade caught, that meant that Kriki was on her own—but there was no way to know if she'd made it aboard the ship or if there were more soldiers waiting for her.

"Do you want to keep fighting, or can we just skip straight to the torture?" Kath said. He'd stopped bouncing and now wiped his hands off on the white material over his belly, as if punching Vi might've given him a disease. "I'll enjoy either option, but it is terribly fun, watching all your hopes fall away."

If she gave in now, that was less time for Kriki to somehow get on the ship and do her work. But if Vi kept fighting, Kath would rightly assume there was some further part of their ruse. Which left only one last card to play.

"Was your mama a worrt?" she asked Kath, her voice pitched to carry. "Because I'm seeing a resemblance."

In the silence that followed, Vi should've heard Dolin's arrow thwack into some soft part of the First Order officer, or at least into a tree or off the transport, if Dolin was nervous. That was their last gambit: Vi said the code phrase, and Dolin, who'd been waiting in the forest, would use his weapons to start a panic, take down anyone he could, and charge in.

But nothing happened.

So Vi danced forward, ignoring the pain in her ribs and belly, aiming for a tight combo of hits and punches. Unfortunately, she was hurt and therefore slow, and Kath knew the same forms she did, and he was twice her size, and he blocked every hit before backhanding her to the ground.

"I never knew my mother," Kath said, cold and clipped. "But I think we're done here. You can barely stand. You're broken, Vi Moradi. Maybe after I get what I need from you, I'll send your fingers to General Organa in a pretty box. Tell her I finally clipped the wings of her Starling."

On the forest floor of Batuu, Vi stared up at him, feeling every heartbeat pulse against her hurt places. The troopers and enemy Batuuans moved in, looming over her, the circle tightening. Still no arrows, still no blasterfire. Dolin must've been captured, or else chickened out. Perhaps whatever his grandmother had told him had finally sunk in and he'd slunk back home to pretend that life outside his village didn't exist. In the open hatch of the transport, Zade was looking like he might spin and fight the trooper guarding him, which would only earn him a blaster bolt in the back. She rolled to her belly to get up again.

Kath squatted and pulled Vi's head up by the hair, forcing her to look at his face. Vi tongued her poison tooth, considering her next move. If she was dead, maybe it would all be over. They would leave. There would be nothing on the planet they wanted.

She was going to die anyway.

She might as well die on her own terms.

She was just about to bite down when she heard an engine rev.

Chapter Forty-Seven

"WHAT THE BLAST IS THAT?" KATH growled, releasing Vi's hair and standing.

Vi let her head fall down, hiding her smile.

She knew that sound.

It was a sound only a Batuu local would know: the rough, growling engine of a crankbike.

Dolin was coming!

As the sound got closer and louder, she realized it wasn't just one crankbike—it couldn't be. It had to be many crankbikes, a whole army of them, some revving high and some spluttering and some deep and guttural, each machine singing its own unique song.

"In formation," Kath told his troopers. "Bind her and toss her in the transport. We can't lose her again. And bring my hat and jacket."

Vi twisted to watch what was happening as a trooper wrenched her arms behind her back again and slapped on the familiar binders. Despite her newfound hope, Vi's body still felt like a bag of sloshing bones as the trooper dragged her up to standing. She stumbled toward the mobile habitat as the trooper hurriedly pushed and prodded her, not wanting to miss the real action. With a rough shove, he pushed her into the transport, where she landed on the floor by Zade as the trooper retrieved Kath's belongings and jogged toward his leader outside.

"What's a murderous spy like you doing in a bucket hotel like this?" Zade muttered.

She struggled to sitting and looked around. "I'm realizing they left us here without a guard," she murmured. "Did Kriki make it on board?"

"I nobly sacrificed myself to draw their last trooper out of the cockpit," he confirmed. "But I never imagined acting heroic would be quite so uncomfortable. Not really feeling much in the old arms, you know?"

Vi pressed herself against the wall until she could slide up it and stand.

"You get used to it," she said. "Now stand up and shush while I get out of these binders."

"You? Can get magnetic binders off? With your hands behind your back? When you can't, like, see the binders?" His jaw dropped, and Vi gave herself exactly two seconds to enjoy it.

"Spy school was fun. Now come on."

As he slithered upright, Vi peeked out the main hatch. The troopers were in formation while Kath pulled on his jacket and strapped his own blaster back on. The roar of the crankbikes had drowned out every other noise in the world, and the very ground was shaking.

Kath was screaming something, but Vi couldn't hear it, and then the cavalry arrived, barreling in from every direction. Arrows and blaster bolts filled the air. Although Vi knew she had to get her binders off, she couldn't tear herself away from the sight. At least two dozen riders roared and screamed, young men and women shooting blasters and skidding their bikes around the clearing, each vehicle a crude but somehow elegant mix of old and new, tech and raw metal, Batuu and everything else.

"The big dolt came through," Zade said by her side. "Look at them! They do breed their farm kids rather brawny around here. Is it the blue milk, d'you think? Or the ronto ribs? If we live through this, I swear I'm going to eat—"

"Are you seriously talking about food right now?"

"What can I say? Being captured makes me hungry."

As Vi worked the slender pin from what appeared to be a simple cuff bracelet and wiggled it into just the right place on her binders, she found Dolin in the crowd outside, wearing an ancient rebel helmet as he tore back and forth across the clearing on his crankbike, hatchet swinging. Waba was not in the sidecar this time, which seemed true to his character. Two of the other crankbikes were upside down, gigantic tires spinning, their riders thrown and unmoving. One of the troopers was down, too, but it was clear the simple Batuuan weapons were no match for First Order armor and tech. Most of the arrows clattered uselessly to the grass, and the Batuuans who carried junky old blasters weren't very good with them. At least there were many more crankbikes than there were soldiers—for now.

Click.

Her binders fell off, and she went to work on Zade's, which likewise clicked off within moments. She replaced the pin in her bracelet and ran to the closed cockpit door.

"Kriki?" she called.

"Eek! Yes?" came the response.

"How's it coming along?"

"More slowly than I'd like. I need more time."

"What if we didn't have much of that?"

Kriki sighed. "Every time you make me panic, my chance of making a vital mistake goes up."

"Acknowledged. Keep up the good work. I believe in you."

"I said don't make me panic!"

Vi smiled to herself. The Chadra-Fan had more guts than she knew. And now Vi's job was to buy yet more time and keep the troopers off this ship.

As she pondered their next move, Zade appeared carrying two stormtrooper blasters. "Mummy, look what I found. Can I keep them?"

Vi took one. "You can keep that one."

"I'm naming it Waba the Second."

They ran to the hatch and peeked out, and Vi was confused by what she saw. There were only three troopers still up and fighting as Kath aimed his blaster from behind the soldiers' armor. Rusko was still up, a blaster in each meaty hand, and Gol was hiding behind him, popping off shots when it seemed safe. Several of the crankbikes were crashed or stationary, their riders dead or injured, but most of the others had disappeared. Even Dolin was gone.

As Vi watched in horror, the last of the crankbikes leapt and skidded back into the forest.

Kath gave the order to turn around . . . and return to the transport.

Chapter Forty-Eight

DOLIN RELUCTANTLY TURNED HIS BIKE AROUND and followed his
friends away from the clearing—well, what was left of his friends. He
couldn't believe they'd come at all—not after how they'd acted when
he'd given his speech, again and again, back at the settlement.

"Not our business," Sylvai had said as he watched his gruffins grazing.

"The First Order isn't real," Houz had grumbled from under his
bike.

"I'm not about to die for some made-up Resistance." This from
Madeli, who didn't even put down her scythe and stop cutting hay to
listen.

And yet, this afternoon, on his way to do his part, he'd heard their
bikes grumbling from far off and found twenty of his people armed
and ready to fight. As it turned out, two stormtroopers had found
their settlement while on patrol and killed his second cousin Tophin
for practically nothing, and now they finally believed, even if their
parents and grandparents had cried and threatened and wailed about
entering the conflict.

And on their way to the clearing, he'd found his second surprise:
Ylena in Savi's speeder, the backseat full of blasters.

Most of the settlement folk had never held a blaster at all. Having them in hand—it was like technologically jump-starting their community through time, giving them an advantage they'd never had before. He'd given them a quick lesson in blaster safety and management, the same speech Archex had given him, and knew that their aim would run true, trained as they were with bows and arrows.

"Please tell me you're going to go far away now," he'd said to Ylena as they remounted their bikes, blasters strapped to backs and thighs.

Her gentle smile had nearly torn him to bits.

"I am," she'd said. "I've done my part. This is all Savi can do, but he sends his best wishes. The Force is with you all today." She'd stepped closer, the blowback from his crankbike making her vest billow. "But promise me you'll take care."

Dolin had felt as if the next hour would determine the entire course of his life. He was filled with purpose, with righteousness, with confidence and strength. He could die today; he knew that much.

So he'd wrapped one hand around Ylena's back and gently cupped her jaw with the other, pulling her close and kissing her, putting all his feelings into it, making it a promise.

"I'll take care," he'd assured her.

She nodded and stepped back, tears in her eyes, and he led his friends and cousins onward, toward the coordinates he'd been given.

And then they fought, and it wasn't at all the crushing wave of triumph he'd imagined, with the crankbikes swooping in and the soldiers running away shrieking in terror. No, the troopers were ready for them, waiting in neat lines, weapons drawn, and there were more troopers than he'd anticipated, and their first volley of blaster bolts sent bodies flying and crankbikes spinning. Someone, he didn't even know who, immediately turned tail and disappeared back into the forest. Although their aim was good, the settlement kids couldn't manage to hit those narrow strips of black where their blasterfire would be most effective, not while driving their bikes. It was chaos, and his gut went cold as he began to consider that Grana was right.

This was a huge mistake.

And people were dying, people he'd known all his life. And he couldn't help them, couldn't stop to hold a hand and whisper warm words about being okay. He had to keep going. Keep driving, keep shooting. The forest floor was slick with blood and oil, and still the stormtroopers were a calm, identical line of monstrous death.

And then the rest of the crankbikes turned around.

And Dolin had to join them in their retreat and figure out some other way to do his part, because being the only target in that clearing wasn't going to save anyone. He was filled with regret and shame and hurt. It was his fault people had died, and their deaths meant nothing. They hadn't even killed all the troopers, hadn't even managed to wound their officer.

Wait. Their officer? But Vi had shot him! Hadn't she?

This entire attack had been meaningless. And to think that he had once thought he would just hide in a tree, taking the soldiers down one by one with his arrows.

To think: He'd thought himself a hero.

He was just another dumb farm kid who thought he could fight something far bigger, just a toddler chased through the garden by the Snarlok when he'd been told explicitly not to get caught. He revved his engine and turned toward home—his real home, where he would beg Grana for forgiveness and stop foolishly dreaming of adventure and just tend the gruffins like he'd been born to do.

But then the strangest thing happened. Someone stepped into his path.

It was a stormtrooper, but unlike any he'd seen before.

This armor wasn't white.

It was red.

Chapter Forty-Nine

THE ONLY PROBLEM WITH KATH RUNNING toward the transport was that Vi couldn't kill him. If she did, he couldn't fly away and set their plan in motion. But if he made it onto the transport, Kriki might not finish. And it wasn't like she could taunt him into hand-to-hand combat a second time. She could barely stand.

If only Vi could reliably hurt him without killing him and make the whole thing seem believable.

"Get ready," Vi murmured to Zade. "They're coming back. And we're way outnumbered."

"And we're all out of farm boys," Zade finished for her. "Leaving us as the only bulwark between our dear little Kriki and these monsters, and, more big picture, as the only hope for the Resistance mission on Batuu. And, oh, they will interrogate and kill us if we fail."

"Look on the bright side. At least we get to hurt them a little first. Remember: We need them alive."

"But not Rusko and Gol!"

"No, we can definitely kill them. Just not Kath."

"But he can be grievously injured!"

"Exactly."

They were on either side of the transport's open hatch, doing their best to stay hidden while shooting, and Vi took aim at a trooper's leg and pulled the trigger. It was satisfying, watching the blasterfire leave a burnt black streak on the white betaplast, but it didn't slow him down. She didn't dare hit Kath, though. As much as it pained her, the entire plan hinged on him being alive, and he was moving too fast, zigzagging around overturned crankbikes and bodies, weaving too much for a certain hit.

She focused on Rusko, but his skin must've been insanely thick, almost armored, as the blaster bolts just skidded off. She landed a shot on the inside of his arm, but he didn't react at all. When Zade shot Gol, he stumbled and fell.

"That's for Kriki," Zade murmured, and Vi nodded her approval.

They took turns aiming for Rusko and the three remaining troopers, but none of their shots seemed to have any effect. They were still running, Kath behind them, getting closer and closer.

Vi's heart sank. It was happening too fast. Kriki wasn't done. They'd been so close, and she could feel her every failure weighing her down.

If only she'd managed to swerve the ponderous Resistance transport to avoid taking the hits that had caused them to crash here.

If only she hadn't passed out in that crash and could've prevented Rusko and the rest of Oga's thugs from stealing the cargo.

If only she'd managed to win more Batuuan hearts over to the Resistance.

If only she'd killed Kath when she'd had the chance.

Every minor miscalculation or case of bad luck had led her to this moment, when she was so close to keeping her people—and Black Spire Outpost itself—safe. Not only for future Resistance fighters, but also for the locals, whom she'd come to love.

Savi and Ylena and the Gatherers, with their friendliness and belief that everything served the Force.

Kriki and Zade and Dolin, who'd joined her even without pay or any promises of a better life, a safer life.

Mubo and Zabaka and Salju and Arta, who'd been kind and helpful, even when they could've been exploitive.

Jenda and Oh-li, who'd done nothing but live simply and refuse to give in to bullies.

She'd tried to save them, to save everyone. She'd put herself into the First Order's clutches—Kath's clutches—using her body and sanity to give Kriki time to do her crucial work.

And yet it hadn't been enough. Sometimes, even your best wasn't sufficient.

Vi and Zade kept shooting, and they took down two more troopers, but Kath and Rusko were still on their way back, hiding behind trees on their way to the transport—and shooting back in turn. Zade cried out and spun away, clutching his upper arm.

"Why does everyone here hate shimmersilk blazers?" he growled.

"You okay?" Vi shouted, not letting go of her trigger.

"I'll live. Everyone digs scars," he said as he returned to his post, still shooting even though his arm was smoking and dripping blood.

Vi was so focused on Kath and his guards that she startled when a gloved hand landed on her shoulder.

"Let me do this," said a familiar but robotic voice in the transport.

Glancing away from Kath, she found a red stormtrooper standing behind her.

It was Cardinal.

Chapter Fifty

ARCHEX KNEW THE RUSE WOULD NEVER hold up under close scrutiny.

As he'd sat in his hidden room in the ruins, carefully painting the stolen stormtrooper armor red with cheap enamel he'd bought on a secret trip to the outpost—and a little high on the fumes, if he was honest—he'd known he was there to buy time, not to fool anyone for very long.

He also knew Vi would be mad, at first, and he had an inborn, or possibly programmed, objection to enraging his superior officer. But even if he thought himself part of the Resistance now, he'd never taken any oath, never even had his tracking anklet removed. Technically, he was a free agent. And you couldn't break the rules if there were no rules to break.

It was also more than a little satisfying, making Vi mad. He would've laughed, if laughing didn't hurt so much these days.

As he kitted up, he felt a deep sense of rightness, even if this armor didn't fit like his old armor. The betaplast wasn't perfect. The red was slightly off—and a bit drippy. He didn't have his cape.

But to anyone in the First Order with knowledge of Cardinal's past, his glaring red form meant only one thing now: betrayal.

He was counting on it.

He touched Vi's shoulder, and as her face went from rage to surprise to understanding to worry, he patted her gently.

"It'll be okay," he said. "I'll stall them. You two get Kriki out through the back hatch."

"But—"

"No buts."

"But, Archex. They'll kill you."

He barked a laugh. "Probably."

"I don't want to worry anyone, but am I hallucinating a red buckethead?" Zade said.

Archex snorted. "I've been hallucinating a drunken idiot for days now."

"Ah. Archex. So it's you. Welcome to the fray."

As Kath, Rusko, and the last, limping trooper made their final break for the transport, Archex stepped out from behind Vi and into the open hatch. Kath skidded to a halt, his jaw dropping in the most gratifying manner.

"Hello, Wulfgar," Archex said with a sneer.

"Captain Cardinal," Kath answered stiffly. "Well, no. Not Captain. They withdrew you from the logs. Completely erased your existence. You're not anything, anymore. You're nothing."

"Clearly." Archex stepped down from the transport. With all the stims in his system, he didn't even feel his leg. "Say, didn't you have an entire squad of troopers when you landed? And now you're hiding behind a local? And here I thought organization was your greatest pride."

Kath flapped a hand at his last soldier and shoved Rusko aside so he could stand directly before his old . . . well, *friend* wasn't the right word. No one in the First Order had true friends. Brothers-in-arms, perhaps, although they'd chosen different paths. Archex had believed in the First Order with all his heart and had longed to pour everything he had into serving it and helping the galaxy, whereas Kath wanted power and authority, and he'd given everything he had to climbing the ladder. There were rumors he'd sabotaged other officers on his way up, but perhaps that was a feature, not a bug. The First

Order was good at promoting people up or down to better utilize their strengths.

"Didn't you have integrity when I saw you last, Cardinal? And here I thought . . . well, if you're working with the Resistance, clearly you have no pride," Kath shot back. His face was pink, his once perfect hair straggling down, his eyes bloodshot.

Inside his helmet, Archex smiled. Making Kath angry gave him more pleasure than anything he'd felt in months. The stims helped, too. He could barely feel any of his wounds. His blood fizzed, his lungs were full of delicious air. And being in the armor? It was like going home.

Even if no one else could see it, he was truly happy.

And then he punched Lieutenant Wulfgar Kath in the teeth.

Chapter Fifty-One

VI WATCHED IN HORROR AS SHE realized what Archex was doing, which was the exact same thing she'd just done.

He was sacrificing himself to give them the time they so desperately needed.

"Stay here," she murmured to Zade, her ears ringing after all the blasterfire. "Don't shoot, no matter what."

He looked at her, panic in his eyes. And surprise.

"No matter what? Even if they take turns kicking him in the tum? Even if they try to kill him?"

"He's buying us time. Kriki needs every second he can provide. Don't dishonor his sacrifice by playing tough guy. Let him do his job."

"Didn't know he had a job," Zade murmured with a shrug. "But yes, sir."

"He chose this job for himself," she said softly.

Vi hurried up to the cockpit, where Kriki was typing so fast it was a blur.

"How're we doing in here?" Vi asked, taking care to keep her voice gentle and calm.

"Well, at first I was freaking out about the blasterfire, but now I'm freaking out about the lack of blasterfire. I was afraid they'd killed you."

"Pfft. Naw. They did shoot Zade, though, which sounds like fun."

"Shoot him? No way. He'd whine too much. Maybe rough him up a little. Stain his scarf or something."

Vi laughed, even though it hurt. Kriki was funny under pressure, probably because she was working too hard to self-censor.

"We got an ETA?"

"Just a few more minutes. So close. Programming in the final message now." Kriki looked up, her jaw dropped. "Wait. If you're up here, what's going on out there? Are they all dead? If they're dead, who'll take the ship up? This one doesn't have the kind of autopilot that can do that—"

Vi shook her head. "Archex is stalling them."

Kriki's horror deepened, her nostrils fluttering with worry. "Archex? But he's . . . I mean, isn't he one of them?"

"Not anymore. Which only makes them more anxious to hurt him."

"Then you have to go help him!"

Vi drew a deep breath. Kriki didn't know how badly she wanted to do just that.

"We each have a job to do. Archex is doing his job to give you the time to do yours. So do him proud. Make it count."

Kriki nodded repeatedly and turned back to her work, fingers flying. "Yes. Yes, I can do this. I can do this quickly and well." Plucking at the gray bead on her necklace, she kissed it and tucked it back where it lived, over her heart. "Now go away. You make me nervous."

Vi nodded and drifted back toward the hatch.

When she looked outside, Archex was on his back on the ground, helpless.

Chapter Fifty-Two

THE GOOD THING ABOUT THE FIRST Order's stims was that they provided everything that an individual might lack at the moment of
greatest stress: strength, confidence, energy, determination. The
bad thing about them was that they masked pain, which meant that
Archex didn't know his leg had given out until he was already falling.

Up until then, he'd given as good as he'd gotten, trading blows
with Kath and the giant shark guy, taking whatever chance he found
to hit or kick his enemies. At least it was personal enough that they
weren't using blasters. And at least Zade hadn't gotten involved and
was sitting in the transport hatch like Vi had ordered him to. The
man's face showed none of his earlier derision and distrust. He
looked absolutely terrified on Archex's behalf, which was gratifying,
if a little too late.

"That all you've got?" Kath said, looming over him.

Archex gritted his teeth and rammed his foot into Kath's knee,
hearing a satisfying sort of pop. Kath growled, bloodless lips pinned
against a scream as he stumbled, and Rusko stepped up to help him.

"Kill him," Kath said to his last trooper. "And you—help me onto
the ship. I'm tired of these games."

Rusko helped him hobble toward the ship while the last trooper loomed over Archex, the faceless bucket staring down. Archex realized for the first time what it felt like to face the flat white mask, to die in such an impersonal way, not knowing who was on the other side. It had been a little like that with Phasma, except he'd known exactly who was behind the mask. He'd convinced her to take off her helmet, but that gambit wouldn't work with this grunt.

"What if you didn't kill him, though?"

Everyone looked up when Vi spoke. She stood in the hatch of the transport, holding her blaster, pointing it directly at Kath.

"Starling," Kath snarled. "And here I thought he was just stalling so you could run away. That's why I let you go: The First Order has an even higher price on his head than on yours. Think about it. You could just walk away right now."

"Maybe," she allowed.

But Archex, of course, knew she would never walk away when one of her charges was in danger. That simply wasn't who Vi Moradi was. And they both knew that Kath would never truly let her go.

Archex could barely breathe now, and the pain was beginning to creep up his leg. When he looked up, he saw that the trooper had a blaster pointed at him but was focusing on Vi. Pain filled him like a cup, and he felt small and broken, like a troublesome child everyone was ignoring. He needed to do something, but he didn't know what. If Vi wasn't shooting Kath, that meant she was still stalling for Kriki, and until someone else started up the fight, Archex was going to stay here, on the ground, trying not to move. The armor was great at repelling blasterfire, but every kick and punch had crunched betaplast against tissue and bone, and he was pretty sure he had several broken ribs and at least a minor concussion. As the stims wore off, he felt it, more and more, every wound old and new.

And yet this strange standoff kept going as if in slow motion, and Archex could only watch from the ground, helpless. He had no way to know if Kriki had finished her work, if his ruse had been successful. And with his face covered, he couldn't communicate anything to Vi without speaking.

"What do you want, Starling?" Kath said tiredly. "You're not shooting at us, so there must be something."

Vi shrugged like it was just a normal afternoon in the market. "You're right, Kath. I'm tired. I just want to be left alone. I came all the way out here, to the middle of nowhere, and you tyrannical megalomaniacs still came after me. Just say I died and let me go about my business. You've got your bounty, right there. So I accept your offer. Take your Cardinal and go."

"Curious, that you would set so low a value on someone who chose the Resistance."

"Yeah, well, we got what we needed from him, didn't we? His intel, I'm sure, is already out of date. And he's pretty useless, as is. Phasma messed him up good."

Archex knew she didn't mean it, knew she was buying yet more time. She had to be. And yet . . . it hurt. That she could speak of him so callously. Even though he knew it wasn't true. It was exactly what the First Order said about the Resistance, that they were worthless scum, the sort of space rats who would turn on each other when times got rough, all their nobility forgotten in the face of a true threat.

"Get off my ship, then," Kath said. "As I'm sure you know by now, there's another hatch. We'll take him back to the First Order immediately and forget you ever existed. Is it a deal?"

Vi looked back inside the transport and smiled. "It's a deal."

And then she shot Kath's left ear off.

Chapter Fifty-Three

ALL HELL BROKE LOOSE.

Still on the ground, Archex was completely forgotten as Kath, Rusko, and the last trooper whipped out their blasters and started firing—but carefully. It was their ship, after all, and even though it could take a lot of heat, they likely didn't want to find out exactly how much. Archex tried to stand but couldn't; between his bad leg and the new wounds they'd inflicted, he could only crawl away, backward, using his one good leg. It hurt more than anything he'd felt in his entire life. When Phasma first stabbed him, these wounds had been numb with poison, and dying had seemed quite pleasant. But they'd never truly healed, and now they sang along with every other hit, every other trauma, a lifetime of damage, a cacophony of abuse that he couldn't escape.

Living, it turned out, was what really hurt.

Archex blinked.

Things were still happening overhead, beyond him. Kath's ear was gone. Vi disappeared into the ship, and Kath, gushing blood down the shoulder of his pressed black uniform, gave chase.

"Bring him!" he shouted to the last trooper as he pointed back at

Archex. "Let's get out of here with something valuable before things get worse."

Archex scrambled back, pain be damned, scuttling like a crab away from the stormtrooper reaching for him even as blood leaked from the black body glove at his waist. The white helmet no longer felt like camaraderie and safety and order; the trooper was a faceless monster, attacking as if in a dream. Archex was panting now, his breath booming inside the helmet, his body broken out in sweat and weighed down by the heavy armor.

Blasterfire erupted from the forest opposite the ship. The trooper lunged and grabbed Archex under the armpits and began dragging him toward the waiting transport. Archex couldn't see, couldn't breathe, and he yanked off his red-painted helmet and threw it away. Finally free, he fought his captor, wrenching himself away and trying to kick out—but his leg was dead, as if the poison had finally wormed its way into every cell. One-legged, his bad lung failing him completely, his flailing wasn't nearly enough to disrupt the soldier who towed him directly toward the very place he was trying to protect. The ship was only a few meters away now.

He couldn't let that happen.

Kriki needed more time.

He had to fight.

With all his might, he ripped his arms away, got his leg under himself, and pulled to standing. There, in the forest, staring right at him, her blaster raised, was Vi Moradi.

Time seemed to stop as he stared at his once-enemy, noting the bruising and contusions on her face, the rip in her gray Batuuan tunic, the blaster graze on her pants rimmed with blood. Her face was set ferociously as she tried to shoot the trooper without hitting Archex, a nearly impossible task from her angle.

Behind Archex, the transport powered up. "Come on!" Kath screamed. "Bring him!"

With that strange clarity he only experienced in battle, Archex finally understood.

Vi hadn't meant what she said. She'd lied to Kath to buy more time—more time for Kriki, and more time for her to sneak around and save Archex. If Vi was here, now, that meant that Kriki had finished her work.

They'd succeeded.

But Archex knew Kath, and he knew that Kath wouldn't leave the planet without him or Vi.

Until he had one of them in his grasp, Kath was doomed in the First Order. He might move the transport to a new clearing, but he would stay here, on Batuu, hunting for the Resistance base and recruits and abusing the townspeople and winning cowards over to their side until he had his prey in hand.

Their only hope was to give Kath what he wanted.

When the trooper again grabbed him and dug his blaster into Archex's armor, right under the armpit, Archex stopped fighting.

He looked at Vi and mouthed words he hoped she could read from across the clearing.

May the Force be with you.

And then he turned away and let the trooper push him onto the ship.

Chapter Fifty-Four

VI HAD BEEN IN BINDERS, IN an interrogation chair, in a tractor beam, but she had never felt so hopeless as she did watching Archex turn around and limp toward the First Order transport. She took aim and shot at the trooper forcefully marching her friend toward his doom, but her blaster bolts just skidded off the betaplast armor. Seconds later, Archex was crawling onto the ship, and time seemed to slow as Vi sprinted toward it, teeth gritted, hoping for some way to save him.

But the hatch door slid shut and the massive transport lifted off the ground and into the air, sending branches and leaves raining down as it sliced through the canopy above.

"I should've killed you ten times!" she screamed at Kath, not that there was anyone there to hear it.

A blaster shot at her from behind, and she spun and shot back, so many times that it made no sense, until the wounded stormtrooper who'd risen for one last fight went down with a lucky shot in the groin.

"Vi?"

She looked up from the ground, where she had inexplicably curled up in a ball. Kriki and Zade stood over her.

"Are you okay?" Kriki asked. "Where's Archex?"

Feeling like she'd aged a century, Vi stood, slapping away Zade's hand when he held it out to help her.

"He's gone," she said, her voice rasping. "They took him. But he . . . he knew it. He let them. He sacrificed himself. He knew that Kath would never leave without one of us, without his quarry. That Kath couldn't go back empty-handed. And if Kath never left, then his ship . . ."

"Wouldn't explode," Zade finished. "That stupid glorious dumb brave idiot! I wish he was here so I could punch him in his dumb neck!"

Vi realized he was crying, and when she touched her face, she found that she was, too. Kriki was softly snuffling, and Vi put an arm around her, pulling the Chadra-Fan close. A landspeeder zipped out of the forest, and there were Ylena and Dolin, who'd been roughly bandaged up, with gauze over his head.

"Did it work?" Dolin asked. "Did you have enough time?"

"I think so," Kriki wailed. "If I didn't, then he . . . then . . . if it was all for nothing . . ."

"Shhh," Vi murmured, pulling her closer. "Don't even let the thought of failure enter your mind."

"Have faith," Ylena said, standing to put her arm around Vi's other side. "The Force works in mysterious ways."

Dolin wrapped his arm around Ylena's other side, and Zade fell to his knees. They all looked up, watching the transport rapidly shrinking until it had almost disappeared against the deep blue evening sky.

"How will we know?" Dolin asked again. "If it worked?"

"We should just barely be able to see it," Kriki said. "Keep watching . . . keep watching . . ."

The ship was a dot, and then a speck.

Kriki's datapad beeped, and she excitedly scrolled through it. "The message is sent!" she announced. "*Resistance spy Vi Moradi deceased during interrogation. No sign of Resistance base. Batuu strategically useless. No natural resources or manufacturing. Miserable place. Returning to fleet.*" She paused. "That's what it said."

They kept watching, but the speck . . . didn't explode.

Chapter Fifty-Five

"SIR, A MESSAGE WAS JUST RELAYED to the *Penumbra*," CE-6675 said.

Kath looked up from the poetry he was creating of Cardinal's face with his fists. "Well?" he asked peevishly. "What did it say? Was it one of our older messages, catching up?"

The trooper at the helm paused, which wasn't a good sign. "I can't tell. It's scrambled. That's, uh, not my area of expertise. The fleet techs will know more, when we return."

Sighing heavily, Kath stepped back and raised an eyebrow at Cardinal.

This man—whatever was left of him under the bloody pulp of his features—was Kath's key to getting back into Hux's good graces. The betrayer, Captain Cardinal, now with bonus Resistance secrets. The thought of delivering Cardinal to the *Finalizer* still wearing this poorly painted armor, this pathetic facsimile of the power he'd once known . . . well, it was just too delicious.

Cardinal was sitting in the same jump seat that had once held Vi Moradi, the harness still stained with her blood—under a fresh wash of his own. Kath reached out, grabbed a handful of Cardinal's sweat-soaked, too-long, ink-black hair, and wrenched up his head.

"I'll ask you again: Where is the Resistance hiding?" he asked.

Cardinal grinned, showing bloody holes where teeth had been.

"What Resistance?" he slurred before laughing. "What could there possibly be to resist?"

He laughed and laughed and laughed.

He almost sounded giddy, and it made Kath uncomfortable.

No person this helpless, this pathetic, should be laughing like that.

So he punched Cardinal again, this time in his already swollen eye.

When even that didn't get a response, when Cardinal stubbornly continued to maniacally laugh, Kath stepped back, chin on his bloodied knuckles. He could hear his heart pumping against the stump of his ear, but he no longer cared. His entire world revolved around making this idiot talk.

"Do you want promises, then?" he asked, leaning close. "Tell me what I want to know, and I'll let you go? Tell me where to find Leia Organa, and I won't return to Batuu and raze this planet to the ground?"

Cardinal looked up, one eye swollen shut and the other bloodshot beneath lashes sticky with blood. Even without his helmet, the man was a symphony in red.

"It doesn't matter," he rasped.

Kath got right up in his face, smelling the hot scent of copper and salt and cheap caf rolling off him. "What doesn't matter?"

Something in the cockpit started beeping.

Cardinal tipped his head back as if staring at the stars outside.

He smiled, a brutal, wolfish thing.

"Nothing does," he said. "You lose."

And then the ship exploded.

Chapter Fifty-Six

IT WAS THE TINIEST THING, JUST a bright flash and a trailing white tail.

But that was all they needed.

Vi screamed, hugging Kriki as they jumped up and down. Zade was rolling around on the ground, laughing madly. Dolin and Ylena were sharing the sort of kiss that felt like the good kind of explosions.

It had worked.

Against all odds, their plan had actually worked.

"I did it?" Kriki squeaked. Then, more confidently, "I did it!"

"We did it," Zade said from the ground. "The world's smallest Resistance cell has pulled off the greatest victory the galaxy has ever known! I mean, probably. I don't pay attention to history, really." He flopped onto his back, smiling. "Ah, but revenge is a lovely feeling."

They watched the white tail until it disappeared, and when Vi looked down again, reality hit her.

Archex was gone, lost in that faraway flash.

Down here, on the ground, they were surrounded by corpses and wreckage—stormtroopers, farm boys, outpost locals, crankbikes, weapons. The beautiful forest smelled of blasterfire and oil and blood instead of growing things, and the trees wore their wounds, bleeding sap. They'd hurt this place. Vi was hurt, too. Her legs wobbled, and she caught herself, but Dolin noticed and put a hand on her arm to steady her.

"Vi, are you okay?"

She shook her head. "No. No. So not okay. Let's go home."

Dolin looked around, too, and his face fell. "I was so busy looking up that I forgot . . . that they . . . my friends . . . that's my cousin Sylvai . . ." He started shivering, his eyes pouring tears. Ylena wrapped her arms around him and pulled his head down into her neck as if to shield him from the carnage.

"Sometimes it's better to keep looking up for a while," Zade said with that rare glimmer of poetry. "We'll come back tomorrow and look down again."

They piled into Savi's speeder, and Ylena piloted them back to the ruins. As they pulled up outside the cenote, Vi almost expected to see Archex hurry out and stand under the overhang, blaster in hand, scanning the clearing for intruders with his usual serious glare. But only Pook galumphed out, his round black screen scanning them.

"Archex didn't make it, then?" he asked.

"No," Vi said.

"My algorithms could've told you that." Pook gave a robotic sigh. "I was almost starting not to hate him."

Zade hopped out of the speeder first. "Me too, droid. Me too. Now come see to our Mother Hen. She's wounded."

"So are you. So is Dolin," Vi protested.

And then Dolin was carrying her like a baby, and she had no idea how she'd come to be in his arms.

"But—"

"Let Pook take care of you first," Dolin said. "Please."

"But your friends. On the bikes. Some are hurt."

He paused, uncertain. "Is it okay? Can I bring them here?"

Vi gave the saddest, smallest chuckle. "Anyone injured by the First Order in that fight is part of the Resistance, as far as I'm concerned. That's what the Resistance is all about. Helping the people who need it most. You don't need a starbird patch or rank to do that."

He placed her gently on a cot in their makeshift medbay, and as she stared up at the ceiling, she remembered Archex helping Pook place the lights. The ruins were a good place for their command center, and they were safe now, but . . . even if Archex had died way up in space, he would always haunt these caverns. While she'd been running around, getting in trouble, he'd been here, left behind, doing the grunt work, steadily laboring to make it livable, to make a place for the Resistance. To make a refuge a home.

Every day, in pain and trying to discover who he was without his armor and cape, Archex had walked these halls and done what needed doing, whether he liked it or not. Even when he felt like it wasn't enough, like it wasn't worthwhile. He'd made the caf for all of them every morning, roasted vegetables and tubers at night. He hadn't complained much, and he'd followed orders, and . . .

Well, great. Vi was crying again.

"Let's make you more comfortable," Pook said, appearing overhead.

"What does that mean?"

She felt the injection before she saw it.

"Pook, what was that?"

"A mild sedative. My scans indicate you have a concussion—again—plus some internal bleeding, and yet another broken rib. And since you refuse to rest, I have made the executive decision to force you to do so."

"But I need to—"

"You don't."

"But you're not allowed to do that! You're—"

Pook sighed. "A droid, and a member of your crew. So until you find a humanoid doctor with a more cheerful bedside manner, you're left with me. Perhaps you will rest more easily knowing that my intellect is vastly superior to yours and unencumbered by a traumatic brain injury and pesky emotions."

The world was going fuzzy and dark, and Vi settled down, smiling.

"You miss him, too," she mumbled.

"Things will not be the same without him," Pook said. "Now do us all the favor of going unconscious."

So she did.

Chapter Fifty-Seven

VI HEALED, SLOWLY. DESPITE THEIR OWN supplies and the superior medpacs they'd stolen from the First Order, she had a long time to sleep in her cot in the medbay, and then rest in her niche in the cave wall, and then sit around the base, feeling her pain and coming to terms with the fact that Archex was really gone.

Dolin and Kriki continued working for Savi, and Waba's nose proved so useful for finding artifacts that they were soon able to purchase some larger pieces of scrap for the facility, including a junky old landspeeder that Kriki was able to fix up. Several of Dolin's friends, the ones who'd fought against Kath's forces and survived, began to frequent the ruins, and some even moved in for good. Vi taught them how to shoot, and Zade taught them how to swear, and Kriki got the flight simulator running so they could practice piloting and one day maybe join the Resistance fleet. The growl of crankbikes pulling up soon became a welcome sound, especially since someone almost always brought a gruffin haunch or a barrel of sour ale to share. Before she knew it, Vi had ten part-time recruits.

Zade somehow wormed his way back into Oga's good graces, and although she wouldn't release his ship, he was allowed in the cantina again, where he discovered he made an excellent and entertaining bartender. It was understood that if he attempted to recruit anyone or shot anyone again, he would be permanently banned. But apparently one brush with infamy and danger was enough, as he settled down and became Vi's source for intel, listening to the travelers and locals alike when they'd forgotten anyone sober was about.

As he said to Vi one night, "Would you ever have thought I'd live past thirty, much less enter into a career of espionage on behalf of the Resistance? For I am an egotistical thing, and there is no I in spy."

"Sure there is, she told him. "It's just really good at hiding."

He cackled at that, and Vi smiled benevolently but didn't tell him that being a spy was about more than listening to drunks and bringing home news of the First Order. Maybe Zade wasn't trained, and maybe he was hyperbolizing, but he'd stepped into the ring with Kath and his troopers not once but twice and lived to tell the tale. And what's more, he'd stayed with them when he could've left. The Resistance needed more recruits like him. No point in bursting his bubble.

Salju came to visit a few times, bringing Vi treats from the outpost and a pretty necklace from The Jewels of Bith, a gift from a few of the marketplace vendors to thank Vi for her defense of Jenda and Oh-li—and for repelling the First Order forces. Salju also told her that her old transport was becoming part of the local habitat, and that the breeding pair of lahiroo that had built a nest there now had a crew of squawking babies.

But most of the time, during the workday, it was lonely. With only Pook around until dinnertime, the corridors were too quiet, too full of echoes. The day came when Vi couldn't stand it anymore. Even though she clearly wasn't yet healthy enough to work, she took the old speeder and followed Savi's Path to the scrapyard, where she was welcomed with open arms. Ylena and Dotti and the other Gatherers hugged her extra tight, and Dolin fussed over her and insisted on pulling her cart and unloading her basket for her. After putting up with their cosseting, she was soon sorting and joking and gossiping like usual, and the voices in her head went mercifully silent. When she found an old trunk filled with dusty brown robes and a few dirt-crusted statues, Ylena was overjoyed and took her hands.

"Savi will be ecstatic," Ylena said. "This is a sign. You've done great things to help this planet and these people, and the Force will smile on you as long as you continue fighting for what's right."

Vi looked down, feeling awkward. "It's just some dirty towels and rocks, but I'm glad you're glad."

Ylena shook her head. "There's so much you don't know, so much you can't see. But the effects of your actions will ripple down through-out the galaxy. One day, these objects you've found will be valuable to someone, and to the Resistance." She shrugged. "And today, I sup-pose, they'll help pay for more Resistance supplies. I hear there's a long-range comm in town that isn't too busted up."

"Now you're speaking my language."

Vi had to take frequent breaks, and by lunch she was already tired. There was mysteriously an extra flatbread for her, as if Savi had known she was coming. Or perhaps he'd sent one along every day, knowing that one day she would be back. It didn't matter. To have someone thinking about her, taking care of her—it was a nice feeling.

That evening, she took the speeder into town, trundling slowly along behind the others. She didn't have to wear a mask or a wig, and she relished the familiar scents of roasting meat and spiced, popped grains. People waved or nodded, and Vi returned their greetings and smiled, grateful that she no longer had to hide her identity. With her belted green wrap and Salju's gifted necklace, she finally fit in among them, and it felt right.

When she went up to order a round of drinks for her friends, Zade met her at the bar, leaning over in that way he had that made every-thing seem like a delicious secret.

"Oga wants to see you," he said. "N'arrghela wanted to wait and drag you out of the bathroom for old times' sake, but I told her you deserved more respect than that."

"That's a lie. I bet you offered to do the dragging yourself," she shot back with her old grin.

He shrugged innocently. "Who could say? I'm an enigma. Steely Carl is waiting for you in the hallway."

Vi cocked her head. "Who?"

"The Talpini. I don't know his actual name, so I just made one up. He doesn't seem to mind it." He polished a glass, or tried to. The bar rags were too old and greasy to do much good. "Not a bad guy, when you get used to the staring."

Vi paid him for a round and set off for her meeting with Oga. She found the Talpini squatting in the hall, chewing on what looked like a bone. He stared up at her.

"I'm told Oga wants to see me."

He silently rose from his crouch and opened a nearly invisible door in the stone, and Vi walked in. As her eyes adjusted to the darkness, she realized that Oga's cantina must've been carved using the same methods as the ancient ruins. Past the open areas, the feel was the same. Whoever the ancients had been, they'd been powerful, and there was still so much to learn about this place.

"Chowbaso." Oga gestured for her to come in, and she did.

The Blutopian mob boss sat behind her desk, and other than the tooka-cat curled asleep by her elbow, they were alone. Rusko was dead, Oga's other minions were notably absent, and the Talpini had already disappeared. It was just them, not that Vi believed for a second that Oga was without her own defenses.

When Vi was close enough, Oga leaned back and crossed her arms. "I'll never say it on record, but I'm pleased with you. I know well enough that the Kath man was thinking about acting against the outpost, and from what I hear, you ran him off."

Vi inclined her head. "The Resistance exists to protect the people."

"Don't care about 'the people,' whoever that is. I care about *my* people, my businesses. And you protected *them*." She reached into a bowl of clamfruit and noisily ate one before continuing in her guttural Huttese. "Not pleased that you killed Rusko, though."

"I didn't kill him. He chose the wrong side and exploded."

Oga raised a shoulder as if Vi had scored a point. "See, that's why I don't like choosing sides. And I'm still not on yours."

"Oh?"

Oga pointed with a clammy finger. "Don't make the mistake of thinking you know my mind or that you have my ongoing friendship. Nobody has that. If the First Order people show up again with proper coin and manners and an officer who shows me deference, they're welcome here until they cause trouble. Black Spire Outpost is the only thing I'm loyal to, and the best thing you'll get from me is tolerance."

Vi grinned. "Tolerance, and free drinks?"

Oga sneered and threw the clamfruit shell at her, which Vi nimbly avoided. "You and your folk are welcome in the cantina as long as you're paying. Your mouthy one is a good bartender, and I don't mind him listening in—which I know he's doing—as long as he doesn't give any more speeches. So you just don't go making me mad or messing with my business matters, and I'll let you be. I know there's a bounty on your head, but that's true for a lot of people who come here, and I don't want it getting around that Oga Garra can't be trusted. Just follow my rules."

Vi nodded. "I will."

"And tell your Chadra-Fan that there's a job open at the Tech Bay, if she wants it. With Gol gone, she's got the most knowledge. She'll owe me my due, but otherwise the place is sitting open, and somebody needs to take care of it. Can't have a bunch of junk gumming up the streets."

At that, Vi really did smile. "Kriki will be overjoyed."

For the briefest moment, Oga's button eyes twinkled. "And you'll find a little something at your headquarters."

"A little something?"

"Don't echo at me. Annoying spy tricks! I reckon the only thing you're missing is a long-range comm and satellite codes, and I just so happened to find such a comm."

Vi snorted. "Did you now?"

Oga waved a rubbery hand. "Just sitting in the forest, all alone. It's a bit bashed up, but I'm sure you and Kriki can fix it."

Vi crossed her arms and considered the Blutopian, and Oga returned her stare as she stroked the tooka-cat with a clamfruit-wet hand.

"What's the cost?" Vi asked.

"Whatever do you mean?"

"I've spoken to enough people to know that Oga Garra never does anything without expecting payment. And the tallies are coming up uneven."

Oga threw back her head in a rasping laugh, causing the cat to squeak and skitter away. When she leaned forward again, there was no humor in her face, and she steepled her long, gray fingers. "I want you to owe me, Vi Moradi. I want you to know that I hold the key to everything you need to survive here, and that I can take it all away in an instant if you go against me. Upset the balance in my outpost, and the scales shift. I expect this Resistance of yours is going to need a lot of fuel."

"That it is."

"Well, then."

Vi inclined her head in a respectful nod. "Well bartered."

"And you." Oga flapped a hand. "Now go away."

When she returned to camp, sure enough, there was a familiar cargo crate holding her long-range comm. Kriki soon had it up and running using the included codes, and Vi and her recruits gathered around it.

"Magpie for General Organa," Vi said, then rambled off a code.

There was a long, crackling pause before Vi heard that familiar voice; this comm, like much of the Resistance's gear, was too old to offer a visual.

"Magpie! So you're still alive down there. I knew you could do it. How goes the fight?"

Vi's throat went tight. "The fight came and went. Thanks to a new recruit named Kriki, we managed to program the First Order ship to relay a message to their fleet, telling them I was dead, that there was no Resistance base here, and that the planet was of no significant value. And then the ship blew up due to a technical error, also courtesy of Kriki."

Beside her, Kriki was practically buzzing with pride.

"That's great news!" Leia said. "The first good news I've had in a while. Please congratulate Kriki for me, and all your team."

"They're here. They're listening."

"I can't believe it's General Organa!" Kriki finally squeaked. "I can't believe you're real! I mean, of course you're real. Sorry. This is Kriki, by the way. Hi."

Leia's voice was warm, and Kriki's fur puffed up with delight when she answered, "It's nice to meet you, Kriki. On behalf of the Resistance, thank you for your work. Thank you all." For a moment, everyone glowed with pride, but then Leia's voice went businesslike again; the war wasn't over, after all . . . "Magpie, how close are we to having a functional command location there?"

Vi looked around the cavern, with its crates and rough table. "We have a basic facility, and we're adding more to it every day. We have rough barracks set up, a makeshift medbay, training grounds, bathrooms, and a kitchen. Pook is doing a great job with construction."

"And doctoring and security," Pook added. "Basically, all the critical tasks at which humans generally fail."

"Sounds like Pook. And how is Archex doing? We lost connection with his tracker."

The room went quiet as heads bowed. "General, he's gone. We lost him in the fight. He . . . he sacrificed himself to save me and keep our headquarters safe."

Vi imagined Leia, somewhere across the universe, bowing her head, too. "It's not even close to what he deserves, but I'll award him a posthumous medal at our next ceremony. I wasn't so sure about him at first, but it looks like you were right."

"He was a good man," Vi agreed. "And he gave his all for the Resistance."

"May the Force be with him."

"I think it is."

After a moment of silence, Leia sighed. "I'm glad your mission was a success. We might be sending you ships earlier than anticipated, if you can handle it. Do you have recruits?"

"We do. And several of them show great aptitude for flying."

"More good news. It sounds like Batuu was the right choice."

Vi looked around. Kriki, Dolin, Zade, Ylena, and the new recruits were alert and ready, if shyly clustered, hearing the voice of the fabled Princess Leia for the first time.

"The people here give me hope," Vi said. "They make me remember there's something worth fighting for."

"Then keep fighting for them," Leia said. "Just like Archex did."

Epilogue

SEVERAL WEEKS LATER

VI WAS OVERSEEING A NEW BATCH of recruits at target practice when her comlink dinged. When she put up her hand, the blasterfire immediately ceased, and all eyes followed her.

That was good. They were learning.

"Captain Moradi, there's an urgent message for you," Pook said. "Top secret." For once, the droid sounded alert and anxious instead of bored, and Vi's curiosity was piqued.

"Keep practicing," Vi said to the murmuring recruits. "I'll be back."

The ruins were a busy place now, and Vi was grateful for the activity and work. They had over a dozen new recruits, and she spent most of her time training them. Kriki ran the Tech Bay and was able to get them good deals on fixed-up machines, while Dolin kept up his work at the scrapyard with Waba. Their encampment had expanded beyond the ruins and out into the clearing, as Vi had imagined it would, and an old X-wing was parked there when it wasn't being used for flight training. She was proud of her work here—and knew Leia was, too. Hence the promotion.

When she reached the room they'd reserved for communications and strategy, she checked that she was alone, pressed a button on the long-range comm, and said, "Magpie here."

"Magpie, it's Green Leader," came a familiar man's voice. He sounded out of breath and desperate. "Look, it's bad news. Someone has informed the First Order that the Resistance command location is functional. And that you're not dead. And now they're coming for you."

"Who?" Vi asked, goose bumps rising on her arms.

"We don't know. But Kylo Ren is on his way, along with the Seven Hundred and Ninth Legion. Those are his elite stormtroopers, chosen by Kylo himself. We're sending help, but—"

The comm cut off abruptly.

Vi knew this feeling well—that crystalline moment when everything went wrong, when calm and quiet became anxiety and work. She allowed herself one flutter of panic—Kylo Ren himself? With the 709th? She'd heard of them. They would be much harder to deal with than Kath's squadron had been. She had to hurry outside and tell her recruits, send word to Savi and to Kriki in town. Even Oga would want to know that Kylo Ren would soon be in the outpost.

She began walking, then jogging, then running outside. Who knew how much time they had left? Green Leader hadn't finished his message. And what kind of help was coming?

But when she left the overhang and stepped into the clearing, all her recruits were pointing up at the sky.

"What's that?" Houz asked.

Vi took a deep breath.

"That," she told him, "is a First Order Star Destroyer."

"What does that mean?"

She looked around the clearing, met every eye.

"That means it's time to fight."

Acknowledgments

The more books I write, the worse I get at writing acknowledgments. Not because there are fewer people to thank, but because there are more, and I'm carrying so many different stories in my head that there's not room for much else. So please know that I'm grateful for everyone who helped bring this book to life and everyone who reads it or reviews it or tells a friend about it.

Loving thanks and ronto wraps to my beloved husband of seventeen years, Craig, without whom I wouldn't be a writer or know quite so much about Noghri. Thanks to my sweet Padawans for the hugs that kept me going through long days of editing and my mom for watching those Padawans while my husband took me out to eat real food in between the bowls of gluten-free cereal that sustained me while I was on deadline.

Endless thanks to my revered editor, Elizabeth Schaefer, who is a joy and inspiration and seemed to make this book happen out of sheer force of will, as well as Tom Hoeler, who supported me through some challenging edits and even accepted my frantic texts during *Game of Thrones*. Big thanks to publicist extraordinaire David Moench and the entire Del Rey team. Keith, Scott, Julie, Erich, Melissa, Anne—thanks for letting me hang out behind the booth at nearly every event. Thanks to Matt, Pablo, and Leland for making sure I didn't make any huge mistakes in canon. And thanks to Michael Siglain for giving me so many chances to tell stories in a galaxy that's meant so much to me my entire life.

Here's a new one! Thanks to the Walt Disney Imagineers, Margaret and Stacey and everyone I didn't almost hyperventilate over during a phone call. Thank you for giving us the wonderful gift of Galaxy's Edge and for letting me be a part of it.

Thanks to my agent, Stacia Decker, for steering this crazy ship.

And to the *Star Wars* Writer Scum, thanks for shooting the pudu at the bar and being there for laughs, tears, and DMs about secret things: Chuck Wendig, Kevin Hearne, Ty and Daniel, EK Johnston, Zoraida Cordova, Daniel José Older, Jason Fry, Rebecca Roanhorse, Claudia Gray, Tim Zahn (and the Zahntourage), Cavan Scott, Christie Golden, Beth Revis, Charles Soule, Jody Houser. And while we're at it, thanks to Denton Tipton and IDW for the chance to tell stories in the Star Wars Adventures comics!

And you.

Thank you for picking up the book. Thanks to everyone who comes to see me at a con or book signing or at *Star Wars* Celebration. I love putting your pins and patches on my jacket and vest, and I love seeing your fan art, and I love feeding sneaky tidbits to those of you who keep hoping I can somehow make Millicent canon. Thanks to my friend Cathy for saying hi in Target and putting up with the fact that my Writer Brain makes me hard to wrangle as an IRL friend. Thanks to Hal for my beloved Cardinal helmet. Thanks to all the Phasmas who let me take pics and to Sebastian and Calvin for always saying hi. Thanks to the 501st for making me an Honorary Member, which fills me with so much honor and pride that I get giddy. The Star Wars fandom is the most kind, enthusiastic, giving crew I know, and I hope you like the book.

Till the spire!

ABOUT THE AUTHOR

DELILAH S. DAWSON is the author of the *New York Times* bestseller *Star Wars: Phasma, Hit, Servants of the Storm*, the Blud series, the creator-owned comics *Ladycastle*, *Sparrowhawk*, and *Star Pig*, and the Shadow series (written as Lila Bowen). With Kevin Hearne, she's the co-writer of the Tales of Pell. She lives in Florida with her family and a fat mutt named Merle.

whimsydark.com
Twitter: @DelilahSDawson
Instagram: @DelilahSDawson

ABOUT THE TYPE

This book was set in Minion, a 1990 Adobe Originals typeface by Robert Slimbach (b. 1956). Minion is inspired by classical, old-style typefaces of the late Renaissance, a period of elegant, beautiful, and highly readable type designs. Created primarily for text setting, Minion combines the aesthetic and functional qualities that make text type highly readable with the versatility of digital technology.

STAR WARS DATAPAD

Enhance Your *Star Wars*: Galaxy's Edge Adventure

Traveling to the planet Batuu? The *Star Wars*: Datapad is an essential tool when it comes to living your own *Star Wars* story—hack into droids, scan crates, tune into transmissions, translate languages and more!

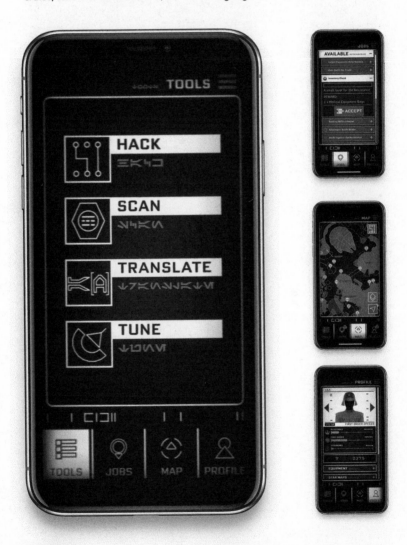

 Available only through the Play Disney Parks app, the *Star Wars*: Datapad will guide you deeper and deeper into your adventure at *Disneyland*® Park in California and *Disney's Hollywood Studios*® in Florida.